Wakefield Press

This Excellent Machine

Stephen Orr was born in Adelaide in 1967 and grew up in Hillcrest. He studied teaching and spent his early career in a range of country and metropolitan schools. One of his early plays, *Attempts to Draw Jesus*, became his first *Australian*/Vogel shortlisted novel, published in 2002. Since then he has published seven novels, a volume of short stories (*Datsunland*) and two books of non-fiction (*The Cruel City* and *The Fierce Country*). He has been nominated for awards such as the Commonwealth Writers' Prize, the Miles Franklin Award and the International Dublin Literary Award. *This Excellent Machine* is the first volume in an anticipated trilogy of childhood novels.

Stephen Orr is married and lives in Adelaide.

By the same author

Fiction
Attempts to Draw Jesus
Hill of Grace
Time's Long Ruin
Dissonance
One Boy Missing
The Hands
Datsunland
Incredible Floridas

Non-fiction
The Cruel City
The Fierce Country

This Excellent Machine

Stephen Orr

Wakefield
Press

Wakefield Press
16 Rose Street
Mile End
South Australia 5031
www.wakefieldpress.com.au

First published 2019

Cover designed by Liz Nicholson, designBITE
Edited by Margot Lloyd, Wakefield Press
Typeset by Michael Deves, Wakefield Press

ISBN 978 1 74305 613 4

A catalogue record for this
book is available from the
National Library of Australia

Wakefield Press thanks
Coriole Vineyards for
continued support

One by one as you swung monkey-wise from branch to branch in the wood of make-believe you reached the tree of knowledge. Sometimes you swung back into the wood, as the unthinking may take a familiar road that no longer leads to home; or you perched ostentatiously on its boughs to please me, pretending that you still belonged; soon you knew it only as the vanished wood, for it vanishes if one needs to look for it.

J.M. Barrie

After a little I am taken in and put to bed. Sleep, soft smiling, draws me unto her: and those receive me, who quietly treat me, as one familiar and well-beloved in that home: but will not, oh, will not, not now, not ever; but will not ever tell me who I am.

James Agee

LOOKING BACK, I can't say what made 1984 so special. A succession of failed driving tests? The man in the picture in Mrs Donnellan's house? Mr Champness telling me the difference between regent and king parrots? Datsuns (always Datsuns)? Or maybe it was our journey north, and the search for Lasseter's Reef. Looking out my bedroom window to see a couple of dogs going their hardest under a rosemary bush. Dave Donnellan (put out for sun) singing his mum's songs. Or Curtis, forever telling me I was a dickhead.

No. A place, person – time – can only be known by knowing the things that went with them. Mixed with them. Coloured and flavoured them. That's how I see it, now. We all lived and breathed and shared fruit because of those small moments of grace.

'I know you.'

'Sorry?'

'Clem ... Clem Whelan.'

'No, he's in Grade Seven.'

The old girl looked over the gal fence. 'That went straight through my flyscreen.'

I didn't reply. It didn't look good. We'd been throwing lemons on the oval and I'd chucked one over her fence. It'd hit something and the others had run away, but I'd done the right thing and climbed the Moreton Bay to see what had happened. And then she'd peered over, hair rollers and all. 'Clem Whelan. Your pop fixed my car one time.'

'My pop's a train driver.'

'Don't lie to me.'

About then the bell sounded and everyone ran into class. I was left with the old woman, who cleaned the senior and junior open units. Every day at three pm, sliding the gal back, climbing through with her vacuum and buckets, walking across the oval, starting her hoover while Mr Gottl was busy with long division.

'Truth's better than just about anything,' she said.

'I was throwing at Kenny but ...'

She didn't reply.

'Sorry.'

'Now you feel better, I bet.'

And then, Mr Gottl himself, calling me in. 'Carn, Clem. What you doing?'

As I clung to the tree I said, 'How much you reckon it'd cost to fix?'

She shrugged. 'Doesn't matter.'

'Why?'

She reached up, and I could see the old turkey giblets dangling under her arms, and she threw the lemon back.

'Clem!'

I caught it. 'We got English now.'

'Go on then. Watch yerself next time.' And she was gone, but not gone, really. She was always there, vacuuming the carpet they stuck down with gaffer tape, cleaning the tables that Stephen Prawer drew dongers on.

Grace, 1976 style. Moments that allowed us to be wrong, impatient, stupid, but still carry on. Forgiveness, although it was more than that. Repeating endlessly. Two am rock bands pounding the piers of the Polish hall as everyone lay awake cursing Bill Hailey. But it would stop, eventually, and we'd fall asleep, and the next morning it'd all be forgotten, mostly. Man worked hard laying pipes, man needed to blow off a bit of steam on Saturday night.

Grace. 1977. Mr Gottl again. I mustn't have been as innocent as I remember. Or maybe someone had put me up to it. Either way, there I was in the open unit they usually kept locked at lunch. I went straight for Mr Gottl's desk. Bingo! The old biscuit tin.

You'd often see him searching for change. But this was more than I could've hoped for: a five and ten dollar note, straight in the pocket. I can't remember why; I didn't really need the money. It wasn't like we were poor, mostly. And it wasn't like I didn't know better. But everything had to be learned the hard way.

'Clem?'

I looked up. What could you say? Mr Gottl seemed surprised, shocked, but (initially at least) more because he didn't understand. Me, Clem Whelan, the kid in the hand-knitted cardy, top of the class for speed and accuracy. He just repeated my name, stepped forward, took the money and threw the biscuit tin (I'll always remember the flick of the wrist) across the room. Took my earlobe and pulled me out the door towards the office. What was I thinking? He dragged me, bodily, across the asphalt, past monkey bars, Barbie girls, towards *the office*. A few stopped to stare, surprised that it was me, Clem Whelan, not Barry or Stephen.

Mr Gottl let go of my ear, but took my arm. He was slowing. I could see his face, lined with anger, or frustration, or confusion. Clem Whelan: Friday afternoon certificates (Quietest, Fastest, Most Considerate), stealing from his biscuit tin.

He stopped, released my arm and said, 'Why?'

My head might've dropped. I might've bit my lip. But then he stepped back and said, 'Go on.'

We were standing under the pine trees, alone, halfway across the car park, halfway to the office. Grace. Surrounded by Datsuns. I stood, waiting, confused.

'Go!' he said, choking on the word.

So I walked away. Glanced back to see him standing, thinking.

January

'Plenty of options,' I said to Pop.

'Such as?'

'Helping you.'

Holding the old fuel filter in his hands, Pop took a few moments to decide. It might last another thousand kilometres, but to be safe, it should be replaced. 'What's the point? Get an apprenticeship. Do it properly.'

'But you can teach me.'

He wasn't sure where everything fitted. He'd stripped most of the Fairlady's engine (Datsun 1500 Sports) and laid the bits and pieces on an old bedsheet he'd spread on the crumbling concrete. He was thinking, perhaps, of putting it back together. If it could be put back together. There was a manual on the bench, sitting open, its torn pages some indication. But enough? He had to think hard about every spanner turn. 'You shouldn't rely on me,' he said.

'I know most things.'

'Not enough.' He placed the filter on the ground and continued. Leaning over the engine, he started unscrewing the oil filter. 'What else?'

'A copper?'

'Can't see that happening.'

'Plenty of other apprenticeships. Printing, fitting and turning.'

He didn't want to stop me. Maybe I'd say something intelligent. Maybe not. But it was worth the wait.

'Just gotta accept it,' he said. 'Back to school. You got the head for it.'

'So?'

Then he looked up, half-shitty. '*So?* Use your brains. That's where the money is.'

We'd had the talk a hundred times. The doctor-engineer-lawyer persuasion. 'So?' He placed the filter on the ground, studied the pieces then shook his head.

'What's wrong?' I asked.

'Nothing's wrong.' Returning to work. He undid the clamps and removed the battery. 'Early Datsuns weren't much.'

'What about the Laurel?'

He glared at me. It wasn't about the Laurel, but what I should do with myself. It was only a week until I started matric. I wasn't interested, and if I didn't resolve it now it'd just be nine months of Bruce Dawe and Gross Domestic Product.

'Your mother wouldn't have a bar of it,' he said, fighting with the battery, working it free, attempting to remove it. 'Gis a hand, will yer?'

So I took it, lifted it, placed it in the little square he'd drawn on the sheet, with the word BATRY, so he'd know.

'Now, let's think,' he said. He put his hand to his head and massaged his temple, as though this might wake the sleepy cells in his brain. Although, even then, standing in the shed that hot day, month, year, I knew, we all knew, the bits and pieces were starting to drift and settle in other places. But the sheet was comprehensive enough. He'd sat there, the previous evening, copying the names from the manual, labelling them, saying to me, 'You'll help us with that Fairlady tomorrow?'

'Sure, Pop.'

'Should have it done in a few hours.'

Mum had said, 'Don't be stupid, Dad. Forty-odd tomorrow. You don't wanna be out in the shed working.'

And he'd turned to her. 'Wait for it to cool down and we'll be there in April.'

She'd given him her look. Not the hot-shed look, but the you're-too-old look, the save-yourself look. She'd turned to me for support but I'd just said, 'I can help.' So she'd fallen silent. *Kingswood Country* silent. Ted and Bruno and other cars, other neighbourhoods.

Back in the shed, Pop wiped his hands and said, 'Your mother's relying on you.'

'I hate school.'

'What's that got to do with anything?'

I studied his face – chicken skin with six or seven liver spots, a bulbous nose with fuse-box capillaries, smokers' teeth, big ears with hairs. 'What about a teller?'

'You can do that after November.'

'Or the public service test?'

'Why'd you wanna be a public servant? Sit on their arse all day …' Which made him think of work, and all the bits that still had to come out. He started removing spark plugs and leads, placing each on the sheet in its numbered spot. 'I've always regretted not finishing school. Then you gotta spend yer life doing this.'

'But you like it.'

'You do anything long enough you get used to it.'

I didn't believe it. He liked cars, and wouldn't be anywhere else doing anything different. Forty, fifty degrees, it didn't matter; he wasn't happy unless he was in the shed. It was his version, minus the titty calendars, of the garage he'd worked in for fifty years, before he'd retired, or been made to. 'Anyway,' he said, 'what about your Nan?'

I knew he'd mention her. Nan, sitting with her Dickens, her New World Encyclopedias, saying, Clem, you done yer homework?

Yes, Nan.

I found this bit here, about the planets.

I finished, Nan.

And all the moons of Saturn and Jupiter. Isn't that what they were asking about?

I finished, Nan.

But Nan would never accept that. You were never finished; you could always do a bit more, make it better. Twenty years of scrubbing pub floors, that's why you had to know the moons of Jupiter, and how the rings weren't really rings.

'She'd turn in her grave,' Pop said, removing the last of the leads.

That made it difficult to argue. I knew that's one thing she'd want: me as a matriculant, university, perhaps, probably, definitely. 'What about some sort of management—'

'Jesus, Clem!' He knocked his head on the bonnet. 'You just go on and on. It's decided!'

No, it's not, I thought, but dared not say.

'What's the big bloody deal? A few months outa yer life then you can go do whatever you want. But … for your mother's sake.'

I wasn't all that worried, but thought it worth a try. He or Mum might've said, Of course, get the paper, apply to a few places. Manager at Tom the Cheap grocery, that'd be okay. Earn a bit of money, help with a car on the weekend. It was worth a try, but it wasn't worth getting him pissed off.

He waved a spanner in my face. 'Nan's every second thought was you and Jen. None of us got a decent education. Now you can get your degree for free. Why wouldn't you?'

I smelled the rooms, the labs, the fingernail-yellow paper in the books; heard Mrs Dent praising Shakespeare; saw the lads with their too-tight shorts on the oval kicking balls that would last until lunch, beyond, into a future of shallow trenches and full-forwards and seven kids with mixing-bowl haircuts. Which was reason enough, perhaps, to do as Pop asked. 'Didn't say I wouldn't go back.'

'Well, stop going on about it.' He sat, picked up his Port Royal and started rolling a smoke. After he got it tight he licked it, lit it, sat back and inhaled.

What you thinking about? I wanted to ask, but didn't. What was the point? Life was just something you got on with, apparently.

I guessed it was Nan, dead ten years, in her little spot in the wall at Centennial Park. 'I suppose she did buy all those encyclopedias,' I said.

'She did.' He drew back, and took in most of the too-thin fag.

'Every week, eh?'

No reply. But I saw her, hobbling back from the newsagent with that week's volume. L–M. Lithuania. Limes. Presenting it to me and Jen and saying, Look after it. Only another five weeks. N–O. New Guinea was a revelation. No one bothered with bras. As well as which, they were good for projects. P–R. Perth. Princeton. Poland. A whole world beyond Lanark Avenue, described in the most superficial detail.

'Do you want me to finish?' I asked.

'Wait.'

He was savouring the last few centimetres, but other things as well. Him and Nan, somewhere, fixing something, cooking it, polishing it.

I stood, pulled the darts from the board and started playing. They hit the iron, and clanged, but Pop didn't say anything. The smoke was drifting, settling. I got a few in and said, 'Wanna go?'

He glared at me like I was stupid, like I'd just ruined something important. So I tried again: three, five, double score. 'Must be fifty degrees in here.'

No reply.

He was wearing heavy, torn overalls. But they were part of the performance. Hot, but you had to be hot. There was a car to be fixed, and this James woman wanted it back by next Monday. 'We should go in, Pop.'

'Not finished.'

His eyes returned to the roof, the tube trusses, the wires gaffer-taped on, finishing in power points that hung loose. The shelves with old carburettors and fuel lines and seatbelts. A workbench piled high with tools no one used.

'What you thinkin' about?' I asked.

He studied the sheet. 'What goes where.'

The expanding iron groaned, but he didn't notice.

'How many volumes were there?' he said.

'Eighteen.'

'Right.' And he was examining them too, Frankenstein and Henry Ford, holding a magneto, but mostly, Nan taking them out of the bag, handing them to us kids. 'Eighteen … home needs a set of encylopedias. It's civilising.'

Now I'd re-mastered the art of the dart throw: jerk, release, let the weight do the work. They were all sticking. *Civilising.* That was important, I guessed. Otherwise you just had four fibro walls and creaking floorboards.

He stepped on his smoke, glowing beside the dozens, hundreds, he'd ground in over the decades. Since he and Dad had built the shed. Which had come before the house, of course. Looking at the hundred nuts and bolts and sheets of iron. Thinking: Right, let's go.

Now, he took a moment to think, consulted the manual (not that he needed to) and disappeared below the bonnet. I threw a few more darts. Noticed the chalk scribble, the addings-up on the blackboard beside it. All the numbers formal, structured, the same. 'Who wrote this?' I asked.

He checked. 'Yer dad.'

I studied the numerals, as if they might tell me something. The chalk was still sitting on the wooden frame. I picked it up and traced the numbers. Perhaps this would provide some clue about my missing father. Who'd left no clothes, toiletries, papers. Nothing. But the father, I guessed, who was standing beside Mum, and toddler Jen, and baby me, in a photo in Mrs Donnellan's house. A photo they'd all missed in their conspiracy of denying me a dad. A solid, real, smelling, speaking, remembered old man. Mine was a ghost dad. A bit of chalk, a pair of shoes, but not much else. A whispered comment from Aunty Maureen before she realised me and Jen were listening. But Mum hadn't realised Mrs Donnellan hadn't realised. And there he was, this grinning man standing with the family that time had forgot. 'Was he any good at darts?' I asked.

'He was okay, I suppose.'

'Could he beat you?'

'What's the point of throwin' those things?'

Always how it was. Dig, but the ground was hard. Dad, apparently, had caused it all. Then Jen was in the doorway. 'Mum says youse should come in.'

Pop didn't reply.

'Pop?'

'Gotta get this done. If you wanna help you can get us a drink.'

'Bloody hot in here. Clem, Mum says—'

'We're workin',' I shot back.

'Doesn't look like you're working.'

'We're working,' Pop growled, and she retreated. I heard the fly door slam and Mum going off and 'Xanadu' fading in and out of the ether.

Pop laid more parts on the ground. Then he stood back and said, 'Gotta go down to Repco.'

'Want me to come?'

'No. Get going before—'

But it was too late. Slam. Slippers on the pavers. Mum at the door. 'Dad, come in. This is bloody ridiculous.'

'I gotta get this done.'

'It can wait till tomorrow. There's a change coming.' She glared at him.

'Clem said he'd drive me to Repco.'

She looked at me, as if I was part of the problem. 'Then you're both inside, right?'

'Can't stop workin' cos it gets a bit warm.'

'At eighty-two you can. You will.'

Datsun 120Y. Four angry cylinders; plenty of rust, seatbelts that didn't retract. Sink-hole bucket seats with cushions. Radio hissing *eastbound and down*, although north-east, actually. Working despite the dust and Coke spray. A glove box full of gas bills and two-for-one pizza vouchers, and a fuel gauge that didn't work, of course.

All of which might lead you to ask, why hadn't Pop fixed it? But that was, and is, life: mechanics with their shitty cars, teachers with their innumerate kids. But despite all this, it just kept going, and now it was my turn. L-plates. Seatbelts (done yours up, Pop?). I checked my mirrors, started the engine and reversed into Lanark Avenue. Driving too long in first before stopping, indicating and turning into Dragon Street, past the basketball stadium with its sub-floor vents for disposing of uneaten lunches. I stopped again, listening to the clunk of the spastic blinker. Pop said, 'You don't need to keep stopping.'

'You're meant to.'

In his day (so the speech went) you could walk into a police station, hand over a couple of quid, fill in a form and whacko, there was your driver's licence. He couldn't see the point of all this mucking around.

'That's what they look for in the test,' I said.

No reply.

'Lose eight points, you're done. If you don't come to a full stop—'

'Okay, I got yer.'

We turned onto North East Road: two lanes of normally heavy traffic, but it was mad dogs and Englishmen, so there were just a few trucks, a bus, and I said, 'Went up the back of one of those.'

'Eh?'

'I was riding behind a bus and it slammed on the brakes, and I went up the back.'

He refused to be drawn, although I knew he was listening.

'Just picked up my bike, got onto the footpath …' I wrestled into fourth, braked hard, nearly did it again.

'Watch yerself.'

I waited to get around. 'No one stopped, asked how I was. Even the people walking past. Didn't I ever tell you?'

He didn't say I had or hadn't; whether he remembered or not. Maybe he was searching his head, the chip-crumb memories.

We drove in silence. Me, following the rules, him, trying to remember. 'What did I say we needed?'

'Plugs, leads, filters, coolant, and more oil.'

He turned to me. 'I didn't say that, did I?'

'Yes.'

'We've got plenty of oil.'

'That's what you said.'

'Ah.' As he imagined the drum, I suppose, and listened to how it sounded when you knocked on the side. 'Well …'

Stoplights. We rolled. I applied the handbrake, but it didn't make any difference. How about we tighten it, Pop, I'd asked, and he'd agreed it needed to be done.

'Just thinkin' …'

'What's that?'

'If that quack's right.'

He was starting to think that the doctor might know best. The proof was everywhere. After all these years you couldn't ignore the lost bankbooks and shoes left on the lawn and the forgotten name of the orange stuff on your dinner plate.

'If he's right?' I said.

'Then you can help.'

He'd told me this a few times, but I suppose he'd forgotten that too. 'If I forget things, you can remind me.'

'Of course.'

'Don't make a big fuss but, you know, tell me where I put things.'

His wedding ring, in the nail jar. I'd only found it by accident.

'Everyone forgets stuff,' I said.

He knew he could trust me. As we continued up Holden Hill he said, 'You can help me out with ... remembering things?'

'Course I will, Pop.'

'But you gotta get back to school.'

'I guess so.'

'Keep the grey cells workin', eh?'

I parked at Repco, locked the door (that you could open without a key) and we went in. The smell of fresh rubber, everything old, worn or cracked resurrected in a plastic wrapper. A nursery of gasket seals and rims. Although Pop didn't see it this way. He picked up a fan belt and said, 'Can't see how they can charge six dollars for a strip of rubber.'

'They charge what people'll pay.'

'Well, then people are stupid.'

He wasn't a Repco man. He knew people in the trade and could get everything at cost. But not today. It was too far to drive to Barron for a few plugs and leads. 'Suppose we're just gonna have to pay it.'

Jacks with none of the paint scratched off; lengths of carpet to put on your dash; artificial lemons to hang from your rear-view;

manuals, hundreds of them; but again, according to Pop, you wouldn't buy them here.

'Carn.' He approached the counter and deposited his bits and pieces. A middle-aged man smiled and said, 'How are you, Doug?'

'Good. You?'

The man sorted the items. I suppose he wanted to say, Jack, my name's Jack, but he couldn't.

Pop noticed his badge. 'Just these few, Jack.'

Jack had his shirt half-open and there was a cauliflower chest with a gold chain, and you could see his big nipples through his Repco shirt. 'Clem, isn't it?' he asked me.

'Yes.'

'You still driving that 120Y?'

Pop piped in. 'Goes like a charm, eh, Clem?'

'It does, Pop.'

'Drive it into the ground, I reckon.'

Then Jack said, 'How's Fay?'

Pop knew what he didn't know. 'She hates the heat.' An attempt to disguise whatever it was that connected Jack to Fay. 'Always complaining, isn't she, Clem?' As he looked at me, half-desperate.

I smiled at Jack. 'Does Mum still see Raelene?'

'Not so much.' He rang up the items and started placing them in a bag.

I could see the look on Pop's face. Fay, his daughter, was somehow connected to Raelene. But who was she? Jack's wife? His daughter? Or did she work here?

Jack pushed the bag across the counter and waited. 'Let's call it twenty-five dollars.'

Pop paid him and there was some small talk and we left. On the way home he asked, 'Who was that fella?'

'Mum used to work with his wife. He'd stop out the front, and pick her up.'

'His wife? Raelene?'

'She'd come in for a cuppa, remember?'

Not a word I should've used.

'See, you coulda told me that, Clem.'

'I just did.'

'No, you coulda said, Mum and this … Raelene …' He checked the bag. 'We can get it finished today.'

'Tomorrow, Pop. It's too hot.'

'Tomorrow, if you help?'

'Of course.'

'I'm not gonna pay them bloody prices. I need a manual for that Valiant but I'm not payin' that sorta money.'

'I can drive you to Barron one day.'

'Good-o. Soon?'

'Soon.'

Pop still had his full licence, but knew he wasn't any sort of long-distance driver anymore. So it was me, on my learners', who did most of the long trips.

I stalled at the lights.

'Careful, you'll have someone up yer arse.'

Lanark Avenue. Three roads, dissected by two. A trilogy of fibro houses on knee-high stilts. Asbestos boxes reclining in the sun with feature windows to let in the heat, a couple of diosmas and a citrus out the front, for old time's sake. Weak concrete for long driveways with Kingswoods and Datsuns. A viburnum reaching to powerlines carrying *Matlock-Love Boat* electricity. Homes like the magazines promised. No more cracking walls. No, this was all finely clipped Santa Ana, kids on rugs on Saturday nights when you had to escape the house.

Lanark I: from the Patricia Avenue flats to Dragon Street

Lanark II (us): from Dragon Street to Fleet Avenue

Lanark III (which led to school): Fleet to the mound (more on that later).

I (1–22) was childhood, II (23–67) the middle bit, III (68–92) old age, and beyond. Anyway, this is how I imagined it, and still do. A three-part road for a three-part life. We were number 31 – another fourteen years and I'd arrive where I'd begun. But Lanark Avenue was, and is, all of a human life, many lives, lined up behind brick cladding over your asbestos. It was, and is, the world boiled down to basics. Everything I've ever learnt or come to understand had its template, example and elaboration there. People, behaviour, jobs, what goes in your mouth and out the other end, living, dying (mostly slowly).

Pop said, 'Here.'

'What?'

He indicated two cars in front of the Polish hall (63–67, apparently they'd demolished a couple of houses to build it). Polish as in folk dances, cooking, music groups and, on a Saturday night, rock bands.

'Try yer parkin',' Pop said.

The gap was just big enough. But then again, you could get a 120Y in anywhere. Attempt number one; I connected with the gutter.

'Come in at more of an angle,' Pop said.

Number two; too far from the gutter.

'How many goes they give you?'

'Three.'

'Right, well, you gotta get it this time.'

Just right, but then I pumped the accelerator and shot back, clunked the other car's bumper bar.

'Jesus, Clem.' Pop got out, went around and had a look.

I followed. 'It didn't seem that close.'

We studied the dent.

'You barely touched it.' He scanned the deserted street. He could knock on a few doors, explain, or … 'Get in.'

'Shouldn't we—'

'Just get in.'

The thing was, we didn't know any neighbours this far down Lanark Avenue, and it was just a little dent and, if you didn't tell anyone, they wouldn't notice.

Driving the rest of the way, Pop said, 'That doesn't make it right.'

'Should we go back?'

'That wouldn't make it right either. It was just a bomb. I mean, if it was something posh …'

I smiled. 'Then you would've stopped?'

'Maybe.'

We passed the Donnellans (33). David was there, in his wheelchair, under his tree, watching. We waved; he lifted his hand, almost. His mum, Val, or brother, Peter, put him out most mornings, and afternoons, and he'd sit for hours at a time, watching the traffic, waving to Ernie on his way to the Windsor. Like a pot plant, and no, I don't mean it that way. They'd just put him out. Better than sitting inside all day, watching television, staring at the four walls.

We got out, and Pop looked over the fence and called, 'How are you, David?'

He mumbled something.

Pop must've felt social. He wandered into the Donnellans' yard of dead lawn and cracked Bay of Biscay, a few old fruit trees, mostly dead. 'Bit hot to be outside, isn't it? Want me to take you in?'

'No.' David shook his head.

'Righto. Got something to drink?'

'Mum'll bring me something soon.'

David Donnellan: rugby player, law graduate, then recluse (as the street whispers began). Ambulances coming and going. All of this, dimly remembered from my own early years, overheard (Aunty Maureen, again), assumed.

'Okay,' Pop said. 'See you, David.'

Muscular dystrophy. But what did the name matter? Plenty of people around Gleneagles were running rough. Plenty of cancer. The Famous Disappearing Marinelli (a heart attack, the same way Sid Donnellan had gone in 1958), a girl with Down syndrome around the corner, a couple of spastics. We didn't mean it cruelly; it was just what they were called. You looked out for them, went and told their mum when you saw them heading towards North East Road.

Coming in, Pop tripped on one of the cracks. 'Fuck.' Ever since David's wheelchair days no one had watered anything at number 33. No sign of Val at the end of a stinker, standing in her dressie, watering the fig tree that grew in the same way rabbits bred. No Peter Donnellan, in the early hours (before the sun had spread across the horizon) in his slippers, sprinkling the burnt clivias.

Pop nearly turned back, nearly said, Water yer fuckin' lawn, but you couldn't say anything to the Donnellans. Life had shat on them.

Six years at university, and he'd never practised. I'd mentioned this to Mum during one of my why-should-I-go-back-to-school speeches, but she'd said (quite rightly, I suppose) David Donnellan was different. *Really* unlucky. Which was true. Peter, who'd graduated with him, had made good money in family disputes, divorce, that sort of stuff, before drifting into a premature, hand-knitted retirement.

As we headed down the drive, Pop said, 'Used to hide in our shed. Look at him now.'

Six pm. A day that refused to cool. Me on my bed, strumming my thirty-dollar guitar. *Nobody told me*, struggling with chord changes, as Jen played Daryl and the boys at top volume. *Summer love is like no other love.* Of course, I was interested, so I tried the progression, D to A minor, or was it C – it was hard to tell. 'Turn it down!'

No reply.

'Oi!'

'Fuck off!'

'Mum?'

A voice from the lounge of Leyland wanderings. 'Jennifer!'

'What?'

'Turn it down.'

'Tell him to shove his guitar ...'

I wasn't fazed. Lennon's white-hot words filled my bedroom. Along with the Nazis. See, genius. Sweaty hands and fingers, D strings and the bit between leg and balls. But what did it matter? I looked at the poster on my wall for inspiration: the great man, circa 1975.

'*Turn it down!*'

I waited for the sun to drop, but that was still hours away. The heat rising from my shag-pile savannah. There was a ten-dollar fan, but that just spread the love. So you just sweated and waited for a change, which always seemed to be a day, a week, eternity away.

A woman's voice: Mrs Champness. I sat on the end of my bed, trained my telescope and focused. Wendy, with her roller-hair and apron. I knew everything about her. Luckily, my window aligned with the Champnesses' driveway, so I could see straight down the side of their house, into their yard (mostly). The shed, and clothes line, and aviary that Les sat in front of for hours at a time. He stood over his wife, shouting something like, *Always gonna … what about we eat?* Wendy just took it, the washing held firmly under her left arm. She moved to get around him, but he blocked her path. She half-stumbled into a lavender, but he blocked her way back. So she just stood waiting, as he kept shouting: *Wait forever, wouldn't I?*

She tried again, brushed against him; he pushed her, she fell onto the ground and the washing went onto the drive. She knelt, started gathering it, but he was leaning over her, letting her have it: *If yer good and fuckin' ready.*

I felt bad for her, but what could I do? Grow red and blue polyester flesh, a rubber mask, utility belt? Fly across the road, pick up Les, rocket up a hundred metres, drop him, so that he came crashing down (in a pile of flesh and bones) at her feet? No Marvel hero could save Wendy from Les. She was stuck with him. I'd told Mum and Pop, but they'd just said, 'That's for them to sort out.'

Let your love come easy and free …

'Turn it down!'

'I did!'

It must have been the fifth time she'd played it. It wasn't right.

Les followed Wendy, shouting in her ear, but she ignored him.

She picked up a singlet or teatowel she'd missed and went in. I trained my TK25 on their yard, in their windows, through their fly door and down their hallway. There were dark figures moving, but no more voices. What would Kirby's Fantastic Four do? What did it matter what they'd do?

Shit! Some old girl walked past, looked in my window and saw me. I sat still. I wasn't spying, as such – just gathering information, attempting to come to some understanding. Sociological observations that would definitely, probably, perhaps, come in handy one day.

I looked up and down the street. Down Ronald and Hester Glasson's (30) drive. They were the Howard Hugheses of Gleneagles, keeping to themselves, trimming the hedge that screened them from the prying eyes (and telescopes) of suburbia. They had a big gal fence and, behind this, fruit trees that kept them from our world of dragsters and going home to Gravox. Ironic, really, since they ran a lamb's wool seat-cover business from their back shed and every Saturday morning there'd be cars the length of Lanark Avenue, and Mr Glasson out measuring seats. Then he'd go in and return a few minutes later to fit the covers. Mum, Pop, Les Champness and Val Donnellan had all whinged, but never said anything to the Glassons. It was only a few hours on a Saturday morning, and there was always a chance you'd need your own cover one day.

There was nothing in Nan's encyclopedias that could explain why Les shouted at Wendy, or Ronald and Hester refused to mix. I'd attempted to understand them. Employed various schemes: Terman's, Maxwell's Graduated Percentile. In the absence of facts I'd improvised, made my own method, based on observation and careful note keeping. I had a little book in my drawer.

12/i/84 LC shouting at WC again. Not drunk, just manic ...

These records stretched back years. Every neighbour had their own page.

3/vi/79 LC put his fist through a wall. Pulled out his hand, continued feeding the birds.

I'd got a lot of use out of my telescope since my ninth birthday. It was only a Kmart number but it did the job. I don't think I'd ever looked at a star, but that was okay.

5/ix/80 LC falls within the imbecile range (20–49).

I'd sticky-taped the key to the front cover. Borderline deficiency (70–80); moron (50–69); with possible characteristics of each group. For example, 'idiot' (below 20): stooped walk, inability to form full sentences, tendency to follow organised sport.

This wasn't me talking. It was encyclopedic. I was just trying to understand.

LC. (Terman's). Approximately 95 (normal or average intelligence). Which makes his case intriguing. Is he aware of his own behaviour? Or is it the grog?

It could've been. I watched as he came out with a beer and sat on his front porch. He drank, looked across the road and in my window. Shit! I moved the telescope and peered through the curtain. His head didn't move. Wendy came out, handed him a plate, and went back in. He started eating and his eyes moved east.

'Tea.' Jen stood in the doorway. 'You still perving on people?'

'It's not perving.'

But she was already down the hall, at the table. 'Mum, he's watching people again.'

I followed. 'Mr Champness is shouting at Wendy.'

'None of your business,' Jen said.

'Didn't ask you, and next time, knock.'

Pop was sitting at the table reading, the broadsheet spread over sliced bread and a half-drunk schooner. 'Not in the mood for you two prattling.'

'Tell him, Pop. It's illegal, isn't it, watching people through that thing.'

He wouldn't be drawn. There was old news to be consumed; stale bread. Last night's rewarmed roast.

Mum came in, put the plates down and said to her dad, 'Not at the table.' She said it every day, and he read it every day, before putting it away. That was the pattern: break rule, apologise, do it again.

There was nothing worse than re-warmed roast. The meat turned to leather, the vegetables to small, explosive devices that rolled across your plate. Mum said, 'How would you feel if someone was looking in your window, Clem?'

'Exactly,' Jen, added.

'I'm not lookin' in anyone's window.' I tackled the ball-bearing peas. 'I's just watchin' what's goin' on. He was right in her face again, and she just stood there.'

No reply.

'It's not right, is it?'

'At least they're minding their own business,' Jen said.

Mum had already accepted the Champnesses' situation. She wasn't so sure about me. 'You could see people getting changed.'

'Yuck!' Jen said.

'I don't look at that. I can't see in—'

'How would you feel?' Jen continued. 'Pullin' on yer dacks and you look out—'

'I didn't ask you.'

'I'm just sayin',' Mum said. 'People are entitled to their privacy.'

A few years ago, Mum had found my notebook of suburban observations, studied it, asked me why I was so interested, and I'd told her it was scientific. But she wasn't happy with that; it wasn't quite right for a twelve-year-old.

Pop was chewing, his teeth clunking. Old meat took a bit of work when your falsies didn't fit.

'How is it?' Mum asked.

'Good.'

That was it. All food was good. If someone'd gone to the trouble of cooking it, that's what you said, no matter how awful it was.

Mum was curious. 'He hit her?'

'Pushed her.'

She took a moment to chew this over. 'It's a pity.'

'What?'

'Cos they're Catholics. They'll put up with anything. Pope won't let them ...' She trailed off. There was no point getting Pop started on the Pope.

He said, 'If she's stupid enough to stay with him.'

'It's not that simple,' Mum argued.

'It is.' As he worked on a slippery potato.

'Where would she go?'

'There are places. Shelters.'

'Not at her age.'

Pop gave her one of his are-you-stupid looks.

'What?'

'Nothin'.' Conversation never went the way you wanted.

'I asked her once,' Mum said, as a sort of excuse for doing nothing. 'Remember, Dad?'

'Yeah.'

'And she wouldn't talk to me for months after. Then one day she was at the door with eggs, and it was all forgotten. So I never dared again.'

All this presented as proof of the importance of suburban autonomy. Every man and woman to his or her own quarter acre.

'Who else you been lookin' at?' Jen asked.

'Enough!' Pop growled. He stared at his granddaughter. 'He's not hurtin' no one.'

She was a small dog, deciding whether to bite his ankle or lick his hand.

Mum said, 'Eat yer tea.'

Plates were cleaned, mostly. Pop mopped his gravy with bread; licked his fingers. With the food eaten, he returned to his paper. 'Just lookin' at the price of new cars.'

Mum started clearing the dishes. 'We can't afford a new car.'

'Cheaper than fixin' that thing.'

'Well,' she sang, from the kitchen, 'that's why we got you.'

'Comes a point.'

And returned. 'It's that clapped out, is it?'

'Wouldn't get nothin' for it, so Clem could have it.'

'What about me?' Jen asked.

'You get the bus.'

The end of the Datsun? What was Pop thinking? It could be made to keep going. Forever, if need be. There was a fella round the corner with an old Buick that still purred. And Datsuns were better than Buicks, surely. They were excellent machines. Thrown together in an afternoon, admittedly, but thought out, so they'd last. Bowed wheels? So what? On Terman's scale, genius or near genius (140 and over). What were Holdens? Dullness (80–90). It'd be like selling your own child. What was he saying? 'I can look after it, Pop.'

He burped, and covered his mouth when it was too late. 'We'll see.'

Backyards are a map of life. As kids, we wander aimlessly, and everything's so big. We jump off the roof of the tool shed, and because our ankles are strong, our legs supple, we just roll, then climb up and do it again. A few years later we're too busy with *what if?*, the side door to the shed, to Datsunland, shotgun reloads and MP-40s (after watching another episode of *Combat*). The fence, the border with other countries, inner worlds collapsing under the weight of Mrs Donnellan's weeds. Dogshit songlines to be followed, dead grass where Pop always parked cars, leaving engine blocks, piles of tyres and pipes that shouldn't be thrown out because you never know when they'll come in handy.

Maps, and hikes through wattle jungles that were only an hour, or afternoon, but were all hours, and every afternoon. Trails that lingered, although they were overgrown with experience, bitterness, an unemployed indifference that was always calling, Back, back, remember how there was a tiger here?

I was still there, putting the old pool ladder over the back fence, climbing into the lane behind Frontline Ford, around the corner and out onto North East Road. I went into Don's fish shop. Don-the-Greek, Pop called him, because if you were a wog you needed to be reminded, and we had to remember. Wogs didn't live in Gleneagles. It was likely (Pop had said) Don lived in Croydon, and commuted to his hot little shop along the road of many Kingswoods. Not that we didn't have any ethnics. A girl called Alice Wong, who lived with a hundred other Wongs in a brick house on Dictionary Road.

'Hi,' I said.

Don didn't acknowledge me; never had. A childhood of empty bottles, five-cent refunds, so if you got ten you could afford a bag of mixed lollies. So, he'd probably worked out I was never going to make him rich. *The Australasian Post* for Nan, when she was alive. Walking home with a handful of Gold Coast meter maids in too-small bikinis and cowboy hats. 'Minimum chips, please.'

He gave me a minimum chips look (*has-it-all-come-to-this?*). Eighty cents' worth, as the Dukes tumbled inside a telly perched on top of the fridge.

I sat and waited. More *Post*s, *Wheels*, and a view of an empty fish tank that had never seen water. A good idea, I suppose, when he opened. A great white moment. But getting around to things, that was the problem. Filling it, buying the fish, and how was that going to boost profits? All people wanted was flesh, and chips, and maybe a hint of the exotic with a pineapple fritter. For me, a potato fritter. That was value for money.

Don shook his basket and watched the chips fry, waiting for the perfect shade of brown. The other hand on his hip. A urine-coloured apron and shirt open to his breastbone, revealing a proper Mediterranean rug and a gold Christopher. Nine o'clock shadow and gold fillings. Which is why I loved to sit and watch Don cook my chips.

I stood, examined the lollies, the teeth especially, and the pre-packed bags that were full of the crap no one wanted. Me and Jen, circa 1978. Mixed lollies, please? No, I like the raspberries. (Don's growl): Full a raspberries. (Jen): I don't like jubes.

'Pretty warm, eh?' I said.

Don didn't turn. 'Hot.'

I sat on the front step, eating. Don had returned to the paper, and the little bits of batter that had been frying all day. When I finished I returned to the lane, the pool ladder, and the yard. Got over, pulled the ladder back and headed in. Mum'd say, Where you been? I'd have to lie. Another Peter Parker moment.

'Oi!'

I looked around.

'Here!'

There was Curtis, peering through the gal, a sheet you could lift back, climb through, into another world. France, or Senegal, perhaps. People with a different language. Unfamiliar clothes on familiar lines. Same weeds, but other trees, and tomatoes that had been trained.

I climbed through into next door. 'Whatcher doin'?'

But I could see the cigarette in his hand. Sterling 25s: good value. I always paid half. He took one out of the box, lit it off his and handed it to me. We sat behind a mound of dirt and settled in with our smokes. One of the great pleasures of life. The peppermints rattling in the bottom of the box, although I guessed Mum would smell it.

'Where y' been?' he asked.

'Don's.'

He stubbed out one, and lit another. 'I wouldn't eat his food.'

'Why?'

And he explained how Don stepped out the back of his shop, went into a little toilet, pissed, re-holstered and walked back in without so much as attempting to wash his hands.

'So?'

'And you eat his stuff?'

'It's deep fried. That'd kill anything.'

But Curtis wasn't so sure. Wog piss was strong piss. Given, you wouldn't taste it in the rancid oil, but those bugs (he insisted) can live in the vents of volcanoes, so I'm sure they can cope with Don-the-Greek's chip fryer.

'You been spying on him?' I asked.

He gave me is *surely-not* look. 'At least I don't catalogue the whole street for ASIO … y' dirty little perve.'

'At least I don't watch people takin' a piss.'

'He doesn't shut the door. I was sittin' here smokin' and I heard the *stream*.'

'The *stream*?'

'Yes. Strong, golden, deep-fried. Going on for several minutes (that man must have an extraordinary bladder). As he fumbles his appendage, collecting billions of Escherichia. Oh, and havin' a bit of a pick at the same time.'

'You're so full of shit.'

'That too. The door ajar, but you can see. Flush. No attempt at a wash. Then in comes Clem Whelan. *Minimum chips, mister.* You, are, such, a sucker.'

'You are full of shit.'

We continued smoking with due diligence.

Curtis said, 'You can buy the next pack.'

'Why?'

'He's getting suspicious. Asked how old I was.'

'Yeah, but you look older than me.'

Although I didn't think he did. Neither of us had turned seventeen. I'd started shaving in Year Nine, but he'd taken another twelve months. 'He knows my Mum. If I buy them …'

'Bullshit he knows your mum.'

'He does. She goes in there for Pop's smokes.'

Curtis wasn't sure. He guessed the old guy in the deli didn't really care how old he was. Sixteen was as good an age as any to get started. His mum came out the back door. We ducked, lowered our cigarettes, and he said, 'Ssh!'

We watched as she unpegged the washing, looked around, called, 'Curtis!' then went back in, mumbling (loud enough to hear), 'Little shit.'

The Burrells were blood neighbours: Curtis, who I'd travelled, tumbled and struggled through school with; his brother, John, who'd melted into the ether of juvenile delinquent homes, always returning like a bad smell before stealing something else, welcoming the paddy van (again) and disappearing for another three or six months; Anne and Gary, who seemed the whitest of white-bread parents, starchy, medium-sliced, obsessed with the fate of their two irregularly shaped sons. Children as loaves that hadn't cooked in the middle, or had risen into un-sellable rhombi, or burned on the bottom.

Curtis, with his sharp teeth and little knob-ended nose, sucked obsessively on the last few millimetres of fag. 'Your Pop's gettin' bad.'

I still had half a cigarette. 'How's that?'

'I walked past him yesterday and said hello and he just looked at me.'

I stopped to think, to study the streaky sky, full of everything I knew about Pop. 'He just takes a bit of reminding.'

Curtis sat up, put out his smoke and said, 'I told him who I was. Curtis. Curtis Burrell, from next door, and he said: You don't have to tell me, I know who you are, Curtis.'

'You just gotta keep reminding him.' Knowing this wasn't really the case. Via Mum, via the doctor, who'd told her the circuits were crumbling and you had to get ready to deal with the fact: he was leaving us. 'Something's gonna get all of us,' I said. 'Like you, with the smokes.'

'So what? You get a good fifty years, that's enough. I have no intention of sitting in some home pissing and shitting myself and … forgetting.'

'You may not have a lot of say in it.'

'That's why you gotta keep smokin' a lot of these.' And he grabbed my smoke and inhaled. I reclaimed it. 'It's a pity,' I said. 'It's gonna be interesting when he …'

Curtis was watching me, thinking. 'You'll have to put a lock on the door.'

But this wasn't him being mean. It was just Curtis. It had always been his way. At age nine he'd decided he'd had enough of childhood. He got up one day, went out for breakfast and said, Good morning, Anne, Gary.

Two open mouths.

How are you both?

According to him, his mum had said, *Anne?*

That okay? We've gotta move on. I can't watch *The Hulk* forever.

Although he was having his own Hulk moment. Bruce Banner caught in the gamma radiation of early adolescence, and childhood. An alter ego filling with air, stretching, straining at the joints, ready to explode in a glumph of green.

Then, he'd told me, he'd told them he'd packed his toys in boxes and sealed them, and would they mind driving them to Vinnies? He'd had enough of all that. They needn't worry about toys any more. Just books. Is that okay with you, Gary?

Gary had said, Where the hell is this coming from?

He'd said, I thought you'd be glad. I'm tired of Uncle Harry too – all that how are you *matey* crap. What's the point? I'm ready, you're ready. I've given Clem my comics. I think he'll take a while, if you know what I mean.

All of this was, and is, apocryphal, of course, but it makes for a good story. He'd seen the world, and decided that childhood was a con. Children were kept childish because adults felt guilty about forcing them to grow up too soon, although that's what they really wanted. So, a game was played. An education that should've taken eight years was spread out over twelve. Gainful employment was denied. Mummy, Daddy, I want an Evel Knievel was invoked, and the whole dreadful process drawn out. But it needn't be the way. What do you reckon, Anne?

Apparently his dad had hit him so hard he'd gone flying, but I don't think anyone would believe that. I suspect he saw it somewhere on telly, or a movie. In the same way childhood and adulthood blurred, so did fantasy and reality. There was never a line. Just oil in water. Like his brother with his hand on a pack of fags while the deli guy was in the back room.

Curtis smiled, and I knew it meant trouble. 'I got some good stuff,' he whispered.

'What?'

'Well.'

He half-ran, crouching, across the yard. I followed. There was a watchtower cubby house, built on stilts, and we climbed the metal steps and went inside. This had always been our refuge. A sort of Colditz unescaped; a fifteen-foot meat locker full of all the wrong things. There was a hole in the floor, and a fireman's pole, and when you had to go in for tea you'd slide down. On the day of his premature graduation into adulthood Clem had asked his parents (apparently) if it could be dismantled. It would just be an uncomfortable reminder. A week later, of course, we were back inside, planning the invasion of the Greater Reich, laid out below in shades of gun-grey and eucalyptus. From up here (there was a window looking out in each direction) I could see our backyard, into the shed, Pop busy inside; across the road, Les Champness asleep on his porch; the roof of Don's shop.

Curtis lifted a floorboard, produced a packet of smokes, opened it and said, 'Can't say a word.'

'Go on.'

A tightly rolled smoke. But I knew what it was.

'Where'd you get it?'

'John's. There were a few in his drawer.' He smelled it, offered it to me for a sniff. 'Shall we?'

It couldn't hurt. He lit it, inhaled, and offered it.

'Nice.' A herby taste in the mouth. 'Is one enough?'

'Let's see.'

Back and forth, but it was such good quality, it lasted. Then, the sound of the gate between drive and yard. We knelt, looked out the window and saw Gary walking with a roll of aluminium over his shoulder. He stopped, checked no one was watching and continued towards the shed. Arrived, put down the roll and fiddled with a padlock. Removed it, took the roll inside.

Curtis smiled. 'Foreignies.'

'Are you high yet?'

'Yeah.'

Although you never really knew with Curtis. I couldn't feel a thing. I watched the shed. 'What's he doing?'

'His *stash* …' And he inhaled a gain. '*Stash* …' Almost eating the word, rolling it in his mouth, salivating.

I didn't need an explanation. Gary Burrell worked for a steel supplier. There was always a bit left over, and it was a shame to waste it. Like excess nectarines left in a wheelbarrow on the footpath. Like the gear in John's drawer. John himself had learned the lesson early, and made the logical extension. Unfortunately, not as successfully as his dad. In a whole-street sense, no one really made the connection. Crime was in the eye of the beholder. What went around came around (if you waited till after closing).

'He'll smell it,' I said, returning the smoke.

'No, he won't.'

I watched over the ledge as Gary came out, locked the shed and walked towards his back door. He stopped again, sniffing the air. I grabbed the joint from Curtis, snubbed it out and whispered, 'Ssh!'

Gary went inside, happy with his day's work.

'I got others,' Curtis said, shaking the box.

'Clem!'

I saw Pop standing on our back porch. 'Come on, yer mother needs a hand.'

'Gotta go,' I said.

'I'll save 'em,' he replied. 'Our *stash*, eh?'

Oh, and acting, that's another thing he was good at.

We are defined by walking. Movement, away from the familiar, towards the unknown. As if there's some promised land, or wizard, or Hardy Boy adventure; 31, 33, 35, and on, past the basketball stadium car park and the flats on the corner of Lanark III. This walk, I sensed – still do – is one I took before I was born. Always alone. There's a destination, but I'm not aware of it. Vaguely, paddocky, with streams and stone ruins from some Walks of England documentary.

So I keep going, towards Holden Hill, to buy a replacement D-string for my guitar. Mum bought it for my sixteenth birthday, but regretted it now. It'd come with a crappy music stand and *Daily Exercises for Guitar Beginners*. Not that I was interested in that; I only needed three chords, and attitude. Elvis under the sheets, until I mastered E and A formations, then the world was my oyster. Minor chords and an expanded repertoire that lasted well into the night, at which point Mum would call out, If you don't stop—! Followed by Jen, He can't even play it. Followed by Pop, grumbling something about an arse-up Segovia.

Lanark Avenue was cut short by the mound that ran beside Delhi Avenue. My theory: all of the dirt they'd piled up when they'd graded the suburb. So much of it that one day someone had said, That'd make a nice feature, wouldn't it? Then someone had planted grass, but that had died, a few trees, and they were still struggling, a blue metal path with more cracks within cracks. It did serve a purpose, though.

Brawls.

Scene: Barry Davis taking a screamer on Stephen Prawer, who goes down, feels his back, stands, takes a swing at Barry and connects with his cheek. Along comes Mr Gottl, pulls them apart and sends them to the office. Followed by the cane, or detention. Then, left alone, Stephen says to Barry, 'Three-thirty, on the mound.'

School bell, a tidal surge through the gates, a hundred kids on the mound, Stephen and Barry throwing down their bags, and straight into it. Fists, kicks, bodies held down, released, thrown around. It wasn't pretty, but it was a part of everyone's primary education in Gleneagles. For some, the highlight.

It was always over quickly. One of the neighbours would come out and the crowd would disperse, but Stephen and Barry would keep going, loose teeth and sore ribs, scratched faces, black eyes.

The neighbour would take them by the scruff, but they'd kick, seeking flesh, until they were delivered to the front office. Then we'd go home.

'Hey.'

I turned to see Ernie Sharpe (35), walking his poodle, Fi-Fi. 'Weather,' he said, nodding towards the dark clouds, off to the east.

'Good, eh?' I asked.

'Her place'll stink like piss.'

Her being Mrs Donnellan, the cat lady of Gleneagles. She had a dozen, maybe more, and Ernie was always on about them.

'Think it'll rain?'

But he never answered stupid questions, or bothered with small talk. 'I told yer mum we should call the council.'

'About her cats?'

'You're only allowed two.' He stopped and waited for Fi-Fi to dry-piss.

'Pop hates them. Says she doesn't get them fixed.'

'Course not.' He pulled her on. We turned another corner and passed Gleneagles Primary, a pebblecrete monument to a Sunburnt Country. Centenarian pine trees and the car park of Mr Gottl's moment of grace. 'Always rootin' each other. And I found a load of kittens in me shed.'

I felt a few spots of rain. 'What did you do with them?'

He wasn't about to say. There was some chance I'd tell Val, and then he'd be in trouble. 'Back to school, eh?'

'Next week.'

'How much longer you got?'

'Last year. Matric.'

But he wasn't interested in that. 'Government wants to sack them.'

'Who?'

'The teachers. They hate teachers. I know they're a lazy pack of bastards, but you need 'em, I s'pose.'

'Good if they sacked all ours.'

Ernie had the bone. 'They reckon if they sack a few thousand, make the classes bigger, they can save ten million. That's the sort of people we got running the place.'

He seemed to be enjoying his afternoon soapbox. Thirty years a unionist had left him with a simple world view: workers worked, bosses screwed them, politicians couldn't give a shit, as long as they kept their jobs.

'At least yer mum didn't send you to St Paul's. That'd be even worse.'

Like Pop, he hated the Catholics.

'Ten million, and we'll have a bunch of boneheads, but they can't see that.'

Soon it would be Marx, and the red flag, and that bitch Thatcher needs stringing up. Tripping over words, spitting, shaking his head in disgust.

'What you gonna do with yourself after that?' he asked.

I shrugged. 'Work in a bank.'

'Ha!'

I knew what this meant: banks were evil. The reason workers couldn't get ahead.

'I thought you was gonna be a mechanic, like yer pop.'

'Maybe.'

Fi-Fi stopped, looked up at him, and he knew. He picked her up and we continued walking. 'Anyway,' he said, resting his hand on my shoulder, 'you got your whole life ahead of you, so don't be in a rush.'

'I'm not.'

'My dad expected me to be a boilermaker, but my mum said, let him choose. But you couldn't choose, not back then. At fifteen I was already welding boilers. I don't think I enjoyed a single day.' He put Fi-Fi down, but she refused to walk, so he picked her up, and we continued. 'Every day I'd think, give it another six months …' He faded, lost in another world, another life. 'Your mum says you got a good brain.'

'Did physics, but dropped out. I didn't get it. I like history.'

'What sort?'

'European.'

I could hear his smile creaking. 'I could help you with that.'

'How's that?'

'Marx and Engels. It's what they saw in the mills. Kids, half your age, losing hands. No education, nothing. That's what you wanna study. I got some books on it.'

'Maybe you could help me.'

'Oh yeah, I can help you. Look at that place ...' He indicated the infant school of Gleneagles Primary: an old, wooden building with the gutters falling off, the roof rusted away. 'Main thing is, use your eyes and your brain. See things for what they are.'

'What's that?'

But, I guessed, if you had to tell someone ...

'See you, then,' he said, carrying Fi-Fi home.

I'd never trained my spyglass on the Sharpes. But I'd started a file on them.

3/v/82 Ernie and Val Doonican. Walk Tall. He has the lot. Twenty or more records. He showed me, asked if I'd like to listen, or borrow one. Now I can hear them of a night from my window.

I walked the kilometre or so along North East Road: Toyotas, the side entrance to the school, the deli (soft porn and Sterling 25s), Savings Bank, and chicken shop. Camelot Motors, with its yard full of clapped-out Datsuns. Then Holden Hill Music. 'D-string, please.'

And more of the same as I walked home: four lanes of traffic, arteries pulsing with Sunny four-doors and King Cab utilities. The sky cracked and flashed and it rained and I just walked. Always walked. Light; heavy, a downpour that laid itself thick and syrupy on the hot footpath and road. Steaming under my feet.

12/iii/79 Pop reckons Ernie's gone mad. He can't handle the heat. Reckons he saw him running in his undies down Dragon Street. Mental instability? Ida was chasing him, calling for him to come home. But it doesn't sound like Ernie.

It got heavier. I could feel it on my arms, through my T-shirt and on my legs. I was saturated, but it didn't matter. Wet sneakers, spongy with every step.

I waited in the kitchen as Mum dissected the cakes, laid them in Tupperware and sprinkled them with cinnamon. 'Pre-reading,' she said.

'What?'

'*Pardon*. Pre-reading: biology, cells, animal groups—'

'*I know*, but what is it, exactly, I should be doing?'

'Gwen's son, Ted, he—'

'Christ.'

'*Pardon?*'

She indicated the crucifix above the door, but it was only there for bad language. 'She says he's been lookin' over his books for weeks.'

'He's an idiot.'

'He's trying.'

'He failed every test.'

'*He's trying.*' And she glanced at Jesus, obviously more pleased with Ted. She sealed one of the containers. 'Take that in to Val, will you?'

'Do I have to?'

'And then help Pop. He's having problems.'

'He took the whole thing apart.'

'Well, help him put it back together.'

Mum had reached a crisis point. Long ago, she'd decided all men were unreliable. There was Dad, of course, scissored from the pages of family history, but (as she pointed out) you didn't have to look far to see who was running the world. Ida Sharpe, tipping Ernie's whiskey down the sink; Val, with one in a wheelchair and the other too lazy to scratch his arse; Anne Burrell, with a pair of little crims and a light-fingered husband; even Wendy Champness. See, she'd say, it's us women holding the world together. The world being Lanark Avenue. What about Hester Glasson? I'd ask. Well, who knows about her? But I'm sure if you could see over that fence you'd find her cutting and sewing while he counted the money.

I jumped the fence and headed for Val Donnellan's front door. Cats, everywhere, including a big tabby with a missing eye where Ernie had thrown a rock at it. Gravel, part desiccated weed mat, two narrow tracks where David came and went every morning and afternoon. The porch where me and Jen had tackled *Hamlet*. Peter Donnellan was up a ladder, covering a fruitless mandarin tree with a net, itself full of holes. 'Hey,' I called, and he replied, 'Hello to you, Clem.' The lawyer in search of plump mandies, and other things. His Catweazle beard and Christ-like hair tied up with a band; his Vinnies pants and dad's old work shirt. A budget sage, in the shade of his own ambitions.

I knocked and heard Val calling, 'Someone get that.'

I waited, and waited. Then the door opened, and Val stood smiling. 'Clem. What cha got there?'

'A cake. Mum made it for you. Said she had too much mixture.'

But it was never too much mixture. If you were making one you might as well make two. I handed it over and stood back, trying to think of an excuse.

'Come in for a cuppa?'

'She wants me to help Pop.'

But that never worked. So, a few minutes later I was sitting in her kitchen – more Jesus, more melamine – waiting for the kettle to boil.

'White with two, wasn't it?' she said. Apparently she still couldn't remember. More likely, it was part of the routine, the tea ceremony: the warming of the cup, the clockwise stirrings of the pot, the drawing-out of conversation. I watched her old hand with its tremor (although she never spilt the tea). The spot where the pot went; the same chipped plate for the biscuits; the same biscuits; the Cornish Seascapes tablecloth with its permanent stains. 'School soon?'

'Next week.'

'Looking forward to it?'

'Yes.' Just in case it got back to Mum.

'Fay says you got a good brain.'

She'd been saying that for years, despite increasing evidence to the contrary. I'd been clever in primary school; made beautiful macaroni murals, had a spotless speed and accuracy record, and what was true then was true now.

'David left with honours,' she said, looking across at her son.

He just nodded and smiled and jiggled a bit so the wheels on his chair scraped on the lino floor.

'He used to study all night ... all hours. You were determined, weren't you, darling?'

David twisted his head. You could see how the muscles wanted to do one thing, him another. He strained, released, but managed to look me in the eyes. 'Go over everything, twice, thrice,' he said. 'I can help.'

'That'd be good.'

Val was admiring her damaged son; her scrunched-up boy-man. She was beaming, proud of the second lawyer in the family. The degrees hung in the hallway, close to her second Jesus. Yellow parchments with crests and copperplate signatures proclaiming Peter and David Donnellan bachelors of law, 1969. David, still waiting for his first case; Peter, doing what he needed to do to be called a lawyer, although everyone agreed, he was no Perry Mason.

'I always told your mum,' she said. 'He'll do something creative. Remember those plays you used to write?'

'Yes.'

'That's something you could do. That one with the sock puppet ... you had us all laughing.'

I feigned some sort of look, mouth open, lost, as if I had no recall, no memory of sock puppets and Alf Garnett-inspired rants on the porch of number 33. Val knew me as a seven-year-old, and always would. Size didn't matter.

'Your hands were so small ...' She put down her cup and examined each of my fingers. 'Remember when you tried the piano?'

'For a while.'

'We thought you'd go good on that with yer long fingers. They're still long, aren't they?' She stared at them, but seemed to be moving beyond digits. 'Fay reckons you've got a guitar?'

'Yes.'

'Reckons yer not half-bad.'

Although Mum would never say that to me. 'I was thinking of starting a band.'

David moved in his chair, as if this idea excited him. I turned to him and said, 'You were in a band, weren't you?'

'Yes ... folk band. I played the drums.'

They were still in his room, but you couldn't mention them. Mum reckoned it would've been better for Val to sell them instead of leaving them where he could see them every day. 'Pretty hard, eh?' I said. 'To play the drums?'

He managed to nod. 'If you wanna get good ... it takes forever.' Then his head dropped, and he was gone.

'Your dad ...' Val said.

I waited. 'Did he play something?'

She picked up her tea, and drank. 'I think Fay said something about it.'

'What's that?'

'I can't remember.' But her face suggested she did. I knew, she knew, she had no right talking about him. If it got back to Mum there might be all sorts of trouble. Instead: 'Pop still gettin' plenty of work?'

'Still does a few, but it takes him forever. I think people get sick of waiting and go other places.'

'Likes his cars?'

'I help him when I can, but there's not much work. Not enough to make it worthwhile. But if he wasn't doing it ...'

'Yes.'

That's all. One word, which was hundreds. *Yes.* Val thinking perhaps: He'd go downhill even quicker. 'He used to have five or six lined up out the front. People knew him, and they came, and paid him good too.' She wrapped her hands around her cup again. I took a few gulps, to move things along as quickly as possible. But then thought, Why? Where am I going?

'Good man, your pop.' Her head dropped; she was off, again, holding the tea and cinnamon cake, but not eating. Stopping, refilling her cup before smiling at me. 'More?'

I had to say yes.

Despite what Mum said, Lanark Avenue had had many good men. Pop had told me about Mr Donnellan, gathering his wife, his two beaming boys, and setting off for Australia. Leaving behind the broken bricks and grey, exhausted hours; the small tobacco shop that had never turned a profit.

A plot in Lanark Avenue. A few new mates, copper-topped stumps, a floor, walls, roof, and hi-ho, off we go. Gleneagles Primary (in the years before Mr Gottl) and High, and university and LL.B. Sun, rosemary, and a single cat. A gravel path and a porch with a blind, so it could be made into a stage for the neighbours' kids. And Mr Donnellan, sitting before his PVC Penzance, drinking tea with his wife and saying, If I went tomorrow, I'd be happy.

Why's that?

Cos I bought those tickets.

Val had told me this story over and over, as I sat in her kitchen drinking tea, imagining Mr Donnellan coming home, embracing his stiff-muscled son, saying how bloody beautiful life was in Lanark Avenue. She'd told me all about him. A bow tie on Sundays. Braces that pulled his pants up his bum (as she and the boys laughed). How he helped Pop build his shed of many Datsuns. How he mowed his lawn every Saturday morning, in praise of the Australian way; pruned the roses in the first week of July; brewed beer that always went bad; told his sons how, one day, with a bit of hard work, they could be running the country.

How he woke up one autumn morning in 1958, went out to pick the paper off the drive, leaned forward and dropped dead with a stroke. How they all ran out, but how he was already halfway cold.

And that's where she'd stop talking about him. Because, by

then, David would be crying. Fourteen-year-old David, running out with his brother, shaking his dad, refusing to concede that life would change because of this moment.

The tea was so strong you couldn't drink it. But I had to. It stayed on the gums, under the tongue, so I soaked it up with more of Mum's cake.

'Your Pop'd do anything for anyone,' Val said. 'Compared to him ...'

She cocked a thumb in the direction of Ernie Sharpe.

'If we could move, we would, wouldn't we, David?'

'Yes.'

'Nothin' against no one else ... *but him*.'

Every conversation came back to Ernie and his hate of cats.

'I was saying to David (wasn't I, David?) that he won't be happy till we've gone. Then he can see this place knocked down, and he'll have a party, I suppose.'

'What's he been saying?'

She indicated a picture on the wall and told me it was Slapton, a beach her and Mr D'd go to before the boys came along. 'Threatenin' to call the council again. Only three are mine, I told him, but he says they're all mine, and I never fixed none. But I did. Didn't I, David?'

'Yes.'

Tea and cake. I couldn't afford to take sides.

'But it's not like they're hurtin' anyone, are they, Clem?'

'No.'

'I do put a bit of food out for them, but it'd be cruel not to. They'd starve.'

I tried. 'What's he want you to do?'

'I dunno.'

'What's Ida say?'

'She keeps out of it.'

The conversation slowed. Another picture of another beach, in Wales. 'Maybe you could sell some,' I said.

'How would I go about that?'

'Put an ad in the paper.'

She took a moment to think, then said, 'I'll give it some thought.'

'Maybe Ernie'd help?'

'*No*, not that man. He poisons them.'

'Really?'

'Not sure what he uses, but he buries them in his yard. I've seen.'

'What?'

'Little graves. I've seen them. I could call the police. I might.'

'Give it a bit of thought, Mrs Donnellan. I could help. Trap them, perhaps.'

'I will.'

And with that, the ceremony was over, the pot empty, until next time. I shook David's hand and left them alone, together, to save the leaves that they could use again.

Escaping the house wasn't always about avoiding the heat. Sometimes Jen and the Abba habit that had gone on too long; Mum and the *Drearies*; Pop listening to the races, Our Velocity two lengths in front; slammed doors; the toilet hissing for hours if you didn't lift the lid and jiggle the stopcock.

Mum had planted a fern. It had spread out against the sun, so you could sit on the wobbly seat and imagine you weren't in Gleneagles. Until the Ford mechanics started changing tyres, or put on their Motörhead radio. Always noise. As if there was some thought to be avoided.

Vagueness in conversation …

Volume thirteen. Memory loss: Alzheimer's. I smoothed the page and studied the photo of an old man – big, scared eyes, mouth open to any possibility. More old people looking at him, as if to say, Are you Harry?

Forgetting people or places …

Lanark Avenue was Pop's universe. He knew, had known, every

planet by its name, its issue (small, delicate moons trapped in orbit), its day and year length. He'd say, No, Mrs Lifton, her daughter moved to Perth, but now he had no idea who Mrs Lifton was. He'd given up on Lanark I and III. Now, it was just us, and Val and Peter and David (on a good day); the Burrells and the Glassons, because he loved how Ron could cut a sheepskin to fit any car.

Life expectancy after diagnosis: eight to ten years …

It had been four years since Mum had first taken him to the specialist. So what happened next? Nappies, bed sores, a body in the lounge room; a lump that had to be fed, and turned and toileted? The thought was tiring, and by thinking it, nothing was solved. Instead, I heard the rustle of cigarette foil, mints in a box, sage on my tongue. I left the book, climbed through the fence into number 29 and looked around. No one. Across the yard and up the metal steps, into the cubby. I lifted the floorboard and retrieved the packet, the three tightly rolled reefers that promised an escape from everything.

Whistling. Anne Burrell came out, unpegged a singlet and went back inside. I heard her calling something to Gary, a slammed door, and *Synchronicity*, loud on Curtis's radio.

'Shut that fuckin' thing up.'

Gary, again, coming out in his singlet, unpegging a shirt, and heading in.

The music quietened. Silence. I watched and waited.

31/vii/81 Curtis won't admit it, but I think Gary's been at it again. I stopped to get him on the way to school, and Anne ducked into her bedroom.

I jumped down the steps, three at a time, and ran towards the house. All the way around, then I stopped under his parents' window, and listened.

'You gonna iron this?'

'Do it yerself.'

I crept around the side of the house, opened the gate and dragged it on the concrete. Closed it, stood under Curtis's window and knocked. The music quietened, the window opened and he looked out. I said, 'Should we have yer smokes?'

'They're having a session.'

'Come on … I'll wait in the Rosies' yard.' I jumped the fence and ran across the road to number 26. Down the drive, into the backyard. I sat on the step and waited for Curtis. Knee-high weeds, skeletal trees, the back door open, as it had been since the Rosies moved out in 1978. We'd often go through the place: the rooms full of flattened boxes, old magazines and rat droppings; leaves that had blown in the open doors and windows; a few of Vicky's dolls. Mum reckoned everyone knew what had happened in the backyard, and who'd want to live in such a gruesome place?

I took out the first smoke and smelt it, considered it. There was no point waiting. A puff: the shed with the collapsed roof. Another: what must've been a veggie patch, although we'd pissed in it a hundred times since they'd gone.

Curtis appeared and sat beside me. 'What y' doing?'

'Felt like one.'

'They're not yours.'

I offered him a go; he accepted, which was his way of forgiving me. 'I'm gonna get my fuckin' nuts crushed when John gets back.'

'You said he wouldn't miss them.'

'I lied.'

It didn't bother me. 'I don't think he'll be in a position to say much.'

He took the next smoke, lit it and started. 'Do you know where he is?'

'McNally's.'

'Do you know what goes on there?'

'I could guess.'

The light was dropping, the sky streaking with illicit haze. Curtis said, 'Where do you reckon?'

I stood, and motioned for him to follow. My bet was the old lemon tree. 'He wouldn'ta needed much height. Just enough to keep his feet off the ground. That's a common misconception – that you need a long drop. But people do it in wardrobes.' I stood beneath a big bough. 'See, and he was a clever man, so he'd know his knots.'

'Why would he know his knots?'

I wasn't about to discuss it. 'I reckon he would've put it here.' I ran my hand over the branch, feeling for the groove, a mark, any sign.

'There's nothing there.'

'Seven years – the wood woulda grown back.' I moved closer, inspected every inch. 'See, a little mark, just here.'

He squinted. 'Bullshit.' Then he walked back to the steps and sat down.

I followed, produced the third smoke and lit it. I could feel myself drifting, floating in the purple haze of another summer day survived.

'How do you know he even done himself in?'

'Common knowledge.'

'Urban myth.'

'Why else are they still trying to sell this place?'

'Cos it's a loada shit.'

Oswald, Tina and the holy daughter. Well, at least that's how I remembered her: red cheeks and big blue eyes, a little grin, too-perfect teeth, sitting beside me as I tried to read about what Harry the dirty dog was up to, her saying, Shouldn't you know some words by now?

I know some.

Grinning more. No, you don't!

Do!

Because even then the small tortures were pleasurable.

It was almost dark. Some of the tall grass rustled. 'Rabbits,' Curtis said.

'Rubbish.'

'Les told me he used to have some. They got under the wire, and he never found them. Mum reckons they get under our house.'

'My arse.'

He shook his head. 'No rabbits … but he hung himself?'

'Hanged.'

'What?'

2/vi/76 Spent an hour with Mr Rosie. He teaches at Gleneagles High. Showed me all his books, and said I could borrow some.

'I liked him,' I said.

'Who?'

'Oswald. But he was pretty highly strung. Smart, though. You oughta seen how many books he had. Pop still reckons that's why he did it: too many books.'

'So you're better off stupid?'

'Apparently.'

More rustling.

'Les said he had six, and they all got out. Four females. I mean, they woulda found somewhere, wouldn't they? Rabbits can adapt to anything.'

It was worth a try. I stood, mostly stoned, and ran through the tall grass. Round and round in circles, stomping on the ground. 'Come on, bunnies. Let's have yers.' I waited. 'Any come out?'

'Yes.'

'Bunnies?'

'Big one. Green and pink.'

'You're hallucinating.' I returned to my step, and although I trod lightly, and happily, I realised I was covered in burrs. I sat down and started picking them off.

Curtis said, 'These smokes are probably not good for you.'

I smiled. 'Says you.'

He leaned against the Rosies' fibro, cupped his hand to trap escaping smoke, and said, 'Pain relief … for people with cancer.'

'Mum reckons Ossie mighta had depression. And if that was the case, nothing was gonna help him. But he was a decent fella. I remember: *I have heard what the talkers were talking, the talk of the beginning and the end, but I do not talk of the beginning and the end …*'

'What the hell's that?'

'Walt Whitman. *I do not talk of the beginning and the end …*'

'Of what?'

'Whatever you want. Life. This smoke, which has nearly gone.'

'Savour it.'

I tried to be serious. '... *the talkers were talking* ...'

It was pitch black, but there were a few puffs yet.

'Monday, eh?' Curtis said.

'I tried to convince Mum ...' But I just melted onto the concrete step, into a big glub of laughter. '... to let me quit ... *school, my darling* ...'

'*School* ...' We embraced, and continued melting.

'But she wouldn't let me. Said ... fuck, I don't know what she said.'

We fell about, sucking the stubs.

'Like, you must go back to school, *you naughty little boy.*'

'No luck?'

'*Naughty, naughty* ... fuck, look, there's yer rabbit.'

We were off after it, down the Rosies' drive, the road, stopping in front of number 35. I watched the cooling house. 'You know what Mrs Donnellan reckons?'

'What?'

'Ernie's been killin' her cats.'

We tried to stand still, but failed, but supported each other.

'She reckons he's been ...' But there was no point standing in the middle of Lanark Avenue. The Sharpes' lights were out. Ernie would be at the Windsor. Ida was probably at someone's place, making up for a lost husband. 'Come on, if we don't do it now.'

We ran down the Sharpes' drive, into their backyard. I whispered: 'Mrs Donnellan reckons he's buried them *somewhere hereabouts.*'

Then we stumbled, and ended up on the parched buffalo. Rolled in some of Fi-Fi's dried shit.

'If we can see, I can tell her. *She can call the cops.*'

So we crawled, inch by inch, around the Sharpes' fence line, feeling for lumps, fresh soil.

'Who was that poet?' Curtis asked.

'Whitman ... *the beginning and the end* ...'

Then we sat up. My god, it was wearing off. Curtis said, 'I don't reckon he'd kill her cats, would he?'

A mound of soil. The size of six or seven cats. And fresh earth. We examined it, felt it and worked the loose soil. 'What do you reckon?' I asked.

He put his nose to it and smelt it. 'Doesn't smell … pussy.'

I checked. 'No, but he could have them deep.'

'Shall we look?' We started digging and removed a bucket load before a light came on in the house.

'Ssh!'

We dared not move. What if she stepped outside?

I said, 'Into the bushes.' And we dragged ourselves, inch by inch, into the cover of a woody diosma.

We heard the shower, and guessed Ernie was home.

'Run!'

Down the drive, the road, into our respective homes.

'What's that smell?' Mum asked, and I told her it was something Curtis's dad was smoking.

Mum was at my door. 'I've laid out your uniform.'

Then Jen. 'Get outa bed.'

'Fuck off.'

Then Pop. 'It's gettin' late.'

'*I'm coming.*' When I went out for breakfast they were gathered like some grand inquisition. Jen said, 'You can't be doing this every morning.'

I didn't reply. What was she, a shopgirl, a hairdresser's apprentice? I studied the badge: 'Feres Trabilsie Hair Saloon'. I said, 'It's *salon.*'

'What?'

'A hair salon, not a saloon.'

She read her badge. 'What would you know?'

Mum delivered my scrambled eggs. 'Eat up. It's a big day.'

'You should think yourself lucky,' Jen said. 'I didn't get to do matric.'

Like she'd had to go work in a mine. But that wasn't the case at all. 'Cos you failed Year Eleven.'

'Smug little prick.'

'Mum, she called me—'

'Cut it out!' Pop said, arranging his paper on the table. 'Eat yer bloody breakfast.'

I found a fork, and a reserve of energy, and said to my sister, 'How's Feres?'

She wiped her nose on the back of her hand.

'You do perms yet?'

Mum walked in, sat down and knew straightaway. 'Got all yer books?'

'Yes.'

'All covered?'

'Yes.'

Pop and I had sat, the previous day, laying out contact, covering books, flattening them, popping the air bubbles.

'Try and look a bit enthusiastic.'

'I am.'

Pop peered over the top of his paper. 'If you make up your mind you'll do well. We could be sittin' here toasting your health. Cheers to Doctor Whelan. But you gotta have the right attitude.'

'Not a bad one,' Jen said.

'You don't wanna be fixin' cars forever. Medicine ... engineer, that'd suit you.'

'I guess you're right, Pop.'

'Just thinka what Nan woulda said ...' He trailed off, trying to remember. 'Thinka Nan ... Colin.'

Colin? No one said a word. Mum sipped her tea; Jen fixed her hair, again. Who was Colin? An old mate? 'I reckon you're right, Pop. And if I became an engineer, what sort do you think?'

His face lit up. 'I love the way they build *suspension* bridges. Start with the pylons, then the cables ... supports.' But even bridges seemed to elude him.

'What about a chemical engineer?'

'That's what you wanna do, Clem. Stick to the books.'

Limited use, I guessed. Manuals could only tell you so much, but you had to know how things went back together. Newspapers, too. They told you what was happening in Lebanon – but you had to know where Lebanon was, and what all the fuss was about. I noticed the back of the paper. 'Boy George ... what a fag.'

And Jen: 'He's got great hair.'

Pop studied the photo. 'What's that, a boy or a girl?'

'Gets his hair done at Feres Trabilsie's,' I said. 'Jen can do it like that, can't you, Jen?'

'Get stuffed.'

I was trying, but it didn't matter. Mum was still watching him, her eyes darting from egg to paper to face; to our rich green Berber; the television whispering in the corner. Pop bit into toast and his falsies clunked. 'Dad,' she groaned.

'Not my bloody fault.'

'We need to get you new ones.'

'They'll last another coupla years. What's the point?'

'You can't eat properly.' She stood, gathered the plates and went into the kitchen. 'Clem, get your uniform on – I gotta drop your sister too.'

Pop took out his bottom plate, inspected it, licked it and put it back in.

'That's disgusting,' Jen said.

He spat out both plates, pulled back his lips and did his best white pointer.

'*Pop!*'

He laughed, then put them back in. 'Happen to you one day.'

'I brush my teeth.'

'So did I. None of this was my fault, was it, Fay?' Then he leaned forward, for the familiar story. Usually we'd tell him we'd heard it, but not today. 'When I was nineteen this fella told my mum I had gum disease, and all me teeth'd have to come out. Mum said, all of them? Yes, missus. Sooner the better. I can do the lot for ten quid, but I gotta do 'em today. Today? Yep. They get infected, could turn septic.'

I sat forward. 'And your mum believed him?'

'Yes. Pair of pliers, thirty minutes later it was all over.'

Jen didn't look convinced. 'Then what?'

'Then he said, Here, pop these in.' He took them out again.

'Pop!'

'Dad, put them in!'

He did as he was asked. 'Same pair … fifty years. Not bad, eh?'

I returned to my room, my uniform, my bag full of lovingly covered books. As I got ready I heard Pop say, '… she was a fuckin' Catholic too.'

Mum: 'Who?'

'That Ellman woman. And he did her for the same price.'

'That's horrible,' Jen said.

'Way it was done back then. She couldn't have afforded to keep a kiddy.'

It seemed strange, that he'd lost track of me, but remembered some girl from fifty years before.

'Eileen Ellman. And she coulda died, too, the way he did it.'

'How?' Jen said.

'He had a concoction.'

I sat looking out my window. Another year: more of the same. There was a machine that I'd be fed into and processed, filled with information and a shred, perhaps, of understanding. For this to happen I'd need a clean uniform and polished shoes and a diary to record my daily output as a function of daily input. I'd need to be on time, and have the right attitude, whatever that was, so I could absorb the same stuff another ten thousand kids were absorbing. And this little machine would chug, all year, until it ran out of petrol. Then it'd stop, and someone would say, Ah, yes, slight effort, and give me a card that said '63' and tell me what university courses 63 could lead to.

I saw Les Champness walking down his drive in his pyjamas

and slippers. He leaned over, picked up his paper and headed back. I wondered if Mr Fantastic might fix him. Stretch out of his window, take him by the singlet and say, You watch yourself, mister.

No, Mr Fantastic wouldn't fit into the drabness of Lanark Avenue, 30 January 1984. It was too hot for him already. The colours bleached from his costume, in the same way we'd all been bleached, into a light blue school shirt, grey pants and white socks. Lennon, too, still on the wall, still praying for peace.

Les went in. Assuming the machine kept working, you could fix people's pipes, or make seat covers, and then they'd give you an asbestos box on stilts. You could carpet it, put an aspidistra in the lounge room, and make more people to feed into the machine.

I heard Pop say, 'The mafia runs the church ... never been a Pope to stand up to them.'

In a way, it didn't matter what he said, as long as kept talking, as long as the machine kept working. Even if he forgot bits, or made some up. The sound of his voice; that's all that mattered. Honey-flavoured, beer-smelling. As long as he kept talking. Imagine that? Pop silent, sitting in a corner, looking at us like we were strangers. So, every little bit of it, every whisper, every scratched nostril and clunked falsie, every rustle of the paper and race call, every fart – excellent! All of it, excellent. Enough to make you happy, even if you were looking down the barrel of another year at school.

Curtis jumped the fence from 29. Same school bag, I noticed. Old shirt and pants, shoes with a bita polish, perhaps. He approached the window. 'Can I geta lift?'

'Come in.'

He was gone, around the garden, across the path that led nowhere, towards our front door. I went out to greet him, and Pop was on his feet, holding his head in his hands. 'He had a horse called Skeffington,' he said.

'That's it, Skeffington,' Jen said, trying to calm him.

He turned on her. 'But you wouldn't know. It wasn't Skeffington, was it?'

'It was.'

'It wasn't!'

She was scared. She clung to her handbag, full of product.

'Yes, it was, Dad,' Mum said. 'Skeffington. Bill Brown had him, remember?'

Curtis knocked, and entered. 'G'day, Mrs Whelan, Doug.' Smiling. 'Jen.'

Pop said to him, 'What do you want?'

'I was gonna get a lift to school, if that's okay?'

'Skeffington?'

Curtis took it in his stride. 'That's it, Doug. He was a good horse, wasn't he?'

Pop was unsure. 'Over long distances. You know him, Skeffington?'

'Yeah ... you were talking about him the other day.'

'I was?'

Curtis pulled out a chair and motioned for Pop to sit. Then he sat opposite him. 'My dad prefers the trots, but he knows a good horse. He's got a part-share in one, but it's come last in three races.'

'Well, Skeffington never came last.'

Again, I turned to Mum, and she was lost in Pop's eyes.

Curtis said, 'Mum reckons horses are like flushing your money down the dunny, but Dad says she doesn't get it. I see what he means, though. There's nothin' better than a nice horse, is there, Doug?'

'No, there's not.'

Jen said, 'We're gonna be late.'

Mum asked if I'd cleaned my teeth.

'Yes.'

'You have not,' Jen said. 'You're disgusting.'

Pop seemed to have rallied. Skeffington. It was definitely Skeffington. 'I'll drive yers.'

'No, you won't,' Mum said. 'You stay and read the paper.' And she opened it for him.

'I'm not useless.'

'Didn't say you were. How's about you do the dishes?'

'I haven't got time for that. I've got six cars waiting.'

'Six?'

'Couple, anyway.'

We kissed him, and left him with his cold cup of tea. As we got in the car, Mum said, 'Thanks for your help, Curtis.'

'No worries, Mrs Whelan. I tell you what we should do …'

Mum tried to start the car. It groaned, then shook.

'We should take him to the races. That'd be good, eh?'

Yes, I thought. The races. Perfect. Curtis was always the good ideas man. And it came to him so easily (120–140: very superior intelligence).

'Good idea,' Mum said, fiddling with the choke. 'We'll ask him.' She tried again. An automatic sigh, like a pair of old, diseased lungs emptying for the last time. 'Shit.'

'Battery,' Curtis said.

'I can't be late,' Jen added. 'Feres blows his top.'

Mum turned to her. 'Well, it's not my bloody fault.'

We watched as Pop emerged from the house. He waved at us. 'Hold on.' He went to the shed, opened the door and switched on the light.

'But it's in pieces,' Mum said.

But then, the sound of a purring Datsun, the gunning of an accelerator, and the Fairlady backed down the drive.

'Jesus,' I said. 'Yesterday it was …'

Pop pulled up beside. 'Come on then, get in.'

February

Day three. A timber art room with a clunking fan, half-hanging from a ceiling, transmitting light from an iron-roofed day. I completed an outline of Mr Fantastic. 'They'll let us?' I asked.

'Of course.'

Mr Andrews, our new art teacher: jeans, sandals, a decent week's growth, a couple of earrings in each lobe, red eyes from booze and drugs, or so we imagined. Nick Andrews, the first teacher who'd let anyone near his first name.

'They'll let you,' he said. 'Don't worry about them.'

Them. The administration: Miss White, the deputy; Meadows, the principal. Nick didn't seem to be one of *them*: the people who said *we've* decided to reschedule exams, or *we've* considered both positions. Maybe he was one of us, although what about the degree, teacher training, job interview, fear of disciplinary action (we'd heard stories)? 'This place is so depressing,' he said, having just described his last contract in the bush, and an art building he'd left covered in soup cans. 'Every building's beige, like someone got a good deal on it. It's enough to churn the bowel.'

We all smiled. It was going to be a good year.

'Curtis, isn't it?' he said.

Curtis looked up from his sketch: a bloated dragon with some sort of perm, an exploding head straight out of Feres Trabilsie's *Head Start to Beauty* (Wednesday evenings: 7.30–7.35). 'Yes, Mr Andrews … Nick?'

'Tell me about White.'

Curtis smiled. 'Well, every Friday morning she lines the girls up …'

One of the girls said, 'She's a bitch.'

We waited for Nick's response, but he was busy with his own sketch.

'… and inspects their fingernails. Says they gotta be short.'

'Why?'

'Typing.'

'Cos she's a moll,' another girl said.

We waited again, watched our experimental teacher, but he said nothing.

Curtis was just getting started. 'Inspects their dresses, doesn't she, Kristen?'

'Too right. She's got a ruler, and measures from your dress to yer knee, and if it's too long she sends you home.'

We saw it! Nick smiled. The only teacher, ever, who'd sided with us against Miss White. Then he noticed me and said, 'Clem?'

I felt like a little kid.

'Nice old name.'

'You reckon?'

'Let's see.'

I held up my sketch: Mr Fantastic wrapped around a telegraph pole, hands around some villain's neck, his string-o'-pearl teeth glowing in the night.

'Nice work. Next thing, trace it onto an overhead.'

This was his plan: to turn his art room into some sort of multicoloured Taj Mahal in the asphalt waste of pebblecrete change rooms and glass-sided boxes, transportables, a few terminal gum trees and various sheds for the gardeners to sleep in and the dope heads to smoke behind. The designs were free choice. It was to be our first project for the year. Ten linear metres of baby-beige-shit walls. We'd be responsible for design, colour scheme, painting and sealing. And this mural (he claimed) would be a lasting testament to our creativity, still admired in decades to come by fresh-faced Year Eights in search of inspiration. 'You asked Miss White?' I said.

'Don't worry about Miss White.'

'Or Mr Meadows?'

'He seems reasonable.'

We laughed; he looked up. 'Why's that?'

'*School is a tide*,' I half-sang. '*We ride it into shore, harness its energy, and it delivers us to the sands of fortune.*'

Nick Andrews seemed amused. 'They all have some crap like that.'

They. More evidence. This man was the John Lennon of

teachers. But how had he survived? Didn't they all gather in the staff room and laugh at us, suck smokes, drink diesel coffee and call us arse-jockeys and little crims?

'Trust me, it'll be okay. Long as it's quality work. You into comics, Clem?'

'Na.'

'He's got a big pile in his bedroom,' Curtis said.

I glared at him.

'And he still reads them.'

'Fuck off.'

Nick watched me, but didn't respond.

'Keeps them next to his telescope,' Curtis said.

'Telescope?' Nick seemed interested.

'Spies on the neighbours.'

And all the girls turned up their noses. 'That's disgusting.'

'For astronomy,' I said.

Nick was grinning. Later, I'd understand his technique: start an argument, watch the fireworks, quote a few philosophers. That was the only way, he'd claim, you could become an artist: get dirty, wrestle in the mud and pig shit, fight for every view, have it criticised and dismantled. Then, perhaps, you could worry about drawing and painting things.

As for Curtis, this was one of his worst habits: turning on his friends to widen his own circle of admirers. 'Curtis, as you'll find, is full of shit,' I said. 'I like astronomy.'

Curtis sat up. 'He showed me, he can see into people's backyards. Like Mrs Glasson, in her knickers and bra and …'

The cries almost drowned him out. Nick had rolled a smoke, and was looking for matches.

'He called me over to have a look.'

I punched him.

'You did!'

Well, I had, but I hadn't been looking. She'd just come out, all flubber and wrinkle, pulling a few dresses off the line, and I'd been watching Les Champness at the time, but there she was.

One of the girls said, 'You can get arrested for that.'

'I didn't!'

Nick said, 'That's your idea, Clem.'

'What?'

'Forget Mr Fantastic, paint what you know.'

'Mrs Glasson?'

'Exactly. Point of view of the telescope, with your neighbour, maybe all of them ... a montage.'

'You reckon I could paint them on the art room?'

'Why not?'

'Mr Meadows—'

'Bugger Mr Meadows. This is art, that's what we do.'

I grinned at his grin. It was like I'd been waiting forever to meet a Nick Andrews. Like he'd taken off his guitar, climbed down from my wall and started sketching.

The day unravelled. Lunch: Twisties inside an excavated roll. Sarah Scarr and her anaemic offsider collecting bottles for refunds. All lunch, every lunch, since primary school. A commendable work ethic, especially since everyone threw old fruit at them and called them scabs. The meatheads on the oval kicking out-of-season footballs, stopping to lie down, smoke, and off again. That was Gleneagles High – no blazers or First XV rugby; no Head of the River or polished shoes. Not much of anything, really. As though someone had said, I suppose we should make a school, and someone else had replied, Well, money's a bit tight, but I suppose you're right. A paddock was found, paths laid, boxes brought in on the back of flat top trucks, craned into position, wired, filled with what passed for teachers, and everyone was happy. Except the kids.

Lunch. What was a thinking man to do? Four-square with the Year Nines? Or just sit and talk, again? Same conversations, same laughs. Like when Lars Westermann let Wendy Vaughan hold his thing in the AV room while we were watching a film about metals. Mr McGarry: *You disgusting little shit!* The lights coming on, Lars zipping up, laughter and applause (although this mightn't have happened).

I walked home alone. Same roads, same unmowed lawns; same Toranas on stumps. I waited, crossed North East Road, past Don stocking his freezer with Paddle Pops. Around the block, down Lanark Avenue, again.

I knew it would all be waiting. The world never changed: Pop in his shed, Mum in her kitchen, Jen home already, because Feres (70–80: borderline deficiency) only gave her four hours a day. *It's magic, you know.* All was quiet in the Sharpes' front yard. It was too early for Ernie to head to the Windsor, Fi-Fi in tow. But Peter Donnellan was out, dressed in Ghandi-white, on his knees pulling gorse from his garden of almost every weed in the world. He looked up and said, 'How was school?'

'Shit.'

'Really?' He wiped his forehead, and squinted to see me against the sun. 'Why's that?'

'Another year of it.'

He returned to work. I wanted to ask him why he was bothering. He had a small pile, but they'd already seeded. I liked Peter. Like Dave, he'd worked out who he was, and settled on the disappointment. He'd taught me the pointlessness of qualifications, ambition, the need to get ahead. To him, the pulling of a weed, the netting of a fruit tree, the placing of his brother in his spot in the yard, were what mattered. I could see, even then, how you could be happy. Like everyone in Lanark Avenue, I guessed. All failures, in their own way. Then he said, 'You've always said that.'

'What?'

'School. Even when you were a little tacker. Remember? You'd walk past, I'd say, How's school? You'd grumble.'

'I didn't.'

'You did.'

I couldn't really argue with this. Peter had been there since the beginning. Since Mum and Dad had brought me home from hospital, and laid me in my cradle, and Mrs Donnellan had brought her sons in to see the new baby. The stuff I'd been told about. They'd probably congratulated Mum and Dad and asked about a name and said, Clem, that's a nice old name, and even (probably) heard me crying at night.

'Been watching you walk past all these years,' Peter said.

'Yeah.' What could you say?

'And you've always been in a rush to get home.'

'Just glad to get away from school.'

'Perhaps.'

Maybe, I thought, home was the place to be. Because it would be the same at four as it had been at eight. 'Got a good art teacher,' I said. 'Lets us call him Nick.'

He just worked.

'Well, keep at it.'

I was in shorts and sandals, of course, with my Clem Whelan satchel, cowlick and stick legs. And he was gardening, and I was telling him about my teachers, and art, and Mr Fantastic, and I felt bad that I'd changed, but he hadn't. I always felt bad; like these people had ossified so I could grow up.

'What do *you* reckon I should do next year?' I asked.

He shrugged. 'Keep studying. It teaches you how to think.'

'I know how to think.'

He smiled. 'Yeah, guess you do. You used to say you wanted to be a pilot.'

'Na.'

'Then a mechanic.'

'For Pop.'

'Then once you said, I'm gonna be a writer. A novelist, like Dickens. And you had this book planned. You told me, remember?'

I waited.

'It sounded a bit like *David Copperfield*, but I didn't say anything.'

I thought about it. It made sense. It was like he was saying it for a reason. 'What do you reckon?'

'Gleneagles needs a famous writer. You could fit the bill.'

I almost laughed. 'Any ideas?'

But he didn't reply. And I didn't need a reply. I could still hear Nick Andrews telling me to do what I knew. 'You're gettin' sunburnt,' I said.

But again, he didn't reply. He'd done a square metre of weeds. That was a good day's work.

I woke to the smell of freshly mowed lawn. Neat, and Lanark respectable. Ready to be rolled on, ball-thrown on, sat on, with the abridged *David Copperfield* Peter Donnellan had remembered. Summer nights on Onkaparinga rugs, because the house was too hot. A tranny (on the end of three extensions) playing Sherbet. The last of Don's lollies. As it got darker, and you couldn't read, but you kept reading, because what else could you do? As Mum called, Clem, come in, the mozzies'll eat you.

I could hear our mower: Pop, out back, tackling the quarter acre of grass my dad had planted in the days of fresh fibro and Peter without his Catweazle beard. I knew I should get dressed, go help, but the smell was holding me down. The mower, reshaping garden, house and street, God's voice promising a Paradise of all things orange, brown and Nana Mouskouri.

Morning glory! But I rose, sat on the end of my bed and gazed out at the wire fence. Gary Burrell, of course. In exchange for a few slabs. Fences were important. They extended pride, but defined privacy. Still, nothing could keep the strays out, and you had to check for dog shit before you ran under sprinklers. The Donnellans were front-fenceless, but that wasn't a yard anyone would want to enter. You could tell people by their fence. Les had built a wooden number, but it had rotted away, and leaned, casting Dr Caligari shadows on long summer nights lit by a cheesecake moon.

And between fence and lawn, a path that Jen had once wheeled me around as I sat in the hot-steel barrow, burning my legs. Hurry up, I'd say, thinking she was doing it for my benefit. But no. The barrow would tip, I'd go tumbling and she'd cover me with the aluminium dome, sitting on it, laughing, as the temperature rose, and I shouted and kicked, wet with sweat, until Mum came out and pushed her off.

A shirtless Les Champness came out, entered his aviary and sprinkled seed. He extended a finger and waited for a bird to settle before kissing it. More than Wendy ever got, I guessed. I thought of Nick Andrews, found a pad and started drawing the birdman. The stumpy legs, fat arse and belly that made him lean forward. Dozens of birds at his feet, pecking between his toes, as he talked to them. Man boobs, of course, bloodhound eyes and a bit of hair you had to get close to see. I stopped, examined him, and felt pleased. So on the second page, I continued. Wendy as Eve. This time from imagination: hair rollers and a net to keep them in place; black dress with apron, and a bowl to gather nectarines; slippers; and a plain expression that came from plain features.

I examined my work and saw gaps in my Creation. Ron Glasson had come out to measure someone's seat, so I drew him, arse view, but you could make out his Olive Oyl legs and long, scarecrow arms.

And this is where I sat, sketching, waiting for victims, focusing on faces and slumped shoulders and June Sharpe with her unmistakable cleavage. As the mower droned, and I felt bad that I wasn't helping.

I studied the twelve images, and felt pleased. This was the world I'd made. It smelled of cut grass and tasted of stewed apricots. It had light and dark, seasons, pimples, corns, animals and hernia scars. The void had been filled. Water, even, in the form of the sprinkler with the high-pitched hiss.

Pop wheeled the Victa up the drive. Then he disappeared out back and returned with a bag of clippings. I leaned forward and put my face to the flyscreen. 'Wait on, Pop.' I pulled on shorts and sandshoes and ran out, claimed the Victa and started. There wasn't much to mow. It just stirred up dust and dead grass. Soon, I could taste it on my tongue, feel it in my nose and ears. Ernie went past with Fi-Fi and waved. More cars pulled up for seat covers and Ron came out and looked at me like I was spoiling business. 'G'day, Mr Glasson,' I said, and he managed a smile. Pop sat down on the verandah and I called, 'In the shade.'

'Eh?'

'In the shade.'

Push, conquer, turn and return. It was all very muscular. After a few minutes Mum came out with drinks, placed them beside Pop, tried to move him, gave up, and went inside. Moments later Jen came out, got into the 120Y and drove off after saying something to Pop.

As I worked I watched my grandfather use a stick to move dirt in the garden. He picked up stones, examined them, spat on them, rubbed them, and threw them away. I switched off the mower, waited for it to die, and sat next to him. 'Finished.'

He handed me my drink and said, 'Good job.'

'You shoulda called me, I would've done the back.'

'Na.' And he shooed me, along with the flies.

He picked up another stone and examined it.

'What's that?'

'Quartz.'

I knew what was coming.

'You're hot as hell,' I said, as I drank.

'I'm fine.'

'Get your blood pressure up—'

'I'm fine! Don't need it from you too.'

Mum must've been on at him about the family history. The little vessel that'd pop, and that'd be it. But perhaps he didn't care, perhaps it would be better than dying forgetting. 'You getta good line, it leads to gold,' he said.

'Yeah?'

'I still regret it.'

I didn't reply; the story would come anyway. About his Croat mate, Arno, and how he'd gone to Coober Pedy and found a shitload of opal and made millions and returned to Europe and built a mansion, and a school for his town and blah, blah, although he knew it probably wasn't true.

Then he turned to me and said, 'It's not too late, you know.'

I waited. Next, he'd say: You and me, we could do it.

'For what?' I asked, dutifully, as the mower cooled, as Ron returned to his shed, as Ernie passed carrying Fi-Fi.

'The map.'

'It's a long way.'

'Not so far.' As he tried to convince himself, again. 'Even if we hired a four-wheel drive.'

'We'd have to, eh?'

'Plenty of water, coupla of spares. Make sure it's in good nick. We could do it.'

'We could.'

'Big adventure?'

I waited for the word. *Lasseter.*

'I worked it out the other day. Three days driving, coupla days looking, perhaps. Day digging, then home. Less than a week.'

He waited for my approval.

'Three days?'

'Four if it's hot.'

'Where would we stay?'

'Motels, or camp out. I'm not too old for that.'

It all sounded so simple. As it had for years. Ever since that day, when I was six or seven, when he'd led me to the shed and opened the big toolbox he always kept locked, took out a piece of paper, unfolded it and showed me. 'There ... see?'

'What is it?'

The name on the top. *Lasseter.*

He'd run his finger along the Stuart Highway, then the road west, into a blank of sandy dragons and hellfire. 'Look!'

More roads, with scribbled names, pictures of a mountain range, valleys, 'NATIV PYNES'. Like some idiot pirate had drawn it.

I'd asked. 'Where's this?'

'*Ah.*' And he'd tapped the side of his nose. Then, in a whisper, 'But look.'

At the end of the journey, a cross, and the words: 'Lasseter's Reef'.

Then he'd said, 'Years ago I was drinking in a pub and this fella comes over. Says, Son (I still had hair back then), I've only got a few days left. And I said, Till what? He says, To live. And I'm thinking, Why are you telling me? Then he says, You're young, starting out, you could do with a break, couldn't you? I says, I s'pose so, mister. He says, Well, could you or not? There are plenty of other people drinking in this pub. Well, I'm thinking, You stupid old prick, but then he puts this map on the bar. Says, Me and my dad found this reef of gold twenty years ago. Hundred yards long. Worth millions. I studied the map. He says, We left it there so we could go away and raise enough money to return, with machinery, take it all out, properly. But then me dad died, and I got sick, then better, then hit the bottle, then forgot about it, got sick again, better again, now I'm *really* sick. And I looked at him and tried to decide. Worth millions? Could I get that lucky? Or was he just … mad?'

I'd been amazed. I'd said, 'Is it real?'

He'd said, 'Well, that's what I had to decide. Then this old fella says, Son, you decide.'

I'd waited. 'Pop, if this is real, and there's gold there …'

'Exactly. So, I was thinking, one day soon …'

'We could go look?'

'Yeah, what d'you reckon?'

'It's worth a go.'

'If it's not there it's not there.'

Then I'd asked, 'Pop, why have you waited so long?'

He'd flattened the map and replied, 'I'm not sure. But the thing is, Clem, now you know about it too.'

We'd both sat in the shed, staring at the cross, like it was glowing, like it had chosen us, said, Come on, boys, you've had some hard times, but that's all over.

Now I wiped the sweat and dust from my forehead and said, 'What d'you reckon, Pop? Coupla million?'

'Yeah.'

He had the look. Like he'd once doubted but had overcome these feelings. But this belief, this conviction had come too late and now he was old and unable to go searching for the thing that might save him, and us, from a fibro existence.

'I'm not getting any younger, you know.' He picked up another stone, examined it, discarded it.

'I know, Pop.'

'I can still drive. And if it is there ...'

If, I thought. If. The glue that held everyone's life together. If Les would just calm down; if Ron would come over and talk; if John would stop stealing.

'If we found it and made a claim it wouldn't do me much good but you and Fay, and Jen, and your kids. That's what I'm thinking about.'

Which seemed reasonable. All you had to do was go and look and if the old guy in the pub had been a fruitcake, so what? This is what I had seen in the shed that day, and what I could still see now. It wouldn't do any harm to go and look.

He said, 'You still believe the map's right?'

'He wouldn'ta made it up, would he?' I wondered if this was the wrong thing to say. Ever since I could remember, Mum had said, 'That bloody map. Some old drunk gives it to you and you actually believe him? Dad, come on.'

'Yes, I do believe him. Why shouldn't I?'

I was getting feeling back into my hands. 'That's very famous, Lasseter's Reef. People have been searching for it for years.'

'Too right. But the thing is, that day in the pub I got lucky, but I let it go, Clem. I let it go. We gotta reclaim it.'

'Yeah, we do, Pop.'

The map was still in his toolbox, and he still showed it to me, explaining where it was, and how we'd get there. He'd planned the route, the stops, the motels, the lot. It was all just a matter of faith.

Luckily, Sunday morning was no longer Baptist. It had been, for years. Mum would drop me and Jen, Bibles in hand, hair combed, faces washed. Me in my best slacks, one of Pop's shirts, cardigan, and freshly ironed hanky. You couldn't spit in church, or anywhere near it, and hell awaited those who wiped their nose on the back of their hand.

Val Donnellan had a cross on her wall, and I'd asked her, What do you think the chances are, really? She'd told me it was a sure bet. Jesus, apparently, had saved her. He'd jumped down from his cross and explained how there were worse things in life than crucifixion. But she'd told me, You'll have to wait, make up your own mind.

It continued, even in the Burrells' lounge room. Curtis, the premature adult, lying on the couch in his pyjamas watching *Songs of Praise*. A village choir and an old man with an accent like Ernie's saying how God had saved him from falling off a cliff. Curtis mimicked him. '*I took one step back, to focus me camera, and I slipped ...*'

Anne Burrell walked past and said, 'Curtis, there's no need to be disrespectful.'

'*Ah, then I was falling, doon, doon, I went!*'

We cracked up. Anne returned to the kitchen.

I said, 'Don't ask Pop about the Catholics. He had a sister, and she went blind.' I whispered. 'His mum had the clap.'

'The clap?'

'You know, cos she had no ...'

The dishes stopped rattling, and I waited.

Curtis listened to the old fella on the telly. '*I reached up, and praise the Lord Jaysus, a hand!*'

'Curtis!'

'It's on the telly.' He leaned forward, and said, 'Had no what?'

'Contraception. So she'd got the clap, and it got in his sister's eyes as she was emerging and she went blind.'

He sat back. 'Catholics. I'll put them on my list too.'

It wasn't just a mental list. An actual one, four pages long, starting with clumsy kiddy scribble (the mailman), progressing through his primary school years (Mr Gottl), high school (all teachers, principals, office staff), up to the most recent, a few days before (Les Champness). And now, Catholics.

Curtis said, 'So your aunt couldn't see?'

'I never knew her. She died before I was born.'

He sat forward. 'They're no better, you know.'

'Who?'

'The Catholics. This AIDS thing. They reckon it'll wipe out half the planet. The Christians reckon it's some punishment from God. That's what we're up against, Whelan.'

You could never quite believe him. 'Half the planet?'

'It can wipe out a whole village in a few days.' Then he sat back, eager for the next testimonial.

'Not much point doing matric,' I said.

'Guess not.' As he listened to a teacher talking about her lambs. '*Franger, eh? In everything we learn, Jesus. The way a flower opens, sends out its smell. It's His design, isn't it, dear Clement?*'

Anne came in and sat on the lounge. 'Just don't say a word, Curtis.'

He checked his watch. 'I won't.'

'No matter what he says.'

A give-me-some-credit expression. 'That's it. He's back for good?'

Anne glanced at me, as if I shouldn't be party to the discussion, but then guessed (I suppose) I'd heard and seen it all. 'You staying, Clem?'

'Should I go?'

She didn't answer. Instead, she returned to Curtis. 'Even if he has a go at you.'

'Okay! I get it. *The way a number divides … that's proof of His love.*'

The car in the drive, footsteps, then voices. The door opened and Gary entered with a bag, threw it on the ground and said, 'I can't stay.'

Anne looked at him pleadingly. 'Just for half an hour?'

'I gotta pick up some gear.'

'On a Sunday morning?'

'Yes.' It was a stop-asking yes, and Anne knew better.

John entered, stood in the doorway and said, 'Hasn't changed much.'

Anne approached her son, tried to embrace him, but he resisted. 'How you feeling, John?'

He barely acknowledged her. 'Thought you were gonna get some new curtains?'

'They're coming.'

He noticed his brother, and the television. 'What, you gone all religious?'

'*The Lawd Jaysus Christ, Johnnie. He can be yer saviour!*'

'Still full of shit.'

Gary held his son's shoulder and said, 'I gotta pick up a few jobs.'

'Want me to come?'

'No, you unpack. I'll see you later. Mum reckons we should go out for lunch.'

Curtis smiled at me and returned to his hymn. I knew what he was thinking: They'd never take me out to lunch. They're scared of him, Clem. Scared of their own son.

Gary left, and Anne seemed lost. 'All done. Now we can get on with things.'

John asked about Pop and I said, 'He's okay, but he's forgetting more.'

'That's shit.'

He had a soft spot for Pop. They'd sit and talk, and John would listen to all the stories: childhood, early jobs, Nan, and the thousand things he'd had to do to keep his family afloat. John would often help him with a car. And although he was a little thief, nothing went missing from Pop's shed. As for me – I was too much like Curtis, the eternal pain in the arse. But he said, 'Tell him I'll come in and say hello.'

'I will.'

He walked down the hall, and the springs suggested he'd thrown his bag on his bed. Anne stood in his doorway. 'Do you want me to wash any of that stuff?'

'It's done.'

'What, before you left?'

No response.

'If you want it done again?'

'Why would I want it done again?'

Curtis had kept his promise and stayed quiet. The paradise of being an only child had finished. Now he was the silent son, the seeker-of-peace. '*Hear us Lord, incredibly bored ...*'

'Shut up!' John called.

'Curtis!' Anne echoed.

'Sorry.' And whispering. '*Popery on a ropery. For washing private parts, and the residue of farts ...*'

'Did you think about what Dad said?' Anne asked.

'I'll give it a go. When's it start?'

'Tomorrow.'

'Fuck. Tomorrow? I just got home.'

Curtis had told me. Gary had spoken to someone at work and they'd found a few hours sorting metal, and if John worked out they'd train him on the forklift, and one thing might lead to another.

Anne said, 'If you don't feel ready, we can ask if—'

'I'm ready. Didn't say I wouldn't.'

'Those forklift drivers make good money. I been tellin' yer father he should do it.' She was trying her best. 'Do you want me to get you a drink?'

'Mum ... just leave us alone, will yer?'

'I just want you to feel ... relaxed.'

Springs, floorboards, and the door closed. Anne emerged. All in all, it hadn't gone too bad. Curtis said, '*Doon, doon I went, but not all was as bad as it seemed.*'

'Clem?' A distant voice, possibly Jen. 'Where are you?'

It seemed strange. Jen never wanted me for anything, except to shout at, or sit on. I stood, went to the door, but she was already half up the drive. 'What's wrong?' I said.

'Pop in there?'

'No.'

'We've been looking for him. He's wandered off.'

I followed her down the road, to Mum, standing in front of our place, arms crossed, crying. I said, 'When's the last time you saw him?'

'He's never wandered off, has he?'

'He's prob'ly down the shops buying smokes.'

'I told him, not by yourself.'

Curtis had followed me, and Anne and John. They stood waiting. It was the old John, the neighbourhood John. He said, 'Is he okay crossing roads?'

Mum didn't know what to say.

'I'll go round the block, make sure he's not wandering there, eh?' He was off, running, and Anne watched him go, half-hopeful.

I suggested we call the police but Mum wouldn't have a bar of it. 'Maybe he wanted to buy some parts?'

By now, Peter and Val had come out, and Ron stuck his head over his fence and called, 'Everything okay?'

'Pop's wandered off,' Jen replied, but he just said, 'Let me know if I can help,' before disappearing down his drive.

'I drove right around but I couldn't find him,' Jen said. 'I checked the shops, Don's, the car yard.' She turned to me. Usually she'd never seek my advice, after all, apparently I was an idiot. But now, she sensed I might know.

I took a deep breath. 'Mrs Burrell, Curtis, could you look ... east?'

'Righto,' Anne replied. She walked off, stopped, returned for her son, and they got in her car and drove off.

Meanwhile, I told Mum and Jen to drive the length of North East Road, and Val and Peter to look down everyone's drive, in backyards, sheds, anywhere he might've wandered. 'Thirty minutes,' I said. 'We meet back. If there's no sign we'll have to call the police.'

Mum and Jen climbed into the Datsun and drove off and Val headed across the road and knocked on Les's door. Peter stood behind her, looking back at me, thumbs up, like he knew something I didn't.

I tried our place first. 'Pop, you here?' I searched his room, noticed his glasses on the dresser, his smokes beside his bed. From room to room, the toilet, bathroom, shed, even behind the incinerator. 'Pop?'

For a moment it was like he'd already gone. The place seemed empty without him. Silent. Somewhere, I thought. Somewhere …

Yes, perhaps? I ran down the drive, along Lanark II and III, across the mound, and stopped in front of Gleneagles Primary. 'Pop?'

I went in. A hundred square metres of asphalt, and a dozen four-square courts. The lunch shed, set out with the same budget pews we'd been made to sit on to drink our government milk before being allowed to play. I turned, and there, in the shadows, Pop, busy with a stick of yellow chalk. I approached him and said, 'Everyone's looking for you.'

He studied me: the body, the face, but not me. Then he leaned over, and continued drawing outlines on the concrete.

'You gotta tell people where you're going, Pop.'

He stood. 'Can't do that, can I? Then they'd know.' He held up his map, and indicated the cross, and the word: *Lasseter*.

It wasn't the first time. A year ago, he'd come into my room one morning and said, 'Come on.'

'What?'

'I'll show you how we're gonna do it.'

He'd waited as I got dressed, then led me outside, opened the map, showed me the first leg of the journey and said, 'What's it say?'

I'd looked. 'Six hundred and seventy-three.'

'Which direction?'

'West.'

So he'd used a compass to find west and we'd set off, down Lanark Avenue, Pop counting each step. 671, 672, 673 … We'd stopped in front of the primary school. Then he'd showed me the map again. 'What now?'

'Seventy one east.'

He'd found east, started walking, and counting. 68, 69, 70, 71 …

We'd stopped again. The map, again. I'd said, 'North, twenty-one kilometres.'

Compass. Turn. March. Stop. We were in the milk shed. I'd said, 'What now?'

He'd indicated. 'See here, a few valleys, a river, this seems to be a path.'

'This is Lasseter's Reef?'

He couldn't see that I couldn't see. 'This is how we'll do it. We have to practise. See, that's where this fella in the pub went wrong. He didn't prepare.'

Then, he'd taken out a piece of chalk and started drawing the topographical features from the map onto the ground. I'd waited, and watched, wondering how any of this might help.

As I wondered now, watching him do it all again.

'Val and Peter and Anne and John are all looking.'

He just kept working. 'John's home, eh?'

'Yeah.'

'Good-o. We can go in a minute. When we're sure.'

'And Mum and Jen are driving round. Mum's gonna be crook at you.'

'She'll be okay. But you mustn't tell her, Clem. She'll put a stop to all this.' He held my arm, and fixed my stare. 'Promise?'

'I promise. But we better go, cos if we're not back Mum'll call the police.'

He was drawing what could've been a mountain, although the gold was in a desert. 'She won't call the police. She's not that stupid.'

There was nothing to do but wait. I sat down and said, 'That all to scale, Pop?'

'Bloody oath.' He held up the map. 'Here, seven kilometres east.' And he took seven steps, to make sure.

'You scared the shit out of us. We thought you were lying dead on a road somewhere.'

'I'm not that far gone.' He drew a yellow cross in the middle of the floor. Stood back, smiled and said, 'There she is.'

Happy, he sat down beside me. 'You think it's there, Clem?'

'I reckon.'

'Not just saying that?'

'No, of course not. But you gotta tell us when you go off. You know, with your forgetfulness.'

'Don't worry about me.' He was surveying his sketch. 'I don't need a map, I got it memorised. But we'll keep it so we can give it to a museum after we find the gold.' Then he turned away, staring out across the oval. 'It's important you believe, Clem. Nan never did. She thought I was an idiot.'

I waited. Same story, but it had to come.

'That night I went home and showed her, and she laughed at me. I said bugger you, I'm goin', and she said, No, you're not, you got work in the morning. And next week. Next year. And she kept me at it, Clem. Like whatever I wanted didn't matter.'

He waited.

'Always another day, Clem. That's what they say to you, these women. She'd look at me and then at Fay, crawling round on the ground, and say, You go, you lose your job, who's gonna pay the bills?'

He was studying every chalk mark. Every footstep he'd delayed, every mile he'd talked himself out of.

'I remember once, I packed the car and said, That's it, and she said, Good-o, you go, but there won't be no coming back. I got in the car, and started it, and she stood watching me.'

He'd never told me this bit before.

'And then I switched off the engine, and she went in … and I wonder, I wonder, Clem, what would've happened if I'd driven off.'

'She would've had you back, Pop.'

'You reckon?'

'Of course.'

'I might've found it, and we might've moved to New York, lived the high life.'

I almost laughed. 'New York? Maybe you woulda bought a Roller, Pop?'

'Yeah.'

He stood, turned on all six taps in the water trough, and waited for the overflow to wash away his map. 'Can't have anyone knowin'.'

We transferred our best sketches onto transparencies, took a few projectors outside and connected them with extension cords. Soon we had outlines on the wall. Most people had chosen one or two, but Nick had agreed to let me have three. I'd shown him my sketches, and he'd loved them. Mr Glasson, rear view, big arse wobbling as he fitted someone's car seat. Mr Champness standing Zen-like with outstretched finger with finches. And finally, mower and me, surveying the yard, as a stray cocked its leg on mine. Piddle, too. Small drops soaking my socks. Nick had laughed and said, 'We've gotta have this one.'

Lesson three: Tuesday 9 February. We stood drawing our final images on the art room wall. Curtis, a duck he'd traced from M (for Mallard); the girls, Boy George and the Thompson Twins (although I'd told them they'd date). There was a boy called Matthew, a Catholic whose parents couldn't afford St Luke's, and he was tackling St Paul on the road to Damascus, although it looked more like North East Road. And, finally, Lars with some sort of moonscape.

Despite the heat, it was the best lesson ever (not that there was much competition). Nick stood back, supervising, suggesting, smoking. He indicated Mr Glasson and said, 'Do you think he might recognise himself?'

'Not a chance.' Although I'd given up on Mr Fantastic, I'd retained a comic sensibility, and the Glasson cleft was its own Grand Canyon, the cheeks their own subcontinents. 'Faces are overrated.'

'How's that?'

'A nose, mouth, eyes – you know what you're getting. But as for the arse …'

'And what's the story with the bird man?'

'Across the road. He has an aviary, and spends hours watching them. I thought this could suggest he's talking to them.'

Mr Champness was Fantastic too. Oversized belly, so he looked like an inner tube; big nose and bulb eyes; more hair, so he couldn't complain.

Nick examined my final sketch. 'Why's it pissing on you?'

'That's good luck.'

'How?'

I'd painted DOG on the side of the mongrel. I showed Nick how the word reflected on the 120Y parked in the drive. 'I see,' he said. 'It's a religious painting?'

Pencils on timber; Nick waited, hid his smoke as another teacher walked past.

Curtis was getting braver. He'd elected Nick a minor saint. He had that book, too, stolen from the school library. When we were in Year Eight (some time after his conversion to Adulthood) he'd started sticking saints on his wall. Every day a new one appeared, cut out of *The Lives of Saints*. Saint Scholastica, Our Lady of Lourdes. By May he'd covered half a wall. Anne had protested, but Gary had said, Let him go. John had called him a freak, and defaced Saints Fabian and Agnes before losing interest. But Curtis was unperturbed. Every day: snip, snip, Clag, smooth, and the appropriate prayer. I'd asked him why. He'd said, They musta done something right. I'd said, But you don't believe in God. He'd said, The saints were human. So instead of Status Quo, Curtis had Timothy and Titus. This phase had lasted until September, when he'd seen a documentary about Darwin and stolen a copy of *Origin of Species* and, a few days later, asked Gary if he could get some paint from the shed.

Curtis turned to Nick and asked, 'Who are your favourite teachers?'

Nick was only so stupid. 'They're all pretty decent.'

'What about Mr Moore?'

'What about him?'

'He got sent here from another school. Mum read about it in the paper.'

We all waited. Even saints didn't kill themselves on purpose.

'I heard he got drunk, and there was this Year Twelve …'

'Righto, let's stick to the art,' Nick said.

'And she got pregnant.'

'No!' Nick said, turning on him.

Silence. Curtis knew what he'd done, and it was bad. Nick knew what he was trying to do, and looked disappointed. 'Whatever Mr Moore did's his business.'

I finished my sketch and asked for paint. Nick inspected it, and agreed. I went inside, squeezed a tub of skin colour, found a brush and returned. Curtis, apparently, was making amends. '*Day was departing and dusk drew on …*'

'He's remembered all of Canto II,' I said. 'Believes it will give him some sort of intellectual—'

'Fuck off, Whelan.'

I started painting Mr Glasson's arse.

Nick said, 'This kid reckoned he got her pregnant, but he didn't.'

We all waited.

'See, that's the thing, Curtis. You believe everything you read.'

'I don't.'

'There was a hearing. She'd never liked him, and she'd set out to get him. But Mr Moore, he's the nicest—'

Miss White appeared from behind the change rooms. Maybe she'd been hiding, listening, although she often patrolled during lessons. 'He is nice, isn't he, Mr Andrews?' she said.

He tried his best. 'Yes.'

Regardless, she stood back and studied the sketches. 'It was nice of Mr Meadows to agree.'

'It was.' More a he-hasn't-actually-agreed reply.

'It'll add to the … amenity.'

'I hope.'

Then she came closer, stood behind me, with her arms crossed. 'What's this?'

'Rear view.'

'Of?'

'This man, he's fitting a car seat.'

She took a moment. 'That's a funny thing to paint.'

'I told them to do what they know,' Nick said.

She moved along, content with Mr Champness. But then she saw the dog and the urine. 'This one's a bit off.'

I explained the God–dog reference but she wasn't interested. 'I'm trying to hint at a spiritual life. You know, God's always watching out for us, even when we mow the lawn.'

She studied me like I was stupid, or taking the piss. 'That's your belief?'

'Yes.' I guessed I could invoke Sunday school if necessary. Then I noticed a small crucifix around her neck. 'My family … we're Baptist.'

'*I am not Aeneas, and I am not Paul!*' Curtis said.

'Sorry?' asked Miss White.

'*Who thinks me fit? Not others. And not I.*'

I glared at him. He always chose his moment.

Miss White turned to Nick and said, 'Can I have a word?'

They walked around the corner, and we listened. Curtis moved closer, hushed us, and stood listening. A minute, more, and none of us spoke. Then he sprinted back, and Nick returned. He sat on one of the tables, took out a smoke and lit it.

'Everything okay?' Curtis asked.

After school, Mum was waiting, and I drove home. 'Another few weeks and you can do the test,' she said.

I didn't reply. It was my way of saying perhaps.

'Then you can drive Pop around.'

'Great, that's why I'm getting my licence?'

'One of the reasons.'

We pulled onto the main road and someone had to slow so he tooted me, and I gave him the finger. Mum said, 'Do that and they'll fail you.'

'He sped up.'

Of course, if she saw Dad in me, this was further proof of a bad attitude. Maybe he'd done the same thing, taking his unhappy life onto the road every day, abusing a world of agreed-upon rules and common sense. 'I'm busy with school,' I said.

'I don't see you doing much homework.'

'I do.'

'Still, you need to get yer licence.'

I slowed, indicated, and drove around the back streets. There were a couple of kids playing, and apparently I was going too fast, and she said, 'If you knock one of them over ...'

'I'm not gonna knock anyone over.'

'You won't listen to anything anyone ... just like yer ...'

I glanced at her.

'Eyes on the road!'

'Like who?' I pulled into a driveway, practised a three-point turn, and continued. 'Like Dad ... how?'

'Gotta have the last word on everything.'

'I wasn't gonna knock over—'

'It's not the point.'

This was usually where the conversation stopped. Where she'd guess she'd given away enough. Occasionally it'd be, He was an angry man, and I'd say, How? And she'd say, Always saw the bad in everything, and everyone. You couldn't live with it, Clem, believe me. And I'd say, He mustn't have been that bad.

'Just cos I'm a bit slack at driving.'

'Careful ... school crossing.'

I slowed, but it wasn't slow enough. Then I said, 'What sorta car did he have?'

She gave me the idiot look. 'Who?'

'Dad. When you met him. What did he drive?'

'What's it matter?'

'I don't know much about him.'

'Trust me, it's best that way.'

'How?'

'Enough.'

'But I only asked what sorta car he drove.'

I could see her head gently shaking. 'That's not what you asked at all.'

'It is.'

And what she didn't say: car, life, behaviour – you want it all, don't you? 'An EH Holden.'

'And didn't you say he rode a motorbike?'

She turned. 'What's the sudden interest?'

'Well, if you told me stuff, if you hadn't thrown away all the …' I stopped. I guessed it'd come back to bite me.

'Don't talk about what you don't understand.'

'But why did you throw away the pictures?'

'Head home!'

I slowed, turned and did as I was told. 'I think it's a reasonable question. He was my father.'

'You never hear Jen asking.'

'That's her problem. You say you don't wanna talk about him, but I can only assume—'

'You can't assume anything! You weren't there. You don't know.'

Time to stop. We'd been here before. Now she would become irrational, sulk, refuse to talk to me, offer one syllable responses or ignore me all together. 'Sorry.'

'He never owned a motorbike.'

'That's all I wanted to know.'

'That's *not* all you wanted to know, is it?'

She had a point. But you couldn't blame me for trying. 'There's a photo of him in Mrs Donnellan's.'

'Well, there you go – now you know.'

'It's not much to go on.'

Silence, as we cruised the main road.

At last she said, 'It was him or me, and you wouldn'ta wanted to be brought up by him.'

'Why's that?'

'Trust me.'

And then I felt I couldn't continue. Whatever the reason, I'd have to hear it from someone else.

She said, 'Here,' and indicated a space between two cars. 'Try your reverse parallel.'

'I know how to do it.'

'Show me.'

I indicated, slowed and positioned myself. Reverse, angle, in, straighten. 'Okay?'

'You don't have to get smart.'

'I was just saying, is that okay?' I pulled out, continued along a road lined by factories and warehouses, an industrial island in the middle of Windsor Park.

Then she remembered. 'I was cleaning your room …'

'I can do it.'

'That book of yours.'

'What?'

'Where you write what you think of everyone.'

'You read it?'

'I's hoping it was schoolwork, but no.'

The Datsun just kept going. I said, 'It's not what I think of everyone, it's a book of observations.'

'Why?'

'I dunno. It's just interesting.'

She wasn't happy with this. 'How do you know everyone's IQ?'

'I don't.'

'But that's what you write. Mr Champness, you said—'

'It's just a guess, based on what I observe.'

She didn't get it. I couldn't explain.

'It's just me thinking aloud. I don't mean anything by it.'

'No one's better than anyone else, Clem.'

'I know.'

'They could write things about you.'

'They're welcome to.'

'You look at Dr Scheer. He's clever, but nice. He can afford to think he's better than us, but he doesn't. See, that's the mark of the man: how gracious he is.'

'Well, sorry.'

'Ernie Sharpe, fifty-eight points … what was it, moron?'

'It's just a classification.'

'Like we're all insects.'

I'd had enough. She was like a mower starting on a very big paddock. I made a U-turn and headed home. When she said we needed to do more, I shrugged.

'Maybe tomorrow.'

So she said, 'And the way you describe people. That bit about Wendy.'

'Christ, how much of it did you read?'

'You don't know what she's been through, so you shouldn't write stuff like that.'

3/v/82 She ran away from him. Down the drive, the road, and didn't come back till after eleven. Quite pathetic, really, that she can't stand up to him. Or at least call the police …

'Been through what?'

'None of your business.'

'See, that's just it!' I pulled over. 'How am I meant to know things if no one tells me? If you won't tell me. If you burn all the …'

The car idled. I'd made my point. You had to be honest with kids, or they'd assume the wrong things.

A city red with fire. The distant ring of hills surrounding us, alight. A northerly pushing flames up hills and down valleys, consuming homes, halls, whole towns, cars full of mums and kids attempting to escape. Even from this distance we could see how fires were growing, joining and consuming the ranges no one had back-burned for decades. We were told there were people dying. Someone had a tranny and we listened to the reports and learned that half the state was on fire. Every metropolitan and country unit was fighting the inferno. They'd run out of men and trucks and some of these sat burned-out, too, black bodies smouldering through the afternoon. By two pm (they let us out early), as I walked home, the streets of Gleneagles were full of smoke.

I turned into Lanark Avenue to see people in their yards, arms crossed, talking, looking to the hills. Peter Donnellan, clutching his rusty scythe, cutting arse-high grass. Mum had said something to Val, and she must've got him onto it. Mum often said her bit. Listen, Val, we'll come and give you a hand with that rubbish out the back. You call the council and they'll come and collect it. What d'you reckon? And Val would never disagree. I guess she knew things needed doing, but didn't know how. One in a wheelchair, and the other in his room (aged forty) reading Proust. What could you do?

'Hi, Peter.'

He stopped and looked up, surprised. He was always in his own world. 'How are you, Clem?'

I studied the hills. 'You reckon there are many dead?'

'They say there's eighteen already, but when they search the houses ...' He continued working.

'You should borrow our Victa,' I said.

No reply. Why would you bother when cold steel could do the job?

'Do you want me to go get it?'

And without stopping: 'No, thanks.'

It seemed a funny time to be scything. Shouldn't we all be gathered, muttering consolations, watching the fronts surge and recede? Plus, he was red-faced, the veins in his temple pulsing to the day's irregular rhythms. 'I could do it for you,' I said. 'Have it done in ten minutes.'

Again, no reply. As though he was doing it because of the day, not despite it. As some sort of mea culpa on behalf of Lanark Avenue, or all of Gleneagles. Perhaps, if he worked hard enough, the wind would drop, the flames die, clouds gather, rain fall. A scything Jesus, complete with beard full of biscuit crumbs, yellow-

tipped fingers, like his mum, long fingernails, because who did he
have to impress?

'Is it heavy?' I asked.

'Very.' He offered it to me. I put down my bag, took it and tried
to copy his actions. He sat in his brother's shady spot, lighting a
cigarette, and seemed pleased. I wasn't sure if this meant I should
keep going. 'You ever seen it like this before?' I asked.

'Not this bad.'

The Donnellans' yard was its own disaster: fist cracks full of
weeds and rat holes with snakes (Mum said she'd seen one). It had
its own Mediterranean climate (in the shade of an olive tree) and
libraries of old catalogues that had blown about for years.

'Hard work, eh?' I said to Peter.

He smiled, smoking with the fag cupped in his hand.

Fuck it! It was too hot for anything. I sat down and he offered
me his smoke. I accepted, dragged, returned it.

'I know all about you,' he said.

'What?'

'I've seen you and Curtis, on the way home.'

'Just have one occasionally.'

'What would your mum say?'

'She prob'ly knows.'

He didn't care. Six years at law school had taught him that rules
were only for the people who made them. 'It's a bad habit.'

'I got a bad attitude.'

He smiled again, and punched my arm. 'This isn't the kid I
used to babysit. You don't remember, do you?'

'Course I do.'

'Yer mum'd come in and say, I gotta go to town, you wouldn't do
me a favour? And she'd present you two, and a pack of chips. Then
I'd get out the Monopoly and you'd get bored and five minutes later
you'd be chasing cats around the backyard and Mum'd be calling,
Clem, leave them alone will yer?'

We started to laugh, but it was too hot.

'Then you'd come in and we'd sit you down in front of the Channel

Niners, and you'd be off again. I remember you on the roof.'

I could hear sirens from the main road. The world might be burning, ending, even, but there was no world beyond Lanark Avenue.

'But then it got dark and yer mum wasn't home so we bathed you and put you in yer jarmies and then it was even later, so we put you to bed, and I read to you. You don't remember that, do you?'

'No.'

'*David Copperfield*. You just said there's no pictures, but I read anyway, and you listened and fell asleep and later, when yer mum came in, I scooped you outa bed and carried you next door.' He waited, and closed his eyes for a few moments.

Further down the road, people had run out of conversation and gone in. You couldn't stop fire with words, so what was the point?

'She was lucky she had you,' I said.

'That's how it used to be. Not so much now. Like him' – and he indicated number thirty – 'and his seat covers. Like it's gonna make him millions.'

'Sorry if I was a bitofa shit.'

'Didn't say I cared. Just remember. That used to make Mum's day, when yer mum asked. She's always loved having you and Jen … Me, David, too. We knew what it was like.'

It seemed cooler now, but that was just David's shade.

I said, 'Maybe it was worse for you. You knew your Dad.'

'Better, worse, doesn't matter. You get on, eh?'

'But … how he died.'

'Doesn't matter how you die. Days after he'd gone, me and David decided, Righto, let's make this work. We had the house looking nice, me on the dishes and hoover, David cooking, making beds.' He turned again. 'You just gotta decide how it's gonna be.'

'I didn't get to decide.'

'It coulda ended worse.'

'How?'

'It's not my place to say.'

He stood, returned to his scythe and continued.

'Why not?' I asked.

'He was a good man, your dad.' As he swung. 'We helped him paint Jen's room, and yours, before you come home from hospital. He bought cots, and all the gear, had it nice. Doted on yers. Used to parade you up and down the street. He was a changed man for a while. Your mum thought things'd come good.' He stopped again, realising he was about to say the same thing. 'He even hired a photographer, and he set up in your living room and took photos, and they gave us a copy.'

Me and Jen in soft focus. I stood, approached him and tried to take the scythe. 'Here, let me, you're gonna have a stroke.'

He wouldn't yield.

'What do you mean, a changed man?'

'Just saying, don't think he didn't care about you. Don't think it was that simple, why he went away.' He realised he couldn't go back. The grass fell in sheaths, and sat neatly on the ground.

'You can't tell me half a story.' I'd never seen him like this before. Maybe it was the heat, the smoke, the ash in the air.

There was no point pursuing it; he wasn't about to reveal any more. He'd let my dad slip out of his box, and knew he had to go back in. He stopped, surveyed his lawn, then went inside.

Curtis rode past. '*Forsaken now, like some old, mouldering thing …*'

He'd predicted it, I guessed. But if you're pessimistic enough, you see everything coming. Peter Donnellan was Curtis Burrell's arch enemy. They fought, and insulted each other in speech bubbles. Good versus evil. Beard versus clean-shaven. See, life is simple. You can boil it down to a comic book plot. Jaysus, and the Baptists' heaven, versus Dante's and Curtis's hell. Even at sixteen years of age, I wondered if everyone saw the world like me.

There was a rosella on the fence. I stepped towards it and held out my hand and it fluttered onto my finger. I looked around; the street was deserted, but the fires were still raging. I picked up my bag, threw it into our yard and crossed the street, bird still perched on my finger. Up the gravel drive to the porch where Les always sat. 'Mr Champness?'

And a voice, above the wind that had stripped the skin off the road, the sides of tress, the gravel and fences. 'Round here.'

I walked down the drive and found Les beside his aviary, pegging a sheet to the wire to keep the wind out. 'I found this one,' I said.

He studied it. 'It's not mine.'

'Where do you reckon it came from?'

He'd never said more than a few dozen words to me. Just when we were getting in the car, and he was out watering, and Pop called, 'How are yer, Les?' and he just waved, or said, 'Hot.'

'Eastern rosella. They're not uncommon.'

'I've never seen one. Nice colours, eh?'

'Yeah.' He examined it quickly, but didn't seem interested. Perhaps because he hadn't bought it, fed it, adopted it. Still, a bird was a bird.

'What do you reckon I should do with it?'

'Let it go.'

I shook my finger, waved it in the air, but it didn't want to go. 'How do you …?'

He took it, put it on the top of the fence, and watched it for a while. 'Doesn't seem to want to do anything.'

'Maybe it's hungry?'

But he just looked at me like I was stupid. 'Right.' He reclaimed the bird, opened his aviary and placed it on a perch. 'Another one to feed.'

Not exactly the response I was hoping for. I turned to the hills, the fires, and said, 'Pretty bad, eh?'

The same look – like he just didn't get me.

'I just remembered … was it true you used to keep rabbits in there?'

'No.'

A fairly clear message. I walked off.

'I know you've been watching.'

I turned. 'Sorry.'

He pointed to my room. 'That yours?'

'Yes.'

'I see the reflection – and the telescope, when the curtain blows.'

I could feel my heart racing. 'Mum got it for me. I like astronomy.'

'You're not gonna see many stars looking out there.'

His eyes, I thought, reflected the flames.

'You better watch yerself, Mr Whelan, or I'll be over to have a talk to your mum.'

'Yes, sir.'

Words? No point. I crossed the road, realising I lived far too close to this man.

Mr Sharpe, returning from the Windsor (where he tied Fi-Fi to the verandah post while he drank with mates for hours on end; where Fi-Fi had learned to stay away from the main road; where the publican, a Mr Loussier, had placed a bowl of water for the dog and sometimes, after tea, scraps from the half-eaten roasts-of-the-day), could be heard coming from some distance. *'Next door to me, next door to me, the girl next door to me.'* He stopped in front of 31, sat on the fence, farted, and continued; *'A dog with a healthy bite, a nibble on his pants last night.'* Although he was facing away from me (and greeted Mr Champness, sitting on his porch) he knew I was watching. 'Have you made a note, Mr Whelan?'

I sat silently.

'Does it read a little something like, *Mr Sharpe, coming home sozzled* …' He checked his watch. *'Ten minutes late, so perhaps he found a friend.'*

Fi-Fi struggled to sniff a fence post, but he jagged her back.

'Mr Sharpe believes in portergaff …'

'Is that you, Mr Sharpe?'

'Evening, Clem. *He's as regular as clockwork. The old girl, Ida, is always complaining, but Mr Sharpe says a man needs a drink at the end of a long day.* Don't you agree, Clem?'

'Yes, Mr Sharpe.'

And called, 'What do you think, Mr Champness?'

'Eh?'

'Man needs a drink at the end of a long day?'

But Les wasn't about to buy into it. He returned to his paper.

'I don't make any notes, Mr Sharpe.'

'Mum reckons you wanna be a writer?'

'I observe but ... I don't write it down.'

'Her brother belongs to the boxing 'pros', And he knocks a rat-a-tat on the tip of my nose.'

'Give it a rest,' Les called.

'Sorry, Les. Just having a word to young Whelan here.'

Les shook his head. 'He's been warned, too.'

'How's that, Mr Champness?'

'Just get home, Ernie. You're a disgrace.'

'Next door to me, next door to me ... You there, Clem?'

'Yes.'

'Every street has one, don't you think?'

'What's that, Mr Sharpe?'

'A disgrace. But there's a lot worse than grog, sung without licence or fee, except in music halls.'

'A lot worse.'

'Like miserable old cunts like him.'

We both watched the pages of the paper turning.

'Where I grew up, Clem, people looked out for each other. Two up, two down, and the kids on the street. Someone like him' – and he said it discreetly – 'they'd be let know. *Workers of the world unite!*'

'Get home!' Les called.

'Mr Sharpe is quoting Marx again. He was an old Red, organised for some union, and he lives in the past. Do I, Clem?'

'No, Mr Sharpe.'

'It's all o'er the town that I can't sit down.'

'Which union was it?'

He turned. 'You interested?'

'Yes.'

'Come on, let's go.' He indicated, pulled Fi-Fi along, and jogged home. I slipped on my sneakers and followed. Life was long, and there was a lot to be learned. As I walked down the drive, and turned towards number 35, Les said, 'You oughta keep away from him.' I didn't reply.

I knocked, and Ida let me in. She was wearing her too-tight leotards, T-shirt and wrist bands. There had been sightings in the neighbourhood, generally when she went out to check the mail. And on the telly, Richard Simmons offering encouragement. She offered me coffee and said, 'Is Ernie behaving himself?'

'I reckon.'

Fi-Fi was already dozing on the lounge, a belly full of chicken schnitzel. She was an overweight poodle, dragging her guts along the pavement between the Windsor and Lanark Avenue, wearing off the hair (you could see where).

'He's in his study,' she said.

I followed a hall of more old-world colourised photos to the lair: a desk, a portrait of Marx and Engels on the wall, bookcases full of hardbound volumes with titles like *Theses on Feuerbach*, and *The Modern Theory of Colonisation*. I guessed Mr Sharpe was smarter than he seemed. Here was a world of European history, economics, politics, as well as the remnants of Ernie's past: photos of him and other men with banners proclaiming '8-8-8'.

'Sit here,' he said, and lifted a pile of papers from a seat. I did as I was told, and he placed a photo album across my knees. 'This is how I got started,' he said, indicating a black-and-white photo with a young Ernie, continental sideburns and slicked-back hair. 'Age thirty-two, I was elected shop steward at Morphett's. They made switchboards.' He and several other men stood in front of a banner: 'Electrical Workers' Union of Great Britain'. 'I met a lot of good men, and they educated me.'

'How's that?' I asked.

'The history of capital, and how greedy bastards use it to better themselves.'

Another photo showed a slightly older Ernie, this time in a suit and tie, speaking into a microphone at some sort of public gathering. 'Here, I'm about forty. This is a few years after we migrated. That's the Waterside Workers' Hall.'

'You were some sort of official?'

'Again, Electrical Workers' Union. Secretary … Comrade Sharpe.'

'Comrade?'

'Too right. Workers stick together, Clem. That's where we got our strength. Of course, things are different now. The bosses have got the upper hand. And do you know why?'

Ida came in with the coffees. She'd thought better of it, and put on a dressing gown. 'Ernie, don't bother him with all that.'

'He wants to know, don't you, Clem?'

'Yes.'

So she shook her head, and left.

'I'll tell you. The workers were too scared to strike in case they lost their jobs. See, you gotta stick together. One in, all in, or it doesn't work.'

There were dozens more photos, charting his rise, fall, and journey towards irrelevance. At the end he said, 'You interested in politics, Clem?'

'Sorta. We're doin' the Russian Revolution in history.'

His eyes lit up. 'See, one in, all in.'

'But didn't Stalin murder fifty million people?'

'Well, that number's always exaggerated, and he was trying to make a new sort of society.'

He spent another ten minutes explaining how, if Australia was communist, Packer and Hancock would have to splash the cash, and we wouldn't be living in fibro huts on the edge of civilisation. This seemed a bit dramatic. They were comfortable homes, and a lot of people in communist countries lived in worse. Still, there was no point bringing this up. Ernie knew best, apparently.

He reclaimed his photo album, searched for another book and opened it. '*The modern bourgeois society that has sprouted from the ruins of feudal society has not done away with class antagonisms.*'

Communism seemed like a good idea. Sharing the goods. Gary

Burrell did it; I'd seen the evidence in his back shed. And maybe that was justified.

Ernie said, 'You can borrow this,' and placed *The Communist Manifesto* in my hands. 'As true now as the day it was written.'

'But Russia's pointing all those missiles at us,' I said.

He sat forward, whispered, as though ASIO might be listening. 'Well, they've got no choice, have they? We're with America, and America's all about the factory owners. But they're closing down, and what's happening to the workers?'

'Sacked?'

'Exactly. That's what America stands for. That's why the Russians are onto them. Makes sense, doesn't it?'

I wasn't sure it did. 'Pity if we all go up in flames.' I noticed a Russian flag on the wall, hidden by a filing cabinet sprouting fifty years of papers.

'Cost of living rises but wages don't,' he said. 'Man can barely support his family now, but if you got capital.'

I guessed education might lead to better jobs, and income, and maybe that was easier than starting a world revolution. But I supposed not everyone had the brains to become a doctor, so it was proletariat versus slave master.

'Take your dad, for example. He'd spend ten hours a day laying bricks, and I remember, he told me, lucky if he brought home ten quid a week. Now, you—'

'Laying bricks?' I asked.

'Yes.'

'I never knew he did that.'

'He was a sub-contractor. The fella that built the homes got paid, the contractor got paid, and your dad, he got whatever was over. Some weeks, he told me, he couldn't afford petrol. Mortgage first, of course, then food for you lot.'

Laying bricks sounded like hard work. But I'd always assumed he'd lost interest in domestic life, his family, me, Jen. 'How long did he lay bricks?'

Ernie backed off. 'Not sure. Just at the beginning. Before he …'

'What?'

'Left … or had to go.'

'Had to go?'

'I dunno, ask your mother, it's none of my business.' He sipped his coffee and gazed out of the window. 'I was just saying, if he'd been in a union things mighta been different. Ten hours a day out in the hot sun, and not enough to support his family.'

'Do you know why Mum doesn't say anything?'

'Her business.'

'It's like everyone in the street's been warned off.'

'Rubbish, we just say what we know. You don't go sticking your nose in other people's business.'

I held the manifesto. I wasn't sure that it was going to help me, or that I really cared. You had to work your own life out before you could worry about other people's. I needed my own revolution, and John Lennon seemed more relevant then Vladimir Ilyich.

'Ern!'

Ida. Ernie jumped up, ran down the hall, into the kitchen. I followed.

'What?'

'Look!'

Ida pointed to the kitchen window. A few metres away two cats stood on a fence strut going their hardest. Ida knocked on the glass but they didn't care.

'Dirty bastards!' Ernie said. He ran into the laundry, found a bucket and started filling it with hot water. 'Filthy bloody creatures.'

Apparently his ideals didn't extend to Val's tabbies. He ran out, threw the water, and they squealed, and jumped.

I stood on his back porch, watching, half-laughing, as the drama unfolded. I looked up to see Val, staring out of her kitchen window, seeing me and pulling the curtain.

Ernie called, 'Why don't you keep them locked up?'

No reply.

'Place smells like piss.'

Then he came in, threw the bucket in the trough and returned to kitchen. Again, I followed, and he said, 'I wanna have a talk to your mum. It's about time we did something.'

I didn't know what to say. The cats didn't bother me. I guessed that Ernie was more a hates-the-boss than loves-the-worker sort of person. 'I better get going.'

'Righto. Read the book, get back to us. We'll talk, eh?'

Ida had started filleting fish. She had a pile of bones, heads, fins. She emptied them into newspaper, wrapped the bundle and presented it to Ernie. 'Go on.'

'Cosa them cats I gotta bury them,' he said to me, going out the back door, picking up his shovel and digging a new hole.

I watched him work, and realised we only ever know part of the story.

Pop let the chain run through his fingers. It glided through the gears, and the engine started to lift. 'Steady it,' he said.

I held the side of the block, positioned it so it would slip into its cradle.

260Z Sports. Pop had developed a reputation for Datsuns, and people came from all over. This time, a man named Harper, who'd said, 'I got her new, but she never had enough grunt.'

A new engine. And although Pop hadn't ordered it yet, he'd decided we should remove the old one first.

'Righto, help me.' We pushed the hoist from either side. The engine rocked, so I steadied it. There were holes where he'd unscrewed the oil and air filter, where the transmission and exhaust manifold had been removed. He'd bought another manual, sacrificed another bedsheet, laid it on the ground, drawn the outlines and positioned the parts of the puzzle.

'Down.' I held the engine in place as he worked the chains again. The block lowered, but he was in no rush. It settled into the cradle and the chains loosened. 'Done.' I helped him return the hoist to its spot in the corner. Then he said, 'Good job.'

He walked around it, wiped it with a rag, and said, 'Still get a decent price.'

If he could see it through, find a buyer, manage to mount a new block. Mr Harper was in no rush. Pop took out his papers and Port Royal and started rolling.

'What next?' I asked.

He surveyed the parts on the ground.

'No rush.' Like he wanted to enjoy each moment. Perhaps (I wondered) because it might be his last. Mum had already given him a lecture about the sheet. His was becoming a world of templates. If memory failed, it had to be helped. Like the list he'd made of every Datsun he'd ever fixed. Starting with the Fairlady 1500 (1967), through to the 720 (1984). In between there was the 510 Sedan, Roadster 2000, 240Z Sports and dozens more. He'd cut out their pictures, and made a calendar. Stuck each one to a board he displayed on his bench. A life in Datsuns.

Mum came in with salad rolls, put them on the table, noticed the sheet and shook her head. 'Bring in the plates when you're done.' Before turning and going in.

Pop positioned his teeth, bit into the roll, and his falsies clunked. He used a finger to push them back in. 'Soft rolls,' he grizzled.

I smiled, and examined the Datsun calendar.

'I remember each one,' he said, standing beside me.

I pointed to the 300ZX (1980). He said, 'Fella named Jones. Just around the corner. But he smashed it up a few months later.' Then he sat on his stool.

'Didn't you do Ron's car one time?' I asked.

'One time, but I don't think he was happy. Never asked again.'

I sat beside him. 'Wonder what he gets up to in his shed?'

'Makes car seats.'

'What he *really* gets up to?'

He continued working on his roll. 'You're too much like yer father.'

'How's that?'

His falsies clunked again, slipped, fell, and he caught the

uppers in his hand and replaced them. 'You been thinking about our friend?'

'Who?'

'Lasseter.' He sat back against the iron. 'We gotta stay focused. I don't want it interfering with your studies. I was thinking the school holidays.'

'I guess.'

'When we get this one fixed we'll have some cash, then we can buy supplies.' He put down his roll and unlit smoke and went to the corner. Produced a crowbar, shovel, spade, and a pick. 'All ready to go.'

I noticed they were new.

Returning, he said, 'Metal detector, that's what we need.'

'How much?'

'I need to make a few phone calls, do a bita research. Main thing is, you're still with me?'

'Of course.'

'We can't give up now. People might laugh, but I haven't told the full story.'

I waited.

'It was verified,' he whispered.

'How's that?'

'After I got the map I contacted this fella at the university and he said bring it in. So I went in and he examined it and said, Doug, I reckon you're onto something.'

'How did he know?'

'*He knew.* I went home and told Nan, and said, You can choose to believe me or not. But before that, I want you to come and meet this fella. So, she gets dressed up and we go back and he tells her it's not a fake. It's at least a hundred years old – the age when the reef was meant to be discovered.'

'And?'

'She tells me I'd believe anything. Then I knew I was on my own, and I have been, all these years. Which is why you gotta promise to help me, Clem.'

'Of course.'

He stood, walked around the engine and said, 'I know someone'll get me a good price.'

'I'll drive,' I said.

He returned and sat down. 'Hurry up and get your licence. It's been a long wait. One time yer dad promised to help.'

'When was that?'

'Before he ...' He thought about it. Obviously, some sort of memo had gone around the street.

'He promised to help?'

'He had a Holden, before your time, and he said, Doug, I'll go, as long as you promise, seventy–thirty split.'

'You agreed?'

'Course I agreed. But then things went pear-shaped.'

'Pear-shaped?'

He must have remembered. 'Doesn't matter. As long as you're still—'

'*It does matter.*'

'Just be grateful he ...' His head dropped; he lit his smoke.

'Pop?'

'Need the throne.' He stood, and made his way back to the house.

Missed, again. I walked over to the Datsun wall and studied the Fairlady, the Roadster. Ghost cars that no one talked about.

March

The Rosies' weeds had set seed, died and settled in a composted square full of cat shit and rubbish that had blown in from the road. But I could still remember when it was freshly mowed, Mr Rosie sitting on the step with me, telling me about high school. 'One trick's filling the head with paper and flushing.'

I went in the back door: the laundry lino lifting, the rusted square where they'd had their trough, spilled toilet cleaners and bleach still colouring the floor. Tina, a few months after Mr Rosie had gone, telling the movers what to take, as I watched from my window and saw what was left of Oswald Rosie being loaded in the back of a truck.

He was still there, looking out the back door. Did you read the Dickens?

Yes.

And?

It's okay, but a bit … unbelievable. Have you got anything else?

He led me to his study, and the bookcase that reached to the ceiling. I said, All we got's encyclopedias.

That's okay.

Planet of the Apes?

It's about a world where the apes rule, and the people are in zoos.

That sounds okay. I leafed through the pages. Can I borrow it?

I stood where the bookcase had been and remembered the movers bringing out boxes of books, and thinking, if no one wants them … But you couldn't say anything. Tina and Vicky standing in their driveway, and Mum sitting next to me, watching and saying, It's sad, isn't it?

What?

What happened.

What happened?

Well … Mr Rosie's gone.

I know, but what happened to him?

Nothing.

I felt the walls, the window frames, as if Ossie might still be there, somehow. As if I could say, I saw you the other day.

Where?

Sitting on your front step.

And what I wouldn't say: staring at the ground, for an hour, like you were looking at something, although you weren't.

I's getting some air.

The master bedroom. There was a hole in the floor and you could see the ground. Like he'd fallen (Curtis's theory – explained in Cantos II). But I knew how it'd got there. Kids breaking in, a year or so after they'd moved. We'd heard them trashing the place, and Pop had rung the cops, and when they'd arrived you could see them scampering, climbing the back fence into other people's yards. So now Mrs Donnellan's cats had a way in, and their piss and shit was everywhere. (I wouldn't tell Ernie, cos he'd just use it against her). There was a built-in wardrobe, and Tina had left a few rugs that sat folded, ready for use. Oswald (I imagined) placing one over his wife, kissing her, saying, It's okay if you find someone else. Before going out, finding a rope and choosing the tree.

Just make sure you stay away from Mr Sharpe, he said to me.

Why?

You don't wanna hang around gloomy people.

Why's he gloomy?

Cos things didn't work out the way he wanted, so he's still … shitty.

But he's funny.

When he's drunk.

He's a communist.

No, he's a misery guts.

I just play with Curtis.

That's okay.

Are you a communist?

No, but I have the book. And he found it, and showed me, seven years before Ernie.

The toilet, as I remembered it. A ballerina for the paper, a scum ring, although it still flushed okay. The kitchen, stripped clean, and back to the laundry. The screen door, and me knocking, and

Mrs Rosie answering, Vicky clinging to her leg. Is Mr Rosie home?

No, Clem.

Oh … Although I knew he was. I'd seen him walking up and down the drive in his pyjamas.

I was gonna get a book.

Can you come back tomorrow?

That you, Clem? The voice from the bedroom.

Go on, then, Mrs Rosie said, as Vicky stuck her tongue out at me.

I went into their bedroom and Mr Rosie was in bed, still in his pyjamas at two in the afternoon. He said: You finished those already? And I returned my pile.

Come on then. He took me into his study and filled my arms and said, How you feeling?

Strange question, cos there was no reason not to feel okay. I noticed he hadn't shaved for a week, although it was term time, and his eyes were red, like he'd been crying. I'll get started on these now.

Good-o.

I went back outside. Walked around the yard. The empty shed, with its cracked slab and oil stains, the beams that held up the roof. The louvres, cracked, diffusing the early autumn light. There'd been a Torana, and Pop had serviced it. The car Tina and Vicky had finally climbed into, before driving off. As we watched from the lounge, and wondered.

I went outside and studied the branches again. That was Pop's explanation – although how he'd known? A few months after Vicky and Tina had left, me, lying in bed, listening through the walls. Pop saying, Hung himself.

Mum: Rubbish.

Went off his medication. She found him hanging from the lemon tree.

But I checked, and there was only one lemon tree, and the branches all poked up, although there were a few that'd been chopped off.

'That you, Clem?'

It was Mrs Champness, peering through a hole in the fence.

'Just having a look,' I said.

'It's a disgrace, isn't it?' she half-sang. 'There could be snakes in that grass.'

'Do we get snakes around here?'

'Yes, we do. Les found a brownie in the aviary. It was after the birds.'

It was Lanark Avenue, and everyone was close, and you could smell them and hear them, and every day they got a little closer, if you weren't careful. I could hear Jen, Depeche Mode (again), and Mum mixing cupcakes. I could smell Wendy's powder, and someone had permed her hair like pavlova.

'Shame, what happened,' she said.

'What's that?'

'Oswald. Nice fella. But I wish they'd do something about this place. It's a disgrace.'

'Did he leave them?' I asked.

She gave me that look, and thought better of it. 'Yes, he left them.'

'I heard he killed himself.'

'Who told you that?'

'Just heard.'

'Don't know about that. Think he just left.'

I got the that's-all-you-need-to-know look. She must've known I was a snoop; Les must have explained it all.

'He was good to you, wasn't he? Like a father, eh?'

'Sort of.'

'That's what I'd say to Les. Pity Clem hasn't got a dad, but at least he's got Oswald.'

'Yes.'

'You were in there two or three times a day sometimes. Tina must have got tired of you, but Oswald never said nothin', did he?'

'No.'

'Very patient man. Suppose that comes from being a teacher.

Not like Les – he wouldn't have the patience for kiddies. But Oswald. I can still remember you on his back, piggying you up and down the drive, and you pretending to whip him, and him goin' like a horse … Can you remember that?'

'No.'

'And Vicky, I think she was a bit jealous.'

It was the way she said these words that made me think.

'He could see you had a brain and he didn't want it to go to waste. You were lucky to have him.'

I could feel my heart racing. *Lucky*? Of course.

'Not that Doug's never done his best, but he's old, eh? And a boy needs a dad.'

Oswald. But maybe someone else, earlier. Someone carrying me. I said, 'Do you remember when I was born?'

'Long time ago.'

'And Dad bringing me over, for you to have a look?'

She took a moment. 'I reckon he mighta.'

'Was he happy?'

'Well, you would be, wouldn't yer? I reckon he was over the moon. I reckon he couldn't wait to tell us all, to show yer. I reckon it was the day after you came home from hospital.'

That was enough. I turned, ran home and flew through the front door, into the kitchen. The mixer was still going. 'Mrs Champness reckons he showed me around.'

Mum stopped the mixer. 'What?'

'Wendy reckons Dad showed me to everyone. Said he was over the moon.'

'Guess he was.'

'So why would he leave?'

She switched it back on, studied the mixture.

'Why?' I switched it off. 'He didn't want to go.'

'Don't talk about what you don't know.'

Jen appeared from her room. 'Why you upsetting everyone?'

I ignored her. 'He was showing me around the whole street.

He'd painted my room, he'd done everything to get ready. Why would he go?'

She switched the mixer on.

Jen said, 'You're such an arse.'

Pop came in from the shed. 'What is it?'

I turned to him. 'I just asked about Dad.'

Four people in a kitchen, waiting.

'You made him go!' I said to Mum.

'I didn't!'

Jen took my arm and tried to pull me from the kitchen. I shook free. 'I just want to know!'

'Enough!' Pop shouted.

Silence, again, apart from the mixer. Mum started crying, turned, and ran from the kitchen, the house.

Jen said, 'You're such a selfish shit!'

Pop was always the practical one. He turned off the mixer and glared at me. 'Certainly wasn't the way to go about it, was it?'

'What way is there?'

'Wait.'

'How long?'

'As long as it takes.' And he went back to the shed.

The murals had weathered. Mud-splattered, with chutney smears from an unloved sandwich, Mr Champness's other finger inserted up his nose. Someone had scraped the legs and arms off a koala. It was always going to happen. We'd warned Nick. So, he'd come out with repair pots, to fix things, and said, 'If you keep at it they'll stop.'

Curtis had disagreed. 'You oughta see what's in the boys' change rooms.'

The school that time forgot. Society, anyway. Tweed-jacketed nose pickers fondling igneous rocks as boilers hissed sweet nothings to puberty blue Leeanes in search of homemaking skills. Some schools put their slow learners into remedial classes, and at least tried. At Gleneagles they were placed in an opportunity class.

Followed the groundsman around all day, pulling weeds, fixing fences. A message to the rest of us (or according to Curtis, trying to impress the canteen sluts): '*Lasciate ogni speranza, voi ch'entrate.*'

Nick had sealed the murals and we'd signed them, and the rest of the school had called them gay, and piss-weak, but, inspired by our Great Leader, we'd ignored them. 'The life of the artist in a cultural urinal,' he'd explained. Going on to say how the place was all sport because dull people liked dull pastimes. 'Artists have always been victimised. Anyway, you really want to end up like …?' But had stopped, realising he had a few footballers in the class.

So, we'd moved on to portraiture. A girl called Tracey had volunteered, and sat at the front. Nick had gathered us around, shown us how to draw axes, tilt the head, get the dimensions right, add a nose and mouth. Then he'd given us paper and charcoal and said, 'See what you can come up with.'

These were the best lessons. Gathered in our uncoolable hut, serenaded by Split Enz, talking. I had a head, decorated with a pig snout and a chin that stuck out like Clutch Cargo. Curtis had bloodshot eyes, gaunt cheeks and canine teeth protruding from her mouth. 'Like a wolf,' I said.

He howled, and everyone laughed.

It was about now Nick would begin his sermon. Not that he'd mean to, or probably care, but he couldn't help but tell the truth. 'They reckon they might boycott LA.'

We waited. Who? Why?

'The Olympics,' he said, no doubt realising we were all dolts, dragged up in a suburban soup of meat, Chryslers and the Ted Mulry Gang.

'The Reds?' Curtis managed.

'Iran, China, the lot.' He stood behind Curtis. 'Who's that?'

'Her.' He pointed, accusingly, like it was Tracey's fault.

'Maybe more on the cheeks … and her teeth don't look like that.' He sat down and turned up the radio. 'I reckon Big Brother wins.'

'Who?'

'You haven't read *Nineteen Eighty-Four*?'

'No.' Although I remembered it on Ossie's bookshelf.

'A dictatorship. Big Brother tells everyone what to think. Watches what you're up to in your home.'

One of the girls pulled a face. 'I wouldn't let 'em.'

I thought of my TK25 and wondered if I was some sort of Big Brother, or maybe just a pervert.

'They control the newspapers, telly. Twenty-four hour *Blankety Blanks*.'

I could hear Ernie Sharpe.

The girl said, 'Plenty of good articles in the paper.'

'Like?'

'AIDS. They reckon that's gonna kill half the globe.'

'Bullshit,' Nick said. 'That's the other thing they do. Make you scared so you stay in your job, and house, and buy stuff.' He slowed, realising the sermon was dragging. 'And plenty of sport. Like we're all part of some big team, and we just gotta win and we'll be happy.'

The biggest of the footballers was named Barry, and he said, 'What a loada shit.'

Nick sat forward. 'How's yer sketch, Bazz?'

He showed him.

'Anyway, Winston Smith thinks dangerous thoughts.' He paused, sharing them, anticipating the reward. 'And he pays for it in room 101.'

'What happens?' I asked.

Nick must have known I'd be the one to ask. 'He questioned the leaders.'

'About what?'

'Newspeak. The Prole sector. Why it wasn't different ... better.'

This revelation didn't seem to interest anyone. But for me, it was about the most important thing I'd ever heard. 'So the book reckons we're *told* what to think?'

'Exactly.'

'By newspapers?'

'And schools, politicians, organisers of Olympic Games. The guy on the telly flogging refrigerators.'

Tracey said, 'That's crap. This is 1984, and no one's watching me take a shower.'

Barry smiled, but thought better of it.

If you're going to form a world view you've probably done it by the time you're seventeen. Taken in the facts, made the connections, read the books (between the lines), listened to the dissenters, suspected the rich, famous and beautiful, the ball-kickers, the guys with the longest sideburns and shiniest suits. Found yourself hating the kids getting all the trophies (knowing they're quite ordinary, but will always be praised). Felt yourself being pushed to the margins of some world you've barely entered. Known you don't belong, like no one can see you, or cares about you or what you think. And when you say all this, you feel there's someone about to put you back in your box, or room, staring through the glass for more clues, watching the wheels go round and round, not cos you want to control anyone or anything, but you want to know the truth. 'So what you're saying,' I asked Nick, 'is that we go to school to learn *not* to think?'

'Thinking takes effort, and people are lazy.'

Gavin Davies came in late. He threw his bag on a desk and said, 'I's at the dentist.'

Nick indicated the pile of paper, the charcoal sticks, and Tracey.

'Hey, Mr Andrews, you're not gonna like this.'

'What's that, Gav?'

'They're painting over our murals.'

Nick ran for the door, shouting, 'Hold on … *you fuckin' cunts.*'

We dropped everything and followed him outside. The groundsman had already painted over Les Champness. Beige, although you could still see the outline. He had a couple of the opportunity kids with him, and they were stirring more paint. Nick approached him, pulled the brush from his hand and said, 'What the fuck do you think you're doing?'

He just stood back. 'Miss White told me to.'

Tracey said, 'Nice work, dickhead.'

Curtis walked over, picked up a lid and tried to put it on a can. One of the kids pushed him away but he said, 'Watch yerself!'

The groundsman wasn't interested. 'If you got a problem take it up with her. I do what I'm told.'

Nick stormed across the asphalt to the office. We followed. He looked back, saw us, but said nothing. Maybe he realised we should see what came next. As he always said, it was an artist's job to question.

Curtis caught up with me. 'They got Les first.'

'We can repaint him.'

We followed Nick into the foyer. He burst into White's office, stormed out a moment later and approached the desk. 'Where's Joy?'

The girl told him she was teaching.

'What room?'

She checked. 'Seventeen.'

He was off again – up the stairs, along the corridor, past posters showing how to factorise quadratic equations. He walked into room seventeen. We stood back. He wasn't dangerous, but she was. We heard him say, 'Did you agree to have them painted over?'

I imagined the old girl standing with arms crossed, her mouth half-open, like a cleft anticipating a fine, rounded specimen.

And softly: 'You never asked Mr Meadows.'

'So what?'

'You can't go painting school buildings without permission from—'

'*So what?*'

Silence.

A whisper. 'Can I see you outside, Mr Andrews?'

We ran to the end of the hall, turned and stood listening. The girls giggled but Curtis hushed them.

We heard Joy White say, 'Where's your class?'

'Waiting in the room. The girls are crying cos their work's been painted over.'

Curtis said, 'Shut up!'

'Well, if you really want to know, I, and Mr Meadows, thought several of those images were inappropriate.'

'How?'

'People's bottoms.'

Curtis nudged me. 'Nice work, Clementine.'

'And the one with the girl giving the finger.'

'You want them to paint flowers?'

'Don't put words in my mouth. Giving the finger to someone who looked like the Pope. Was it the Pope?'

'It was a statement about birth control.'

'And you think that's appropriate for a high school?'

'They're Year Twelves.'

'That image was seen by younger children. One told his mother.'

'Listen, Joy, these kids can think for themselves—'

'And she rang regional office and complained. And they rang me.'

As Nick had explained, the truth was a slippery eel.

'The point is, you coulda talked to me before you started painting over it.'

'You had no right discussing Mr Moore with them.'

Silence.

'It makes me wonder what else you talk about. You're not one of them, Nicholas. You're a teacher, apparently.'

One of them. The distinction that mattered.

'I heard what you said,' she continued.

'If they ask ...'

'No, they're children.'

She was wearing him down with facts.

'You're gonna paint over all of them?'

'Yes.'

'They're not all offensive.'

'You should've asked. They'll attract graffiti. They already have.'

'But I ...' Like he realised there was no point. Maybe it had come from a life believing in the redeeming power of art. Like Curtis said: *abandon all hope*.

Saturday morning. Curtis had worked out that hot women (his words) liked to have funky cars (his words). Personalised plates, Playboy stickers and car seats. Therefore, my room was the place to be. As they arrived, parked, went in to see Ron Glasson, re-emerged, waited for him to measure up. Curtis was there, focusing, describing, saying, 'D'you reckon she's got a boyfriend?'

'Look at her … probably. Anyway, what are you gonna do? Go out and tell her you've been perving on her?'

'That's not how it's done.'

'Do tell.'

'Stroll out and say something like, Some sheep died for you. Then stop …' But he realised there was no way. 'Just watch I s'pose. Look how short she wears that—'

Mum. A quick knock and she came in, handed me a pile of freshly ironed shirts and said, 'What are you two up to?'

Curtis said, 'Clem's showing me how his telescope works.'

Mum glanced out the window. 'That's a bit unsavoury, isn't it, Curtis?'

'What?'

'You know …' There was no point continuing. 'How's John settled in?'

Curtis pushed the telescope towards me. 'He worked with Dad for a few days, but chucked it in.'

'Why?'

'Cos he's John.'

'What's he gonna do now?'

Curtis stared at the shag pile, as if this was a question he shouldn't, couldn't answer. 'You know … Mum's a bit worried.'

Mum must've thought, fresh clothes, new day, no time for dragging your tail. 'I'm sure it'll work out. Some people need a while to find their way, don't they, Clem?'

'Why you asking me?'

She didn't reply; smiled; lifted an eyebrow. 'He keeps a book, don't you, Clem? Where is it?'

I'd hidden it.

'Writes down all his thoughts … don't you?'

I refused to reply.

'Like Anne Frank. And he's made little notes about everyone. I'm sure you're in it too, Curtis.'

'He can write what he likes, Mrs Whelan. Doesn't bother me.'

Mum realised it wasn't going to work. 'Says a bit about Mr Glasson, don't you, Clem? Reckons he's—'

'Mum, thanks for the shirts.'

'—got a dozen children lined up behind sewing machines, making the car seats. Apparently Ron had some sort of sect, and multiple wives …'

I stood and helped her from the room, but she was giggling.

'… and now …'

I closed the door and reclaimed the eyepiece. 'Sorry.' Mr Glasson had gone, but the girl was standing, fanning herself with one of his brochures. 'She's getting hot.'

Curtis grabbed it. 'They're fuckin' enormous.'

'Why'd he quit his job?'

'Sacked. Told some guy to fuck off. He'll end up back at McNally's.'

'You reckon?'

'Those dicks he went to school with, round the block. I saw him with them … There's an older brother, and he's been to prison.'

'So what can your parents do?'

He looked up. 'We should take some photos.'

'Isn't that against the law?'

We waited. Mr Glasson returned with car seats and started fitting them.

'They're doin' break-ins again?'

'Probably.'

'Shouldn't you tell someone?'

'Why? It's not my problem. It's better when he's gone.'

Curtis just didn't get it. Or did, but didn't care. John was like some stranger who sometimes stayed in their house. It'd started with shoplifting: chips, drinks from Don's, a few titty mags, then (not realising he was on CCTV) a session with his mates snapping antennas off Fords in the car yard. Police visit number one. Then, they'd broken into Gleneagles Primary, stolen radios, cassette recorders, petty cash and an overhead projector they'd later smashed in a creek (covered with their fingerprints). Visit number two. This time they'd arrested him, taken pictures and dragged Anne and Gary to the station to see what their future would look like. Court date, good behaviour bond, but then they were back at it. Shops, till, money. More visits. Court. Three months at McNally's. Released. One of them had distracted the girl at the BP and John had cleaned out another till. Another visit. Another three months.

This pattern had repeated for three years, most recently stopped (Mum had told me) when Anne had discovered cartons of cigarettes in the cubby house. She'd placed them in a shopping bag, driven to the police station and asked them to pick him up at school, so she didn't have to go through it again. Or Gary; Curtis; the rest of Lanark Avenue, with its tolling bell.

Again, court, McNally's, this time for six months, with the threat from the judge that next time it'd be adult prison.

'Your mum's done her best,' I said.

'Who gives a shit? The sooner he's gone … I *want* him to steal. I'll dob him in, then I'll get another six months of peace.'

This didn't seem unreasonable. Anne had tried, but wouldn't turn on him again, I guessed. Gary had given up years ago. But, it seemed to me, and Pop, that at some point someone would have to deal with him.

Curtis kept describing what he was seeing: a black bra that was dirty, *dirty*. 'I should try.'

'Bullshit.'

'*L'amor che move il sole e l'altre stelle.* The love that moves the sun and stars.'

'Hello?' Ron's voice, from the road.

Curtis shot back behind the curtains. 'He's seen us.'

Ron: 'That you, Mr Whelan?'

'Ssh!' Curtis said, slowly dragging the telescope away from the window.

'And that device of yours?'

I glared at Curtis. 'He saw you?'

'The breeze blew the curtain.'

We listened. Silence. Maybe he'd gone back in to the call the police? Or maybe he didn't care. Maybe he was finishing the job.

'Have a look,' I said.

Curtis moved sideways, glanced. 'Safe.'

We looked out. Ron Glasson looked in. 'That you in there, Clem?'

Steps, along the path, on the porch, and a knock on the door. 'Fuck,' I said.

The girl was standing, watching, her arms crossed, her car seats half-fitted. I strained to hear Mum and Mr Glasson talking at the front door. 'Wasn't me,' I said to my supposed friend.

Then they were at my door. Mum and the man who'd never stepped foot in our house, our garden, our lives.

'Well, what have you got to say for yourself?' Mum asked.

I waited for Curtis to confess – black bra, latches, popping out, the love that moves the sun. I had to think on my feet. I'd seen where dobbing got you: the mound, a disaffected son, broken antennas and a life of misery. There was only one thing to do. 'I was just showing Curtis how it worked.'

'You were bloody not,' this stranger said. Never more than a quick wave, and G'day, and now here in the land of my most intimate apparel, and moments. He stepped forward, grabbed my telescope, folded the legs and placed it under his arm. 'I see you, lookin' at people all the time. It's got to the point I can't step out the front of me house without wondering if my fly's done up.'

Mum glared at me. No words, but I could see she was saving them.

'Man deserves a bita privacy, doesn't he, Mr Whelan?'

'Yes, Mr Glasson.' I waited for Curtis. He was studying the carpet.

'What would your dad say?'

'What's that got to do with it?'

He shook his head. 'You'll get this back when I'm sure you won't …' He leaned over to the window. 'Coming, Mrs Hill.' Then stormed from the room, the house, number 31.

Mum said, 'Happy?'

'What's Dad got to do with it?'

'I warned you.'

Curtis stood, smiled at Mum and said, 'I better get going.'

Of course, I thought, you bastard.

He scurried from the room, strolled past the girl, and lingered, and I thought, You've gotta be kidding.

Mum said, 'He coulda called the police.'

'*It was him.*' I indicated the figure talking to the girl. 'He was looking at her.'

'Rubbish.'

'How did Ron see? Look, the sun's in his eyes.'

She wasn't going to concede. 'What's it matter? It's usually you. I can't believe … I warned you, now everyone in the street will know.'

Then she was gone. My telescope. Curtis. Mr Glasson.

So, the world had asked for it. I found my notebook under the bed and opened to a new page.

14/iii/84. The Fantastic Four were no more. Mr Fantastic vowed to make new friends. The Invisible Woman had accused him of horrible crimes. What did she know? He'd been burned, again, by the Human Torch, and decided enough was enough. Even the Thing had deserted him. He rose from his bed, pulled on his zoot-suit, took his guitar and flew from the room. The evil Glasson was holding the girl hostage …

'Been havin' a perve?' Jen asked, standing in the doorway.

'Fuck off!'

'Clem!' Mum called from the lounge room.

'You're old enough to buy a magazine,' she said, smiling, and I threw a book at her.

The girl got her covers and drove off. Mr Glasson went home. Curtis called. 'Sorry.'

Half an hour later there was a knock, more voices, then Mum at the door with my telescope. 'Don't know if I should give it to you.'

'Was that him?'

'Hester. And she gave you this.'

She dropped the telescope, and a map of something, on my bed. I looked.

Map of the Constellations: Summer.

Sleepy Gold Coast days, high socks, sandshoes and a walk to Southport for milk and news. Meter maids, too, in Hills Hoist bikinis. All so strange, as I read, in my shed, in Gleneagles. Apparently they walked around, finding expired meters, feeding them. 'What do you think of that?' I asked Pop, showing him a picture of the sisters-at-work.

He glanced up from under Mr Harper's bonnet, shook his head and continued preparing for the re-assembly.

'You ever been to the Gold Coast?' I asked.

'Who'd wanna go there?'

'It says it only rains a coupla days a year.'

He was filing an engine mount, removing rough edges. 'People can get it too easy.'

I knew what he meant. You had to struggle: cold weather, rain, bills, a dodgy brain. 'Says here: *the Smiths are studying chemical engineering* ... as if.'

'Where d'you find that?'

'In the pouffe.'

'What a loada rot. Put it in the bin.'

He descended, greasing mounts and cleaning transmission lines. I studied the Smiths: same height, boobs, tummies (as I imagined the grimiest, leather-studded ecstasy imaginable) and cloaks with sequins. 'You'd go soft in the head, wouldn't you, Pop?'

'Shoot me if I ever play bowls, Clem.'

This was one of his mantras. Bowls, apparently, meant you'd given up on life.

'Anyway, you wanna chuck those old magazines. Nan doesn't need them anymore.'

Strange he'd mention her. It'd been ten years and the person, I suppose, had been replaced with the *idea*. 'She used to love the *Post*, eh?'

'For some unknown reason.'

The crosswords, mostly (this one finished, complete with question marks and copperplate notes). Stories about Perth plumbers rowing around Australia; one-armed kids winning soccer grand finals; Noelene Brown moving from screen to stage. And the story of eighty-seven-year-old dementia patient Costa Poglou, who'd gone missing from his nursing home, and the police and SES and a whole neighbourhood had searched for him for two days. But it was all right, the article explained, because people with dementia *did* remember. Costa had walked seventeen kilometres, a dozen suburbs, over main roads, through shopping centres (the CCTV proved it), paddocks, drainage ditches, to the spot he and his wife had built their first home. Now, it was gone, replaced by townhouses. But he'd made it, stood in what had been his veggie patch, and the man who lived there now (an accountant with two gleaming boys) had asked, Can I help you? And he'd said, My house? Where's my house? And the accountant had realised, and tried to show him around (as best he could) before taking him inside for a cuppa, and calling the police.

So maybe it was all in Pop's head. Every clue; every answer. I recognised his writing and said, 'Seventeen down: *She married the Sentimental Bloke.*'

'Doreen ... *Christ*, get rid of it.'

Every week Nan'd send me or Jen to Don's with a handful of twenty cent pieces. Enough for the *Australasian Post* and fifty cents' mixed lollies – no teeth.

'You should keep them as a reminder,' I said.

'Don't tell me what I should do.' As he kept spraying lubricant. *Sorry.* Although you couldn't say it.

'I can remember everything I want. And if the rest's gone … so what?'

What he chose to remember. What he could remember. The photos we still had of him and Nan and Mum and me and Jen at a picnic, a rug and a thermos of tea, sandwiches. That's the sort of thing you had to remember.

So maybe I could keep the *Post*. Maybe, in a decade, it'd tell me things he couldn't. The bits he'd kept in a box, and tried to forget. Nan getting in the car, but him not seeing her, even out the corner of his eye. Clutch, reverse, handbrake off, and back he went – Nan thrown out, but the door slammed shut by a post, and by the time he'd heard, and braked, she'd hit her head on another post, and was unconscious, hanging with one leg half-in, half-out, bleeding from the nose.

I kept reading. 'This musta been one of the last she read.'

'What's that got to do with anything?'

Wouldn't you think to ask? Do you remember yer nan, Clem? Can you see her when you close your eyes? Do you want me to talk about her, remind you how she helped you with your homework (little letters copied like the teacher drew them); walked you to school, and back; patted you to sleep when you were a bub, when your mum was tired, and there was no one else around to help (except Val, but she knew when to say when)?

'Righto, let's go.' He stood, approached the hoist and wheeled the engine towards the car. 'Come on, then.'

I stood on the other side, holding the block steady while he positioned it.

'You remember the sequence?' he said.

'Sorta.'

He'd done it without a manual; insisted he remembered everything: crankshaft, transmission, electrics. 'Righto.'

You had to trust yourself. If you started writing everything down your brain would become less elastic. If it worked out you didn't need it, it'd stop performing. So, he started pulling on the chains on the hoist. The block lifted.

'Is that right?' I asked.

He stopped, fiddled with them, tried to work it out. 'This one down … like this, isn't it?'

'Yeah, that one, Pop.'

He tried again. It lowered.

I said, 'Stop.'

And I turned the block, so it might fit. 'None of these bolts line up.'

He seemed unsure. 'So we're ready?'

'Go on.'

He pulled the chain again, and the block lowered. Down, until it approached the bolts. Then he stopped again. 'This isn't right, is it?'

'Nearly there.'

He studied the coming-together, then bit his lip. 'You reckon?'

It was simple. We'd done it a dozen times before. There were holes, and they'd align, and we'd bolt them, and then connect the parts that'd eventually make Mr Parker's car run again.

'Righto.' He pulled the chain but the block was unbalanced and the left side dropped before the right. It fell heavy and wrong and scraped against the engine well so that it was pressing down on the side of the car. He stood back and said, 'Fuck!'

I came around. The engine had pushed out a body panel. There was no more tension in the chain, so he pulled it through. 'What a mess.'

'We've gotta lift it.'

'Explain that to him.' Indicating the damage. 'Forty years … never done that.'

'We gotta put it back, attach it.'

He walked from the shed, across the yard, towards the house. Mum was hanging washing on the line. 'What's wrong, Dad?'

He went in.

Following, I said, 'The engine dropped.'

'For goodness sake.' We found him filling the pot with tea. 'What's wrong, Dad?'

'I'm givin' it away.'

Mum said, 'Cos you hada bita trouble?'

'Go look what I done. Used to do that blindfolded.' He lit the stove, filled the kettle and placed it on the ring. Out of sequence. He always boiled the water first.

'Come on,' Mum said, 'Clem'll help you fix it.'

'Enough!' he said.

Jen, standing in the doorway. 'What's wrong?'

'Mind yer own business!'

Mid-term, and my first essay was due. I scribbled a few hundred words about the Russian Revolution before stopping to listen to Lennon, in bed with his own uprising. Mum was always on at me to study, every minute, It's an investment in your future – but I couldn't see it. So many years of grind, long division and King Tut dead at fourteen. It was all in the past, and all I wanted was alcohol, sex with real women, money and freedom. Wait, just a bit more, but I didn't believe it. More, stretching into my twenties, beyond, mortgage, babies, old age, forgetfulness and a shed with an abandoned Datsun. So life had to be lived now. But how? One thousand words: *Outline the causes of the 1917 Revolution.*

Fuck.

Ernie's book had come in handy. I'd ploughed through it: sitting waiting for minimum chips. Don: Whatcher reading?

The Communist Manifesto.

Loada rubbish.

How's that? As I turned to the appropriate page and read about the proles rising against their capitalist oppressors. As Don scratched his arse, wiped his hands on his apron and shook my chips. Capital. You need capital, I explained. Then you can invest in a chain of fish shops and employ other people to work in them, and manage them, and you can retire.

I'd read Marx on the toilet, in the car, waiting for Mum at the shops, during lunch (as Curtis made Twistie rolls), at home (as we watched *That's Incredible*), forcing myself through the word sludge in search of meaning. In the same way I'd searched the Fantastic Four, Beatles' lyrics, bird books, bus timetables, anything that might explain how the world worked. Manuals, newspapers, textbooks, IQ percentile rankings, *The Guinness Book of Records*, encyclopedias (V–Z, the leftover world from the alphabet of things). Maybe, when all of this brewed, stewed and boiled, there'd be a picture of the world that made sense.

I'd even read it to Ernie, when I took it (heavily annotated) to ask questions. 'So Marx is saying there have always been class divisions, and always *will* be?'

'No, not always. He was saying it's how we let people walk over us. We need to organise. That's what you should say in your essay.'

On the wall, a black-and-white photo of a 1969 Conference of Union Leaders: beer bellies and sideburns lined up in anticipation of a lost Russia.

'Can I hold on to this a bit longer? It's helpful with my essay.'

'You can keep it. But the thing is, are these ideas living, or dead?'

'Ernie!' Ida, at the door. 'He's not interested.'

'Yes, you are, eh, Clem?'

'Yes, Mrs Sharpe. See.' Showing her my underlinings.

She just shook her head. 'Well, you got your disciple at last.'

Now I had something resembling an essay. I wondered if it was any good. There was only one way to tell. The Donnellan brothers were the best Lanark Avenue could muster. Two degrees, twelve years of university, cast in the weeds of number 33. Doctors of letters waiting for a right to wrong, a chance to show Val she hadn't wasted a lot of time, money and faith. I went next door and found David in his spot. Showed him the essay and said, 'Don't know if this is any good.'

He read a few lines, and seemed interested. 'History?'

'Modern European. Just wanna know what I should add.'

His eyes followed the lines, but then dropped into the grass, through the plum foliage, down the street towards a man painting the Polish hall. Like he could, but couldn't; knew, but didn't have the energy or willpower. This, I supposed, was the worst thing of all. To know you no longer wanted to be, to fix, to raise and re-lower and bolt in; to realise the thing that used to churn in your belly had been shat into a garden of caltrop and soursobs. 'What do you think?'

'Peter,' he managed.

Of course. The brother who'd become. Who'd taken over the family, but laid it to rest in the brick-clad collapse of pier and asbestos sheeting.

'Righto,' I said, reclaiming my essay.

A few minutes later I was sitting with Peter at the kitchen table. He placed my essay on the melamine and read. 'It needs an edit.'

'Could you?'

He found a red pen and started correcting. 'You know, if we have a good go, I could get you an A.'

'You reckon?'

'Easy. You've thought it through, and there's evidence. I always thought there was something stirring in the grey cells.' He tapped my head. 'Though it's taken a while.'

He corrected, and I watched David, searching up and down the road where nothing was happening. 'Do you reckon he gets bored?' I asked.

'Here, look ... needs a footnote. Sounds like you just made it up.'

I checked. 'I'll add it later.' But returned to David. 'What about when he needs the toilet?'

'Rings his bell.'

I waited. 'What's it called?'

'What?'

'What he's got.'

'Muscular dystrophy.'

'Is it bad yet?'

He looked up. 'Not yet. Next coupla years. Which worries Mum.'

I'd overheard conversations between the mothers. The

invocation of nursing homes, carers, nappies, machines, hospitals. Years of thinking and planning and avoiding doing anything, yet. Like the future would fix things. But my experience suggested the future just fucked things up.

'So, like, when she's gone?' I dared. 'What happens then?'

He seemed surprised I didn't realise. 'Well, I'm his brother, eh?'

'Yeah.'

'Course I'm gonna ...'

The thought had crossed my mind. If he'd worked as a proper lawyer, earned a lot of money, he could've had a nice place and car and holidays, and when Val went, he'd be able to pop Davo in a home where he'd get looked after properly. But people in Lanark Avenue didn't do that.

'Might have to make some changes, inside,' I said.

'Yeah, we're applying for some money.' And he indicated a letter on the table. 'So we can redo the shower.'

Something I'd often thought about. The impractical bath, the poky receptacle. 'How does he ...?'

'Mum or me, we gotta use a flannel.'

Enough said. I wanted to ask, but dared not. A mother, with a son that age. See, this is what I mean. What book tells you about that?

Write an essay. To understand, they say. But that's not understanding anything. And why couldn't the topic be: *How do mums clean their disabled sons?*

'So you'll look after him?' I asked.

He didn't answer. Such an obvious question, I suppose.

'Here you say: *The persuasive powers of Trotsky were enough to convince the Russian people* ... but not all of them, surely?'

'Ernie.'

'No doubt. He's a good talker, but that's about all.' He circled the passage, and continued.

David was ringing his bell. Val came into the kitchen, rubbed my head and said, 'Keep at it, you two.' Then she filled a glass with water and went out to him. I heard the door slam, and saw her placing the drink in Dave's hand, help him lift it, wipe the water from his chin, talk to him, and kiss him on the head.

'That's what they don't teach you,' Peter whispered, as he worked.

'Sorry?'

But again, no reply. Val stood behind her son and looked at the things he was looking at. Ron and Hester's closed gate. Les Champness's shuttered house (a burst of late summer heat). A crow in the middle of the road, picking at something. But nothing, really. Just the possibility of a car driving past, or a skink crawling across the garden, or someone walking along the footpath. Even Ernie, who would acknowledge David because he wasn't responsible for the cats.

'I could help,' I said.

'What's that?'

'If I'm still here. You know, if you need help.'

He almost laughed. 'You've got Doug.'

'Mum can handle him.'

'Don't worry. I've been looking out for him since … the beginning.'

I knew that. The pictures on the wall. The brothers in a pool their dad had rigged from canvas. Him, Val, watching on. A photo for every year: the boys in short then long pants – Year Four through Twelve, then sideburns and beards, university, graduation gowns. Dozens of photos in the long hallway David was wheeled down dozens of times a day.

'He's the only one who'll listen to me,' he said. 'And I'm the only one who'll listen to him. So it works out okay.'

The endless Peter–David drone, heard from our own kitchen several times a day. Over the six pm news: the number of Russian warheads aimed at Australia. D: That's because America didn't deal with them after the war. P: Rubbish. This was always going to happen. Capitalism will eat itself, and it'll take us with it.

'It's strange,' I said. 'I couldn't look after my sister.'

'How do you know?'

'She hates me.'

'That doesn't mean …'

'But you're different. Brothers, for a start.'

'No different. You'd do it. You will, I guess, somehow.'

Val had gone. David kept scanning the street: left-right-left …

'Course she's worried,' Peter said. 'Not that he won't get looked after, but you're leaving something unfinished, aren't you?'

I guessed he was right. A child had be fed, groomed, educated, and eventually launched into the world. Then he or she would drift away from the shore, and find a current. But David would remain moored, bobbing in the waves, waiting for a release that couldn't come. He'd need to be cleaned and repaired, but couldn't go. And if that were the case, no one would. That's why Peter mowed his lawn with a scythe and allowed his beard to gather at his knees. Because there was no rush. Home was forever; you couldn't leave.

'Some of the phrasing,' Peter said. 'Subject, object … who's been teaching you English all these years?'

'*The Brady Bunch*.'

'Apparently.' He looked up. 'Done.'

I studied the essay, covered with red scrawl. 'Needs some work?'

'Write another version, taking in all my suggestions. Then bring it back and we'll have another go.'

'It's that bad?'

'It is. You want an A?'

'I guess.'

'You can't guess. You need to *want* one.' He waited. 'There's a million kids out there writing the same essay.'

I thought of giving some statement of personal beliefs. About the man, and the system, and one thing you can't hide is when you're crippled inside, and how I didn't want to play the game, although looking back now, I had no idea what the game was. Me being a dickhead, probably. Disguising my laziness and lack of originality as attitude. The John Lennon of Lanark Avenue. Although Lanark Avenue didn't need one. What it needed was an A, so the next generation didn't have to live in fibro houses.

'This is how it happened,' Peter said.

'How what happened?'

'My dad. When I was a little fella I came home with a D for maths. And he sat where you are, and I sat here, and he said: We travelled all his way, went to all this trouble, and you bring home a D.'

I waited.

'I felt sort of bad, and said, I'll get an A next term, and he said, I hope so, cos your mum'd be heartbroken if she thought ...' He stopped, remembering, I suppose. 'So then he dropped dead, guessing I couldn't do better than a D. At which point, Clem, I could've said one of two things: Well, what's the point? He'll never know now. Or: I promised you an A. I'll get an A.'

I waited. 'So?'

'But when the results were in the teacher said, Peter Donnellan, eighty-four, B, and I was gutted. I said: What do I gotta do to get an A? She said, Work harder. Then I told her about my dad and what I'd promised, and do you know what she said?'

'What?'

'Maybe next term.' He smiled, and shook his head. 'What a bitch!'

'She wouldn't—'

'But I explained to Mum and she understood. After that I was a different boy. I did what it took, Clem.' He waved my essay under my nose. 'Gotta make the choice. You gonna do it again?'

'Righto. Next week.'

'By Thursday.'

This is what Pop had told me about the Donnellan boys: mowing lawns until the mower broke, then cutting by hand. Delivering newspapers. Up and down the street, knock-knock, Can I wash yer car, Mr Rosie? Gathering bottles and taking them around to Don's, hanging the washing, cleaning the toilets (until David started feeling stiff), whizzing their way through childhood in search of coins, cleanliness, and high marks. Pop would say, 'They were stand-outs, Clem. You wanna be like them.'

'It's not like they're that successful.'

'Are you kidding? They made something of themselves, Clem. And do you know why?'

'No, Pop.'

'*Cos they had to.*'

Peter said, 'You do five subjects. I can help with more.'

'You don't have to.'

He jiggled his hand through my hair and said, '*Clemmy baby, who's all grown up?*'

'Get off.' As I pushed him away.

'*Don't need Uncle Peter's help no more?*'

'I'll …'

But he was up, and had me in a neck hold. 'I wiped yer bum, I may as well help with yer essays.'

'You did not.'

'Bullshit.' He called, 'Mum!' Then he grabbed my arm and took me outside to Val, who was removing clothes from the line. He said, 'Tell him. When Fay left him here, and you were busy, who wiped his arse?'

Val wouldn't be drawn. 'Bottom.'

'Who?'

Val just smiled at me.

'See,' Peter said. 'No secrets, old boy. Fixed that; I can fix your grammar.'

And here, I thought, seeing where he was standing, the spot you helped me pitch a tent, in preparation for cub camp. Where we spread the canvas, put it up the wrong way and had to start again. Where David brought out Coke and chips and we three (having barred Jen) sat drinking, and you said dirty limericks and your mum came out and told you not to corrupt me, I was only nine, and you said, We're only trying to help.

He dragged me around the house, pulling my arm so it lengthened, Mr Fantastic-style. Standing me in front of the faded verandah, he said, 'You, in a dress.'

'Bullshit.'

And he went to his brother, and turned his wheelchair so he could join in. 'Didn't he, Davo? Clem in a dress, and this was his little stage. We all gathered out front and Jen raised the awning and he turned on the tape player. *Dancing Queen, young and clean only seventeen …*'

'Never did.'

'*You can dance …*' Pointing at me accusingly.

'I remember,' David said.

Val had come around, without her washing. 'You did,' she agreed.

'*You can dance …*'

'Why would I put on a dress?'

David was giggling, but he kept turning to check the street. Peter jumped onto the verandah. 'And we all applauded. Me and Davo, Mum, Mr Champness, Doug, everyone.'

'Never happened.'

Art changed. Radio off. Lead on cartridge paper, as we all worked. Me, Mr Bulljaw: part-man, part-bull, with horns twice the size of his head. Big nostrils with clag-grey mucus; demonic eyes venting steam into a Lanark afternoon full of unsolved crime. Bulljaw could talk – 'Yield, Champness. Unhand her!' – as he bleated and farted, rising into the sky, the stars, the outer reaches of the universe.

Nick had said, Think back to when you were a kid. You picked up a pencil, you wanted to leave a mark. What was it?

I'd had to think, but then remembered Mr Bulljaw. I was six or seven, the owner of my first *Fantastic Four*. I'd traced the figures against a window, coloured them and stuck them up around my room. Peter Donnellan had seen my Human Torch and said, Not bad, but …

What?

What about *you*?

Me?

Your own superhero. Someone who lives in the crawlspace and comes out when there are problems. I'd said, Give me a few days, and a few days later there I was at the door to number 33, showing Val, David, and my mentor. Saying, Mr Bulljaw.

Val: He's a nice lookin' superhero. What's he do?

I'd explained. How he'd charge crims, gore them on his horn, fling them across the universe. I'd explained the source of my inspiration (B–C, pp. 34–35, Beef Cattle) and waited for praise.

I'd like a copy, if I may, Val had said, and it's still there, in a frame on her wall.

I nudged Curtis and said, 'What do you reckon?'

He just shrugged and drew an Uncle Scrooge with dollar-sign-eyes. There were fairies and footballers and Jodi Lodge (the girl who never spoke) attempting a dog, although it looked like a sausage with eyes.

'You can still see the murals,' I said.

Nick wasn't happy. 'He's gonna do another coat, just to make sure.'

'That's bullshit, eh?'

He just turned the page of his book and kept reading. I said, 'My neighbour's a lawyer and he reckons they've got no right.'

'Clem, it's not about … what sort of lawyer?'

'He doesn't work anymore.'

'He never worked,' Curtis said.

'He *did*. Told me he wasn't cut out for it.'

Nick didn't want to buy into it. He switched on the radio. Classical, quiet.

'He used to be good. We've got this neighbour who used to hit his wife …'

Curtis poked me.

'And she asked Peter … our neighbour, if she'd help him.'

'When was this?' Curtis asked.

'He told me.' I could remember Wendy scampering across the road, Les coming out, asking, You seen Wendy, Clem?

No, Mr Champness.

As he walked up and down the road, stopping in front of the Donnellans'. Wendy?

Looking at me slyly, though I wouldn't say.

You in there?

Picking up a handful of gravel and throwing it on Val's roof.

I saw yer. You want a fight, I'll give you one.

Then Peter had come out and said, Go in, Clem, and I'd gone in, but stood at the door watching. It'd started calmly, but the voices had loudened and I'd heard *respect her wishes* and *court order* and *it's not acceptable*. Then Mum and Pop and Jen were behind me and Mum'd said, Come away, it's none of our business. Pop had said, Les is gonna do him, and Jen had pushed to see, and Mum had pulled us back in and closed the door. I'd gone to my room and looked out and saw Les pushing Peter, and Peter stepping back, then turning and walking in, then Wendy emerging from the front door, approaching her husband, taking his hand and leading him home.

'Problem was,' I told Nick, 'he didn't like conflict. Always wanted people to get along.'

'Painting over murals? What law's that?'

I shrugged.

'He should stick to ... what's he do?'

'Preserves apricots,' Curtis said.

Nick laid down the book. 'Despite what I mighta told you, Clem ...' He stopped again. 'They listened to Lennon cos he had money and wrote songs. But for you and me ...'

I studied Mr Bulljaw. 'Peter said you should've stood up to them.'

He returned to his book. 'They give you a letter first.'

We all waited.

'So it looks like they've followed some procedure. But it's already decided. You've gotta go, it's just a matter of how.'

'They did that cos of the murals?' one of the girls asked.

'Because I was discussing other teachers.'

Curtis bit into his lip. 'That was my fault.'

'No, you asked. Then there's a second letter.' He held up a piece of paper. 'That's how it's done, Clem. *You think you want a revolution?*'

We continued working. I said, 'I can get Peter to look at those letters.'

He closed his book, picked up a Stanley knife and piece of plastic and said, 'Who's done?'

I held up Mr Bulljaw.

'Let's have you, Clem.'

The class gathered and he laid the plastic on a cork mat, and on top of this, my bull-hero. He used a pencil to trace over it then started cutting lines to make the shape. 'Like this,' he said. 'Major lines thicker, the hair, here, thin for effect.'

I could see it. I returned to my spot and continued. We all did.

Nick sat at his desk, folded his arms and said, 'That White woman has a face like a car accident.'

One of the girls explained how she'd never been married, and how it was always the way with that sort.

'Which poses the question: is it morally acceptable to hate someone?'

'Of course,' Curtis replied.

'You'd know,' I said. 'We're probably all on his list.'

Nick seemed intrigued. 'You've made a list?'

'No point wasting time with dead ends,' Curtis explained, then I told everyone about Curtis's premature adulthood, his first cigarette, vodka from Gary's cabinet.

'Am I on the list?' Nick asked, and everyone asked, although Curtis explained he didn't make a point of discussing his list and how, when he died, it'd be published, with full comments, so people could know their shortcomings.

'What about White?' one of the girls asked.

He was enjoying it. '*Late forties, single, sexually frustrated. There were, no doubt, ambitions, but she failed to realise them and set about making the world pay.*'

We all laughed. Even Nick, who said, 'Your first mark.'

And we waited again.

'The most important.' He stood, approached me and looked at Mr Bulljaw. 'All done?'

I nodded.

He picked up the stencil, approached a cupboard, found a can of black paint and said, 'Come on, you lot, bring yer stencils.'

We followed him outside. He shook the can, laid Mr Bulljaw against the wall and sprayed. A few minutes later there seven bull-men. Then he said, 'Get all the cans. Let's see what we can do.'

You're so small you can't see above the clothes rack, so you wander, run, hide in women's skirts, parkas, shirts. Someone's looking for you, but you feel safe: your legs are poles, feet, wheels, and it's only a matter of time. So you run again, stopping to check yourself in the mirror, back into the bushes, deep into the darkness. *Clem!* It's safe. So you emerge, walking in circles, dipping into discount boxes.

I sat up, looked out and saw people waiting for covers, and Mr Glasson drifting from car to car. In, out, making small talk, measuring seats.

'*Come, let's drink it while we have breath, for there's no drinking after death …*'

Ernie making his way along Lanark II. Stopping to rest on fences, cough, fart, wander in and out of his own jungle.

'*Down among the dead men …*'

Resting on our tube steel, lighting up, pulling on Fi-Fi's lead so she wouldn't get any ideas. 'He makes a nice cover, missus. You'll be happy.'

And the missus just smiled at him.

'He did mine a coupla years back, eh, Ron?'

He just continued measuring.

'Specially on a hot day,' Ernie said. 'Y' don't want to burn yer legs. Wool allows your skin to *breathe*, eh, Ron?'

He'd had enough. 'Ernie, Miss Stephens doesn't want that smoke in her car.'

'Sorry, missus.' And he stubbed it on the fence. 'Wash 'em every coupla years, they'll last. Good quality, eh, Ron? Where do they come from?'

'Sheep.'

'I know that, but what sorta sheep?'

'Merino.'

'Yes, best sort. Spanish. Fought a civil war over sheep … *Down among the dead men let him lie!*'

'You reckon you should get home?' Ron asked.

'What's the rush? Then you got the missus on at yer. Yours go on at yer, Ron?'

'No.'

'You watch that, Miss Stephens. Nice new seat covers, you don't want some drunken old bastard …'

It was unusual to see him this gone, this early. The Windsor only opened at ten. I knew he could get tanked in under an hour, but not in perfect dog-walking weather. Fi-Fi pulled on her lead, but he held her back. '*While the lads of the village slept.*' Burped. 'You run your hands through that wool, missus. Merino. Spanish Civil War. Fascism. And it was all a prelude to Hitler. The communists were against Franco … you heard of Franco?'

'Ernie!' Ron said. 'What are you goin' on about?'

'It's a public place, isn't it? I'm entitled to sit on this fence. Aren't I, Clem?'

I had to stop myself.

'Clem?'

The girl Stephens was sitting on the bonnet, grinning.

'You give a guarantee on those, Ron?'

'You're an embarrassment to the street, Ernie.'

'At least I talk to my neighbours.'

Ron turned to the girl and said, 'If you want to park in my driveway? It might be quicker.'

She nodded to Ernie and said, 'Nice to meet you, Mr …?'

'Comrade Sharpe.'

She got in, started her car and pulled into number 30. Got out, and Ron followed, and continued his fitting.

'Little bitch,' Ernie muttered, standing, continuing.

You can't know where you're going, when you run through

menswear. This is the world, as you swing from tree to tree, wiping your nose on someone's new slacks. The idea of buying something, wearing, altering, are all irrelevant. The clothes are rough-skinned bark you can rub your back on. You can stand inside jackets, and put your arms in the sleeves, although your fingers mightn't reach the elbows.

Down among the dead men ...

Someone sounded their horn for Mr Glasson to hurry up. Hester ran out and spoke to them and told them to be patient (I guessed).

Lacewings, fairy dust, and a trail. As the bell rang. I closed my eyes to hear. Yes, a bell. Then Ernie and David and something about cats. Then, louder, a frantic ring. *You wait and see what I'll do ...* Unmistakable. So drunk so early.

I half-ran to the front door. Mum said, 'What is it?' but she was busy with the Brasso, so there was no point. Down the drive, to see David and Ernie going their hardest.

Ernie: 'You don't think I will?'

David: 'Mum?' Ringing his bell, until Ernie tore it from his hand and flung it to the ground.

I walked around. There was a man in a Valiant, waiting, watching from his uncovered seat.

Ernie pointed to a cat, and her litter of seven or eight kittens, playing in the grass. 'That's disgusting.'

'What's wrong?' I asked, stepping forward.

'I could get 'em and ...' Ernie moved towards the kittens and David tried to block him with his hand, then moved his wheelchair.

'Mr Sharpe?' I said.

'Stay out of it, Clem.' He approached the kittens, leaned down, but they darted under the house. 'Little shits.'

'*Mum?*'

'No point stressing David,' I said to Ernie, 'it's not his—'

He moved his face a few inches from mine. 'You oughta seen it. Dozens of them, out in the sun, crawling all over his lap and ...' He stopped, noticed the man in the Valiant and said, 'What are you lookin' at?'

The muffled voice. 'Go easy, mate.'

'Not your fuckin' mate. Who are you anyway, parked out the front of *my* house? He hasn't got a licence to operate a business.'

I picked up the bell, placed it on David's tray, but he didn't touch it. Ernie just stood, tottering, studying the ground.

'Is your mum home?' I asked David.

'Shops.'

'When will she get back?'

David was watching Ernie, unsure. 'Mum's tried to get rid of them. She gave some to Miss Davis, but they came back.'

Ernie noticed the kittens re-emerging and ran at them again, caught one and threw it across the yard.

The Valiant man got out and said, 'Oi!'

'Fuck off. She's got hundreds. They piss on everything.'

Val and Peter approached from Lanark III with their bags of groceries. Ernie saw them and drunk-jogged towards them. 'Another litter. You said you were gonna do something.'

Val looked around: me, the Valiant man, a terrified David. She hurried over to him, straightened his hair and asked, 'What's he done?'

Ernie seemed to have sobered, or perhaps it was the grog talking. 'You got at least three tabbies, and they've got litters, and then there's the older ones.'

'Ernie?' I said.

'Bloody catfights outside my winder every night. And that smell, when they mark their territory. Then they chase Fi-Fi round the yard, I seen it!'

'No,' Val said.

Ernie moved closer to her; Peter put down his groceries and moved between them.

'I tried to grow a few vegies, but they dug 'em up. And they're into our bins. You wanna come and clean that mess up?'

'Mr Sharpe,' Peter said, pleading his case.

'And you can move, you little faggot.' He pushed him aside. The Valiant man stepped forward; I stepped forward; Mr Sharpe was a few inches from Val. She shielded her face, lowered her head. David said, 'Leave her,' but no one could hear him over the voices, the chaos.

I took three steps, and was between them. 'Quiet!'

The noise stopped.

'Me and Curtis,' I said. 'We've got an idea.'

Ernie wasn't worried about me – just the cats, running around the garden; Val, covering her face and mouth, like someone had died; David, helpless in his chair.

'It'll work,' I said.

Ernie turned. 'What will?'

And I explained.

A few minutes later, Ernie went inside.

'Come on,' I said to Val.

I waited in the hallway as Val and Peter helped David onto his bed to rest. The door was ajar, but I didn't look. I heard Peter plug in the radio, and soon there was Chopin, and the blind was drawn and I felt that this room – bare-threaded and fibro, awkward corners with ill-fitting furniture – was much the same as mine: a place to go when everything else failed.

I studied photos: the brothers in a rowboat, life-jacketed and buck-toothed, waving to Val on the shore. Sitting in the kitchen, studying, and I could see the clumsy Indian's grave marked in upper- and lower-case serif. Funny, really, how it all came down to a photo. Mr Bulljaw, flying through suburban air, admiring the house he'd built. Completing circuits circumscribed by the main road, the primary school, the substation at the end of the road. And next to this, the only photo of the man who was probably dad.

Gone.

Val came out and saw the problem. 'Ssh, he needs a nap.' Beside his brother, in a wicker chair, reading about Stephen Hero.

She took me into the kitchen, closed the door and said, 'Cuppa?'

Always the cuppa. But I agreed, and as she filled the kettle she said, 'It's not gone.'

'No?'

She reached up to the bill box, opened it and produced the yellowing photo. 'You keep it.'

'But why …?'

She shovelled tea into the pot. 'I'm the one who keeps the peace.'

I waited.

'Your mother, sitting there, and she says, Clem's been looking at that photo in the hall. What was I gonna say?'

I studied the fat face, the brown eyes, the black hair that burst out of his head, down his cheeks; the small lips and little dent in his chin that, I supposed, I'd inherit.

'Put it in a book,' Val said. 'Somewhere she won't find it.'

'She can't tell you what to do.'

But she just filled the pot with hot water, sat and waited. 'She was adamant. Said you'd been asking questions, and it was best you didn't know.'

'Why?'

'You can't unknow things, can you? Then you've got seventy years of it.'

She said this like she knew it better than anyone.

'That's all your mum's thinking. It wasn't that he was a horror.'

She poured the tea, silent. With Val, silence only meant one thing. She was deciding. Then she touched the photo and said, 'In a book, or under a cupboard?'

Tea, hot, brown and photographic, like all the tea she'd ever poured, and drunk, all the days, the ticking Tower of London on the wall. Then she said, 'Firstly, he built that house, and he did a pretty good job.'

'I knew that,' I said, as a way of telling her she'd have to start the story closer to the end.

'We all helped where we could, whether it was painting, or planting the garden. Until it was real decent-looking and your mum, and dad, they were happy.'

I settled in for the tea.

'Then came Jen, and you, and he was the proudest dad alive.

He, *he* was the one who'd walk you … around the block, stopping to show everyone. You, especially, cos you were the blondie, with the blue eyes, and handsome … still are, eh?' She stopped to think. 'It's not my place to tell you.'

'I'll never say.'

She had to be sure I'd put this, too, under my wardrobe. 'Whatever anyone might say about him, he was a hard worker, at the start at least. He laid bricks.'

'A bricklayer?'

'For about year. Bit longer. Up at six, off on his motorbike.'

I'd seen the handlebars hanging from the shed roof.

'Home at four. Did his back in, but kept at it. Hated it, but kept at it. He had these babies, and wanted to support them. That's what he was like, no matter what anyone says, he wanted to do the right thing.'

It sounded hopeful. Bricklaying. You'd have to be determined. Building other people's houses. People who could afford to build in brick.

'Maybe that's all you need to know,' she said.

I waited. 'It's not.'

'Not a word?'

'No.'

'The company he worked for went broke, and he lost his job. Your mother said he stole from them and they sacked him, but he told me that wasn't the case. Then he couldn't find work. Sat at home, days on end. He got frustrated and you'd hear him shouting. David and Peter went in a few times but …'

She didn't seem to want to continue. 'It's not my place to tell you.'

'I know, but it'd be good if you did.'

'I think things were tough, money-wise, and your dad had some mates, and they'd always be over, and he'd be off with them till all hours. Then came the police …'

Now it seemed clear.

'He was locked up for a while, but came home, then there was more shouting and we'd sit here and worry about your mum and you kids. Can you imagine?'

'I guess.'

'The one good thing your mum did, with a bita help from Doug, was tell him to leave. And when he came back she got a court order to keep him away. And one day, when she tells you that, you gotta thank her. She wanted you and Jen safe, so she got rid of him, and it wasn't an easy thing for her to do.'

'I guess.'

'Him out the front at four in the morning, throwing bottles on yer roof, until Doug went out and shouted at him. You can't remember, but one day she'll tell you, and you gotta say thanks, right?'

'Right.'

'Cos that …' But she stopped, like she'd run out of batteries. 'You're not upset?'

'I guessed it must've been something like that. For mum to hide the photos.'

'Now you understand why.'

'I suppose. But she coulda told me. I woulda been okay.'

'You were just a kid. Still are.'

I went home. Past the open door, Peter asleep beside his brother. Down the drive, stopping to search our roof for broken glass. I went into the shed and took down the handlebars, but they told me no more than Val. My dad was a sort of John Burrell, and maybe Pop was trying to help him, still.

I knocked on Ernie's door. 'Mr Sharpe?' And a muffled voice. 'Get that, will yer?' Mrs Sharpe replying, 'I'm on the toilet.' Then silence, as every man and woman stood and shat his ground. Then Ernie called, 'Who's there?'

'It's me, Clem.'

Silence, again.

'Mum reckons you got a net?'

Ernie and Ida, still communicating (just) after forty years.

Ernie didn't seem to care about what he did, wore or said. He'd smoked his life down to the butt. Once, Mum had said to Ida, I've got a few tickets to a nice restaurant, and Ida had asked Ernie, and of course he'd said no. Mum had told him you had to keep working at a relationship, and he'd said something like, Within limits, invoking a coal mine that had been worked clean. Ida had cried (I heard) and told Ernie she hated him and he'd said he couldn't give a shit, and that'd ended that.

So, that was my view of married couples.

'Mr Sharpe ... should I come back later?'

'No, what is it?' He opened the fly door.

'A net.'

'What for?'

'Me and Curtis ... the cats.'

'Follow me.' He walked out to the shed, switched on a light and went in. 'It's here somewhere.'

I waited as he searched a dark corner.

'What, she complaining about me, I suppose?' he said.

'Sort of.'

'I was entitled to say what I did, Clem.'

'You upset David.'

'I can't be responsible ...' He checked the rafters. 'Maybe I got a bit worked up, but that doesn't change things.' Clearing his throat, he spat into the darkness. 'They're wild. Sisters rootin' brothers, and their mum. One instinct: kill. All the birds I see lyin' on the lawn.'

'They were pretty upset.'

He found a torch, turned it on, and moved around.

'That David, he's ...' But thought better of it. 'And as for that horse's hoof.'

'Peter?'

'You ever seen him with a girl? Woulda been one, surely, after all these years.'

'I don't reckon. I think he just likes his own company.'

'Perhaps. Although they keep it well hidden, Clem.'

I couldn't believe it. There were a lot of other explanations, but that one made the least sense. 'Woulda had a boyfriend, wouldn't he?'

'Well, he wouldn't be parading him down Lanark Avenue. They meet in clandestine places.'

It was a funny thought. Peter paying the rent. 'He told me he was engaged once.'

'He never was.'

'Yeah.' I started searching piles of tools that hadn't been used in decades, metal offcuts, courtesy of Gary. 'But he never talks about her.'

'I never heard nothin' and I've been livin' next door to him for years.'

'You should ask him.'

But he just made his you-don't-know-the-half-of-it face. 'Well, maybe not a poof, but strange.'

'But you called him one.'

'I never did.'

'You did, I heard.' It wasn't my job to lecture Ernie, but he seemed to want to hear. Perhaps he trusted my opinion.

'I shouldn'ta said that, I suppose.' He sat down to rest, and think. 'He's not a bad fella, as such.'

I sat next to him. 'And Val's okay?'

'Well … She did a bloody good job, bringing them up. Not too many women …' He turned to me, half-worried. 'I didn't say anything too bad, did I?'

'You pushed her.'

'No?'

'You did.'

He dropped his head and studied the concrete. 'I should say sorry. But she's the one with the cats.'

'And she's agreed to my plan.'

'I wasn't too nasty?'

'You called her a few names.'

'Well … she's never been the sort to come in with a cake. But she's always in your place, and that upsets Ida.'

'Maybe she's scared of you?'

'You scared of me, Clem?'

'No.'

'There you go. Ida's tried to be friendly, but no, hardly a word.'

'You should take her a cake. Change your ways.'

He sat staring into the shadows. 'Not at my age. It's just, Ida. Still, I shouldn'ta pushed her.'

'She wanted to talk but you ...'

'Just goes to show, young Whelan, stay off the grog. You sneak one in?'

'No.'

'But you have a smoke, don't yer?'

'Don't tell Mum.'

'Stay off them, too. Look at Yul Brenner.'

'Who?'

He read the side of a box in front of us. 'Musta been years.'

Soapbox Speeches. In texta. He opened the box, retrieved a pile of papers, and sat. 'I thought I'd chucked them.'

'What are they?'

'These,' he said, blowing dust from the sheets, 'were my *Kapital.*' Then he read. '*Comrades, gather round and hear what they have in store for you.*' He waited, eager for an opinion.

'For who?'

'The workers. *Even as we speak, managers are counting beans, working out how many jobs they can shed, and where these jobs will go.*'

I didn't get it.

'See, the date, 1973. The managers at Alcott's were already deciding how they could send work overseas. *Be sure, comrades, each of your jobs will be sold down the river.*'

Maybe he could hear the applause.

'*You cost too much. Foreigners work cheap. Be assured: this country will have no manufacturing by 1990.*'

He was in full flight: a factory of eager ears, raised voices, red flags.

'*First, the machinists will go. We know that's coming. I've seen the tenders. Hong Kong. That's where they'll make your children's pants.*'

He stopped for breath. 'That was a good bita writing, eh, Clem?'

'What is it?'

'A speech I wrote when I was a delegate.'

'It's good.'

'But I never gave it. I was scared of public speaking. More than six people, forget it. So, this is where it ended up – with the others.'

He took the paper-clipped soapbox speeches out and read the titles: 'On the Rights of Electrical Workers', 'How the ACTU Has Let Us Down'. Then he tipped them out of the box, and another. After this, there was a small mountain of paper on the floor. He said, 'Every Sunday I'd sit writin' 'em, while other men actually got up and spoke, and took control.'

He had enough to make a decent fire. They smelled cat-pissy, but everything in his shed smelled cat-pissy. 'Why didn't you get someone to read them for you?'

'Doesn't work that way, but if I could get this lot published …'

And I thought, No, not really. 'Communism isn't so popular now. Not with all those missiles pointing at us.'

'Taken.'

'But you're right, they make a lota stuff in China now, don't they?'

'If people hada listened we wouldn't be losing our jobs. And my other speeches. Coupla hundred, I once counted, and a not a word was spoken. How's that for a waste?'

'Bit like Peter,' I said.

'How?'

'Six years at university, and he mows his lawn with a scythe.'

'You gotta be careful, Clem.'

'How's that?'

'What you do, you make matter, or else you might as well settle in for the day at the Windsor.'

This seemed reasonable. If worst came to worst there was always a stool beside Ernie and a trip outside every hour to make sure Fi-Fi was still on her chain.

'There they are!' Ernie said. He stood, picked up a couple of fish nets and presented them to me. 'Good luck. Make sure you get them all.'

'You gonna help?' I asked.

'I'll watch.'

Val and Peter stood on their porch. I approached with the nets and said, 'All ready.'

Val saw Ernie, crossed her arms and stepped back into the shadows. He was content to stand in full sun, on his cracked concrete, watching.

I said, 'I reckon this is the best way. They look after them real good.'

'Go on then.'

I dropped the nets, returned home and found the keys to the 120Y. Came out, and drove into the Donnellans' yard. Parked parallel to the house, got out and sounded the horn. 'Curtis!'

He came down the street, followed by John, who again, stood watching. He said, 'No way you can get all them.'

Peter fetched the Whiskas, and bowls, opened three cans, emptied them and tapped the sides with a spoon. The cats knew what it meant. They came out. Slowly at first, sniffing, looking at us and making sure.

'Go on,' John said.

'Wait,' I whispered.

They took their time, watching us, fighting for the best share.

Ernie almost laughed. 'Problem is, they're smarter than you.'

'Go!' I said.

I had my net over a tabby, and most of her kittens. Two got away but John chased them across the lawn and gathered them by the scruff. 'We should just drown them.'

'No,' Val said, turning away from the spectacle.

Curtis had messed up. He'd got an old girl, but all of her kittens had scampered. Peter jumped to it – from the porch, across the yard, scooping them into a laundry basket.

Then to the 120Y. Ernie came over and held the back door open. I emptied mine, and they ran about on the seats and the parcel shelf, but Ernie shut them in. Curtis handballed his tabby, and Peter emptied them, one by one, into the Datsun.

Ten minutes of this and we had an empty yard. We all stood looking, but the final few had gone. The others were dancing around in the car, bouncing off the roof, jumping, fighting, and probably pissing. I said, 'Now's the bit where I drive them to the pound.'

Everyone waited: Ernie, grinning; John, shaking his head; Curtis, blank. Val turned and went in.

'They'll look after them,' I called.

Peter, shrugging; even David, from his window.

Then Pop came out, down the drive, saw the car and the cats and said, 'Whose idea was that?'

I wasn't sure what to say. Fi-Fi wandered out, and started barking at the car. Ron Glasson's head appeared above his fence.

'Well?' Pop asked.

'I thought we could drive them to the RSPCA.'

'Bugger me.' He opened the door, and the cats jumped out.

'Fuckin' hell,' Ernie said.

'Thought so,' John said, smiling.

Pop turned to Ernie. 'How about we use your car?' He put his head in and smelled it. Retreated. Turned to me. 'You can clean it, right?' Then went back in.

I studied the picture of Dad. His arms, which might've been short, his hands, building our house, my room. I noticed the cornice, and wondered if he'd stuck it on; the window frame, if he'd cut it to size; the paint, even, which he might've applied. The house might've smelled of him; the cuts, the sanding, the joining were his. But if there was any pride, it had gone. When these mates (who were they? Ex-crims, slicked-hair and barbed wire tattoos?)

sat around our dining room table, and said things like, You don't need to worry about money, that's easily taken care of.

I opened my wardrobe, lifted the jumble of shoes and deposited him in the mess of shoelaces and Fantale wrappers. He could wait there, in the same way I'd had to. He could think about what he'd put me through, and feel bad. He could come to realise that he should've replied: No, fellas, I got too much at stake. I'll get a job, soon.

Pop, outside, setting the sprinkler on the lawn, turning it on, stopping it, moving it, trying again.

24/iii/84. The lawn isn't so important. It's the idea of lawn. Related to sport, in the suburbs. Running, sweating, recording scores, winner, loser, the team as tribe. One man as part of many, so that any failure (or insecurity) belongs to all, not one. Therefore, the possibility of bliss, each week …

Pop sat on the fence and watched the fountain. There were gaps, but if you watered enough it'd all get wet, surely. He liked watering. It didn't make the grass any greener, because you couldn't make summer any cooler, the sun any kinder.

When I checked again he was talking. Les and Wendy Champness, in their church clothes, clutching Bibles. I sat back, but peered from behind the blinds. Wendy said, 'A big year, I suppose?'

'Long as he doesn't screw it up,' Pop said. 'Got a good head, make a good engineer, long as he doesn't get any ideas.'

'Like what?'

'That guitar … writes his own songs. Thinks he's John Lennon. Then there's that mate of his. We wanna keep them apart.'

'You can't,' Les said.

'Clem reckons he's made a list of everyone he hates.'

'We on it?' Wendy asked.

'Then there's the brother …'

They all bowed heads. Les said, 'I just make sure we lock the place when we go out.'

'Yes,' Wendy said.

'Off to church?' Pop asked.

'Yes,' Les replied. 'See if he'll forgive us this week.'

'For what?'

'Nothing in particular, Doug. Them birds too noisy?'

'Na, they're okay.'

'Take care of yourself.' And they continued, hand in hand.

Raised voices from number 29. Anne versus John, by the sound of it. Pop stood, took a few steps, then waited.

'Wasn't me.'

'Carn, tell me.'

A vase or something like it smashing.

Pop walked from our yard, along the fifty or so metres of footpath, and down the Burrells' drive. I ran out of the house, across the yard (the grass soggy under my feet) and jumped the fence, then hid under the windows. Inside, the voices continued. John said, 'You've got no bloody idea.'

'It wasn't me.'

I heard Pop knocking and say, 'Anyone home?' and for a moment the voices stopped.

'Come in,' Anne said, and I heard the screen door open and close.

Pop said, 'I haven't been in to say hello since you got back.'

Silence. I moved around and sat on the verandah. I could imagine the choreography, the three figures in awkward counterpoint.

'Settled in?' Pop asked.

A long pause.

'John?' Anne said.

'I heard!'

'I wanted to give you a while, get back on your feet. You don't want some old bastard like me …'

'John?'

'I heard him!'

'You okay?' Pop said.

'The discussion, Doug, was about … why don't you tell him, Mum?'

Nothing.

'How someone must've said something for the cops to know. And you'd think, wouldn't you, Doug, someone who's got it in for you. But you wouldn't think your own mother.'

'Well,' Pop said, 'there's no use—'

Rustling, like Pop might've come between them, like he was holding John back.

'Nothing of the sort,' Anne defended.

'I was about to tell Mum what happens at McNally's. I've told her about the meals and the way they make you play basketball and how you can only watch telly for an hour a day, but I haven't—'

'Come on,' Pop said. 'I got somethin' to show yer.' And a long, slippery silence where I guessed Pop was holding John, walking him towards the door.

I stood and hid around the corner. They came out, and Pop was leading him by the arm, down the drive, towards number 31. I followed at a distance. They went into the shed and I stood outside, listening.

'There,' Pop said. 'Nice mess, eh?'

A minute where, I guessed, John walked around the car, studied the problem and said, 'You gonna leave it like that?'

'Yep. That's the end of my efforts, mechanic-wise.'

'But he's gonna want it fixed, isn't he?'

'I'd say. You wanna have a go?'

It seemed strange that he'd ask John, but not me.

'First up, you're gonna have to lift it again.'

I listened as John gathered the chains, attached them, then started pulling them through the gears.

'Easy enough, but it's done a bit of damage.'

And I imagined Pop checking.

'Yes, that'll need fixing. Clem said he'll have a go.'

Clatter, tools, then the clicking of a wrench. 'All this will have to come off first, Doug.'

It continued. I imagined Pop watching. 'Seems hard to believe your mum'd dob you in.'

'Well, she did.'

'You've had some pretty wild days, John. Old bastard like me, might guess how it'd end.'

'How?'

'I've seen it.'

'So what?'

'Things can get away from you. Then, it's all fucked up, for good.'

Pop knew that John was good with a spanner. But Dad had been good with a saw, so you had to fix the big things before the little ones. No point building a house you couldn't live in, or having a car you couldn't drive.

'Clem's dad,' Pop said. 'You know what happened to him.'

'Dad told me.'

How come he knew, before me? Had everyone in Lanark II discussed it?

'Stick to the manual,' Pop said. 'Transmission there, see. You could get it going, eh?'

'What about the panel?'

'Have to think about that. Your mum mighta said something.'

'You know?'

'No, I don't. But listen, boyo, if I thought it'd help you *I'd* call the coppers. What d'you think about that?'

No reply.

'And if she did, good on her.'

'You don't know what goes on …'

'At yer little prison? I could guess, but you knew, didn't you?'

A silent minute. Pop said, 'You could just about hammer out those panels, then undercoat it, spray it yerself.'

'He'd tell.'

'Not if it was done properly.'

Pop was nothing if not practical. Some things needed fixing, some weren't worth the effort. Some things you could throw out, some things you couldn't. 'Don't bother with it, John. I'll tell him I buggered up. I'll tell him he can take it to Golding's, and I'll pay to have it fixed.'

'It's not that big a job.'

'You're busy with other things.'

'What about Clem?'

'He's busy with study.'

'I got a bit of time spare, if you want.'

I could see Pop's face. 'Well, if you reckon. If you think we could do it?'

'Easy.'

'I could give you half the money.'

'I don't want it.'

'You need it. Fixin' things, that's the best way to pay the bills, isn't it?'

'I guess.'

Again, silence, as the hoist creaked under the weight of the engine.

Curtis's theory was that if they kept making rules at this rate there'd be nothing we could do. This, in response to the announcement that the canteen was being converted to healthy eating. And we all knew what that meant: no more pies and hot dogs, Coke, chocolate milk and chips. This would impact our ability to make Twistie rolls, the staple of our school diet.

'No one beyond the first oval,' Curtis said. 'No groups of more than three. But how are they gonna stop that?'

'Quietly!' Miss White said, from behind her telly-screen glasses.

'No talking,' Curtis whispered.

'Curtis!'

This was the result of stencilling. We'd arrived for Monday art, waited outside the room (with its little white patches where Bulljaw had been painted over) then, Miss White walking towards us.

'Fuck, no,' Curtis, and a few others had said. 'She's relieving.'

That was bad enough, but I sensed things were worse. Remembered Nick waving his letter, with the suggestion he'd given up caring. Remembered the look on his face, like he'd decided.

The tone of his voice, defiant. And I knew: he'd gone (or had been made to go). His comment about the small, smoky-smelling dictatorships that ran the world, and how you could beat them for a while, but not forever, because most people didn't care enough. The Queen proved this. Religion, too. Most people enjoyed being led, even by bad leaders. It saved thinking and acting for yourself. Ernie had explained this, too. Stalin was no different from White.

He'd gone. Resigned, probably, but maybe they'd tapped him on the shoulder.

When she'd arrived I'd said, 'Where's Mr Andrews?' and she'd replied, 'He's away.'

'Sick?'

'I believe so.'

But I'd known. *I believe so.* That was code. Mr Andrews had been dealt with. Mr Andrews was given a chance, but had refused to change. Then she'd said, 'I'm moving our lesson. Room seven, please.'

'Not in the art room?' I'd asked.

'No.'

Another bad sign. Dictators always controlled their environment, curtailed the possibility of escape, mentally, and otherwise.

We'd gone to room seven. Sixties curtains and fifties wood panelling. Lino: as brutal as the day it was laid. High windows you opened with a pole, just to make sure no one felt the breeze. A blackboard with dried spit-bombs, and a 1982 date.

Curtis glared at White and said, 'She's on top of my list.' He raised his hand. 'Miss White?'

She looked up from her marking.

'What's happening with the canteen?'

'What do you mean?'

'Are they getting rid of the Twisties?'

Everyone laughed.

'Yes,' she said, returning to her work.

'Why?'

'So you eat healthy.'

'But what about our Twistie rolls?'

She laid her pen on the table. 'I don't care about rolls. There'll be salads, stir fries …'

And you could hear the groan, although you couldn't.

'Anyway,' she continued, 'what's that got to do with art?'

'Nothing, but not everyone—'

'On with your work, please.'

Work: a sheet with printed axes. We were meant to sketch a dog from *Art Appreciation for Australian Schools* (1963): the arch of the back, the bend of the legs, the droop of the head. It was meant to take fifty minutes and if we finished we should read, because that's what teachers said if they couldn't think what to do. Mine was coming along nicely, although it wasn't much of a dog. Curtis was drawing a combination dragon–Hitler. He'd started with the head and mo and claws and was filling in the rest. 'No borrowing books at lunch,' he whispered.

'Why?'

Then loudly. 'Miss White, why can't we borrow books at lunch?'

'Miss Gillian needs a break. Is this relevant?'

'Sometimes you need to borrow a book, and if she's not around …'

'She has to eat.'

'If we can't borrow we can't work. I had this essay about the Enlightenment …'

'Curtis!' She stamped her orthotic on the lino. 'Are you finished?'

'Can't draw dogs.'

'Well, draw something else.'

'When's Mr Andrews coming back?' I asked.

'I told you, I'm not sure.'

'Is he crook?'

'Clement, isn't it?'

'Clem.'

'If I knew, I'd tell you.'

Lying bitch, I thought. Who was it? You? So, I thought I'd try a Peter Donnellan tactic. 'Someone reckons he was sacked.'

She didn't respond. The clock tried to tick, but didn't. None of our clocks ticked. There was a rule against time, apparently.

'Miss White?'

She took a deep breath and said, 'There might be a new teacher.'

Everyone said their little bit. One of the girls said, 'Cos of what he did?'

She raised her voice. 'Thank you.' And waited for quiet. 'I'll be honest. He's had enough; he said he wanted to move on.'

The raised voices turned to mumbles, whispers.

'Therefore, we've asked for a replacement.'

'*He* said he wanted to move on?' I asked.

'Yes.'

'But didn't he …?' I thought about it. Was this my John Lennon moment? Was I about to incite a riot, demand the truth? 'Was it cos of the murals?'

'It's a confidential matter and I'm not willing to discuss it.'

Bullshit, I thought. He'd been taken out back, and a bullet put in his head. Then they'd airbrushed him from official photos. He no longer existed, and soon, any mention of his name would land you in a shitload of trouble.

'Not fair,' the girl said.

'It was his choice. His personal circumstances.'

'That's not what he told us,' I said.

She sniffed insurrection. 'I think he said something about wanting to move interstate.'

What was the point? The paperwork had been completed, forwarded to regional office, photocopied and filed. *Persona non grata*. And there'd be someone nicer, and more reliable, in his place.

'Not really fair,' Curtis said.

'Why?' White asked.

'We shouldn't have to change teachers in Year Twelve. Maybe he could come back?'

'Maybe you could finish your work?' She stood, stormed across the room, studied his drawing and said, 'That's a dog?'

'I can't draw dogs.'

'That's the point. You try. You get better. *You stick at it.*'

'Like Nick did?'

'Yes, no … what do you mean by that?'

'What I said.'

She returned to her desk, found her detention pad and started writing.

'I mean, we wanted to do them murals, and you lot painted over them.'

'Get your things.'

'For no reason. He let us decide what to do, that's why—'

'Go!' She stood, presenting him with the slip.

He turned to me. 'Again.'

I shrugged, and realised I was no Lennon or Lenin or anyone, really, with a backbone. He gathered his few things, took the slip and left the room, saying, 'Nearly eighteen, but you still won't tell us …'

At recess, as we sat eating one of our last Twistie rolls, Curtis said, 'There's a list of rules in the behaviour room as well.'

I squished my roll innards into a little ball and threw it across the yard.

'*Thou shalt not speak, move about … thou shalt copy the school rules.* Ironic, rules about rules. And Pearson's there, pickin' his nose.'

Pearson, Harry James. Chose the behaviour room. As a sort of calling. Appears to write poetry as he oversees the silent destruction of teen souls. Sonnet form? Types them up and forwards them to journals, and they're published under a pen name …

'I thought you were gonna speak up?'

'What's the point? He's gone.'

It was disappointing that we'd miss a year of Andrews, but encouraging to know you could go through life thinking, doing and saying what you felt. 'No walking through the car park,' I said.

But he didn't seem to care about rules anymore. 'John's been over your place.'

'He's helping Pop fix Mr Harper's car. They beat out a panel and smoothed it, and sanded it back.'

Nothing.

'He's good at it.'

'Hoo-fuckin'-ray. Tell Mum.'

'What?'

'I wish he'd piss off, or die.'

I knew. Violence was kept in kitchen cupboards. Brought home from the shops and packed away until it was needed. Used, returned, and never talked about.

'He might come good,' I said.

'Your pop's delusional. He'll be okay for a few weeks before he robs a shop, pisses off back to McNally's.'

'*Apparently* if you walk past their cars you might pull off an aerial. It's funny that they think that about us.'

'They're paid to deal with us. They've got mortgages. They need money. That's the only reason.' He sat slumped, holding his half-eaten roll. 'Quiche.'

'What?'

'Apparently you can die from eating pies.'

It was no fun being unloved. But we all started off, and ended, this way. 'I think when I'm older I'll go to Greece,' I said.

'Greece?'

'Work on a fishing boat.'

'You're too lazy.'

A long pause. Someone thumping pavers. A dog that never stopped barking.

'There are good bits.'

'Yeah.'

'Like, the best, when the baker's van used to come.'

Six thirty am. The van parked in the middle of the road. Mums in nighties and dressing-gowns drifting out, choosing fresh bread and finger buns. Val saying to Mum, You want 'em looked after tonight?

'That was the best smell,' I said.

Or me and Curtis, sent out in our pyjamas to buy a pipe loaf. Me, to the man: Mum says can you put it on her bill?

'Why'd they stop it?' Curtis asked.

'I dunno.'

'All the good bits end.'

I guessed he was right. It was all coming to an end: the desire to pull on shorts and a T-shirt, go out, hop on your dragster and ride Lanarks I–III for hours. No reason. No result. No arguments or wondering why anything happened the way it did. 'Come on,' I said. 'Before next lesson.'

We walked to the front office. The girl was young, but she could type. I motioned to her and said, 'Mr Andrews, the art teacher.'

She just smiled.

'I need to call him. Do you have his number?'

'We can't do that.'

Curtis leaned over. 'My brother says to say hi.'

She smiled again.

'They let him out.'

The idea seemed to interest her.

'I'll do you a swap.' He found a slip of paper and wrote his phone number in big, blocky letters.

'I could get in trouble,' she said.

'Don't worry,' Curtis said. 'We were never here.'

And she turned, and excitedly opened the filing cabinet.

John had decided: the car could be fixed so Mr Harper wouldn't know. The engine refit, made to purr. The whole package presented in some sort of Wheel of Fortune moment to the world's second most happy customer. He'd made it his business to come every day, and Pop had made sure he was there, to unlock the shed, turn on the power, open the louvres and supply Coke. To stand back, and encourage him.

And it continued, into the last weekend of March. It was still hot, but once you got working you didn't feel the heat. Things just fell into place: rods, bolts, belts.

As John sanded he looked at me and said, 'Why do you bother?'

'He's okay.'

'He's not right in the head.' He blew the putty dust, wiped the panel with a damp rag and examined it closely. 'What do you reckon, Doug?'

Pop stepped forward, turned, walked a few steps and stopped. 'One foot, two, two and a half ...' I'd been watching him for a few minutes, and the behaviour never varied. He was lost in his own world of distance and counting.

'What do you reckon?' John asked again.

Pop said, 'Doin' a good job. Nice and smooth.'

John felt it with his hand. 'Baby's arse. He won't be able to tell, eh, Doug?'

'No.'

John continued working the sandpaper in small circles. 'Curtis was dropped on his head. I've read that list of his.'

I waited, and wondered what Pop was really measuring.

'Everyone he hates. But if you counted all the people who hate him ... And he upsets Mum.'

I wasn't about to buy into it.

'Always on detention. Then she's thinking ...' He wiped the panel again and said to Pop, 'How'd you manage to do this?'

'Wasn't concentrating.'

'Maybe it'll come good. D'you reckon it's ready?'

'I reckon if you reckon.'

John wiped his hands, opened a tin of primer, and started stirring it with a stick. He tried me again: 'I know I've been in trouble, but at least I'm normal. Curtis just likes upsetting people.'

Depends on your definition, I thought. Counting steps. Upsetting.

'He used to record Mum and Dad in their room, you know, and write it all down. I mean, why would anyone do that?'

'It's the sort of thing that interests him,' I said.

'Did the same with me, in the toilet, but I let him have it.'

He slipped on a mask, picked up the airbrush and fed the tube into the paint. 'All ready.' He switched on the compressor, stood back and laid paint in long, smooth lines. Then he stopped and took off his mask and said, 'What d'you reckon, Doug?'

The spell was broken. Pop walked over, indicated a few spots, and John fixed them. 'Long as we can blend it,' he called, above the noise.

Pop sat down beside me and lit a smoke. He was back in the land of the living. Without any concession to the counting, he said, 'You wanna go?'

'Na.' I knew this was John's gig, and we had to make it work. Then he might come good, and Gary and Anne would be grateful. 'Doesn't interest me.' But there was something in John's eyes: an intensity, blue, focused, with sharp lines on his forehead where he concentrated.

John finished, put down the handset and sat next to Pop. 'I reckon we might do it.'

'I reckon.'

He took his smoke, had a puff and returned it. Then Pop said, 'You got a good eye, and good hand, John.'

'You reckon?'

'That's what I said at the start, remember?'

When the twelve-year-old would come over, help Pop with an engine, remove a radiator, change oil.

'I told you there was a future. First time you come, you were knee high. You'd take a tyre on and off, remember?'

No reply. Which meant he did.

'That's why I was so disappointed, but ...'

'What?'

'You might not be interested.'

'What?'

'Johnson's, where I got this paint – crash repairs.'

Pop had already told me. It seemed a good idea. Society had to take care of its lost and lame. We saw that every day, when the opportunity class went gardening. In a way, it didn't seem fair, but it's just how it was.

'Mr Johnson – Harry. I told him about you.'

'Yeah?'

'Said you got a steady hand, mechanical aptitude, been workin' with me for a coupla years.'

The gal expanded as it got hotter; the heat came through onto our backs.

'He said he might have a spot.'

'No shit?'

'But the thing is, before he'd take you on he's gotta know you're reliable.'

John sat up.

'He said, What sorta kid is he? I had to be honest, and I told him you'd been in a bita trouble, but I said, That's only because of some issues at home.'

'And?'

'Which seem to be sortin' themselves out.'

John admired his work, like he was wondering if he'd be up to it – six am starts and long days, weekends. 'So?'

'He didn't seem against it. I been doin' work for him for thirty years, so I guess he trusts me. Said this fella he's got now's leavin' in a few weeks, then I could bring you in for a chat.'

John smiled. 'That sounds good, Doug. You reckon—'

'I tell you one thing, John. I'd only take you if you stayed clean and helped around the house and didn't give yer mother grief every five minutes.'

'I don't—'

'I talk to her, she tells me.'

'Well, they tell you bullshit.'

'No.' He turned to his apprentice. 'That's just the thing. If you're told something.'

'I've always done what I'm told.'

'Breakin' inta delis? Johnson won't put up with any of that. First time you answer him back ...'

John glared at me, like he wanted me gone. I took the hint, stood, left the shed, but lingered outside, listening.

'You say I stole, but what about Dad?'

Pop took a moment. 'I'm just sayin', takes a bita work to hold down a job. I gotta be sure.'

'And I'm tellin' you, there's nothin' wrong with *me*.'

I didn't think Pop really believed there was any excuse. I'd heard his speech about the sins of the father, and how you weren't them, and you had to answer for your own deeds, and other bits of Bible he'd trot out when it suited him.

I noticed the shadow, turned, and saw the broad shoulders, the white shirt, the tie. 'How are yer, Clem?'

'Hi, Mr Harper.'

'Your pop around?'

'I reckon, somewhere. Said he was gonna call you when it was ready.'

'I hadn't heard, thought I'd look see.' He just stood, waiting.

'You wanna come in?'

'Is he in there?' He indicated the shed door.

'Well ...'

But there was no point: Pop's voice, John's, venting from the shed. Mr Harper went in anyway, and I followed.

'Doug? How are you?'

'Glen ... this is John, he's been helping me with yer car.'

Hands shook, smiles exchanged. Then Harper noticed his car. 'You got it back in okay?'

I couldn't watch. I stepped back and leaned against the outside of the shed.

'We were putting it back in and we had an accident ... me and Clem.'

'*Jesus.*'

'You can see, it damaged this panel.'

'Why didn't you call me?'

'I's gonna, but John here, he's got an apprenticeship at Johnson's, reckoned we could fix it, so I didn't want to worry you.'

'It's never had a dent, nothin'. I thought you were good.'

'Well, the engine's runnin' fine. You wanna hear it?'

Silence. That'd be Harper, inspecting the repairs. 'You're never gonna get that to match, Doug.'

'Yes, we will. Teal blue. Trust me.'

'Look, it's a mess. The way it's been knocked out, see, that's not right, and the putty, that's all over the place.'

Pop, lost. 'Well, I'm sorry.'

'Bet yer fuckin' arse you're sorry.'

'Said he's sorry,' John began.

'Did I ask you?'

'I's trying to fix it for you.'

Pop tried his best. 'Righto, we'll have it fixed, Glen. John, come on, you head home …'

'I just reckon it's pretty rude. It was an accident, and we tried to make good. That paint cost me fifteen dollars. I thought you might be grateful.'

'John,' Pop said.

And there was a scuffle.

'John!'

And someone fell against the galvanised iron.

I could go in, stand between them, but I'd seen what John could do.

Mr Harper said, 'Before you do any more damage.' I looked in and saw him removing the masking from the car, close the bonnet, and hold his hand out for the keys. Pop gave them over, opened the shed, and moved. Harper started his car, backed it down the drive and was gone.

Pop said, 'It dunt matter. His choice.'

John looked at him, his hand shaking, but held in place.

'Keep yer cool.'

Later that night, as we ate rewarmed pizza, Pop explained. 'He did good.'

'How's that?' Mum asked.

'When Glen come at him, he just stood there, and when he pushed him, he didn't push back. That woulda taken a bit of doing, eh?'

And Jen said, 'Don't trust him, Pop.'

But I could see in Pop's eyes, the light, the challenge of fixing a car that didn't come with a manual.

April

Holidays. Stale-bread-Curtis, returned to the wrapper. Jim Rockford crawling from his van, wrestling winos in search of the murder dollar. I longed to be Jim. Late mornings, strong coffee and an open-topped drive along the Pacific Highway. Stopping for debt collectors and pimps, the teary-eyed children of nice-people murdered.

Me, the teenage Garner, giving up on Lanark Avenue, wandering the back streets of Windsor, the flaky suburb the other side of the main road. It'd started suburban, like us, but ended industrial. Factories built between more cracked-spine fibro homes. Weedy driveways with old washers, stripped bare, piled high along fence lines. Looking in open doorways, down halls, to mums shouting at bare-arsed kids as, outside, dads collected, stripped-down and calibrated. Always twice as many cars as there were people, cos cars could be cannibalised (I'd learned that from Pop, though Mum'd never let him keep wrecks round the yard). A trampoline for the kids, perhaps, but with a hole, and someone had stacked bricks on it. So there was no distinction between living and making a living.

I crossed the road and entered Don's, bought a Coke and emptied my pockets, hoping there was enough. As he counted, moving uncomfortably in his Marlboro T-shirt, he said, 'You been behavin' yerself?'

'Yes.' Surprised he'd shown interest after so many years. Perhaps it was boredom, the quiet before the Ford mechanics, after the milk mums, the ciggie kids. 'We're right behind your shop.'

'With the pool ladder?'

'Yeah. Me and my sister, t' get over the fence.'

He dropped the money in the till. I wasn't sure if he'd gypped me. It seemed unlikely I'd had the right amount.

'You never buy cigarettes?'

'No.'

'But you smoke them.' And he gave me a strange look.

'Well …' Then I thought, he would've seen me, walking past with Curtis. 'Everyone smokes these days.'

'The *Post*?'

'Nan used to read it.'

He waited.

'Nan and Pop. You know Pop? He comes around for tobacco and papers.'

'I know him.' He returned to his newspaper, spread out on the freezer.

I walked home around the block that was a songline, each blue metal hill and valley one that I'd made, each fence post one I'd watched peeling, rotting and falling into the soursobs. Past the Donnellans', but Davo was inside. Then a voice, 'Clem.'

I turned, looked at the fly-wire.

'You busy?'

I went to Val's door, and straight in, since I'd been invited. She welcomed me, smiled and showed me her cake. 'I guess I should,' she said.

'What?'

'Like you said, about Ida.'

It seemed like a good idea. At any rate, it'd shut Ernie up for a while.

Val picked up a bowl of icing and started spreading it on top. 'I don't know … after all these years.'

I'd told her how Ernie didn't care about Ernie, but Mrs Ernie – that was different. How he hated to see her left out, forgotten, when Donnellan and Whelan were together, babysat, front porch Hamlets, rides in wheelbarrows and the rest of it.

'If it's such a simple thing,' she said.

'I guess.'

'I often watch her, trimming her edges. She gave up on Ernie doin' it years ago. And when she's finished she goes over them again, to make sure they're neat. And I think, that's too lonely. She hardly ever sees June.'

'Didn't she used to work?'

'Years ago. Before your time. Myer. Every day, down the drive, dressed in black like she was going to someone's funeral. Hers, I guess.' She finished icing the cake and searched her drawers for a plastic message.

'You've never had her in?'

'Never. That's terrible, isn't it, Clem? Just cos you don't get along with one person … I don't reckon I ever seen anyone much in there. 'Cept the Avon lady.' She found a 'Happy Birthday' and tried it. 'Too much?'

'It's not her birthday.'

'What about candles?'

'I guess.'

She kept searching. 'When Peter and David were in scouts they'd bob-a-job, and they used to clean his car. And he'd give 'em a few dollars.' She stopped, staring out of the window, seeing it, perhaps. The boys, their arms heavy with badges, Ernie saying, I don't know about a bob.

'Scouts are good for a boy,' she said. 'You liked it, didn't you?'

'Didn't last long.'

'No, you didn't, did you? But you cooked good soup.'

Best left unsaid, I thought. Although, thinking back, the Cohen Cup was my first and only trophy. The 1st Gleneagles Scouts always entered: a statewide cook-off for troops of seven. One for the entrée, one for the soup, two for mains, two for dessert, and a leader. Me as Mr Soup. Rising at six (it was a camp-out) to grate vegetables, boil bones, add peas, the rest, until I had a soup that would, in 1979, win us the cup.

'Only thing I ever won,' I said.

'Nonsense.'

'True. I played sport a few times, but I always sucked.'

Cooking soup wasn't as easy as it sounded. Val had taught me. We'd done it properly. Peter and David had built the fire in their backyard. They'd set up the tripod, warmed the cast-iron pot, then got out a card table to work on. Val had shown me how to grate the vegetables so they tasted best. Flavour, so no one would complain. To cook, just the right amount, so you won trophies.

'Best soup I ever tasted,' Val said, settling on a 'Best Wishes'. 'The secret was the time you took to let it simmer.'

Simmer. Like our own lives. Like Don, guessing it was probably time to say hello. Maybe, in a few years, he'd ask my name. But there was no rush.

Val was looking across at the Sharpes' front door, wondering. 'It seems too late.'

'How's that?'

'After all these years.'

'It's never too late.'

She sighed. 'David chopped the wood, and Peter got the fire going.'

I couldn't remember. I wasn't sure how she could.

'Then the grass caught and Doug came running and shouting and got the hose and squirted the shed, and when it was out, cursed us for lighting fires in summer. Then I said it was for your soup and he said, Well, you need to be more careful. You remember that, Clem?'

'Not really.'

'Well, if I think about it I won't do it.' She took off her apron, picked up the cake, smiled and walked from the kitchen. A few moments later I watched her knocking on the Sharpes' door.

Ernie answered. He just stood looking, waiting.

'Ernie ... Ida home?'

He might've smiled, but I might've seen it wrong. But he called, 'Ida.'

Then they started talking, but I couldn't tell what they were saying. Val handed over the cake, and Ida motioned for her to come in. Ernie didn't say a word.

Peter came in behind me. He handed me an essay and said, 'More corrections. Redo it, get it back to me.'

'That's the third draft.'

'It's still not right.'

He noticed the scene on the Sharpes' porch. 'She did it?'

'She reckoned that mighta been the problem.'

We watched as the three went in, the door closed and a cat wandered across the Sharpes' porch. Then, a van pulled up out front. It passed the side window so we couldn't see it. 'No,' Peter said.

We went to the front, out the door, and saw it: Gleneagles Council Pet Control. Two men got out, checked some paperwork, went to the back of the van and took out two nets. One of them saw Peter and said, 'You Donnellan?'

'Yes.'

'Righto.' He came onto the property, stalked a cat, netted it, and returned it to the van. It squealed and clawed, but it didn't matter. After he'd deposited it, he returned for another. Meanwhile, the second man had caught a few kittens, and put them in the van.

Peter approached them. 'You can't do this.'

The first man said, 'Look at the regulations. Three cats, registered, desexed.' He kept hunting, around the side of the house. Peter followed and said, 'At least wait and I'll collect them.'

'This place smells like piss. You gotta stand back, or we'll call the cops to help.'

He returned to me. 'Mum's gonna be ...' He watched the Sharpes' place. Ernie was standing in the doorway, his face cold, hard.

Another tabby, twisting itself in the net, extending its razor claws and baring teeth. But it didn't matter – he was soon in the back with the others.

Then Val came out. She pushed past Ernie, but then turned back to him. 'You happy?'

He didn't reply.

Ida was close behind, standing with a saucer with a slice of Val's cake. But I guess she knew it'd be her first and last slice.

'I tried,' Val said to Ernie. 'I've always tried, and this is how you repay me.'

'I called, did I?'

'Yes.'

'You should check yer facts.'

But Val wasn't about to listen. She hobbled down from the verandah, the drive, towards the first man. 'Aren't you meant to send me a letter or something?'

'This many cats ain't fair to yer neighbours. They're wild. They'll attack kiddies. I've seen it. If they're hungry, they'll have a go at anyone.'

The men continued their hunt. They sprayed under the house and the rest of the cats came running. Soon they were all in the back of the van, as Val stood watching. At one point she turned to her son and said, 'They allowed to do this?'

'Probably,' he answered.

And she looked at him like she'd wasted money on a useless education.

'What you gonna do?' she asked.

He shrugged. 'We can try get them back. But we'd have to fix them up … three of them, anyway.'

Val turned to the first man. 'Tell me they won't put 'em down?'

'This many, it's hard to give them away. People want dogs.'

To Val, this was the worst thing of all. *People want dogs.* Therefore, they put cats down. Again, she turned to Ernie. 'Hear that? They're gonna put them down.'

He didn't respond.

'Put 'em all to sleep. But they didn't hurt no one.'

Peter took her around the shoulder and tried to lead her in. She fought him, but eventually yielded. But as she went she said, 'You wanna go see … when them little things are falling asleep?'

And then, she was in, and the door closed.

Ida was still holding her slice of cake.

Ernie just said, 'You wanna bit, Clem?'

I showed Pop the picture of Nan's sister. She was standing muddy-kneed in a black-and-white swamp, talking to someone out of shot. 'I forgot her name.'

'Started with S, I think.'

Jen said, 'Sue.'

'Sue,' Pop agreed. 'Nan's sister.'

I made a note in the book in my lap.

Sue Gould (Nan's sister). Tried, but couldn't remember.

Jen started her clippers. She worked her way along Pop's already shaved-down collar line. 'How do you want it?' she asked.

'Nice and short,' Pop replied.

'She died young, didn't she?' I asked.

'Did she?'

Fell off a ladder, 1968, but he had no idea.

I opened the album again, laid it on Pop's lap, and he pushed it away. I indicated another photo and said, 'I remember this fella. He lived at the end of the street. He used to sell sausage from his shed.'

Pop studied the face. 'Giuseppe.'

Giuseppe Palmieri. Moved out (according to Mum) in 1973. But he remembers. Maybe he liked the sausage.

'What was his surname?' I asked.

He seemed annoyed. 'Why you asking me all these questions?'

'Just trying to remember.'

'Palmieri. Giuseppe Palmieri. Used to make red wine. Shit awful.'

I had a method. I'd assigned everyone in the street one point. Then, I'd gone through the album, working out who was who, and assigned each of these people their own point. That made forty-nine. Problem was, that'd be forty-nine questions. And Pop wasn't stupid. Nonetheless, I had to continue. 'Now this one,' I said, showing him, 'is one of mum's nephews, isn't he?'

'Why you asking?'

'Well, I's thinking, we're studying Australian history, and I don't even know half my own family.'

Jen put down her clippers and started snipping his fringe.

'None of that,' he said.

'I can get it nice.'

'I don't want it nice. I want it gone.'

'Right.' As she picked up the clippers and continued.

Pop returned to the nephew. 'Well, if you must know, he was …'
I watched his eyes studying the young man's features. 'A nephew.'

'Was it Joseph?'

'Yes, Joseph.'

He seemed happy with that, although his name was David.

No spark of recognition for number seven.

Jen said, 'How about I leave a bit and you can push it over to
the side, like this?'

'All of it.'

'But you've had the same haircut for years.'

'I once paid this fella to pussy about, but six weeks later I was
back, and he was the most boring bastard I ever met. Telling me
about his kids. So I said to Nan, Clippers. And she did it, for years.
Now you get the privilege.'

'Just seems a waste. I can do colours and perms.'

'What do I want all that for?' He closed his eyes, breathed the
Saturday morning pea soup and let the sun warm his face. This
was his spot, in the middle of the backyard, at the end of three
extensions. Far away from the house and all of its disasters.

I whispered to Jen, 'Is he asleep?'

'No,' he said.

'You're lookin' relaxed.'

'I would be, if you weren't rabbiting on.'

'This one,' I said, showing him a picture of a backyard birthday,
on this lawn. 'I remember this was my sixth birthday. See, you,
Nan, Jen, me, and this kid, remember?'

He squinted to see.

'Wasn't she Ida Sharpe's niece?'

He shrugged.

'I remember, she stayed with them for a few months when her
parents were overseas, and she'd always be in here playing. She was
a real pain, going through our stuff. Remember, Jen?'

'Little bitch.'

'Wasn't she called May?'

'How much longer?' Pop asked.

I noticed a toy in the picture. 'Look, that Tonka truck. It was a fire truck, wasn't it, Pop?'

'Wasn't it, wasn't it, wasn't it? Can't you keep quiet?'

But this wasn't about Alzheimer's. I'd loved my Tonka truck. I could remember lighting fires, putting them out, incinerating plastic cowboys and policemen and watching them turn to glob on the concrete. It'd had an extendable ladder and lights that flashed and bells that clanged, and it was just like the real thing, when you were six.

'Rabbits,' Pop said.

I looked at Jen; we stopped ourselves from laughing.

'Rabbits,' he repeated, eyes closed, head rolling, mouth open.

'What rabbits?' Jen asked.

'Heap of them, gettin' about everywhere ... that's what the fella said.'

'What fella?' I asked.

'Rabbits.'

Babbled about rabbits. Triggered memory. Sixth birthday? Tonka truck. Or was it the haircut?

Jen pushed his head forward so she could trim the edges.

I could remember the cab: the three or four firefighters. The little black hose you could undo, although it was solid and you couldn't squirt anything. Still, you could incorporate your own hose, or a spray-pack, Mum's, from the bathroom, or Jen's, used in early attempts at hairdressing to simulate Agnetha's do. An all-metal Tonka. So you could punish it. Or play with it in conjunction with Evel Knievel.

'Evel Knievel, you remember him, Pop?'

'Rabbits ...'

'Pop?'

'Lasseter's Reef ...'

'Pop?'

'If you follow the directions in the sand ...'

'What do you mean?' I said. 'The rabbits are at the reef?'

He came out of it. 'What?'

'You said rabbits ... and the reef.'

'Did not.' He watched Jen, worried she might have heard. 'What did I say?'

'Something about a reef.'

He glared at me, annoyed that I'd let this happen. 'Great Barrier Reef, eh, Clem?'

'Yeah.'

Something about rabbits became Lasseter's. Strangely, no mention of the trip for the last few weeks. Hard to know what he remembers.

'I hate rabbits,' he said. 'Disgusting animals. Worse than cats.'

'Cats are nice,' Jen said.

'Stinkin'... anyway, won't have to worry about that no more.'

'Why's that?' I asked.

'I rang the council. Told 'em we'd had enough.'

I couldn't believe it. He'd been putting up with cats for years. He was good at ignoring them: on the shed roof as he worked, in season, outside his window at three am.

'They came and took them,' I said.

'Good.'

'Val was upset.'

'She'll get over it. Enough's enough.'

I could see Ernie's face, hear him, telling me to get my facts straight.

'That was mean,' Jen said, although she didn't like Val's cats. Not the sort you saw playing with wool on the back of toilet doors.

'You shoulda said something,' I added.

'No point muckin' around. That's what you pay your rates for.'

Ernie, going inside, content to let me think what I wanted, but disappointed, perhaps, the cake idea hadn't come off.

Jen turned off her clippers, offered Pop a mirror and said, 'Twenty bucks, ta.'

'Take it outa your board, when you start paying some.'

'I gave Mum twenty bucks.'

'Likely story.'

'*I did.*'

'Righto.' He stood, brushed himself off and said to me, 'How did I do on yer quiz?'

I shrugged. 'Not bad.'

'Good. Tell your mother. She can tell that shrink.'

Ellman Street wasn't so dangerous on a Wednesday afternoon. Probably never dangerous, although you could see in the door at the Crazy Horse, men at a bar, and girls with T-shirts that covered way too little. Black footpaths, because they'd waited too long to hose off the vomit. Anonymous doors with steps leading down to basement tatt parlours, with handwritten offers of *masage by the ½ hr.* There were Middle Eastern joints with shishas on the footpath, and an old toothless guy selling newspapers. I went into the Loussier Café and ordered a coffee. There was a boyfriend/girlfriend combo in the corner, he in a sort of Gandhi, no-salt-tax pullover, her in a jumper and poncho. I sat, waited, listened, as he said something about her mother's cooking, and she agreed.

I took out one of my photocopies. *Fight Dementia.* And started reading. *The importance of a controlled, unstressed environment …*

The boyfriend raised his voice. 'You've never once said anything good about her.'

The girlfriend, laughing. 'You're so full of shit.'

I glanced over, but realised I shouldn't have, as they both glared at me.

… in which the person with dementia follows a familiar routine …

I'd visited the library, taken out a pile of books on dementia, and read. I'd told Mum I was going to study meiosis and anaerobic respiration, but this seemed more important. I'd marked pages, then copied the bits I guessed we'd need to know.

… the frustration caused by being unable to meet other people's expectations may manifest …

Mum needed to know; we all did, despite the fact there was no discussion, meetings in Pop's absence, even statements of outcomes of doctors' visits.

He said, 'You'll never move out.'

'I will.'

'If she said jump under a truck, you'd do it.'

Good stuff. I wanted to write it down, but couldn't. Ellman Street, it seemed, could furnish enough material for years.

The girl placed my coffee on the table and I tried to look hip. 'Hey.'

Then he came in. I stood, motioned, and said, 'Mr ... Nick.'

He saw me, came over and sat down. 'How are yer, Clem?'

'Good ... good to see you.'

It'd taken me a while to call. I'd held the number in my hand, sweated it clean, wondered if there was any point, but I couldn't shake the feeling that Nick was gone. I'd phoned, my finger shaking in the holes. Awkward. Enough words to arrange a meeting close to where he'd got a new job as a designer in a print shop.

He called across the café. 'Short black.'

Flat white seemed inadequate. I was drinking Lanark Avenue; him, Ellman Street. He wore an old T-shirt, holey, food-stained; I had a nice shirt Mum had ironed. He'd bearded up, but I'd shaved (the bit I needed to). He'd moved on; I'd stayed behind.

Soon things loosened, and he started telling me about it. 'It was fuckin' ridiculous ...'

Fucking. I was right in the middle of it now. Relationship bust-ups, Nazis, prostitutes, teachers so bad they got sacked. I was living the life. What was that smell? Of course, weed. And by the look of Nick's eyes, he'd been into it too.

'I was called in and they slid this bit of paper over the desk. *Mr Andrews, you haven't responded to our suggestions.* And I said, Cos they're fuckin' stupid.'

'What suggestions?'

'A form they give dodgy teachers. "Guidelines for Appropriate Conduct in the Classroom". You know, be a mature role model ... shit like that. I said, If I do what's on there I won't be much of a teacher. And White said, That's just the point. You're not their friend, you're their teacher.'

He thought about it some more; maybe these were new thoughts.

'That's what I reckon, Clem. These people never succeeded in teaching, you know, at a personal level. They didn't have those skills. So when they got to run things … See, that's the world. Loada bullshit. But if you say that you'll never have a quiet moment.'

This seemed fair. Only the Ron Glassons of the world had peace, and that was because they were always keeping their head down, refusing to engage.

'I told White it was a load of old bollocks and she said, Fine, that means we have to move you on, and I said, What's that mean? She said, How it sounds.'

'Move you on?'

'Apparently there were a few schools I could choose from. Most of them completely feral, or a thousand kilometres from anywhere. Places where, I guess, they figured I couldn't do any damage.'

'And you said?'

'I said, Fuck yers. Take your job and stick it up yer arse.'

I smiled, imagining it. 'How'd she respond to that?'

'*Well, Mr Andrews, that just proves what we've suspected all along.*'

'I can hear her saying that.'

'You poor bastard. Stuck there.'

'Only another few months. I wanted to drop out, but Mum wouldn't let me. I still might.'

'No, you won't. Few more months. You're a smart kid. You need to go to uni. You don't wanna let them get in your way.'

The boyfriend got up and left. She lingered, looking out the window, but not at him. I guessed it was for the best and he'd find someone better, and she would too, and they'd get married and have kids and not even remember this day.

'Anyway,' I said, 'we were all pissed off. We complained, and then started a petition.'

'No fucking way.'

'Whole class signed it, and Peter, next door, said don't give it to the school cos they'll just bin it. He said to send it to regional office, which we did, but …'

'Nothing?'

'Not yet.'

'They'd be an even bigger bunch of pricks than White and her little cocksucker.'

Cocksucker. Good stuff. Lennon in his unmade bed.

'And the fool we've got now.'

'Like you said, coupla months, then you don't have to listen to it. Then you become famous and paint them or write about them and for the rest of history people will remember what you said, not what they've done.'

This was a nice thought. 'It was good with you. We all thought we could, you know, get to do what we *really* wanted.'

'You can.'

'I guess it's only April.'

'You're what, seventeen? Look at me, thirty-three, working for nothing, drawing shit for brochures.'

'Can't you find something else?'

'One thing about teaching. It paid okay. But the more you get paid the more you need to keep yer trap shut.'

Just what Lennon had said.

'So I feel better,' he said. 'When I get up and slip on me pants I know I'm not gonna have to face White, or some other arse. That's more important, eh, Clem?'

'I reckon you're right.'

'That's why you phoned, wasn't it? Cos you wanted to know? I mean, you only go round once.'

Fighting Dementia. Nick noticed, read the title and said, 'There you go. Keep teaching art at Gleneagles then you start forgetting where you left your keys, your car, your house. Quite fuckin' pitiful, really.'

'I guess.'

He smiled. 'You always said that: *guess, guess, guess.* Who's got dementia?'

'Pop.'

He drank his coffee in one go. 'Bit of a shit. What did he do for a living?'

'Mechanic. He loved it … loves it.'

'I hope he's okay, Clem. But I reckon you'll look after him.'

It was then I realised Nick wasn't coming back to Gleneagles, and he wouldn't teach me again. No instruction on media, and drawing line, perspective, or how to think about art, people, life. No more words, even. Nothing.

'You gotta say hello to everyone,' he said. 'Especially Curtis. He's a mad bastard.'

I studied the sheets: shapes to name, number sequences to complete, words to remember (*noticeable circumlocution of synonym substitution*). This need to define and describe always let you down.

'So, I guess I'll be seeing you.'

He waited. 'Keep painting.'

I knew it was my time to get up, go out, walk away. I hope he watched me go, and I guess he would've checked the envelope I left on the table, with my stencil, Mr Bulljaw, and the note saying he could use it if he wanted.

Pop stormed around the house, lifting cushions, searching drawers, upturning the laundry basket and feeling pockets. 'Mighta left it at the servo,' he said to Mum.

'You want me to ring them?' she asked.

'Hold on.' Behind the old bar that'd never been stocked, the magazines on the coffee table, the pantry, even. 'Enough to give you the shits.'

'Stop and think,' Mum said.

He tried, standing in the middle of the lounge room. 'I always put it in the same spot.'

The telephone table, as you walked in: wallet, keys, hanky, smokes, lighter. The essentials, lined up ready for another day. Only now minus his wallet.

'How much was in it?' Mum asked.

'*How would I know?*'

'You don't have to bite my head off.'

'Twenty, thirty … Christ, I always put it there.'

Fighting Dementia. I tried to remember the bit about forgetfulness: names, objects, places. I went into his room, checked his bedside table, in his underwear drawer: singlets, socks, the lot. Nothing. Out to the car, under the seats, in the boot. The shed: benches, a shadow sheet, on the ground, waiting for the next customer.

When I went in he said, 'It'll have to wait.' He was pulling on his good pants, an old business shirt that had seen weddings, funerals and a few christenings. 'Mighta been stolen.'

'Who?' Jen asked.

'That's what happens now. You leave your door open, someone comes in and helps themselves.' He pulled on socks and his shoes, freshly polished.

Mum said, 'Why you doin' this?'

'Gotta try.'

'For *him*?'

He tucked in his shirt, tightened his belt, and Mum said it was John's interview, not his. 'Yer wasting yer time. Even if he gets it. Coupla weeks, you see.'

'It's not how you fix things, is it?'

She shook her head. 'He hit Anne.'

'I'll leave off the jacket.' He felt his pockets. 'Feel naked without me wallet.'

'If you're gonna tell Harry he's some sort of angel—'

A knock on the door. John came in, dressed in a pair of Gary's shiny slacks, a too-thin tie and pointy boots that sent the wrong message. 'How do I look?'

Mum just smiled. She was good at insincerity.

'Is it a bit much?' he asked.

'No,' Pop said. 'He'll appreciate that you've gone to the effort. You done your résumé?'

John showed him the few, stapled pages. I wasn't sure why Pop was doing this. There were limits to how much you could help a neighbour's kid, and it wasn't like Anne or Gary were overly thankful.

'Got a good feeling,' John said.

'That's nice,' Mum replied, still smiling, as if to say, Should we care?

'I'd like to work a bit, then buy a car. A Valiant, eh, Doug?'

'You bet.'

A Valiant. Like it meant so much to us; to see him coming good, and buying a Valiant.

'I'll take you for a ride, Mrs Whelan.'

'That'd be nice, John.'

I noticed Jen's face and knew what she was thinking. Careful what you say, John. Nothing about the place you tried to torch with your *mates.*

'I'm very grateful,' he said to Pop. 'Like … all of yers.'

Mum and Jen just stood back, their heads tilted at strange angles. He said to me, 'If I get in I'll see if they got somethin' for you, Clem.'

Fuck off, dickhead. Any other time you wouldn't piss on me. But, strangely, I hoped he'd get the job, to keep him out of everyone's hair.

'What sorta money do you reckon he'd pay?' he asked Pop.

'Don't worry about that till you get the job, right?'

There was a knock on the door, and the home interview began. Harry Johnson, still in his overalls, came in and slapped Pop on the shoulder. We all said hello, then Mum disappeared to the laundry, Jen to the kitchen and me to the dining room table, and a page of protein synthesis.

'How are yer, old man?' Harry asked Pop.

'I'm alright. You still in business?'

'Trying … this John?'

He nodded.

'Nice to meet you, son.'

Pop sat the pair in the living room, offered beer, tea, then coffee. Harry wasn't interested. 'You stayin', Doug?'

'Can't hurt, can it?'

Harry asked if he could smoke. 'You want one, Doug?'

'No, thanks.'

Then he turned to John. 'So, John, Doug tells me yer good with yer hands.'

'He can dismantle a four-cylinder engine,' Pop said. 'A Gemini, in an hour.' He slowed, stopped, responding to Harry's raised eyebrows. They both waited for John.

'I don't have any problems with that, Mr Johnson.'

'Good … and John, you reckon those skills will transfer to panel beating?'

'I reckon. I've done a bit … anyway, if you take the job nice and slow.' He turned to Pop for approval, who said, 'He's methodical, Harry.'

Harry said, 'You should let John tell me, Doug.'

Pop sat silent.

'Like he said, Mr Johnson, I take me time, study the manual, ask other's people's opinion.'

Bullshit, I thought.

'That's very important,' Harry said, 'We gotta lotta good people, and they'll help you learn if you ask, but if you think you know everything—'

'He's not like that,' Pop said.

'Doug.'

Jen came into the room and handed Pop his wallet. 'Found this in the fridge.'

'What was it doing there?'

'You left it there.'

'Why would I leave it in the fridge?'

But she just returned to the kitchen.

John: 'I reckon I'm happy to listen and learn, Mr Johnson. That's what I been doin' with Doug.' He handed Harry his résumé, and he checked it. 'Didn't finish school?'

'Year Ten, nearly.'

'Pity, good to have a bita maths and English to write quotes.'

'He can write,' Pop said. 'And he's good with numbers … right. Sorry.'

John said, 'School wasn't for me.'

'You didn't fit in?'

He took his time, as Pop had recommended. 'No, just about King Richard and ... I like to get on with things.'

'But what if you get bored with sanding panels?'

'No, I don't reckon.'

'From what I've heard ...'

Pop said, 'All that business, I only mentioned it ...'

Harry stared at John.

'Yes, I have been a bit of an idiot, but there's one thing I'm good at, Mr Johnson. And I wanna have a go. So I guess you'd have to take a risk, wouldn't you?'

'You stole stuff?'

'Yeah. I's a fuckin' ... sorry, I's an idiot.'

'And you're no longer an idiot?'

'No ... I'm not sayin' ...'

'How long you been outa McNally's, John?'

'Not long.' And his shoulders slumped.

'Don't lock you in there for stealin' lollies, do they?'

'No, sir. No, Mr Johnson.' Looking down at the carpet.

'And I wanna feel safe. My business ...'

John looked up long enough to accuse Pop with his eyes. I wondered, again, why Pop was falling for this shit.

'John?'

'Yes, Mr Johnson?'

'You tell me why I shouldn't find someone with a clean slate. Someone's at least finished Year Ten?'

'I don't know.'

Harry sucked his smoke and examined the boy forensically. 'I did six months in prison before I started. Bet Doug didn't tell you that?'

'No, sir ... Mr Johnson.'

'Needed that to wake me up.'

Silence. Just the sound of the washer.

'So I don't mind a few rough edges. What do you think, Doug?'

'I think.'

Harry extended his hand, and John shook it.

'Six months' trial. I'll give you Friday afternoons in exchange for Saturday mornings. Hundred and eighty a week. First time you argue … out you go.'

John tried to disguise his smile. For Pop, it was a tongue-round-the-lips, self-satisfied grin. 'I reckon you won't regret it, Harry.'

'I wouldn't have said if I'd thought that, Doug.' He returned to John. 'Six thirty start?'

'Yeah, I'm just next door. Open at six if you like?'

'Half six'll do. You wanna pace yerself, son. Could be a long sixty years, eh, Doug?'

'Too bloody long, mate.'

After Harry left Pop went next door with John to tell his parents the good news, and I guess Anne would've hugged them, and Gary would've offered them a beer, and Curtis, sitting with the bionic woman, would've said (something like), 'Nice one, John.'

Warm, with a butterfish breeze. Me, lost in the car yard beside Don's. Half an hour pricing my first Datsun, if I ever got my licence. I headed home, past the mysterious number 27, a house that's never entered this story because we never knew its occupants. Some little man, and his wife, who only ever darted between car and front door, and had someone in to mow their lawn. A mystery couple. Maybe the police were after them? Which would've been a problem, considering there was a retired copper across the road at number 24 (next to the Rosies' old place). You'd see him sometimes, on the weekends before he retired, parking his patrol car in the drive, going in for an hour or two. He had a brick house. The only one in Lanark Avenue. Of course, his walls were cracking. You couldn't build brick on Bay of Biscay, but some people couldn't be told.

It was one of those perfect Lanark mornings: a couple of crows in a tree waiting for something to get run over; the smell of someone's mock orange and the sound of a toilet flushing, the lid dropping; lemon, even, from someone's washing; and the buzz from the substation. I walked past the nine-foot fence. The sign (DANGER 60,000 VOLTS) that'd scared the shit out of me as a kid. I'd said to Jen, 'Careful, don't touch it.'

'Why?'

'Do you know how many volts that is?'

'You're such an idiot. Not in the fence. In there, going through the power lines. Why would they have sixty thousand volts going through a fence? Go on, touch it.'

'You.'

She took my hand, and forced it against the fence, and I said, 'You bitch!'

'Sixty thousand volts! You dick.'

Around the corner, past the doctors' surgery (the smell of menthol drifting across the road) and Kentucky Fried Chicken, the colonel smiling. Down the drive, the Peter–David drone, the bell, in the front door and straight to my room, and my desk. The place Pop'd helped me make models when I was a kid: propeller-less Spitfires abandoned on a melamine apron. I took out the ream of paper and flattened it. *This Excellent Machine.* Stolen, of course, from someone's poem. Turned to the first page, and a description of a thinly disguised 31 Lanark Avenue, Gleneagles. The protagonist was a down-market Holden Caulfield. This teenager (Arnold Ruge, courtesy of Ernie's Marx) was rebuilding a motorbike in his shed. Talking to his grandfather (Barry Ruge). Arnold was trying to convince his pop he didn't want to return to school. His pop was having none of it.

You, young Arnie, have got a heap of potential …

But, Pop, I hate the place. I want to get out, see what life's all about.

It didn't sound like me. Maybe that was the problem? Maybe I wasn't interesting enough to fill a whole novel? But I'd been told by my English teacher, Mrs Masharin, to write about what I knew. When I thought about it, I didn't know much. Hadn't been far. Really, was probably quite dull.

I skipped a few pages, and there I was, little Arnie, helping my grandfather assemble a Yamaha. Of course, I hadn't done any research about motorbikes, so most of the terminology was Datsun-speak.

Look at that, Pop. Good as new. You're a deft hand at assembling motorcycles.

I picked up my pen, turned to Chapter Three, and continued writing.

Arnold sat on his bed, looking out his window, watching Mr Lawrence feeding his birds.

I stopped. What if it did get published, and Mum told all the neighbours, and they bought a copy (unlikely) and read it and came storming down the drive? 'Is your son there, Fay?'

Lawrence removed a pigeon, stroked it and released it. It flew about but then returned to him.

I had to write about something else. That seemed easy. But what? I'd spent hours dreaming up spy plots, crime stories, dysfunctional detectives roaming the wheatbelt in search of kidnappers. Cheap, nasty stuff. No, I had to aim high. Literature. And all good literature was autobiographical: Dickens, Salinger, even the Brontës, transcribing their own churchyard dramas.

But then, suddenly, Lawrence wrung the bird's neck, watched it kick, and then dropped it on the ground.

What was that? Why was he killing it, and what would Mr Champness say? (He wouldn't read it, but Ron'd probably tell him.)

I'd already thrown one novel in the bin. Made a hundred pages, and the characters had emerged, strutted their stuff, but one day I'd given in to doubt. I'd promised myself I wouldn't do it again. *The Vagina Cooling Machine* had been my *Stephen Hero*. A tormented man (stolen from Kafka) employed by a large corporation to operate a machine that cooled the nether regions of artificial prostitutes. In time, the man had *become* the machine. He'd started blowing, fainting, sitting up, but, of course, the propylene vaginas were no cooler. So he'd been taken to a wasteland, shot, and dumped beside a dead dog.

Mum had found it while I was at school. When I'd got home she'd pulled me aside and said, 'What's that story you're writing?'

'It's set in the future. People are no longer required for real jobs, so the government invents pretend jobs to keep them busy so they don't get organised and revolt.'

'But what's all that about *vaginas*?'

'That's the job they give the main character. They have artificial prostitutes, so real women don't have to do it, which sorta makes sense.'

She'd stared at me. 'So he has to operate a machine?'

'Yes. Like the Industrial Revolution. See, it makes some important social and political points.'

'Vaginas?' She'd stared at me, unsure how anything she'd produced could come up with that. Maybe, I guessed she guessed, I needed help. The stress of growing up without a father had taken its toll.

'And what does this man do at night?'

'Like us. Goes home, cooks tea and fiddles around in the shed. Maybe he's making his own machines.'

'For cooling vaginas?'

'Yeah.'

But she'd left it there, guessing it was another one of my phases: like collecting snails and painting them orange and watching them crawl up the toilet bowl, fall in, get out, crawl up … But *This Excellent* was nothing like *The Vagina Cooling*.

There was only one thing for it. I gathered the pages, flew out the door, down the drive and into the Donnellans' yard. 'Hey, David. Much happening?'

'It's quiet without the cats.'

'Is yer mum gettin' more?'

'Says never again. She's pretty crook about it, Clem.'

'She'll come good. Is Peter around?'

'In the shed, I reckon.'

There he was, in their never-opened shed, standing beside his old E-Type Jag, pulling weeds that'd grown from the dirt floor. 'Hiya, Peter,' I said.

'Clem.'

Pop had started fixing it once, before Val had told him they didn't have money for parts. In the years since, Jen and I had played in it, pretending to be delivery drivers and Datsun-lovers. We'd shooed the cats (that had built beds out of clothes that had dropped from washing lines), cleaned out the rat droppings and the piles of old newspapers and books that the brothers had stored inside, and pretended.

But it'd gone to seed. Clogged with the dust and dirt that filled the Donnellans' shed. In the spots where the floor had fallen through, the weeds had survived, pale and trembling, inside a car inside a shed.

Peter was at work. Clearing weeds and depositing them in a pile outside the shed, beside rubbish he'd cleared from the boot, under seats, all over. There were a few rat skeletons, and a cat mummy, ready for worship.

'What you doin'?' I asked.

'Cleanin' up.'

'Why?'

But he just ignored me, taking a hoe and chipping at the weeds around the car.

'You know what you said about me writing?' I asked.

'Yeah.'

'D'you remember that other story I showed you?'

'The penis one?'

'Vagina.'

He noticed the pages in my hand. 'You havin' another go?'

'Thought I might.'

'What's it called?'

'*This Excellent Machine.*'

'Good title.' He put his hoe down, took my novel, sat on the Jag's bonnet and started reading.

I sat beside him, told him what it was about, and how I wanted to be honest, and tell the world about Lanark Avenue. He looked from page to person and said, 'What makes you think anyone would be interested?'

'Just guessing. We gotta lot of funny people. Ernie, Ida, John … you and Davo and Val.'

'We're gonna be in it?'

'Nothing mean. Just, you know, loosely.'

'I see.' He continued reading.

'Should I come back?'

No reply.

'Assuming you wanna read it.'

'I will, if you want. But maybe it'd be best to write it first?'

'What's the point if it's crap?'

After a few minutes he returned the pages. 'Not bad. Bit clunky, but I can help you with that.'

'So I should continue?'

'Of course. Like I said, Lanark Avenue needs a poet.'

That was enough. Now, I thought – believed – I was a writer.

Peter returned to the hoe, and the weeds around his car. He said, 'I'll do you a deal. You write me a novel, I'll give you my Jag.'

I wasn't sure.

'It's been sittin' here so long. I was thinking of selling it for scrap. But you could do it up, eh?'

Cobwebs and rust and shit. But somewhere beneath it all, I knew, was a Jag. 'So, I finish the novel …?'

'You get my Jag. Good deal, eh? You don't have to get it published. I don't even care if it's any good. But you gotta *finish* it.'

'You'll help?'

'Course. Show me every coupla chapters.'

He took a broom and swept the dirt from the bonnet, the roof. Maybe he was thinking of me, maybe Pop, maybe John, but what did it matter?

I walked into what had been Vicky's room, the screen kicked out, the last of the window glass smashed. She was still there, calling out, Clem, get home this instant! Then hiding.

And me arriving home from school, at the top of my voice: That you, Vicky?

Not, it's not Vicky, it's Mrs Whelan.

Did you want to come over?

And showing herself. No, I gotta clean me room.

Tomorrow?

Is yer mum making scones?

I guess.

Okay then.

Into the old bathroom, the Rosies' cracked toilet bowl, and a lump of shit on the floor. Graffiti, tags, cartoon cocks in action. We'd called the police at 11 pm and they'd eventually arrived at midnight. We'd wandered over and Pop had said, 'No, they're long gone,' and the constable had said, 'Unless they're gonna put a fence around the place there's not a lot we can do.' So, they'd just poked around, filled in some paperwork and left.

Morning, and you could see the extent of the damage. It seemed a shame, because Oswald had been houseproud, vacuuming his carpet and mowing his lawns every Sunday morning, before retiring to his books. A sort of domestic Prospero, avoiding his suburban void. He was still there, in his ruined house, caught up in Conrad as the smell of wisteria drew him out of his shell. Saying, Clem, what's all this about vaginas?

It's a metaphor.

For what?

How willing we are to ... give everything up.

How do you mean?

Sell out. If the price is right.

Like the telly show?

I walked into his bedroom, again, and hoped I'd find his Conrad. Instead, there was a pile of rubbish where someone had tried to start a fire.

They're gonna burn this place down, I said.

It won't worry me.

What about Tina and Vicky?

No reply.

He'd left fertiliser in the shed, and they'd brought that inside and scattered it around.

I gotta go now.

He didn't look up from his book. Good-o, Clem. Take care of yerself.

I went down the back steps into the yard. I could see Les sitting in front of his aviary, watching his birds. Singlet, shorts and thongs. He was listening, then writing something on a sheet of paper. He didn't look up or seem to care where he was or what was happening. Wendy came out with a basket of washing. 'Sun's out,' she said.

He didn't reply.

'Any good?'

'Na.'

'You gonna enter them this year?'

Again, nothing.

Wendy started hanging out the washing. First, a baby blue jumper (you'd often see her on the porch, knitting), big enough for an old child, or young man.

Les said, 'Why you doin' that?'

'Just am.'

'Stupid.' But returned to his birds.

Another jumper, baby blue, same size, or a bit smaller. It seemed strange. They wouldn't fit anyone at number 28.

'What would people think?' Les asked, as he made marks on his sheet.

'Don't care.'

'Doesn't help no one.'

'Helps me.'

More jumpers, gradually becoming smaller, paler, but always blue.

Les said, 'It's morbid. I reckon you need a psychologist.'

'Perhaps I do.'

'Why'd you gotta keep washin' 'em, anyway? What's that prove?'

'Keep 'em in good nick.'

The last few were small, the very last, baby-sized, like it'd been knitted for a doll. When she was finished she stood back and said, 'Nice bita sun, should get them dry.' Turned, and went in.

I counted seventeen jumpers. Maybe they were for some sort of charity, or refugees, or starving kids in Africa.

I walked down the drive, and home. Mum and Pop were sitting on the verandah, Pop in overalls with his spray-pack, surveying the few weeds that dared grow in his garden. I sat beside him and he said, 'Go on, tell your mother what I scored.'

'What?'

He took some folded papers from his overall pocket, opened them and showed me. *Fighting Dementia.*

'I thought we'd get some information,' I said.

Mum read the pages, returned them to me and said to Pop, 'He's just concerned.'

'That's not gonna help, is it?'

I dared not speak.

'So?' Pop asked, bending over, pulling a weed.

'Twenty-eight out of forty-nine,' I replied.

'*Clem,*' Mum said.

'You weren't meant to notice, Pop.'

'What if it's not that bad?' he said. 'I'm an old bastard, and something else will probably get me first.'

'Don't say that,' Mum said.

'See, Clem? You're thinkin' I'm gonna be wandering down North East Road starkers and people'll be laughing. If you go through life worrying about things ...'

They both looked at me.

'Twenty-eight,' I said.

'Fuck.' Pop reclaimed the pages, tore them into pieces and scattered them to the wind. 'If I hada done it to you, would you have done any better?'

'No, but ...' I stopped, realising I was burying myself.

'Instead of studying me, you could help me.' He handed me

the weed-wand, and pushed the spray-pack in my direction. 'Off you go.'

I checked. 'There aren't any weeds.'

'There are plenty.'

So I started, walking the yard, searching for weeds, hitting the few he'd missed the fortnight before. Then I saw the jumpers again. 'Seventeen of them,' I said.

'It's none of your business,' Mum said, noticing them.

I kept working. Pop said, 'It's very strange.' He took out a smoke and lit it.

'People cope differently,' Mum said.

'With what?' I asked.

'It's none of our business.'

'It is if she's gonna hang them out,' Pop said. He stood, approached his roses and started plucking spent flowers.

'If it helps her,' Mum said, 'then good. If I'd had to go through that.'

'What?' I asked, giving up on the weeds.

'*None of your business.*'

Pop said, 'Cosa the kiddy she gave up.'

'Dad!'

'It's no bloody secret. He's not stupid, are you, Clem?'

'She wouldn't want people knowing.'

'Rubbish. She told you. She knew you'd blabber.'

I sat down, and worked on Mum. 'Told you what?'

She fought to keep it in, but couldn't. 'She had a bubba and gave it up for adoption.'

'Why?'

'She told me once, but …'

We waited. Pop sat and said, 'She's not quite right in the head.'

'No one is,' Mum said.

'Don't see me hanging seventeen jumpers on a line.'

Mum glared at him. 'If she knew I went around telling people …'

'I'm not people,' I said.

'She was only young. Back then things were different, weren't they, Dad? Her mum, who was Catholic, and terribly *decent*, said, You're not having … an abortion.'

'I know what an abortion is.'

'Well, this mother made her have it and give it up for adoption.'

'Did she want to keep it?' I asked.

'She told me she did, but this mother, she was worried about her Catholic mates.'

'Fuckin' Catholics,' Pop growled.

'She had to do what this woman said. No job, no money, no prospects.'

'Any normal person would've let her keep it,' Pop said. 'That's the *human* thing to do.'

'Catholics aren't human?'

'No. What about when Wilf …?' He stopped.

Wilf. I'd suspected. Mum waited, unsure, but decided the story was the best contraceptive. 'The nuns took the boy and gave him to a family, and that was that.'

Pop said, 'Family's gotta stick together no matter what happens. But that *evil* woman … It's always the religious ones.'

Mum slapped his knee. 'Wendy's never got over it. And then to have married him. You gotta feel sorry for the woman.'

As I did. Plenty of them in Lanark Avenue.

'But the jumpers?' I asked.

'It's her way,' Mum said. 'Every year she knits one for him. The size she reckons he might be. Once I asked her why she did it and she said if he ever comes back he'll know she never forgot him, or stopped loving him.'

'Not much chance he'd come back.'

'Worst thing of all,' Mum said, 'was what happened next. A week after she got out of hospital she thought, No, I'm not gonna do it. She stood up to her mum and walked out on her, returned to the hospital and asked for him back.' She was imagining this, I guessed. The stark ward, the nuns, with the smugness Pop told us he wanted to wipe from each of their faces.

'What?' I asked, watching the jumpers move in the breeze.

'They said, They've already taken him. So she had to go home to her mum, and welcome Les into the house, and get married, and all that. But she just keeps knitting, and luckily, Les doesn't say nothin'.'

'Keep off!' Val's voice, from next door. She stood opposite Ernie beside the fallen fence with its rusted wire. He said, 'Get yer facts straight.'

David twisted to see. 'No closer, Ernie.'

'Was a time,' Val said, 'people looked out for each other.'

'What, spreading tetanus?' Ernie asked.

'They never hurt you.'

Pop spread his hands on his legs, studied his fingers.

'Don't you lecture me,' Ernie said. 'I helped with that roof.' And he indicated. 'Nailed every sheet on.'

'You killed them. The lot of them.'

Pop stood and hobbled towards the borderlands. 'Don't you reckon people are sick of hearin' it?'

Silence. Except David's murmuring, as he tried to turn to see.

'It's done. Let's get on with it. I could complain, we all could, but …'

Ernie said, 'She thinks I called the council.' Turning to Val. '*I didn't.*'

'You did.'

'Ring 'em, ask 'em, just stop goin' on about it.'

I waited, watched, as Pop decided.

'Christ, Val, if he says he didn't …'

'Who then?'

'Could've been a hundred people.'

'Why would I have waited all these years?' said Ernie. 'If I don't like something I deal with it, but I don't scab on anyone. *Anyone.*'

Val stared at him, unsure. She turned to Pop. 'Who then?'

He indicated Ron's place. 'Someone who'd had enough, I guess.'

Val went in, and Ernie waited, and said to Pop, 'God knows I woulda been entitled to.'

I've never been able to resist supermarkets. As a child I perfected the art of the Friday sickie. Warming Mum up on a Thursday night, a few coughs (as Jen said, Faker!), slow walk, red eyes (plenty of rubbing). Then, on the morning: I can't get out of bed ... I think I'm gonna chuck (Jen: That's the worst acting ever!). But it usually worked.

And why all the effort? Simple: shopping. Every aisle a world of possibilities: meals you'd never thought of, new lines of cream biscuits, prawns, and a thousand other things we couldn't afford. And here I was, years later (no point faking a gut ache in Year Twelve), walking the same aisles, smelling the same fake citrus, feeling safe. But maybe it wasn't the promise of virus-free chopping boards. Maybe it was the memory of Mum, who'd let me push the trolley, or sit in it, like Blackbeard in search of treasure.

The forecourt (where Mr Gottl had brought us to sing to the shoppers) was filled with arcade games. Four years earlier it had been Space Invaders. Straight after school, bags at the door, line up. Half an hour later (if you were lucky) you got to put your money in the slot and blast aliens. Then Curtis would record your score, and some other kid would beat it, so you'd have to line up and try again. We all lost our techno-virginity in the Gleneagles Shopping Centre forecourt. Until the novelty wore off, and we returned to bikes and graffiti and, eventually, shoplifted pornography.

I passed the record shop (where I bought my John Lennon LPs) and waited outside the butcher as Pop talked to Bruce (the fritz-giver, the mum-chatterer), his team's colours beside a poster of economical cuts. Artificial grass in the front window, and trays of rib eye resigned to their crock-pot fate. Bruce: who was always happy and smiling, probably because he knew people would always want meat, and Coles could never match his quality. Until they did.

Pop came out, handed me the keys and said, 'Go on.'

To be honest, I'd let the driving slip. It was a lot of work, and there were songs to transcribe, personalities to describe, neighbours to watch. I couldn't reverse-parallel, and there was always the bus. But Pop insisted. 'The sooner you take yer test the sooner we don't have to drive you around.'

Right. I got in, belted up and started the car. 'Seatbelt, Pop.'

'I don't need to wear it.'

Maybe he was testing me. 'If we have an accident, you could get hurt.'

'Go on.'

I waited.

'It's my life. If I want my brains all over the road …'

I waited.

'Christ!' He put it on then lit a smoke. 'Do you mind if I have one?'

'Feel free.' As I backed out, and someone else did, and abused me.

Pop put down his window. 'He was first! You fuckin' wanker!'

I navigated the car park. The 120Y was running rough and I said, 'Sounds like the plugs.'

No reply.

'We could buy some, replace them.'

'Put it into Conte's. Get it done properly.'

'Spark plugs?'

'Get him to do it. I couldn't be bothered.'

'But you said he was a crook.'

He took his time with his smoke. 'He's okay.'

It seemed final. He'd decided: no more cars. Even spark plugs, which were the easiest thing of all. 'You know what he'll charge?' I said.

'Watch the kerb.'

But I'd mounted it, and the Datsun's shockers protested.

'Less talk, more concentration.'

I turned onto the main road, indicated and entered the flow. 'Can't let things beat you,' I said.

'If I want a sermon I'll go to church. Just drive. Look, he's gonna—'

And he was right. The Mazda cut in front of me, and Pop reached over and sounded the horn. 'Don't be scared to tell them.'

'Let me drive.'

'People'll shit on you if you let 'em.'

Again, the flow. I said, 'I'm not preaching, but spark plugs?'

'Conte's a good man, he could do with the work. So we'll give it to him.'

I didn't believe him. Pop'd do anything to save a few dollars. He said, 'You're still riding the clutch.'

'I am not.'

'You'll burn out the clutch plate. That's always been a problem with Datsuns. Pull in here.'

I obeyed.

'Reverse around the corner.'

Fine.

'Three-point-turn.'

Easy.

'Right, keep going.'

Back on the road, he fell silent for some time. I crept over the limit, but he didn't say anything. I stayed in third too long, but again, nothing. 'D'you reckon I'm ready for the test?' I asked.

'One way to find out.'

Then he returned to the road. After a while he said, 'I's readin' about Lasseter.'

'Yeah?'

'Everyone thought he was mad.' Again, he looked at me, as if to ask.

'How's that?'

'He reckoned the reef was seven miles long, which is a stretch. But maybe he was prone to exaggeration?'

'Maybe.' Indicating, turning towards home. He saw this and said, 'Go round the block a few times.'

I drove into the basketball stadium car park, found a gravelly hill and tried a start. It was shit, but he didn't say anything.

'People reckoned he was mad. Some fella put up fifty thousand quid for his first expedition, but when they got out there, Lasseter was um and ah and they're thinkin', Christ, what have we done?'

'They didn't find gold?'

'Eventually the whole expedition deserted him and he was left with these camels, and they ran off into the desert, then some blackies tried to help him, but they thought he was mad, so ... he was left alone.'

'What happened then?'

'He walked around a bit, realised, I guess, he was in a heapa trouble, sat down and wrote a note.'

The car was running better now, and I cruised the back streets without indicating.

'Watch fer kiddies.'

'I'm always watching.'

Again, he was wandering the desert, determined. 'He was right at the end, Clem.' And touched my arm, so I understood. 'He wrote: *What good's a reef worth millions? I would give it all for a loaf of bread.* Then he died.'

'Without finding the gold?'

'He had another sheet of paper, and he drew a map ...'

'Your map?'

He waited, then said, 'You're still with me, aren't you, Clem?'

'Of course.'

'Cos if I thought ...' He looked into his lap, mulling it over. Then back at me, 'If I thought you thought I was ... deluded?'

'No,' I said. 'If you trust the map.'

'I do, Clem, a hundred per cent. Nan didn't believe anything unless she could see it. She kept me working ... and I shouldn't have gone along with it. But there were bills to be paid. She hated the thought of me going. That time I bought a tent and a camp oven and a compass, she got real shitty. And when I was working, she put the map in the bin, but she never knew I got it out again.'

I stopped at a light.

'Lasseter was just a few miles short.'

Green. 'But why hasn't anyone returned? I mean, that was fifty-four years ago.'

He threw his smoke out the window and said, 'How'd you think he felt, at the end, so close? But he had a son, and I suppose he thought he'd find the map and get the reef and all would be good.'

I pulled into the drive. 'But wouldn't this son have a claim to the reef?'

'I've got as much right as anyone. Anyone who can find it.'

Mum came out and asked if we'd remembered the bread. I said, 'I knew I was in there for something.'

It was an impressive toilet: fake-tile floor with a drainage hole; cold, catty smell; solid bowl with bakelite lid, so that it thundered in the night. A decent flush, too. I sat listening as Mum cleaned my room. You could stay, and she'd clean around you, looking at what you were doing (When's that Biology due?), or you could cut your losses and retire to the toilet. She was making my bed. 'Be nice if you could put yer socks in the wash.'

Pop's reading pile on the floor. Last Sunday's *Mail*. I checked. Teak swivel luxury on sale for $469, and upholstered PVC telephone tables for $29.95.

'Clem?'

'What?' (I hated communicating while *in officium* …)

'Your bed's full of crumbs.'

'Leave it.'

'You wanna bring mice back into the house? Pop said he saw a rat in the shed.'

I sang: '*Blah, blah* …' Loud enough for me.

'Well, you come and clean it.' As she muttered, 'Rude little shit.'

Three-piece teenage bedroom suite. $119. Nice. Although there was no point wishing.

'You gonna stay in there all day?'

Yes, I thought, if that's what it takes.

'What yer doin'?'

Jen, laughing. 'You better not ask. He might tell you!'

And a little chorus of giggles.

'Get stuffed!' As I fetched paper, to suggest otherwise.

Jen, again. 'Hurry up, I gotta go. I don't want to have to smell your arse.'

She knocked on the door. Code. The lock had broken years ago, so you had to give a thump, wait a second, and enter. Nonetheless, it wasn't a foolproof method. I'd had a few doors open while I was on the job. Pop staring at me and saying, Didn't hear you.

'Carn,' Jen said, knocking.

'Fuck off!'

Then, a full-page ad from Datsunland. Second-hand 180Bs. We all knew it was time to trade up from the 120Y. It had 300,000 on the clock, and the CVs were shot. The suspension had gone and the steering was loose. Still, Pop wouldn't hear a word. All of this, apparently, could be fixed.

Some four-cylinder cars claim more power, some claim bigger interiors, others claim some of Datsun's built-in features. But we believe none of them put it together like Datsun 180B.

The pictured car was a stunner: fresh chrome, new tyres, and lamb's wool car seat covers (as I wondered …).

… inertia reel seatbelts; reclining high-back bucket seats; the parcel tray extends to the full width of the interior; a centre console; arm rests on all four doors; the classic 180 grille …

Jen, again, knocking. 'You're not the only one!'

I threw down the paper and flushed the toilet, zipped up and exited.

Jen stood at the door, sniffing. 'It doesn't even smell.'

'My shit don't stink.'

The cleaning frenzy had stopped, so I returned to my room. Mum was still there, sitting on my freshly made bed, a pile of shoes at her feet. The wardrobe door hanging from its one good hinge. And, in her hand, the photo of Dad. She said, 'You hid it?'

I thought what to do. It wasn't like there was any explanation. 'I didn't want you to … I thought you'd be upset.'

Why had she cleared the shoes out? As though she was looking for it.

'Is this the only one?'

'Well, it's the only one you didn't get.'

Her face changed, like I'd gone from son to stranger. 'Why did I do that?' she asked.

'You tell me.'

She sat up, confused. 'The whole deal … cos I'm a *bitch*?'

'I didn't say that.'

'You don't know what went on.'

'Yes, I do.' Shit! I'd said it. I shouldn't have, but I had.

'What?'

So I told her: the potted history I'd learned from Val. 'See, I'm not stupid. You coulda told me.'

And the look: You don't know why?

'I've had to guess.' And what I wanted to say: when other kids got their dad, not their pop, on the father–son camp; when I looked courtside and it was just you, filing your nails, or Jen, plaiting her hair; when I wished for even the dodgiest of dads (worse than Gary) but realised I couldn't have one, any one.

'Nasty,' she said, standing, throwing the photo on the pile of deceased shoes, boots, worn-down thongs.

'He couldn't have been that bad.' I wanted to say: You made him go. I knew I couldn't. I wouldn't be able to take it back.

'There were drugs,' she said. 'Did you know that?'

I dared not move.

'I put up with the rest, but I wasn't going to put up with that. Not in my house, around you and Jen.' She picked up the photo and showed me. 'Would you have kept it?'

I waited. 'I guess not.'

Then she sat on the bed, studying the photo. 'He was a good man, Clem, and he tried. But he changed. When you got kids you can only have so much patience. I waited for a long time.'

I sat beside her and took the photo. 'I can see, I mean, from what Val said …'

'Val?'

Shit! Again. 'It wasn't her fault. I kept on at her.'

The toilet flushed and Jen came out, washed her hands and stood in my doorway. 'What's wrong?' She noticed the photo and knew, I guessed, although she decided to stay out of it. She went into her room and closed the door.

'It's not like you think,' Mum said. 'I thought it best if we moved on. Nan and Pop agreed. It worked for a while until ...'

'Val didn't mean anything.'

She stood, examined my shoes and said, 'If you want to keep them, put them away. If not, pop them in the bin.'

And she was gone, leaving the photo on my bed. Out the front door, into number 33.

Pop had folded his shadow sheet, swept the floor and packed his tools in their box. Mum'd be happy, although she wouldn't. Neat. Although with dementia, neat wasn't always good. But he'd left a chair in the middle of the shed, and a small table with an ashtray, and smokes, and more magazines. The manuals had been packed away. I couldn't see where. Maybe he'd thrown them. So now he just sat, remembering: the engines stripped and rebuilt; the radiators replaced; the thousands of litres of oil drained.

I could smell smoke, and checked over the fences. From the middle of the Donnellans' yard, a grey haze filling the morning air, spreading low and settling in yards and the lane behind Frontline Ford. I heard Peter saying, 'It's goin' everywhere, Mum,' and Val replying, 'Don't worry, no one's got their washing out.'

I lifted a sheet of iron to see what was going on: Val, carrying the dead weeds from the shed, depositing them on her fire, poking them with a fork and going back for more as Peter continued clearing around the Jag.

I was about to go in when Val said, 'I didn't mean anything by it.'

Peter was too busy working to respond.

'I told you, they shoulda said something to them years ago.'

She dropped her fork, picked up a pile of old newspapers and hobbled across her yard. She threw the lot on the fire, which flared, catching her dress. She patted it, and didn't seem to care that it had taken a chunk of polyester. The grey smoke whitened, rose, spread, and I ducked to avoid it. Then she returned and gathered more weeds.

'It's not like I told him much.'

'He had to know some time,' Peter said. 'He's old enough. What's he, seventeen?'

'I didn't tell him the worst, about that time you spoke to them fellas out front of the house. Standing with their tattoos and cars and dirty-lookin' faces.'

'I remember.'

'And you said it was a quiet street, and one of them told you to mind yer business or else he'd ...' She stopped, frightened by the thought. 'There's a lot more I coulda told him.'

'But she wasn't angry?'

'She stood with that look and I knew, right away, and I said, It's about Wilf, isn't it? And she was about to let loose when she said, Well, if he knows he knows. Not here to blame you, Val.'

'But she was?'

'Too right. Never seen no one change so quick. That's when I asked her in for a cuppa, and she was quite apologetic. Like it was her fault, makin' me promise to stay quiet all these years.'

'About time,' Peter repeated. 'You can't make sense of the world if you don't know where you're from.'

'Too right.'

I sat down against my side of the fence and listened. I could tell everything about them from their voices.

'Poor, Fay,' Val said.

Bottles. A box, perhaps. Peter saying, 'We could get money for these.'

'No, put 'em in the bin.'

'Could keep them, just in case.'

The home winemaking he'd been promising to start for years.

'Just chuck them, you're never gonna do it.'

'Might.'

Weeds. Fire. Silence.

Val said, 'Then she ends up havin' a good cry and sayin', Yer right, Val, it was mean to keep it from them.'

No reply.

'You been so good to me, she says. And I say, Anyone would've done the same, and she says, No, remember, all them days you'd babysit?'

Me and Jen playing on Val's rug with Val Doonican drifting in the window from next door, Peter reading Dylan Thomas aloud, hoping (somehow) to inspire us, as Val made cupcakes for our after-school treat.

She said, 'I told her, It was a privilege, Fay. Then she was crying again, saying sorry. I said, There's nothin' we can't say to each other. I bathed 'em, remember? When you couldn't get home in time? I put 'em in that rotten bath of mine and scrubbed them and dried them off and put them in David's and Peter's old jarmies till you got home. Remember me doin' that, Peter?'

'Yes, Mum.'

The fire flared. I imagined more weeds, more shit they'd left in their shed too long.

'That's what I told her, Peter. I mighta let it slip, but it was cos I cared, cos I couldn't help myself.'

'Look, Mum, we still got this.'

Silence, as they examined whatever it was.

'Should give it to Fay,' Val said.

'Righto.'

I peered through the gap. It was the cast-iron pot we'd cooked the soup in. Five, six years of cats and rats. Keep it, I thought. Then Peter handed her a few lengths of wood and she made her way to the fire, lowered them in, like an offering, and stood watching. 'Lonely,' she called.

'Eh?'

No response, then: 'Some days … though I dunno if I'm ready to start again.'

'Once Clem sees it, ready to go, he'll be motivated.'

Now it was a reliable fire, red flames and clear smoke, rising straight up.

'Don't know,' Val said.

'It'll need a tonne of work, but I reckon it'd be just the thing for Doug.'

Doug?

'Get him interested again. Nothin' worse than when you lose interest, eh, Mum?'

She returned to the shed. 'Who d'you reckon then?' she asked.

'What?'

'Who dobbed us in? It was him, wasn't it?'

'I don't reckon. Whatever else, he's not that sly. He'd tell you.'

'Ron?'

'Perhaps.'

'Or maybe the Ford people?' She came into view, studying her back fence, the lane, the windows of the big factory. *'They weren't hurtin' no one,'* she called.

'Mum, it wasn't them.'

'Mighta been. Quarter of a century, not so much as a wave.' She leaned over, gathered the last of the weeds and returned to the fire. This time, Peter followed her, and they stood watching the flames.

'Doug?' he said.

She took a moment. 'No.'

He looked at her.

'Les, perhaps. He's complained before, remember, about cats hangin' round his birds.'

'No, not Les.'

'Well, it had to be someone.'

'So I stood havering in that moorland dim …'

'Out of place,' I said.

Curtis didn't care. 'Just break, Whelan.'

So I broke. Pocketed the seven and smiled. 'Should we put some money on it?'

He was confident, but not particularly able, and he knew it. Still he couldn't resist. 'One dollar.'

'One?' I almost laughed. 'So you're sure you're gonna lose?'

'Two.'

'*Come on.*'

'I would if I could, but I don't have it.'

'Fine.' I took another shot. Got the one in. Then, again, but missed. We shook hands.

'Two dollars,' I said.

'Perhaps.'

The Gleneagles pool hall sat at the top of North East Road, surrounded by car dealerships, a tile display centre, a lawyer (specialising in divorces and custody) and a few old houses left to rot in a cloud of monoxide. There were thirty or so tables, crammed in, and the place was dark all day.

'*The first quick zest that filled me to the brim.*'

Why? Because Curtis had told me this place was the reason Dante picked up a quill. The Circles of Hell. The Damned lying in torment. We'd never been able to work it out. Dozens of men playing pool in the middle of sunny, productive weekdays. Apparently, not everyone had to work.

'*A friend of mine, who is not Fortune's Friend, is hard beset upon the shadowy coast; terrors and snares his fearful steps attend.*'

'How much have you memorised?'

'Nearly finished Cantos II. But eventually, the whole thing.'

'Why?'

'Can't you see, Clemmy? That's the world described. You wanna understand it, remember it. Don't forget it. Cos they'll try make you.'

'Who?'

He took a shot. '*They.* They'll have you working, and you'll have a nice house and car and you'll think, I've got it all, but really, you've got nothing.'

I guessed he was right. Why else would the *Mail* be trying to convince us that happiness was Berber with free underlay?

'And in the end,' he said, 'the profits go to the mortgage-makers.'

'So you're a communist now?'

'They're even worse. You've just gotta recognise this place,' as he looked around the hall, 'for what it is. *The savage brute that makes me cry for dread.*'

He pocketed the eleven and fourteen and smiled. 'Now it begins.'

The pair on the adjacent table were part-truckie, part-bogan. Each had a paunch emerging from a holey T-shirt – white, purple-veined and hairy, covering the front of too-low pants with arse crack. Thongs and ankle freezers; turkey giblet arms (although they couldn't have been more than forty) and double and triple chins.

I loved the place. Musty carpet, and forty years of tobacco in the curtains someone had hung to try and give the place a bit of class. The besser block walls, covered in graffiti, a songline of stubby cocks and canyon vaginas for all the kids to see. Yes, kids. Cos we'd been brought here earlier in the year for PE. Taught the rules, then marched to the top of North East Road, led in – to the amusement of the Damned – and given a table. They'd watched us, these dark men, and laughed, and made comments loud enough for us to hear. *Come on, boys, watch where you put them cues.* Our pool hall sport lessons had been our favourite. Coke and more hot chips, as the teachers sat in the corner with a ciggie.

We'd popped our hot dogs, and settled in with milkshakes. Shared a stolen smoke, before beginning.

'*I saw him coming, swift and savage …*'

But this time the fatter of the two beside us looked over.

Curtis noticed, but you had to ignore it. We'd seen the broken pool cues. We'd heard how it happened. He whispered, 'Dante … he was a poet.'

The same man kept watching.

'Would you like to join us?' Curtis whispered.

'Ssh,' I said.

Low ceilings, of course, so you wouldn't think about the day you'd abandoned. Maybe it was best you didn't know. Eternity was a long time.

'To be honest, it's all a bit depressing,' I said.

'Yeah.'

Sport lessons were one thing, but *choosing* to wait at the gate? And if you didn't start hating the place at one point, you'd become part of it. The pale faces, like plants left to grow in a cupboard.

'John'd fit in,' Curtis said. 'Place's full of people he could look up to.' He studied the lesser fat man's technique.

'You should bring him.'

'I keep my distance.'

'What's he been up to?'

'Gettin' ready to start work. Two weeks, tops. He'll either punch someone or steal something. He can't help himself. He's a born criminal. Trash.'

The fatter man looked over.

'I see what you mean, Whelan. We gotta move on, don't we?'

Then, from the other end of the hall, raised voices. One man pushed another, and he recovered, said, 'Wanna try?' And his mate: 'Finish the fuckin' game.'

Mum'd be proud. I hadn't told her this was how I was spending the last day of my holidays. 'If John settles, it could make life easier for you.'

'He won't.'

'At home?'

'Struts around like he owns the place. Stands over Mum. Good if he did come here, give someone lip, get one of these over his head.' He gripped his cue.

The three and two, in succession, but then I missed. Curtis countered with three more, and I realised he was winning, although he didn't seem to care. Who needed two dollars? There were plenty of smokes under the cubby house floorboards.

'I could kill him,' Curtis said.

'Why?'

He said it to tease me. 'Plenty of reasons. It could get to the point that I didn't care anymore.'

'You wouldn't handle prison.'

'*Of hurtful things we ought to be afraid.*'

I waited. 'You'd kill him?'

'Why not?' He looked around. 'This place is fuckin' horrible.'

The fatter turned to us.

'*Horrible!*'

'Well, piss off!'

We walked down the hill, past Hungry Jack's, the Gleneagles sing-along shops, auto care, and an empty shopfront where Ron Glasson had once opened an outlet, but failed because of a lack of off-road parking (Pop had said any idiot could've seen that coming). Curtis kept his head down. I asked, 'What's he been up to?'

'I'm not goin' back to that shithole again. I remember it being fun.'

'I agree.'

'Things change, don't they, Clementine?'

'Yeah.' As I smelled the child-happy smell of thick and endless exhaust.

'And it's like, you can't go back. It doesn't work, eh?'

Mrs Masharin was an excellent teacher. That is, she liked me. She had an accent part-Moscow part-Gleneagles, always wore her hair in a bun, sat very upright and dressed in Target frocks, but somehow made them seem special, posh, classy. She wasn't so old that you couldn't lust after her. Thirty, perhaps, with what might have been enormous breasts. Curtis had been the first to point this out, one recess after a hot lesson, and one or two loose buttons. 'She's got 'em packed in, but if you look …'

So I did, and decided he was right. Of course, Curtis took it further. 'There goes the final button.' As she tackled Steinbeck. 'All it'd take is a quick fiddle with the latch and bam.'

'Curtis, quiet, please!'

Now she was reading the results of our short story assessment. Colin Davies had made up a story about a Vietnam vet who goes nuts and blows up a small town.

'I said I'd come back, and I did, but what was here? Who was waiting for me.'

Fuck me. Why was she even reading it? I watched her lips, big, Russian, deep purple. The colour of lust. I could see her tongue moving, banging against her big, white, too-perfect teeth. No doubt she was trying to seduce me with her love of words, and literature.

'I forgot to tell you,' Curtis said. 'Last night I's out the front and I saw this woman and this girl go into the Rosies' place.'

'Who were they?'

'I reckon …'

'No?'

'Looked like them.'

'Did you say hello?'

He shook his head. Masharin was waiting for him. 'Curtis, if you keep talking I'll have to separate you two.'

'Go on,' the Cohen girl said. 'They never shut up.'

Masharin glared at her.

Curtis said, 'If it was Vicky she was lookin' pretty good.' Whispering: 'Tall, blonde … last time I saw her she was like a grasshopper.'

I tried to remember. A good-looking grasshopper, even then. I could still remember watching her through my polished lens, dreaming how nice it'd be to kiss her. 'What were they doing?' I asked.

'Looking around. Threw some rubbish in the yard. Got in a car and drove off.'

'If they come back, I get first go.'

'Fuck off.'

'Curtis?' Masharin was looking at him. 'It's important to be original.'

'Sorry?'

She held up his short story. We could see the C- from the back of the room. 'You have to come up with your own ideas. This man, wandering the underworld … Dante?'

'But I did my version.'

'You even used Virgil to lead him along—' she checked '—Lanark Avenue.'

'That's what I mean. My version. Hell in the suburbs.'

She didn't look impressed. '*It was nearly night, and everyone was coming home ...*' She picked up her version of *Inferno*. '*Day was departing and the dusk drew on ...*'

The Cohen girl said, 'Don't yer get an E for plagiarism?'

Masharin said: 'It's not plagiarism, as such, but, Curtis, I asked for a short story, not a translation.'

He pointed to Colin Davies. 'But he did *First Blood*.'

Davies almost stood. 'Did not.'

Masharin asked, 'What's that?'

'A Sylvester Stallone film.'

'Is not, Mrs Masharin. I made it all up.'

'Like I did,' Curtis demanded.

'At least I wrote a story.'

'A lame piece of ...' He stopped, smiling at Masharin.

She said, 'In contrast, this wonderful piece by Clem Whelan,' displaying it like it had been shot, and hung on a wall, 'is an extract from a novel: *This Excellent Machine*.'

Curtis nudged me. The A was even bigger; you could see it from the moon.

'You're writing a novel, Clem?'

'Yes.'

And she smiled. Not just a like-your-work smile, but something bigger, closer, more intimate. '*Mr Lawrence watched his birds. Counted their songs. To him, each was an affirmation of the sanctity of life.*'

'Please,' Curtis grumbled.

'*As long as they sang, things were good. But when they stopped, at dusk, it made him think there was more to night than darkness.*'

'What the hell's that mean?' Curtis asked.

Colin Davies said, 'Is that what you wanted? I could've written that.'

'No, you couldn't,' she said. 'This is writing of the highest calibre. *The cats were gathered around the wire, trying to get in, and he shooed them. But they returned, hungry. Dozens, desperate for something to eat, and Mr Lawrence saw this, and was determined to stop them.*'

'You're in,' Curtis said.

But I wasn't even thinking about that. More, how Peter might have been right.

I watched how the light settled on Pop's hands, in the fine wire grid set in the glass of the shed louvres. The tremor was getting worse, but nothing more, perhaps, than any old person's shaking. I'd read about it. It was to be expected. Parkinson's perhaps. He lifted a spanner from the bench and said, 'This'll do,' and cleaned it with a rag.

'What do you think?' I asked.

'E-Type?'

'Yeah.

'Lotta work, boyo. You're quite welcome to the shed. Maybe John could help you?'

'I thought you could.'

His hands hovered above the tools. An archaeology of life, a mechanic's, sitting collecting dust. He lifted a paint scraper and said, 'This might help him.' He cleaned it and placed it beside a wrench. 'And you always need a couple of ...' He studied it. 'A couple of ...'

'Wrenches?' I asked.

He glared at me, like this object had never had a name, but I'd devised one, and somehow it fit. 'It'll be a lot of work.'

'But it's a Jag.'

'Clapped out piece of shit. It used to be in here. He asked me to rebuild the motor, and I gave him a quote. He asked me to wait, but months later I had to tell him I needed the room.'

'But it'll be okay? With a bita work?'

He messed my hair. An old thing. A reminder of other Clems.

'Perhaps, but you'll need parts. He's offered to buy them?'

'No.'

'Didn't think so.'

'But he's giving me the Jag.'

He smiled. 'No one never gives you nothin', Clem. He's gettin' rid of some old junk.'

I didn't agree. Jags were worth money, and this was a classic.

'So it's a present?'

'When I finish my novel.'

'What's that got to do with anything?'

'He's trying to motivate me.'

He didn't get this. 'Tell him you don't want it. Hurry up and get yer licence and we'll buy you a 180B.'

I thought about it. A 180B? Clean, easy, simple. I could imagine taking Curtis to town, bars, girls, and steamed-up windows. You had far better prospects with a Datsun.

Spark plug pliers. Pop studied them, wiped them, put them with the other tools.

'You gonna give him those?' I asked.

'He'll need them.'

'But it's your only pair.'

He searched the cast-iron boneyard. 'I got another set somewhere.' As he lifted and dropped, mixed, picked out old shards of plastic and sandpaper and said, 'Haven't I?'

'I've only seen you use those.'

'Well, he can have them. I can buy another pair.'

The pile was growing. Pop reckoned this is what John needed to get him started. You couldn't expect a new apprentice to buy his own gear. He said, 'Later, he can replace them. But for now … if *you* started.' He squeezed my arm.

'So what do you reckon?'

'I'm too old.'

'It'll be like a hobby.'

Then, John was at the door.

'Ask John.'

He came in, and Pop lit up and motioned for him to approach the altar.

'Ask me what?'

'Clem wants to do up Peter Donnellan's old Jag.'

John almost laughed. 'God, Clem, get a Valiant. Something worth the effort.'

Pop held his shoulder. 'Good advice.'

He's not what he seems, I wanted to tell Pop. He hits people. His own mother, probably. But Pop wouldn't have listened. He led John over to the stash and said, 'This lot, to get you started.'

John didn't get it. 'What?'

'This lot. You can have them. You'll need them.'

'Right.' He picked them up, admired them. 'Thanks.'

No attempt to say no, or make it difficult. Just a pair of beady eyes.

Pop had been generous: wire strippers, piston-ring pliers. 'Somethin' to put 'em in.' He opened his cupboard, found his toolbox, brought it over to the bench and emptied the contents. Then he loaded it with John's new tools. 'That's yours.'

John wasn't concerned, but made a show of it. 'I can't take yer toolbox.'

'I got another.'

'No, you haven't,' I said.

'Well, I can get another.' He picked up his map, lost in the mess of tools. Sat down, flattened it on his knee and studied it.

'He's a bit confused,' I said to John, and he emptied his tools from the box. Then he put them in a plastic bag. 'Good of you to do this,' he said to Pop.

Pop was following directions, driving through the desert.

'This is what he does when he's confused,' I said.

John said, 'So I shouldn't take them?'

'Course you should,' Pop called. 'Don't listen to him.' He glared at me, before returning to his map. 'Somewhere round here.' Finding the cross with his finger.

No, don't do it, I thought. But it was too late. John was over, sitting beside him. 'What's that, Doug?'

'A reef.'

'What reef?'

'Gold. Seven miles long. In the outback.'

'And this is where?' He moved his head to get a better look.

'You've never heard of Lasseter's Reef?'

There followed the story: the map's origins, his attempts to look for it, Nan's reluctance, and a philosophical treatise on how a man never stopped searching. I just stood at the bench, listening. 'Pop, he doesn't want to hear all that.'

But John said, 'Yes, I do.'

'Harold Lasseter was seventeen,' Pop said. 'He was riding from Queensland to the Western Australian goldfields and somewhere near the WA–Territory border he stumbled on it.'

'Just sittin' there?' John asked.

'Yep. He kept on towards Kalgoorlie, but got lost, and a camel driver helped him. Took him to this camp, and a surveyor named Harding. Lasseter told Harding about the gold, and he believed him, so they back-tracked, looking for it. Anyway, their watches weren't good enough and they couldn't get a proper fix, but they got close enough and Lasseter wrote it down.'

They both gazed at it.

'Then they returned and tried to get people interested, but folks were making good money on the goldfields. Lasseter spent thirty years trying to convince people to fund an expedition. So this friend of mine, he came across it ...'

John touched the map, but Pop kept possession.

'You know, I reckon I saw a documentary of this,' John said. 'And they said it was all in his head.'

'Not at all,' Pop growled. 'Me and Clem, we reckon it's true, don't we, Clem?'

'We do, Pop.'

'Eleven hundred kilometres west of Alice. Of course, I can tell you this, can't I, John?' He was emerging from his funk, folding the map once, twice, and putting it in his pocket.

'Course you can,' John said. 'It's not like I'm gonna go look, eh? I got this apprenticeship to start.'

I heard voices in the driveway: deep, monotonous.

Pop stood, handed John his prize and said, 'These'll get you started.'

The voices grew louder. The yard gate opened, and there were footsteps. Mum explaining something. 'He's always out here.'

Three figures in the doorway: Mum, a man in a suit, and a copper, a constable. Pop said to them, 'Funny time for a visit?'

No one responded. John placed the bag on the bench.

'I'll leave you, shall I?' Mum asked.

And she was gone.

The man in the suit looked like a detective. *Division 4*. Decent pair of burns, and a suit with arms up past his wrists. He said, 'How are yer, John?'

'Alright, Mr Craig.'

Mr Craig said, 'We did check, and it looks like it was his.'

'So? None of my business.'

'It is.'

'You talked to Alan?'

'He's next. What say we go for a drive? You tell us your side, we write it down again. *Again*.'

'Righto.' He turned to Pop. 'Can I leave these here?'

Pop seemed confused, but not Alzheimer's confused. More, what-have-you-done? Just when I got you a job, and gave you a bag of tools.

They left and Pop sat down and Mum came in to sniff about, then Jen, with her bleached fingertips. Mum said, 'I told you, Dad.'

'I showed him the map.'

No one spoke.

'Mighta been nothin' at all. Them mates of his, eh?'

'Yeah, nothin' at all,' Mum said, going in, followed by Jen.

Pop repacked his toolbox, complete with map. As he worked he said, 'Take this over to Anne, will yer?' He handed me the bag.

'Shouldn't you hold onto them?'

'Na. Once you give something, it's given.'

May

The world could be made and unmade. The jungle was real, if you wanted it to be. The bricks could make yurts, or yachts, or the house you lived in. You signed a contract with yourself, to build, to nest. And years later when you found it under your bed, it was still waiting for the Idea. So I made a shed; a box for holding E-Type Jags, tools, old men and their dreams. It was made from all the bricks in the world, but none of them. It held everything, but nothing. Because it was the act of making that mattered. Like the mythical Wilf, raising high the roof beams, clicking his own blocks together on some long-forgotten Saturday morning.

Still a Saturday morning, and still kept inside by the weather. Vertical rain on our gasping roof. A gale working on the corners, lifting iron, as we waited for the crash. I stopped, studied Legoland and listened to the storm. Les ran out and covered his aviary with its tarp, strapped it down, and spoke to his birds. It's passing, girls! As Wendy waited at the door and said, Come inside, it's dangerous.

'There she goes!' Pop called.

He'd been pacing the house: around the lounge room, the dining room, the kitchen, following the borders, placing one foot in front of the other, and counting. He'd get to the end and say, 'Sixty-two,' and we'd just look at him. Then he'd say, 'That doesn't sound right,' and start again, one foot at a time, estimating when something (the old bar, say) stuck out from the wall.

'Clem!'

I ran out, and realised the real world was calling. Pop pointed out the back window and said, 'We're gonna have to fix it.'

The back fence had lost two of its sheets of iron, revealing wooden posts, and Frontline Ford.

'Come on.'

I followed him out. He was still in his shorts, singlet and slippers. Mum called after us: 'Dad, come and get something on,' but he just waved her away.

He picked up the first sheet of iron and tried to hold it in place. The wind was too strong, and blew him back. He fought it. I helped, but the gale ripped the iron from our hands. 'Hammer, and three-inch nails,' he called.

I ran to the shed. Mum and Jen were standing on the back porch, watching. Mum said, 'Tell him to come in. It'll wait.'

I just shrugged. Pop never listened to me.

'Dad!' she called, but he didn't reply.

Pop had sorted the nails into different-sized jars. Three inch. Then I searched for the hammer.

'Clem!' The voice above the howl, above the voice: Mum. I went out and she pointed to the fence. The two sheets of iron were sitting on the ground, but Pop had gone. She said, 'Jen's gone after him.'

'Where?'

'Through the fence.'

I ran, jumped through the hole, down the lane, past Don's little toilet with its banging door. 'Pop?' To the main road. And there he was, wearing a single slipper, wandering the asphalt. Jen stood calling as cars approached, slowed, drove around him. No one stopped or seemed to care. Soon the traffic had banked up, and one man wound down his window and said, 'Go home, you silly old fool.'

I ran towards Jen, and noticed Don standing beside her, calling, 'Please, come in!'

I joined them. 'Pop, you're gonna get hit.'

But he wasn't listening. He was trying to determine the dimensions of the main road. Pacing the distances across a single lane, two, the lengths of gutter, how far from pole to pole. I could see his lips moving, and the numbers coming.

Mum ran up behind us. 'Dad!'

The cars had banked up a hundred metres. A young man got out. 'You gonna get him, or what?'

We figured it safe, and walked onto the road. The wind had picked up and it was hard to stay upright. Dirt, bits of wiper blades, even an old hub cap. 'Dad!' Mum tried again, but nothing.

Don, still in his greasy apron, stood in front of the cars and lifted his hand. We approached Pop and I put my arm around his shoulders. 'We gotta go in,' I said, but he pulled away and continued pacing.

Mum tried, but he did the same, this time pushing her away.

Motorists were sounding horns, and the sky cracked and opened and the rain started again. Light at first, but within seconds, crashing down.

Jen was determined. She took his arm, but he turned, glared at her and said, 'You can't have it.'

She waited, unsure.

'You can't. It's mine. I was given it. Forty-two paces, from lane to lane.'

She went around behind him and tried to push him onto the footpath. He lifted his hand, struck her across the face and she fell onto the road. He stared at his granddaughter and saw what he'd done. She spat, and it was blood. Don, the drivers, even the lady from the homebrew shop; they all saw it. Pop ran to the footpath, past the dealership, heading north along the main road. Jen, still holding her face, moved to safety. None of the motorists cared enough to pull over.

'I'll go,' I said.

'I'll come,' Mum insisted.

'No, go get the car. Pick us up.'

I ran through rain, dust, leaves. I knew where he'd be. Through blue metal, whipping up across the basketball stadium car park. I sprinted, and noticed him in the distance. 'Pop!'

He heard me above the storm, stopped and turned back, but continued shuffling.

In the primary school gate, of course.

I caught up, went into the milk shed and saw him panting, searching the ground for road and direction. 'That was a bit rough,' I said.

No response.

'You cold?'

I realised Mum and Jen wouldn't know where to look. But I couldn't leave him alone, contemplating lost reefs.

'We need to fix that fence,' I said.

'It'll wait.' But he still didn't look at me.

I was shivering, but he didn't look cold. White, bluey flesh and veins and bone that you could see through tissue.

'They got rid of my map,' he said.

'They always get rid of it. That's why you have to keep drawing it, Pop.'

'I haven't got any chalk.'

'We can come back tomorrow, and you can do it.'

He shook his head. 'Don't reckon.'

'Why?'

No reply. But it was obvious. 'What'd I do, Clem?'

'Happened quick, eh?'

'*What'd I do?*'

'You got confused, Pop.'

He searched the ground. 'I was counting it, Clem. Seemed like if you could work out how big ... seventy-two, three, four steps, and yer right.' He looked at me. 'I didn't break anything, did I?'

'No.'

'She'll be angry.'

'She'll understand.'

'Seventy-three, seventy-four ... you gotta keep usin' it, Clem. Gotta have a goal.'

'What's that?' I asked.

He seemed to settle with the thought. 'If we could find it, even if it was smaller than they say, it'd set you and Jen up for life.'

'The reef?'

'I been checking, and the price of gold just keeps goin' up and up. You'd have enough for your grandkids, and theirs. Imagine that.'

'Be good, Pop.'

'I know it's not seven miles long. Maybe it's seven feet, or inches, but what's it matter? It'd be enough to make you rich.'

I realised that Pop had to find this thing before the counting and pacing and confusion claimed his ability to reason.

'Don't know what I'm gonna say to her,' he said.

He was shivering. I could see his legs. Two long bones, strapped together, with the suspension shot, but functioning, in the same way Datsuns just kept going, no matter how much you punished them.

'Righto,' I said, deciding. 'We gotta stop talking and get organised.'

'What do you mean?'

'You're the one sayin' you left it too long. How you can't listen to your wife, or you'll never do nothin'.'

'You can't, Clem. Women just wanna hold you back. You're a pay cheque to them, that's all. They don't care about gold. They can't see the big picture.'

'Exactly. So, we need to decide.'

'Too right.' He sat up.

'We need to work out when.'

As he thought about this, the rain stopped. And as he thought some more, the wind died down. And finally, before he could pass judgement, the sun popped out from behind a cloud. 'What do you reckon, Clem?'

'I've just gone back to school. That gives me twelve, thirteen weeks before the next holidays. That'd be enough time to get ready, eh?'

'I reckon.'

I studied the concrete for clues. 'We got some stuff, haven't we?'

'Ground covers, that old tent, but I guess by then – when's that?'

'September.'

'We could sleep under the stars. But we might need swags, maps, cooking pots, grills … heapa stuff. But I gotta bit of cash, Clem. You know, rainy day.'

'Good.'

But it didn't feel so good. What if I'd started something I couldn't finish?

'We can get all that. We can go, Clem. I'll even get the Datsun ready.'

'The Datsun? Would it go that far?'

'Of course. Ends of the earth. Main thing is, if we say it, we gotta do it, don't we, Clem?'

'Of course. September.'

'September.' He was upright, animated, the warmth of his blood had coloured his face and body, and he was jumping about, happy (I guess) to be out of his counting cage. 'But one thing …'

'What's that?'

'We gotta keep it secret.'

'I agree.'

'Your mother would find some way to stop it. And imagine, even if it's just a chunk this big …' He held out a flat palm. 'I could end me days sailing the Whitsundays. I seen that in the *Post*. Beaches as white as … bloody white beaches. And these big mountains. Where they filmed *South Pacific*, cos it looked better than that.'

I saw how he glowed. That'd be worth the petrol, surely, I thought.

We shook on it and spent the next ten minutes discussing logistics. It was a three-week break. That was more than enough. And three, four hundred dollars, we'd be set to go. As long as we didn't tell Mum or Jen, which was sort of the same thing.

When we got home, Mum said, 'We gave up looking.'

Jen was talking funny, because Pop's fist had split the meaty bit on the inside of her mouth. But that was all. It'd heal, and as he came in, she said, 'Jesus, Pop, I'm gonna have to look out for you.'

He stood waiting, and she went to him, and he put his arm around her, and she stayed there, like she'd do in her pre-Feres days, when she thought ponytails were an okay hairdo, and Leif Garrett ruled the world.

'I'm just a silly old man,' he said.

And then I could see that she was crying. But she wouldn't lift her head, cos she didn't want us to see. I guess she was scared of losing him, too.

'Nothing broken?' he asked.

A hall with a Country Women's smell and an urn bubbling in the corner. A raised platform and a spot for the mayor and his deputy (I guessed) and someone taking notes. And in front of this, two long tables, a selection of councillors lined up like they mattered. There was a cricket-Gary, with burns and a wide tie, and a Head of English-Sue, with her hair up, studying her notes; a few middle-aged accountants and a strangely out-of-place Kiernan with ponytail hair and a tie-dye shirt.

We sat along a wall, waiting. Peter said, 'We're number two.'

Peter: in a suit he'd salvaged from the back of his wardrobe, yellowing shirt like some nineteenth-century frontispiece, and a woollen tie with a knot like a tumour. His pants were up to his ankles, revealing Menzies socks with crying diamonds and, although he'd polished his old leather shoes, they looked like something he'd worn to school during the Blitz. He smelt like mothballs. He'd combed his hair and beard but it was still Catweazle. He didn't make a convincing lawyer.

'What you gonna say?' I asked.

But he just smiled, like he was withholding a crucial piece of evidence.

There was a portrait of the Queen, and we were made to stand while someone read an oath. Then a sort of town crier said, All ye who have business here, make yeself known, and Peter smiled again, and I said, 'Is this for real?'

Proceedings began. A man named Moore claimed his neighbour had built a fence six inches onto his land, but the neighbour disagreed. Peter said, 'I hate this sort of shit.'

'Weren't you a lawyer?' Six years down the drain, I guessed. But if your heart wasn't in it. 'Did you have many cases?'

'A couple, but I lost them all.'

'You coulda made good money.'

'Les, that was what done it. I shouldn't say ...'

'Go on.'

'One night, there's Wendy at the door, and she comes in and says, I've decided.'

I waited while he decided. He couldn't tell me, of course, but guessed (I guessed) a boy needed to know.

'She says, He hit me again, and Mum puts her arm around her, and I ask her, You want to go to the police? She says yes. So off we go, and they throw Les out and the whole street sees and he screams and …'

A woman looked around and hushed us. Some sort of official (in a pantomime police suit) looked up and said, 'Quiet, please.'

Then, the fence saga went to mediation.

'So?' I asked.

'He was charged with assault.'

'She did that?'

'After some persuading … my persuading, which I never felt good about. But you can't be faint-tickered if yer gonna be a lawyer.'

It was a revelation. But one the street had chosen to forget.

'It'd have to go to court,' Peter said. 'So the day arrived and I went with her. We got out of the car, crossed the car park and she stopped. She holds my arm and says, I can't do it. I tell her they're waiting but she just turns and walks off. And that was it.'

'What was?'

'A week later he moved back in, and that was the last we ever heard of it. The last I ever practised.'

Peter's teeth were yellow. Too many smokes, as he sat listening to scratchy Chopin. It was like he'd perfected imperfection. Come to believe in the crustiness and mothball smell of all people. And having accepted this, set about living with it. There was no point changing yourself, your loved ones, your neighbours. People were, and always would be. You just had to get on with it, make the best of the worst, mow your lawn mechanically, encourage others, spread love like burley on polluted waters, seek the middle path (every day), plan for a future of simple, caring acts (including wiping your brother's arse).

'You never had no more problems with Les?' I asked.

He thought about this. 'He never mentioned it, Wendy never mentioned it and in time it was like it'd never happened.'

The fence saga was adjourned and the clerk summoned Mr Peter Donnellan, of number 33 Lanark Avenue, Gleneagles. He stood, said, 'Wish me luck,' and approached the stand. His singlet stuck out under his jacket. Val had told him to shave, but he'd refused. That'd be like accepting their authority. After all, who'd given these people the right to decide about cats?

'A few weeks ago,' he said, 'my mother, an elderly pensioner who receives an allowance to care for my disabled brother, was told, without notice, her cats were being removed. Then, in a display of bullying and intimidation, two council officers dragged her pets into the back of a van.'

The mayor, his offsider, the councillors, and assembled, seemed to be trying to work him out.

'I appear within the twenty-eight allotted days to ask for the return of these animals.'

The mayor was happy to take him on. 'According to my notes, Mr Donnellan, there were … twenty-three cats, a dozen or so kittens, although the officers suggested a lot got away.'

'That number seems excessive.'

'Well, it's what they collected.'

'Regardless, my mother (who's been suffering under a great deal of stress since the event) wasn't warned.'

The mayor was having none of it. 'Mr Donnellan, the council's guidelines on pets are quite clear. Maximum three cats, and these need to be kept inside, or within fences. The report suggests these animals had been roaming wild. There are children in your street?'

'Some.'

'And if I were one of their parents …?'

Peter opened a piece of paper. 'This photostat, of your bylaw, states—'

'Mr Donnellan, we've limited time. Three cats, under control, vaccinated, desexed, not roaming other people's yards, taking down their washing, piddling on porches. Should I continue?'

'Council make up their own rules and try to convince us—'

'Mr Donnellan! I realise you're a lawyer but tonight is about cats, and fences, not whether you think councils have the right to regulate what goes on in your street. You could always try the High Court. Failing that …' He took a drink of water.

Peter wasn't fazed. 'The point of this evening is to seek the return of six cats. She's been upset without them. She's had one for eighteen years.'

The mayor consulted his deputy. A few words, then he said, 'No.'

'Three cats then. We'll make sure they're desexed, registered, vaccinated.'

'Too late, Mr Donnellan. They've all been destroyed.'

Peter took a moment, then shook his head. 'All of them?'

'Our vet decided. Too wild. Full of disease. No one would want them, so it was best. We've carried the cost, although there was talk of sending your mother the bill for their destruction.'

'The bill?'

'We're not doing animals a favour by letting them run wild. I'm sure your mother cared for them, but I'm not sure she understood compassion.'

'Of course she did,' he said. 'More than anyone.'

'Well, from what I see here, and these photos.' And he offered to show him.

Peter had given up. His shoulders had dropped, and his belly popped out. He looked at the carpet, with its Gleneagles crest showing a dragon with a rabbit in its talons.

That was it. We returned to the car park and I drove Peter home in the 120Y (he did have a full licence, but hadn't driven for years). And all the way, he kept saying, 'How am I gonna tell her, Clem?'

I leaned a ladder against the tool shed, climbed up then slid my arse over the iron and sat on the edge. It was only three metres, but I supposed you could still break something. This had been my Kitty Hawk, where the supersonic action had begun. Six or seven, looking down, wondering if it was survivable, mustering the courage, then throwing myself off, rolling (cos that's how they did it on *CHiPS*). Now, it seemed higher. The thought of jumping, ridiculous. Obviously, something would get damaged. But I wondered if it was because I was less supple, or less brave?

I took out a blank page, flattened it on a clipboard and wrote:

The boy Arnold was scared of heights. And one day, decided there was only one way to fix the problem. So he climbed the shed and jumped off. He felt his knee collapse, and bend under his body, and at first there was no pain. But after a few seconds he became aware of what he'd done.

Pop came out of the shed with his hammer and nails, picked the iron sheets off the lawn and started hammering them back on.

'Want a hand?' I called.

He squinted to see me. 'What the hell you doin' up there?'

'Nothin' much.'

He hammered.

Barry Ruge was angry with himself. For letting his fence collapse (all three hundred metres of it), his house, too. First, the asbestos sheets, then the roof iron, the pipes, cables, then the frame, all of it. Until he and his family were sitting beside a pile of building junk. Him saying, 'I shoulda done something about it,' and his granddaughter, Cicely, saying, 'Listen, Pop, it wasn't your fault.'

He nailed on the second sheet, stood back, admired his efforts and came over. 'You slip off there, we're not driving you to hospital.'

'I've been jumping off for years.'

Soon the rubble sank into the earth. A sinkhole opened and swallowed the family. Barry called to Cicely. 'Listen, love, I was meaning to fix it. But I been busy. I'm sorry ...'

'D'you talk to your sister?' he asked.

'She's okay.'

'Explain that ...' But he just wandered into the house, taking his hammer. Something must've needed fixing. I could see over the fence into number 29. Curtis, climbing the ladder to his cubby house, emerging, hiding something.

This is how it happened. Arnold's neighbour, Colin, had been given a chicken. He'd bought feed, and looked after it. It had put on weight. Then, one day, he noticed a strange thing. The chicken had the ability to walk backwards. He didn't know if this was normal behaviour, so he borrowed a book from the library, but it didn't say anything about chicken locomotion. So, he guessed he was on to something. He showed him mum, but she didn't care, his father, but he was busy welding, his brother, Chopper, but he was busy counting his smokes, so he called Channel Seven.

Curtis came down the steps, crossed the yard and stopped. He was listening for voices inside.

'Dickbrain!' I called.

He saw me, then ran through his own personal gorse, lifted the fence iron and came into our yard. Across it, up the ladder, and sat beside me. 'Good gear.' He showed me the smoke, and let me smell it. 'Anyone around?'

'Inside.'

He lit it, smoked it, offered me a go, sat back and said, 'You used to jump off here.'

'You used to jump from the cubby. That's higher.'

He noticed my new chapter. 'What's that?'

'My novel.'

'Masharin'd love to get her hands on that.' He smoked, offered it to me, but changed his mind. 'And you could get your hands on her.'

'I was writing about your chicken. That day when *Current Affair* came.'

He laid back, laughing. 'Star for a day.'

'That chicken never walked backwards.'

'It chose its moments.'

'Not when the camera was rolling.'

Having spoken to the producer, Colin promised his bird was unique.
A film crew was dispatched, set up in his yard, and waited. The beast
was presented, a bell rung (for this, Colin promised, was its cue), but
the chicken walked forwards. Colin said, Wait, and they waited. Bell.
Forwards. Colin held the chicken and walked it backwards, but when
he released it, it walked forwards. The reporter said, Does it really
walk backwards? Yes. Plenty of times. It's like it knows you're here.

'See, full of shit,' I said.

He sat up, but swayed in the breeze. 'I know I make shit up, but I swear, it walked backwards.'

So the crew packed up and left. But it wasn't the disaster it promised.
That night, we all sat around Colin's telly, and the story ran, and
when they showed the chicken it walked backwards. Perhaps people
couldn't see the trees swaying backwards, or the smoke blowing the
wrong way, or the washing on the line acting strangely. Next day,
at school, Colin was dragged up at assembly, and everyone applauded
and some believed he did have a backwards-walking chicken. But
only some.

'Whatever happened to it?' I asked.

'Dad chopped off its head.'

We watched as John came out, climbed the cubby steps and went inside, then emerged, calling, 'Curtis, you little cunt.'

'Shit,' he said. Loud enough for John to hear. Who looked over, and called, 'Where is it?'

Curtis showed him the stub, and smiled.

'I'll fuckin' kill yer.'

Curtis went to give him the finger, over-balanced and fell. He rolled a few times and sat up, unaware (it seemed) where he was. John was coming across the gorse, towards the flapping iron. Now, as Mr Fantastic, I had to act. I shuffled forward, closed my eyes and jumped.

It wasn't that far. No more than it used to be. I gathered the Thing, helped him up, back to the fence, pulled back Pop's newly repaired iron, and helped him through. We ran into the lane, and the voice followed us. 'Carn here, you little fuck!'

Past Don's dunny, down the lane, around the corner and into the car yard.

'Ssh!' I said, settling Curtis against a Falcon wheel (One Time Owner, One-Off Price $2999).

We waited.

'Curtis!'

He giggled. I heard footsteps between the new and used cars.

'Too gutless to show yourself?' John called.

I could smell fresh rubber. And the cars were particularly clean. Little plastic flags flapped in the breeze. Prayers, although this was no time for devotion.

'Gutless.'

Again, footsteps. I grabbed his arm, moved him again, settled him beside (nearly under) an exhaust pipe.

'You gotta come home sometime.'

Then we listened as a salesman approached John and said, 'Are you looking for something?'

'No.'

And John turned, and walked back down the lane that led to our homes.

Then the same man was standing above us. 'What are you two after?'

'Nothing,' I said. 'My friend here felt a bit sick.'

We stood, crossed the road to Kentucky Fried Chicken, pretended to be cars and went through the drive-through. The girl said, 'We only serve cars,' and Curtis said, 'Broom, broom, I'm a Mercedes-Benz.'

She said, 'Fuck off.'

He said, 'Two-piece feed, but I don't want any wings.'

We walked around the block. Curtis said, 'I can't go home,' and I said, 'You're gonna have to,' and he said, 'Come in with me, will yer?' and I said, 'No fucking way.'

Another unproductive day. My novel, on the tool shed roof,

blowing away in the afternoon breeze, down the greasy lane, onto North East Road, where it was (fittingly) run over.

As we walked I said, 'It didn't walk backwards.'

'It did. I don't believe in God, but I believe in the backwards-walking chicken, because I've seen it, and I know it's real.'

Jen guessed it might make a nice sideline, maybe even a session after a perm. But she had to practise, sound convincing, persuade punters to part with five dollars for a ten-minute reading. To me, this seemed rich. I mean, nineteen-year-old buys a pack of tarot cards, attempts some improvisations and people actually believe her? But, but (and she made a fair point) it wasn't about logic, it was about the suspension of disbelief. Like writing novels, she said, but I said that was an entirely different thing.

She'd spread a rug on the dining room table, scattered a few crystals (they'd come in the same starter pack), rinsed the colour from her hands and sat waiting.

'Go on,' I said.

She shuffled.

Pop, sitting on the lounge, caught up in his own wheel of fortune, said, 'What a loada rot.'

'Is not,' Jen replied.

'It's possible,' I said, in defence of my sister's new hobby, 'that if people *want* to believe, and you help them—'

'Doesn't make it right.' The wheel spun, and he willed it (I guessed) to stop on the Bali holiday. But it was only a vacuum cleaner.

Jen laid out three cards and took a moment to study them. 'I can see something coming ... something you've been wanting for a long time.'

'That's a safe bet,' I said. 'Everyone wants something. Shouldn't you be more specific?'

'Let me finish. The Sun means ... *shit*.' She consulted the legend that had come with the box. 'Optimism, expansion, moving forward.'

I tried to encourage her. 'Year Twelve?'

'Perhaps.'

'Good results?'

'Yes, that's what it means. Good results.'

'Or maybe the novel?'

'Yes, that too.' She studied the second card. 'The Fool: a spirit in search of experience, knowledge. See, it does work.'

I didn't want to say anything. 'I suppose I am in search of experience.'

She held her hands above the cards. 'I can see you getting something you want.'

'What?'

'It's complex. You have to tune into the voices.'

'Whose?'

'I don't fucking know.'

Pop: 'Language!'

'I can see you jumping around, because you've won something.'

I guessed she was doing okay. 'I suppose you'll have to do it a lot to get good.'

'What?'

'The acting.'

'I'm not acting.'

'But you don't actually *see* me jumping about?'

The third card. 'Wheel of Fortune.'

'Hey, Pop,' I called, 'it's Burgo.'

'Take it seriously,' Jen said. 'The Wheel of Fortune is destiny.' She checked the sheet, rubbed a crystal and tried her hardest to stay professional. 'So if you put them together: you have a journey, it will end well, there are good things ahead.'

'Thank god for that.' I noticed the sheet: 'What if you hada pulled Death, or the Hanged Man?'

'I took them out.'

'Why?'

'That's what the instructions say, until you get good. You wouldn't want to tell someone you can see their death and then it actually happened.'

'It seems rather convenient. I mean, if the spirits are making you choose a card, cos that's someone's destiny, and there are a couple missing …'

An ad started and Pop was out to the kitchen, topping up his Passiona, searching for chips, returning so he didn't miss a moment of Adriana Xenides.

Then Curtis was at the door, inside, sitting beside me, looking at my cards. Jen knew that tarot was already on his list of hates.

But he said, 'Cool.' (I knew it was one of his strategies.)

'Jen wants to start a stall,' I said.

Pop settled in before the wheel returned.

Curtis said, 'I think it's intriguing, how people do this.'

Jen just waited.

'I mean, you must have to practise … astral travelling?'

'The instructions say you should relax, shut out all thoughts and ask, Is there anyone there?'

'Do they answer?'

'I'm hearing something, but it's early days.'

Pop farted. We all laughed.

Curtis was good. He said, 'If you need practice, I wouldn't mind knowing what's coming.'

She shuffled her cards, spread them out and picked three.

Pop said, 'Her hair colour's funny.

'Who?' I asked.

'Adriana. No one has purple hair.'

I checked. 'It's auburn.'

'Purple.'

Purple it was. Jen was communicating. I sat waiting.

'So, Curtis, this one here, it's the Tower.'

'What's that mean?'

She checked. 'Chaos. Crisis. See, cannonballs, fire.'

'That doesn't sound good.'

'Wait. This one here, the Moon. Tension, deception.'

He shrugged, checked out Baby Burgess and said, 'I think I'd rather try that.'

'Wait … the Chariot. Honour and willpower. They're telling me you'll face a struggle, and this will cause you stress, but in the end you'll win out.'

He grinned, so she retrieved her cards. 'When yer ready to take it seriously.'

'*I am.*'

Pop applauded. Someone had won the car. There was confetti, music, a husband running down to embrace his wife. Burgo smoothed his mo and Adriana smiled, nicely. 'Good on 'em,' Pop said. 'I like it when a worker wins.'

Curtis said to Jen, 'You couldn't say what's gonna happen to John, could you?'

Pop turned. 'He's got a job, hasn't he? He'll come good. Why do you need cards to tell you that?'

Reluctantly, Jen laid out three cards and studied them.

'Them things are giving me the shits,' Pop said.

Jen wasn't listening. 'Justice. But I don't know if that means he'll find it, or suffer it. Then here, the Devil.'

'Jen!'

'And …'

We looked. A man, hanging by a rope by his foot.

'The Hanged Man.'

'I thought you'd taken it out?' I said.

'I thought I did.'

Pop jumped from his chair, took four long strides and swiped the cards. 'Life's bad enough without all this shit. You should know better, Clem.' He walked from the room, the house. We stood at the front window and watched. He turned into number 29. Down the drive, meeting John on his way out.

'It's all your fault,' Jen said to me.

Me and Curtis left the house, jumped the fence and hid behind an awning. We heard Pop say, 'Well?'

And John. 'What?'

'Don't you what me. They come and take you away and not so much as an explanation.'

'I didn't know you wanted one.'

Silence, as we imagined.

'Well?'

'What, you think I was …?'

A long pause. We could hear Pop's laboured breathing.

'Not a word. After what I done.'

'They wanted to talk to me about Alan. They've got him for knockin' over a petrol station. They thought he mighta hidden the stuff at our place. I brought them back, they looked through my room … that's all.'

Pop was confused, again. 'What would Harry think?'

'I don't know. I didn't do anything, Doug.'

'I tell you, John, if you start up again I'll make sure he knows. Then it's out the front door.'

There was a figure in the doorway, then Anne's voice. 'What's wrong, Doug?'

Pop tried a few words, but they didn't work. 'I's just seein' … about all that business.'

Now, maybe, she looked at John. He said, 'I think Doug's a bit confused.'

'You okay, Doug?' she asked.

'Just a bit shocked,' he managed. 'When I saw them coppers in me shed.'

'That was nothing,' she said. 'They come and hada look around and I made them a cuppa, and they were happy. This mate of his, this Alan, he's still muckin' up. But John's stayin' clear of him, aren't yer?'

And he agreed with her. But only for Pop's sake. He said, 'Thanks, Mum, I can handle it.'

'I only thought—'

'Thanks!'

But still, she said, 'Gary's nearly out of the shower. Wanna come in for a beer?'

'No!' John shouted. 'Go away.'

So she must've gone in.

'That's no way to talk to yer mum,' Pop said.

I tapped Curtis's shoulder and we ran across the lawn, back over the fence, to the six o'clock news.

As we sat waiting for Pop, Curtis said, 'I wouldn't be so sure.'

'What?'

'Alan. He came over the other day when Dad was out, and John told me to keep my mouth shut.' He was digging his heel into our old Berber. Maybe he'd decided the cards were right.

'She found it and hid it,' Pop said.

I stopped in front of the dehydrated meals: curry chicken, stroganoff, bushman's stew (whatever that was). 'Coupla these?'

'Chuck 'em in.'

One of each, and we continued. A billy, lightweight pots and pans. 'Couldn't we take 'em from the kitchen?'

'Then your mother'd know.' He tapped his nose. 'Anyway, weeks passed, and I said, I want it back.'

'You couldn't find it?'

'Na. She was good at hiding things, your nan. After she died, we found six hundred quid under the wardrobe. I'd been gettin' me socks outa there for years.'

Then we discussed tents. I convinced him we'd need one. He wanted dome, I said hiking. He said touring, I suggested a tarp, strung between trees, but he said *Null-ar-bor*. So we decided to hold off. He reckoned Gary might have one, but he couldn't ask him yet, because Anne'd probably get it out of him and she'd tell Mum and that'd be the end of everything.

'I demanded it back. I said, You give it to me or I'll go, then she laughed. I can still remember her laughing.'

We stopped to consider self-inflatable, air, foam, sleeping bags, or swags. Pop insisted on the latter, but I argued cost, seeing how we were only going to use them for a few nights, perhaps a week. He said, 'You're gonna be tired, and you need a decent sleep.'

'What you gonna do with them, after?'

'*After* we'll be rich, won't we?'

I didn't want to say it. I deposited them in the trolley with the mozzie candles and torch batteries.

'She still wouldn't hand it over. Said she'd chucked it. I tipped out the rubbish and started searching and she appeared and I said, Come on. Then she was on her knees helping.'

Gas bottle and a portable stove. I said, 'How we gonna get this lot in the Datsun?'

'You'd be surprised what you can get in a Datsun.'

Lantern, and mantles.

'She's goin' through old chicken carcasses and yoghurt and …' He stopped to remember, barely suppressing a smile. 'I found it, held it up and said, You coulda saved us both a lotta trouble. I wiped it clean, dried it and found the spot, in the shed, where I knew she'd never look – women never do – in a toolbox.'

We made our way to the checkout, our trolley overflowing with camping goods. Pop said, 'This'll do for now.'

We paid and made our way to the car. I said, 'You'll never get it all in,' and he said, 'Faith, child.'

He filled the back seat, the boot, passenger floor well, parcel shelf. But we were still a swag short. 'See,' I said. 'And this isn't everything.'

'Yes, but we'll repack it, and there won't be any boxes.'

You couldn't argue. He forced the final swag in, compressing the rest as it groaned and crushed, but yielded. Then he slammed the door and said, 'See, plenty of room.'

He pulled out of the car park, onto the road, without looking. Someone let us have it, of course, and I said, 'Maybe I could practise?'

'Not with a car full of gear.'

He changed lanes without indicating. 'Shouldn't you use your blinker?' I asked.

'What d'you reckon about John?'

'What d'you mean?'

'Reckon he's up to something?'

'I dunno.'

He slowed, indicated and turned right. The camping mountain shifted. 'I reckon he's come good. It's the job, see. Given him something to look forward to.'

'Perhaps.'

'What's that mean?'

'It's hard to believe ...'

'Bullshit.'

'Well, maybe you're right.'

It was a long, straight stretch. Nothing much could go wrong.

'You gotta have a bita faith, don't you?' Pop said. 'I coulda just given up on that map, but I'm not gonna. And you wait, I'll be proved right.'

'I hope.'

He gave me his doubtful look. 'But you don't reckon?'

'Look!' I called. He'd drifted across the road, and braked, but not soon enough. He knocked the back tyre of a bike and a boy went flying across the nature strip, onto the footpath.

'Fuck!' he said. 'You distracted me.'

Me? But I didn't say a word.

He pulled over, hobbled back and asked, 'You alright?'

The boy was already up, brushing himself off, examining a skinned knee. 'You just about killed me.'

'I did not.'

'I was on the side. Couldn'ta been further.'

'I know,' Pop said. He took his wallet, found a twenty and handed it to him. 'Tell yer mum I'm sorry.'

The boy's eyes lit up, and he felt the paper, smelt it, and shoved it in his pocket. 'Thanks, mister.' Then he was on his bike, and gone.

'I reckon I oughta drive,' I said.

Pop watched the traffic, then said, 'Okay. But just cos you need the practice.'

I stuck the plates to the window and we set off. The old girl purred, or popped, and slid along the road, ignoring the Commodores and Falcons roaring past. 'You really reckon she'll go that far?' I asked.

'Easy. Don't forget, I fit new suspension. She can take a loada weight.'

'But four cylinders?'

'Don't worry. Me and Nan drove to Sydney in a 510 sedan. You remember that one?'

'Sort of.' Although I didn't. He'd never mentioned a 510.

'Anyway,' he said, 'they're long roads, and you get tired, so you gotta share the driving. I'll be relying on you, Clem.'

He stared at the dehydrated food on the floor. I knew what he was thinking: If we'd ever go, or whether all these props were more of the same: an expedition into imagination.

'It all keeps going, doesn't it?' he said.

'What's that?'

'*It keeps going.*'

Maybe he meant the Datsun, but I suspected not. Maybe his body (he reckoned he had a decent ticker, and he'd make it to ninety, like his mum and dad).

'What does?' I asked.

'Even if …' Then he said, 'I can't wait for that first night sleepin' out under the stars. I can just smell the grass, can't you?'

'Definitely.'

'And billy tea. That's the best of all. So hot you can't drink it. With the stars, millions of them, taking the heat.'

I didn't need to say anything.

'It'll be great, Clem. You wait.' He looked out the window. 'Later, when I'm … bad, you gotta make sure yer mother puts me somewhere.'

'Where?'

'A nursing home. I don't want yers thinking I should be at home, if all of youse have gotta spend yer time lookin' after me. You gotta get on with things, Clem.'

I stopped at a light. 'You'll be okay, Pop.'

'I'd be happy in a little room somewhere, maybe with the telly in the corner, watchin' Burgo. That'd do me, Clem.'

I turned into 31 and braked hard. Ernie and Fi-Fi stood in front of the car. I wound down the window, popped my head out and said, 'Sorry, Ernie.' I wondered if he was heading back from the Windsor, but he wasn't pissed, so he couldn't have been. He came to my window and said, 'How's the driving going?'

'Good.'

He looked across. 'How are yer, Doug?'

'I'm alright. Just about squashed yer dog.'

'She's okay. Better without them cats, isn't it?'

'I guess.'

Ernie looked in the back seat. 'What, you goin' camping?'

'No,' Pop shot back. 'It's nothin', right? Nothin'.'

Ernie shrugged. 'Lotta nothin'.'

'It's for a mate.'

'Reckon it'd be nice to go camping, if anyone's goin'.'

'No one's goin'.'

'Good-o.' And he pulled at Fi-Fi, and retreated.

'Prick of a man,' Pop said. 'Go on, get in, before your mother gets home.'

I backed the car up to the shed, and helped Pop unload our stash onto the shelves he'd cleared especially. Then we covered the lot with tarps and piled carburettors and exhaust pipes and bags of fertiliser on top of it all.

Then he stood back and said, 'Not a word.'

'Not a word,' I repeated.

We left the shed and, this time, he locked the door.

Despite not having been to the races for years, Pop seemed more concerned about the dollar coin. 'How the hell are you meant to hold on to it?' A note was real, reliable, big; a coin was small, annoying, easily lost under Don's freezer. He placed the coins in his pocket. 'Enough to pull yer pants down.'

Mum laughed. 'I can just see 'em down round yer ankles.'

Everything was changing, too quickly. The national anthem – a disgrace, Pop had said, the first time he'd heard it, sitting watching the news. *Girt by sea*. 'What the fuck's that mean?'

'Surrounded by sea,' I'd explained.

'Stupid. Everyone likes a bit of a sing-song for the Queen.'

On and on. Green and gold, who made them our national colours? Bob Hawke? A piss-head for Prime Minister. At least Lanark Avenue stayed the same. Everyone too poor to move out.

'Latin Hero,' he said.

Mum studied the form. 'Six dollars a win. What about Lustre Man? Cahill's a good jockey, isn't he?'

'No. Latin Hero. Chondra, perhaps. Six-fifty a win, two-twenty a place. What do you think?'

'Your money.'

So he took the form, and studied it.

I watched the jockeys getting ready, saddling their horses, mounting, prancing about. I, and we, hadn't been to the races for years. Pop had hinted, but Mum had always been too busy. Then, 'What d'you say we go tomorrow, Dad?'

'Y' reckon?'

'You want to?'

'I guess so.'

Which was his way of saying *absolutely*. The races had been a habit, but Nan had broken him of that, too. He'd had a part-share in a horse (Tonto's Pride, the photo still hanging in his room beside Skeffington), but it'd broken a leg. He often told me about it: him and a mate watching from the grandstand, the fall, the sheet, the little pop of the rifle, and all his racing dreams finished.

The gate opened and the horses were led out. Pop had itchy fingers and a pocket full of coins. He said to Mum, 'Ten bucks, what d'you reckon?'

'It's up to you.'

Because that's why she'd brought him: for the memories (of losing, even). He turned to me and said, 'Carn.'

We walked past old men in tweedy jackets, club ties and braces, yellow-tipped fingers and glowing rollies. Wives, of course, studying the hatched, matched, dispatched, and celebrity photos, before taking up their knitting. A few kids, but most of them were in the compound, running around the betting ring, picking up handfuls of stubs and throwing them at each other.

Pop stood in front of Clarry Grimshaw and studied the odds.

'If you win, you could save us the trip north,' I said.

'Save us? But you wanna go, don't you?'

'Of course.'

'But yer right, a bita cash would come in useful. We could buy a Commodore. V8. Be there in no time.' But he stuck to the ponies. 'Right, what'd I say?'

'Latin Hero.'

He got Grimshaw's attention, and gave him fifty dollars, for a place.

'Fifty?' I said.

'You watch. He won't win, but he's solid.'

He led me to the bar: two schooners and a can of Coke. For the first time, he used dollar coins. As we headed back he said, 'Was a time there'd be two thousand men here. Now, look, five hundred, perhaps. And the spirit's gone out of the place.'

'More for people to do these days.'

'Less. Just more of it. That's the way of the world. And don't tell yer mother I put fifty bucks on her. Can you imagine? Say it was five, ten.'

He didn't wait for me to agree, because he knew I would. *Bonis omnia bona*. It'd been years since he'd come to the races, and he'd done a shitload of good. So, now he'd cash in his ticket. That's how it felt. And there was proof: Jen's cards. She'd sat him down the previous evening, cleared his sahasrara chakra and selected the Sun (optimism), Magician (talent) and, of course, Wheel of Fortune (destiny). Put together, this could only mean one thing.

We returned and Mum said she didn't want a schooner, she'd never liked beer, you know that, Dad, so he said, Clem can have it, and she said, He's too young, and he said, What, a few months? He handed it to me and waited for me to drink it. Mum just gave me her don't-you-dare look.

'Stuckey,' Pop said.

'Who?' Mum asked.

'Stuckey, the Bishop, he owned racehorses, dozens of them. Then they made him bishop and people were saying he should sell them. But he wouldn't. Every Sunday he'd get up and talk about the evils of money … but he had his own stable.'

I smelt it, tasted it, but Mum glared at me. It wouldn't be my first. Me and Curtis, up the cubby house with a couple from Gary's beer fridge. Nice and cold, with a smoke, and a shot of Anne's brandy from a jar.

Pop wasn't finished with the Catholics. 'He had prostitutes.'

'He did not,' Mum said.

'He did. His cook told the newspapers. She always saw them there. Some nights two at a time.'

It seemed like a decent story. When it came to Catholics, and the truth, you had to forgive him. I lifted the glass and Mum said, 'Don't you dare.'

Pop said, 'Let him go.'

'We don't need an alcoholic in the family.'

Pop finished his; took mine. 'You can't baby them, Fay.'

The horses waited for the starter. Lights, and they were off. Latin Hero sprinted, broke free, and within a few seconds had two lengths on Enduro.

'Go, you beautiful thing,' Pop said. The beer was spilling and Mum took it and drank it, looking at me as if to say, If this is what it takes.

Latin Hero was three lengths ahead, two, one, then back in the pack, but then surged, broke free again. Pop said, 'See, what did I tell you?'

Mum leaned over and asked, 'How much did he put on it?'

'Ten bucks.'

Cheers, and feet on the old floorboards. 'Beautiful!' Pop called, before sitting and saying, 'I still got it.'

'It didn't win,' Mum said.

'I backed it for a place.' And he was off, down the steps, after his money.

Mum just smiled, content.

'Good idea,' I said.

'What?'

'To bring him.'

'Yes.' She folded her arms, like it was a job well done. 'He used to bring me when I was a kid. I'd just hang around the stables all day imagining I was Elizabeth Taylor.'

'Would he win?'

'Na. He always had his dreams, and dramas. But nothin' real.'

The map, that's real, isn't it?, I wanted to say.

'Then he'd come with …'

Dad. I knew.

'With Ernie. For all the stuff *he* goes on about, he's happy to gamble.'

'Val said you got rid of Dad.'

She sat staring at nothing. 'I didn't get rid of him.' She drank the beer Pop had left. 'There's only so much you should put up with. But he wasn't a bad man, Clem. I won't have you thinkin' that. Val didn't say that?'

'No.'

'He was just easily led.'

The horses came back to the mounting yard.

'He was still your father. Some just stick around longer than others. Look at Val, and Sid. One minute he was there …'

'When was the last time you heard from him?'

But I was intruding, and she wasn't willing. 'Just don't tell Jen. She likes things the way they are.'

I liked the races. If life was a backwards-walking chicken, and only you could see it, then you had to prove your faith. Hand over the cash, wait for your beastie to come good, and if it didn't, continue to believe that tomorrow it would. I loved the smell of cheap cologne and talc and the way they made perfume out of body odour. The men, who hadn't shaved since Friday morning, with gold garters on their shirt sleeves. And polished shoes, because the races were like church, and you had to look the part. The voices and placings and crappy music and some kid calling out for Simon to tell Mum that Dad was gonna be late, and the way you could hear and feel the horses' weight through the earth, into the grandstand.

Mum said, 'Your dad helped Pop buy his horse.'

'Really?'

'But that was before it broke its leg.'

Pop half-ran up the stairs. Damn it, I thought. There was gonna be more. 'Bloody beautiful,' he said, alive, glowing.

'So, what did you make with yer ten dollars?' Mum asked.

'*Nothin*'.'

'Nothing?'

'I invested the lot on the next race.'

'Dad!'

'It's money in the bank.' He showed her the form. 'Classy Chloe. John Frew, trainer. He works his horses, and they win. Twelve-sixty a win, three-ninety a place, either way.' He waited for us to declare him a genius, but Mum said, 'How much did you win?'

'Don't worry about that. Just thinka the money. Coupla thousand of them gold coins.'

Driving home, Mum said, 'Fifty bucks. A week's shopping.'

Pop said, 'You never know – win or place. But if you wanna go back next Saturday?'

I waited at a light. 'I can drive you, Pop.'

But Mum said, 'Maybe it wasn't such a good idea.'

The map was missing, gone from its usual hiding spot (and with the shed locked). Pop had looked everywhere. 'I mighta had it in me pocket, and it mighta dropped out.'

'Where?'

'If I knew I'd look, wouldn't I?'

He searched gaps in the shelves, lifting the tarp to see if it was under the camping gear. 'Hold on … *hold on*.' He checked the lock on the door, turned to the louvred windows, fiddled with them. 'Loose.'

'What?'

'Someone coulda removed them, got in, taken the map, replaced them.'

I checked. They seemed okay. There were even cobwebs.

'Or …' He studied the roof iron, the walls. 'You could remove a sheet, and replace it.'

'Someone's got in?'

'*John*. Remember, he saw the map?'

'He wouldn't steal that. Cash, or ciggies.'

He was taken by the idea. 'No one else knows.'

It didn't make sense. 'Pop, I reckon you left it somewhere.'

'I check every day. You and him are the only ones who know. Unless yer mother made you destroy it?'

I followed him out of the shed, down the drive, the street, towards the Burrells'. There was a paddy wagon in their drive. 'See, he's in trouble,' he said.

'You don't know.'

He whispered, 'Unless it's Gary?'

'Let's go home.'

Too late. Two officers brought John out in handcuffs. He didn't resist. Anne followed, saying, 'Can't he at least pack some clothes?'

'You can bring 'em in, missus.'

Pop walked the last few steps to the drive, and stopped the policemen. 'What's going on?'

They walked around him. One opened the back door and tried to push John in.

John said, 'It's not me, Doug. Alan's stolen some stuff, and said I was with him. But I wasn't.'

Pop seemed confused. But he said to the coppers, 'Aren't you meant to have some sort of evidence?'

They asked him to move; he refused.

'You can't just take people away. It's not Russia. He says he wasn't there, you don't have no evidence, so how can you arrest him?'

'That's it,' Anne said. 'It's all down to that little crim. He lies about everything.'

'You'll need to undo these,' Pop said, indicating the handcuffs. 'And go away and get some evidence, *then* come back.'

I noticed Curtis at the front window – stony-faced, refusing to acknowledge me, or anything going on.

Pop put himself between the policeman and the door. 'We got a lawyer next door. You can just wait. I'll go get him.'

The policeman tried to put John in, but Pop shouldered him, and the cop said, 'You do that again, you're in there too. Got it?'

'He's starting a new job,' Pop said.

Didn't he take your map? I wanted to ask. But he'd changed his mind. The stripes and uniforms and blue lights brought out the best in him.

'What'd he say?' Pop asked John as he was pushed in and the door closed and locked.

'You can't take him,' Anne pleaded. 'He's told you what he's done.'

'I's coming to tell you,' Pop said to him. 'Harry's got a start date. August ten.'

The car grumbled, and filled the air with lead.

'John?'

Anne grasped the back door, and tried to open it. 'We'll have you out in a jiff.'

'August ten,' Pop said. 'I'll tell him. Don't worry about this little prick. We'll sort him out.'

Curtis had gone, but the curtain was still moving. The car drove off, *hmphed* onto the road and cruised the length of Lanark II. Anne turned to Pop and said, 'When it was done, he was at home. They said the third, but he was with us, Doug.'

We went home and Pop returned to the shed to search for the map. I sat in his chair, put on the telly and watched football. It made as much sense as anything. I picked up the *TV Times*, opened it to Sunday and saw the map, flattened between the pages. The highway, the side roads, the cross. 'Pop, I got it!' I called.

Val stood on a stool and attempted to pick small, shrivelled mandarins. She was sure Mum would want them. I held a plastic bag, and she dropped them in. 'Tell her there's plenty where these come from.'

She was still in her nightie, but often was until lunch, or early afternoon. Dressing-gown open, revealing an old age of broken capillaries. Slippers, too, with flapping soles.

'Keep some for yerself,' I said.

'The boys don't eat them.' Plop, as the scrotal fruit dropped into the bag. 'Peter used to throw them at David. I'd come out, callin' at them ...' She stopped and her eyes settled on something near the house. '*Jesus*.'

'What is it?' I asked.

She tumbled, corrected herself and ran towards the back step with the mandarins. Kneeling down, she looked under the house. 'I've never seen him before.'

I knelt beside her and searched the musty darkness. There was railing all around but she pulled it back and said, 'Carn, kitty.'

'Not one of yours?'

'Never seen him. White, with a marbled head.'

I heard a squeak.

'I can see him,' she said. 'Little boy cat ... can you see him, Clem?'

I couldn't, but she had special cat sight.

'Carn, darling.' She ran inside, emerged with a biscuit, knelt and tried again. 'It's only about a metre. You could just about fit under, Clem.'

Val's house? But what could I say? I laid down and eased my head under the floor. It smelt like old stew and gas, or the throne after one of Pop's sessions. I wriggled under, and felt Val pushing me. Soon I was within reach, got him around the neck and started wriggling out. Moments later I emerged into the light.

'Isn't he a gem?' she said, taking him, kissing him on the head. The cat didn't fight her. He knew he was on to a good thing.

We went in – cat, mandarins and me – and she filled a saucer of milk, and cut fritz from a roll and watched him eat.

'*Providence*,' she whispered.

'How's that?' I asked.

'He takes away and He gives.'

'What you gonna do with him?'

She gave me a look. 'He's a bit thin, but we can feed him up.'

I thought of Ernie and Pop and the street and the council, and everyone, really. I could smell cat shit on my shirt. Stale fat. David came in, pulled up to the table and said, 'Where's she come from?'

'*He*,' Val corrected. 'He was under the house.'

David studied him. 'All on again, eh?' And smiled.

'No,' Val said. 'This one's special. He was sent. So we gotta protect him.'

'How?' I asked.

'Keep him in the house, don't let Ernie see, whatever happens.' She picked him up, settled him in the crook of her arm and started stroking him. Soon, he was half-asleep.

Dave said, 'Doug still teaching you to drive, Clem?'

'He's trying.'

And Val said, 'Imagine. You gettin' yer licence. I's only just changing yer nappy.'

'Few years ago,' I said.

'Not when yer our age, eh, David?' She held the cat's head so it couldn't help but look at her. 'I reckon I'll call yer Providence.'

'That's got a nice ring,' I said.

Then to continue the naming, she said, 'I used to bath you and Jen. If yer mum was late home, and sometimes Doug was down the pub with Ernie. Tip water on yer head … and you had them little bum dimples, didn't he, David?'

But he just nodded.

'Bit of a shame.' She picked out a mandarin, examined it, and seemed pleased. 'What you gonna do next year?'

'Uni, perhaps.'

'Be good if you did law, eh, Davo?'

'Yeah.'

'You interested in that?'

'Perhaps. Maybe arts. Writing. I like books.'

'That'd be alright too.' She nodded, and David followed suit. 'Dickens is the go, eh?'

'*David Copperfield*?' I asked.

'That's a good one.' She checked that Providence was real. Examined his teeth, and eyes, then mine. 'Peter reckons you're writin' your own book?'

'It's just a first go.'

'Reckons it's about all of us.'

'Sort of.'

I couldn't help but think of the passage I'd just finished. Annie Douglas, pushing her disabled son down the street, stopping in front of Chris Knowlson's house.

Nice music, Mr Knowlson.
Kamahl. He's my favourite. What about you, Mrs Douglas?
Nat Cole. Nice and smooth.

That's how they'd start off, anyway. Then there'd be issues over barking dogs, and Chris would call the council, and they'd send someone around, and it'd get worse.

'Mrs Masharin reckons you should write about what you know.'

'Well, that's easy, you know us. There's nothin' you could say that'd upset us.'

You and yer dogs, Mrs Douglas. Keep me up all night.
I keep them inside. You're determined to make trouble.

'I can think of plenty to put in,' Val said, sitting forward. 'Remember that sports day, when David and Peter came along?'

I could. Father and son day. Pop had promised to come, but had fallen sick (not that it'd stopped him working in the shed). So, Mum'd asked the brothers, and they'd agreed. They'd walked me to school, and signed up for the 200 metres and longest kick. David wasn't so bad, but when Peter joined the other dads for the shot-put … Business shorts and long socks and sandals, an early Catweazle beard that had already yellowed around the mouth from the smokes. As I called, Carn, Peter.

And Trevor Smith: Why d'you call your dad Peter?

He's my neighbour.

Funny sort of neighbour. Looks like he's been smoking something.

He'd come last, of course, because all the other dads had beefsteak legs and thunder thighs and wore shorts way too small. But as we walked home I said, Thanks for taking me.

No worries, Clem. Any time. Me and Dave know what it's like.

'So you gonna put that in?' Val asked.

'Don't know yet.'

'Main thing is, have a bita yer mum, and Pop. They did most for you. What's it called?'

'*This Excellent Machine.*'

'Right. What's the machine?'

'You know, you go in one end and come out the other … different.'

'That's for sure.' She pointed to a black-and-white photo of a young woman and man. 'Me and Sid, many years ago. You wouldn't recognise me now, eh?'

'I can still see you.'

'And David, there.' She indicated a boy with a dangerous grin. 'Main thing is, don't put *him* in it.' Pointing to number 35. 'He's a horror. Woulda been good livin' here, if not for him.'

Providence was almost snoring.

She gathered her nightie in her lap and said, 'Coupla cats never hurt no one. What sorta person woulda dobbed me in? What d'you reckon, Clem?'

'Maybe it wasn't Ernie?'

She waited, unsure.

'Pop isn't always sure what he's doing.'

'Doug?'

'I mean, he can't drive. He just about killed this kid on a

bike the other day. And half of what he says doesn't make sense.'

'*Doug?*'

'You can't get angry with him, Val.'

'Jesus, but I told Ernie …'

I'd put that in, too. Chris Knowlson in his yard calling, *I don't know what you're on about, Annie.*

You know.

Check yer facts.

'I'm sure he wasn't thinking,' I said. But she must've been remembering the hundreds of times she'd looked after us, the bowls of sugar and bags of mandarins.

'I must talk to Ernie, and say sorry.'

'I shouldn't have said anything.'

'No, it's all good, Clem.'

The front door, and steps in the hallway. Peter came in wearing his council chamber best, his 1969 special. He stared at Providence. 'Mum … what you done?'

'He was under the house. Tell him, Clem.'

'I had to drag him out.'

Peter opened the fridge and poured himself water. 'Well, I did what I could.'

'How's that?' Val asked.

'This Alan character, he reckons John helped him steal vodka. But John swears black and blue. And I tend to believe him.'

'What about Anne?'

'Sittin' in the corner crying. Don't think she knows what to believe.'

'You gonna represent him?' I asked.

'That's the thing,' he said. 'This tall fella comes in – defence attorney – and says, I've got it, Mr Donnellan, is it? And I say, I think I'll take it, but then Anne looks at me, then John, so …'

'You can only offer,' Val said.

'They're nuts,' Dave added. 'Some kid, I bet?'

'Yeah … a kid.' He stroked the cat's head. 'Might be best, anyway. I haven't kept up with it.'

He studied the lino, and knew. There'd be no legal renaissance. Once you'd started mowing your yard with a scythe.

23/v/84 Mr Thomson is the opposite of everyone. Sits, most lessons, reading the newspaper, occasionally scratching his arse, before turning the page and saying, 'Everyone okay?'

Sometimes Thomo would go on about Leonardo, or Titian, and how they were fakes and how their assistants did all the work. Probably because he was a failed artist. He'd shown us his watercolours, all runny and obvious and dull, and told us what competitions they'd won (local council stuff, mostly). He'd produced a Mona Lisa and said, 'Really, it's quite ordinary, but the ages have chosen to remember it.' In the same way they'd chosen to ignore him.

To fix the problem, he read the sport section while we kept busy. Today, it was portraits. I had Jen's tarot cards, so I pulled one, and began. The Devil. Big smile. Black eyes and a couple of decent-sized horns. It wasn't like he was going to check, so what did it matter?

Curtis was busy. Her name was Tracey, and he'd taken a liking. They'd spent a few lunches together, holding hands, sitting behind the Moreton Bay at the far end of the oval. At first I'd joined them, but then he'd said, 'Listen, Clem, me and Trace just wanna talk.'

Now they were drawing each other. Thomo was busy with a kettle and plunger in the corner, tuning the radio to the races, peering out of the window to see if there was anything on the horizon: fame, a better job, talent.

Trace asked me, 'What yer drawin'?'

I showed her the tarot card.

'The Devil, eh? He's got big ears too.'

I didn't reply. She was pretty thick. Curtis could do a lot better, but she was well put together, for her age.

'Aren't you meant to draw a person?' she said.

'He's a fallen angel,' I replied.

She didn't get it. 'But he's not a person.'

Thomo sat down and tasted his coffee. 'Everything okay?'

Like he cared. He was our Nick replacement, but he was no Nick, or teacher, or anything, really. He'd told us he was on a contract and would be out on his arse come December, so I suppose the incentive wasn't there.

'Devil's real, eh, Curtis?' I asked.

'Too right,' he replied. '*While I was with the spirits who dwell suspense, a lady summoned me.*' He put his lips to her neck, and pecked her white skin.

'That's disgusting,' one of the other girls said.

Thomo looked up from his paper. 'What?'

'Tracey kissed Curtis.'

Thomo shrugged. As long as no one got pregnant on his time. 'Give it a rest, Colin.'

'I'm Curtis.'

Tracey said to me, 'You live next to Curtis?'

'Yes.' I continued copying my devil: red leotard with a big arse and ball pouch. Loaded and ready to fire thunderbolts. Like Curtis probably, as he took her hand and stroked it.

She returned to her boy lover. 'That'd be nice, bein' that close, eh?'

'We hang out,' Curtis said.

I examined her dress, undone to the third button. Black bra. That was all it came down to, surely? Curtis was determined to conquer his personal wilderness, desolate for seventeen years.

'Me and Clem have grown up together, haven't we, Clem?'

'I guess.'

'Got up to a lot of trouble, haven't we?'

'Some.'

'Like what?' Tracey said, smiling.

'Can't tell you. I'd have to eat you afterwards.'

'*Gross*,' the same girl said.

Thomo: 'Come on, it's not a coffee shop, I want results. Full face, quality stuff. No bullshit.'

'We used to go in the substation, didn't we, Clem?'

'Yeah.'

'And throw sticks at the high voltage lines.'

'That's really intelligent,' someone said.

'Coulda killed yerself,' Tracey added.

'Not if you know what yer doin'.' He whispered in her ear, '*To do thy bidding pleases me so well.*'

It was becoming obvious. He loved his tight pants, but they probably weren't the best choice, considering. He moved about awkwardly. Tracey's head was still an oval, with a sort of pig nose and elephant ears. She said, 'That doesn't look like me.'

'I can't draw.'

'Why'd you do art?'

'Either that or Home Economics.'

Curtis crossed his legs, but that made it more obvious, so he adjusted his jumper to cover it. The Devil called: big, flaky horns with sharp tips. And red wings, spread to display their venation, and some sort of sword for lopping heads. 'Yep, me and Clem, we were the neighbourhood terrors, weren't we, *mate*?'

'Yeah.'

'Even got picked up by the coppers, once.'

'Did you?' She seemed to like this idea. She held his arm, he crossed his legs again.

'We got locked up for the night but they didn't have any evidence. Reckoned we'd stolen some grog but, you know …'

She added lines to his portrait, and now it looked like a donkey. Then she studied my devil and said, 'You read them cards?'

There didn't seem any reason not to. Thomo was caught up, and the girls were talking about Target and two-for-one dresses. So I opened the pack, shuffled it and selected three cards. Then I studied them, lifted my hand and chanted a few times. 'This is bizarre,' I said.

'What?'

'The Lovers.'

She smiled. 'Yeah?'

'Someone's entered your life, and he needs something from you.'

'What?'

'It's not what you think.'

'No?'

'Not long-term, you know? Something, quick.'

She clung to Curtis's arm. 'You sure?'

'And this card. Strength. This indicates self-control. It's like they're saying, Don't give in to your weaknesses.'

'Lift up thy voice of gold!' Curtis said.

I drew a few more cards until I reached the Fool. 'Of course, the Fool. A spirit in search of experience.'

'What experience?' she said.

'I'm trying … they don't want to tell me.'

The Blessed strained to escape. Curtis kept checking. I guessed his heart rate was up, and he was red in the face, and sweating. He'd given up on the portrait, adding a body and legs and splayed feet. Then, a glowing knob. She said, *'That's disgusting.'*

Thomo overheard. 'What is?'

'Nothing,' Curtis said.

I thought we were in for a repeat of the AV room encounter: Wendy and Lars in the dark as the projector flickered and Mr McGarry explained how they made aluminium. Lars reclining, as it was offered, and accepted, as the whole mystery of human life was summarised in dot point. As a small head bobbed in counterpoint to the marvels of mineral discovery and refinement.

Thomo stood, strolled over, and Curtis screwed up his picture. Thomo took it, flattened it and smiled. 'A portrait?'

'Should I start again?'

'If you think it'll do any good.'

'It can't do any harm.'

Then he noticed my cards. 'How things looking?'

'Pretty good.' I showed him my devil. 'Is that what you wanted?'

'You taking this serious?' he said.

'Yeah. Nick, Mr Andrews, he reckoned I was a good drawer. Mr Bulljaw, we had him all over the art building.'

'Who's Mr Bulljaw?'

'That's open to interpretation.'

Then he noticed Tracey's picture, but didn't say a word. Apparently, being piss-weak was better than being a smart-arse.

Later, as we walked across the compound, Tracey said, 'Where'd you learn to do cards, Clem?'

'I borrowed them from my sister. I reckon I could make a bita money. Two dollars a go.'

'Any takers?'

I described home room, most of the girls lined up, shiny dollars in their palms, as I spouted shit about the Empress (*Mother, creator, nurturer – I can see children, lots of them … How many? … Lots, and wait, there's someone you've met … Go on … He's tall, with brown hair, or is it blonde?*)

'That's such a load of shit,' Curtis said, walking normally, after a difficult start.

'It is not,' Tracey said.

'Think about it. This fool's known those girls for five years. He's had conversations about boyfriends, hobbies, careers.' He stopped, guessing, perhaps, it wasn't going to get him any closer to his goal. 'Come on.' Across the yard, into the main building, to the basement stairs.

'Where's it go?' Tracey asked.

'*To Hell!*'

She laughed. 'This is out of bounds. It's always been out of bounds.'

Curtis checked it was safe, took her hand and led her down. I followed, unsure. There was a door at the bottom with a padlock, but he showed us how the shackle could be removed.

We went in. He switched on a light. A dark cavern with a twelve-foot ceiling and a giant boiler in the middle. Insulated pipes studded with rusted bolts. Knobs and pressure gauges and a little table in the corner where you could sit and read. 'I'm the only one who knows,' he said.

'What if someone comes in?' I asked.

'*What if someone comes in? You coward.*'

He indicated. 'Down there, see, a passageway leads under the main building, and there, the first, second and third wings.'

They were all lit up, yellow, diminishing into the distance.

'This is neat,' Tracey said.

'Old Coward's off mowing the lawns. Come on.'

He led us down one of the passages. '*Through me the road to the city of desolation ... Through me the road to sorrows eternal.*'

'Shut up,' Tracey said. 'You're scaring me.'

The passages weren't high enough to stand; or wide enough to move comfortably.

'I'm scared,' Tracey said.

Eventually the tunnel emerged into a second, smaller chamber. Again, someone had dragged a few tables down, and there was a *Playboy*, and empty spirit bottles.

'This is where Coward hangs out,' Curtis said. 'Wonder why the garden's full of weeds? He gets the opportunity class working then says, I'll be back in a minute, then comes down here, has a quick look through the literature—' and he showed the centerfold '—and relaxes.'

I noticed the glossy pages, and guessed what was expected. 'I gotta learn for the Geography test.'

'Yeah, it's creepy, let's go,' Tracey said, pulling Curtis's arm.

He resisted. 'It's even better under the second wing. Coward's got it nice. A couch, so he can have a sleep.'

She stopped to think about this.

I turned and walked away. As I went I heard him saying, '*So to go on, and see this venture through, I find my former stout resolve returning.*'

June

Pop said he was too old to drive halfway across Australia, so I'd have to get my licence. The September holidays were approaching and I, apparently, still had a lot to learn. I selected reverse, checked the mirror and backed down the drive, almost collecting Ernie. Pop put his head out the window. 'Sorry, Ernie, he' still learning.'

Ernie picked up Fi-Fi. 'Don't worry, she's got nine lives.'

'Where you goin'?'

'Windsor.'

'Wanna lift?'

'Wouldn't say no.' Ernie climbed in the back. 'The gout's been playing up.'

I drove along Lanark II. Ernie said, 'Not out of yer way, is it?'

'Just practising,' Pop said. 'Headin' down for a drink?'

'Quick one.'

Like it was so strange, although I knew they'd drunk together. Walked down Lanark, and North East Road, past Economy butchers and Apex glass. Tying Fi-Fi to the post and heading in. I knew they'd sat together, for hours, discussing the economy and Whitlam and the 620 Bulletside pickup. And I also knew something had happened. 'I can drop you, Pop.'

'No time for that.'

'Got all day.'

'*No.*'

I turned onto the main road, merged and drove with my hands on cold plastic. I tried to think what might have happened. Pop saying, Unions'll be the death of this country. Ernie replying, What would you know? Were you ever in one? Pop replying, They've killed the economy. Then Ernie standing, saying, You're full of it, Doug, and Pop telling him he could shove his manifesto.

'You two used to drink together?' I said.

'Coupla times,' Pop replied. 'Careful, you're straying into the other lane.'

'You should have a beer, Pop. Get you out of the house.'

'Eyes on the road. Stop nattering.'

'You're always complaining how bored you are, now you stopped fixing cars.'

'When did I say that?'

'Why'd you stop?' Ernie asked.

Pop didn't want to be drawn. 'Once you get to my age ...'

'You got all that knowledge, you should keep at it. Man's only done when he stops tinkerin'.'

Pop studied the road.

'You can come in for a drink,' Ernie said. 'My shout. That was all a long time ago and we've moved on, eh?'

'From what?' I asked.

'*None of your business*,' Pop said.

Ernie popped his head between the bucket seats. 'It was a big—'

'It's all done, Ernie!'

And he retreated, stroking Fi-Fi.

We drove in silence.

'You got a good eye,' Ernie said to me. 'Hasn't he, Doug?'

'Yes.'

'You'll be ready in no time.'

'I gotta hurry,' I said. 'I wanna get my licence before September.'

'Why's that?'

Pop turned back to him. 'He just means *soon*.'

'Yeah,' I said, taking my cue. I could hear the cogs in Ernie's head clunking. He knew how to read Pop as well as anyone. He said, 'You goin' somewhere, Doug?'

Pop turned back. 'No, I am bloody not.'

'Calm down.'

Silence, again, as the traffic settled.

'Bit of a drive, eh, Doug?'

'No bloody drive. We can pull over and let you out?'

'Sorry.'

Another bus, but Pop was preoccupied.

Then Ernie said, 'What's this?' And produced a groundsheet from our shopping expedition.

Pop said, 'It's nothing.' He poked my side. 'Hurry up. He needs his shandy.'

Ernie examined it. 'You only need a groundsheet for one thing.'

'Lots of things,' Pop said.

'Like what?'

'Like lots of bloody things.'

'Like driving west?'

Pop turned to him again. 'No.'

'I'm surprised it's taken so long, Doug.'

'Mind yer own business.'

'Last time you said we'd go. What, you goin' with Clem?'

No reply.

'September, before it gets too hot. All that gold … before it's too late. We're no spring chickens, Doug.'

'I'm not goin' nowhere.'

I glanced at Pop. 'You might as well tell him.'

'I could come with you,' Ernie said. 'That's what we agreed on.'

'That was a long time ago.'

I turned into the hotel car park, switched off the engine and waited. Pop said, 'We're here.'

'When would it have been … sixty-five?' Ernie asked. 'Me and your pop had been sitting at the front bar for hours, then he says: I got this map.'

He spent the next five minutes explaining how Pop had taken the map out of his pocket, flattened it on the bar, showed him Lasseter's Reef and asked if he was interested in coming, for a ten per cent cut.

'And that was it, Clem. We shook on it and agreed on a date. But then he changed his mind.'

'I did not,' Pop said. 'Tell him the whole story.'

'That's it.'

Pop turned to me. 'Yes, we agreed on it, but a few days later I get this phone call. That Doug Currie? Yes, who's this? I'm so and so and Ernie Sharpe mentioned you might be looking for someone to come on a trip. Then another call, and another. He'd told the front bar of the Windsor, everyone knew.'

'Okay, I got a bit tipsy, told one of the fellas, but I vowed them to secrecy—'

'And you believed them?'

'Jesus, Doug, I said I's sorry, but that needn'ta stopped us drinkin'.'

There was a short pause; hot asphalt, Fi-Fi panting. Pop said, 'We're here now. You can go have a chat with your mates.'

'I can do some driving, and I'm not a bad cook.'

In the absence of a dog, Pop smoothed his pants. 'I'll think about it.'

Ernie got out, let Fi-Fi down, and she pissed against the wheel. Then he led her towards her post on North East Road, the dangerous few feet between pub and traffic where she'd sat, alone, all these years, waiting for him to stagger out pissed. But, I guessed, she was happy, because she had a routine, and knew that was her spot, and people would give her water and a pat and a crust of their pie. Like her master, aware that everything happened, if you were patient.

Curtis and I crossed the oval and headed for the Gleneagles shops. They'd let us leave early after our midyear exams. School had been a long, agonising wait for the dentist; the pain that came and went. Thirteen years, nearly, since we'd sat together, cross-legged, listening to our Prep teacher telling us what to do if we needed the toilet.

'Too much wasted time,' Curtis explained (school had been the first entry in his list of hates). 'I could read when I was six, maths, nine or ten, and all the rest was bullshit.'

I'd just spent two hours writing about the Russian Revolution. A good dose of Ernie – peasants eating sawdust, watching their children slowly starve, as their landlords dressed for balls. 'How do you reckon you went?' I asked.

'Beautifully.' Curtis took a folded slip of paper from his pocket, opened it and showed me. Dozens of tightly scribbled facts and dates and a palimpsest of causes, outcomes and long-term effects. 'Those teachers are so lazy. I had it on my desk, and no one walked past. White sat on her arse reading a magazine the whole time.' Then he ripped up the evidence and offered it to the wind. 'Beats sittin' with Peter. He really stinks. Do you reckon he uses deodorant?'

'He told me he doesn't.'

'I never quite got him. How can you live that long and never have a girlfriend, or wife? There's only so much wanking you can do.'

'He's different.'

'Lives with his mum. Classic closet homo.'

'He is not.'

'They hide it, Clemmy. Coupla magazines under the wardrobe.'

'You're full of shit.'

'You wanna watch out, he'll be after you next.'

'He's sort of … asexual.'

Curtis almost laughed. 'No such thing. God put it there for a reason.'

'You're the expert.'

He smiled again.

'Go on.'

'No, if she knew I was telling …'

He was busting to say it. Seventeen years of waiting, listening, overhearing, imagining and practising. It wasn't something you could keep to yourself.

'I offered Coward ten bucks a week if he mowed during my free on Thursday afternoon.'

We jumped the fence and headed towards a new, multistorey police station under construction.

'Ten bucks a week?'

'I've been selling John's smokes. Figure it should keep me going for a few months.'

'What about when he comes back?'

'Not any time soon. So last Thursday I told Mum I was studying in the library and me and Tracey …'

'Go on.'

'We wandered down, had a chat, bit of a kiss. Then the bra …'

He'd always said he'd beat me, and he had. He'd said he didn't see why people had to wait so long. Who made the laws? The Catholics, no doubt. But if your stuff started working at twelve, why all the hanging about?

'I can't tell you any more.'

'Go on.'

He just smiled.

We crossed the road and walked in the shadow of the scaffold.

'And?'

'She had a bit of a sook and said, Why did I do that? I told her it'd all be good, and she said, I don't believe I did it.'

'*And?*'

'I told her it's natural. Then I mentioned next Thursday, and she got all shitty and ran off.'

'Did you make sure?'

'You don't worry about that. Remember old Sparrow? *There are only two days every month when a woman can fall pregnant.*'

Poor old Mr Sparrow, who really taught physics, but had been made to suffer Year Eight science. And reproduction. There were only so many overheads he could put up, so much biology he could discuss, before he got to the meaty bits. Wendy, in the corner, grinning. Lars, salivating, and we children hiding blushes, but feeling sorry for him. *When the semen is deposited in the ree-productive tract, the sperms swim at a fast rate* (smiling, to convince us he wasn't at all uncomfortable) *towards the freshly ovulated egg. Upon arrival, he and she have a few words, then unite, and, the rest, is … well …*

'What if it was one of the two days?' I asked.

'Listen, Clem, you don't wanna overthink these things.'

I wondered what I would've done. Sought advice from Peter? Looked up my options in volume six of Nan's encyclopedias? But it didn't matter, because it wouldn't happen. Girls like Tracey weren't attracted to boys like me.

A paddy wagon pulled up in front of the temporary police station. Two officers got out, opened the back and rough-handled a young man towards the station. 'You been to see your brother?' I asked.

'Why would I?'

Number two on his list: John.

We crossed the road and went into the shops, past the butcher, cuts laid out on plastic grass – thigh and rump on their own trickling mattress. 'You actually … *finished* the job?' I asked.

'You don't believe me?'

'You were always determined.'

Standing in the newsagent, years ago, showing me how all the cuts fit together, saying, 'Before I'm eighteen.'

'Good luck.'

Explaining what bit did what, but how you had to be careful if you were doing it in the dark.

We stopped in front of the photo machine. Five shots for a dollar. Curtis fumbled in his pocket. Nothing. 'Got a dollar?'

'Why?'

'She said she likes my arse.'

I handed it over, and he went in, fumbled, waited for the flash, then re-emerged.

'You didn't?'

But he had. Five shots. Half-moon. With a big, ugly crack.

Back to Gleneagles, through the primary school, *Yellow bird, up high in banana tree*, as it had been years ago, when Mr Gottl had first taught us. Still, it seemed a noble thing, keeping the flame burning, as knickers and work shirts blew in the breeze over galvanised fences and lives as rust-proof and make-do as our own. 'I gotta go home and learn,' I said.

The Grade Fours were still lined up, waiting to be tagged, to run to the yellow flag and back, because somehow it'd make their lives better.

'Ten minutes,' he said. 'I can prove it.'

Down Ashfield Street, across the mound to the Housing Trust flats with their pit bulls and stumped Toranas. Number thirteen. Knock, knock. But instead of Tracey, an older woman, smelling of mum.

Curtis introduced himself and asked if Tracey was home and mum agreed, reluctantly. 'You're the one she does art with?'

'I reckon.'

'*Trace!* And who's this?'

'Clem – me mate.'

She didn't like the look of this at all. But Tracey emerged, led us into the garden and Curtis gave her his snaps, and she smiled and said, 'Don't let him see – it's private, eh?'

'He's okay.'

'You wanna come in?'

But Curtis noticed mum, holding the blinds open. 'Maybe not. I better go home and learn.'

'Okay.' Despite seeing the curtain moving, she took his arm, squeezed it and kissed him.

'Can't wait for next Thursday,' Curtis said.

'Ssh!' She punched him.

He turned to me. 'We're goin' to the movies—' And back to Tracey. 'Aren't we, Trace?' And he winked at her, and she said, 'Yeah, that's it, the movies.'

Walking home, Curtis said, 'Think you owe me an apology.'

'Fuck!' As she walked past again. 'Fuck!' Twitched a few times, carried on.

You had to feel sorry for her. Curtis saw the humorous side (of course), imagining what it would've been like having Tourette's in Thomo's class, or Jacob's economics, answering every question with a *fuck*, as they were forced to smile, and continue, Anyone know? Three factors affecting GDP?

I sat on my bed, focusing, watching her continue down the street.

3/vi/84 It's a pity, because she's pretty good-looking. Years ago a couple of kids started teasing her, riding their bikes around her, saying things like, What's it like to be spaz? Me and Curtis watched and Curtis said they shouldn't get away with it and I said whatcher gonna do? He stormed out the door, picked a couple of lemons off our tree, walked out front and threw them. One hit a boy in the temple, and he fell, luckily across the dead grass of the median strip. Then there were words, and they rode off. Problem solved.

I continued watching through the lens that concentrated Lanark Avenue. Of course, there was more to Lanark II than what I've described. The house next to the Glassons, for instance. It was close enough. Between Val and Ernie on the other side. They were called Davies, and the son had a Kingswood that he'd fix most nights, revving it for a full ten minutes. There was a mother, and she always wore an apron, and you could see her lifting the venetians and looking out, and I guess she'd go to the phone and call her sister (or someone) and say, Oh, you wanna hear a story? That strange woman across the road ... you know, the one with the cats?

The husband would come and go, and a daughter, but none of us knew who they were. Mum had tried to be friendly, Val too, but what could you do? Mum reckoned the Kingswood son was selling drugs, and she'd seen John Burrell in there a few times, but it wasn't like she could ask Anne or Gary.

The Collinses lived next to the Davies. They had a kid my age, but we never talked much. Curtis reckoned he *was* a retard, and should be avoided at all costs. By retard he meant too enthusiastic, daily following us (in the early years) up and down the street, saying, 'Mum reckons they should trim them power lines,' as Curtis replied, 'We gotta go now ... you better do yer homework. Whatd'you say yer name was?'

'Ted.'

'Go on, Ted. Channel Niners starts in a minute.'

But one day the Collinses disappeared. Shoved all their crap in a loading van and drove off without so much as a goodbye. Maybe Ted eventually found a friend, but Curtis was very selective. Three was a crowd, especially when Ted ate his own snot.

A nose appeared. Much like my mine. It withdrew, and there was a face, much like mine. And this boy stood back, looked at me, and said, *What's going on?*

I's looking.

At what?

Stuff.

My name's Colin.

He indicated number 29.

Movin' in.

My name's Arnold.

Arnold what?

Ruge.

Can I have a go?

The boy, with vegemite-stained face and a hole in his T-shirt where he sucked on it, came into the house. He walked past Barry Ruge, who was busy filing his corns, and Barry said, G'day.

G'day, mister. I'm Colin.

And that was it. Colin came into my room, sat on my bed and looked through my telescope. My life would never be the same. He focused on his dad, who was helping some men carry a wardrobe inside, and said, We come from Smithton.

Where's that?

In the cuntree.

I said, We've always lived here. Dad built the place.

Who's yer dad?'

Dunno.

Why?

He left.

Why?

Dunno.

Fair enough. And he focused. See, that kid there, that's my brother, Chopper. He's always in trouble.

Yeah? As I wondered what Mum'd say.

Mum and Dad reckons we'll have a new start. People won't be shitty with us. Chopper smashed all the winders on Johnson's deli, and Mr Johnson called the cops, but Dad told him he'd pay, but it was never the same after that. Everyone reckoned we were ... you know, a bit crook.

How long you stayin'?

For good.

This seemed okay. I needed a friend. Even one with food all over his face.

Colin said, What grade you in?

Two.

Like me. I was in One but I was too smart so they put me up. Mum reckons it was because Mrs Jones couldn't handle me, but Dad reckons it's cos I was too smart. Are you smart?

I dunno.

What school you go to?

Gleneagles.

That's where I'm goin'. Can I sit next to you?

I sit next to Alice Fong.

She can move. What's she, a slope?

We sat watching the movers, and Chopper, on the fence, checking out the neighbourhood, until Chris Knowlson went past and started talking to them.

Curtis said, Who's he?

Mr Knowlson. Goes past at this time every day. Comin' back from the pub ...

What, is he pissed?

I reckon.

And who's the old girl with the cats?

Mrs Douglas. She's nice. Looks after me and Cicely when Mum's at work.

Who's Cicely?

My sister. She's a cow.

How old?

The conversation rolled, and Colin insisted on being introduced to my sister, but then said she wasn't worth the effort. Older women were better, especially ones with titties.

Noises from the Champnesses'. A sound like a shoe hitting a wall. Muffled voices.

Maybe Les was on the grog again. I waited, listened, focused on the door (closed), the windows (curtains drawn), out the back, down the sides. If only I could see through walls. Again, a thud, and a voice. 'See it through.'

Silence.

Jen came in. 'Mum told you not to.'

'Ssh! Les and Wendy are at it again.'

'So what? Mind yer own business. *Pop.*' And she walked off.

I waited. This time, a heavy thump, like a piano dropped from a height. Wendy stormed out the back door, paced the yard, and Les followed. He was shouting at her, and she was giving it back. Then he took her arms and she pushed and he staggered back and she moved behind the house and I couldn't see.

Pop came in. 'You spyin' on people again?'

'Les and Wendy are at it.' Pop peered out the window and said, 'Let us know if it gets nasty,' and retreated. Jen said, 'Aren't you gonna stop him?'

They came into view. She was threatening him with a finger. I wondered what I'd do if it turned nasty. Then she walked towards the aviary, opened the door and the birds flew out. Les was quickly behind her, but she pushed him and he fell. He got up, made for the door and closed it, but the birds had gone. So he threw it open and turned to her and said, 'There, you happy?' and she said, 'Very.'

He pushed her, and she fell, and he tried to grab her ankle but she kicked him and he fell again, comically. Then she said, 'Hope you're happy.'

Les watched the birds go. 'Why?'

Wendy went in, slamming the door. Les returned to his aviary, examining it in case one had decided to stay, but none had. So he went inside.

Mum pulled up in the Datsun, took some groceries from the

back and came in. The minute she did, Jen said, 'Clem's watching people with his thing again.'

Groceries deposited on the melamine, she came into my room. 'I thought we'd resolved this?'

'It's Wendy,' I said.

'Clem?'

'She let his birds go. All of them.'

Mum sat on my bed, moved the curtain and checked. 'What happened?'

I explained. 'What should we do?'

'Serves him right. Pig of a man.'

Nothing.

'What d'you reckon they're doing?'

'Ssh!'

Wendy came out carrying a bag overflowing with clothes. She stood in the middle of the front yard, then walked off. But she'd only got a few metres when she turned towards the Rosies' house and walked down their drive.

Mum moved me, and studied the action. Jen came in and said, 'What you doin'?'

'Ssh! She's just standing there … now she's goin' inside. I think she's finally had enough.'

'What should we do?' I asked.

Mum stopped to think. 'Wait.'

So we waited. Minutes, half an hour. At one point Les came out, checked the street, paced his yard and went back in.

'Want me to go see if she's okay?'

'No. He might see.'

An hour, another, and then it was getting dark and cold. Mum told me to keep watching, and went to make coffee, but was soon back. Pop came in and she told him what was happening and he said we should mind our own business.

As the hours dragged, we took turns. Even Jen. But there was no movement from either house. Just the Tourette's girl. Then

Ernie and Fi-Fi on the nightly run, Ernie unable to wait, stopping and pissing against our gum tree.

Soon it was dark. The streetlights cast shadows over what had been the Rosies' lawn, although now it was just dirt. No lights in number 26. No power, I guessed. Mum said, 'She must be sitting in the dark.'

All of us, Jen, me, Pop, Mum, gathered on my bed.

Pop said, 'We better go see.'

'She must be hungry,' Jen said.

Mum: 'Yes.' She thought about it. 'It's dark enough. He won't see me.'

She left the house, crossed the road and went into the Rosies'. We waited. Jen said, 'We oughta call the cops.'

'They'll sort it out,' Pop said. 'They always do.'

A few minutes later Mum returned. 'I told her to come stop here, but she won't.'

'What's she doing?' I asked.

'What's there to do? She's sitting on the floor, looking at the ceiling.'

'We can't leave her there,' Jen said.

Mum thought about this. 'Come on.'

She led the expedition. Jen was told to find a few blankets, Pop to fetch the old foam mattress from the shed, and she warmed leftover stew and slopped it into Tupperware. She packed some of her clothes in a bag, and toothpaste, and a hair brush, and when we were ready, said, 'Dad, you wander over, knock on his door, say you noticed his aviary was open and the birds gone, then take him outside while we get across.'

Which he did. I carried the mattress, and Mum and Jen the supplies, over the road, round the back and into the Rosies'. I ran out to the front yard, switched on the water and returned. Mum was making up a bed.

Jen and I stood watching as Wendy ate.

She said, 'He's just having one of his moments.'

It seemed funny how she apologised for him, considering the cut on her face, and what looked like a black eye.

Mum said, 'Right, you two, home.'

She had the tone. When she had the tone, you obeyed. As we went, she said, 'Clem, get a few candles … and some Dettol, and Band-Aids.'

We checked, then crossed the road. I said, 'See, sometimes it doesn't hurt to look out for people.'

Pop was still talking to Les. Like nothing had happened.

'It's nothing like that. No one censors newspapers.'

'You don't reckon?'

We were our own Winstons, sitting in the front seat of the Jag, smoking. Peter had rolled a few, set them up on the dash, told me to keep it mum.

'Someone rewrites news to favour the government?'

'It's more complex than that. The paper needs revenue so it tends to print the sort of things … Player profiles, stats, cigarettes, grog. That's all people care about.' He stroked Providence. He was a nice cat, quiet, happy to sleep, licking the hand that fed him. They kept him inside, and every now and again Val or Peter would put him in a bag, smuggle him past Ernie's, go a few blocks and walk him on a lead.

'So all this has to go.' He dropped his smoke in the ashtray, resting my Orwell essay on the steering wheel and crossing out a paragraph. 'Winston had no choice. Let's talk about individuals as cogs in a big machine.' He made notes on the side of my essay.

'What about the next paragraph?'

He referred to the question: *How did truth-telling cost Winston Smith his life?*

'Love,' he said, as he continued reading.

I felt the dash: real leather. The knobs: heavy, tarnished metal. The clock, even, with its glass face. 'Nice workmanship.'

'You gotta earn it.'

'I know.'

'How's it going?'

I ground a smoke into the bottom of the tray. 'I'll have it finished by October.'

'I'm looking forward to it. Paragraph three is too abstract, you'll have to try again.'

'The upholstery might cost a bit.'

'They can patch the leather so you can't tell. How do you spell *dilemma?*'

'Dunno.'

'You should. That's how the trouble starts.'

'The windows work okay?'

He spat tobacco from his lips as he tackled clumsy syntax.

'And the engine, nothing major?'

'Doug'll be able to help yer. Classic twelve cylinders. New plugs, filters.' He smiled at me.

'He's lost interest.'

'Na, it's in his blood. He just needs something to get him going.'

'So the car's for me? For finishing my book?'

'That's what I said.'

'Not Pop?'

'No, not Pop.' He caught on. 'I mean what I say, Clem. It's a loada junk, but it can be fixed. Everything can be fixed with hard work.'

'I guess you're right. Pop still reckons his map …'

Peter looked over. 'His map?'

I thought about it. On one hand, Pop had made me promise; on the other, you could trust Peter with anything.

'He has this map and he reckons it shows Lasseter's Reef.'

'*Lasseter's Reef*? But it's not real.'

'He reckons it is.'

He smiled his you-can't-put-that-in-an-essay smile. 'So it shows where there's gold?'

'He wants to find it.'

'When?'

'He wants me to come, so I gotta finish driving.'

'So you can go the outback? In the Datsun?'

'I guess.'

'But it's just a folk story.'

I explained Pop's lucky day at the pub; his series of false starts; Nan's map-napping; the John Burrell false alarm; the years of planning and hoping. 'It might be real, and it might not. But he thinks it is, and I reckon he should go.'

Peter said, 'Good thinking. Although, when he drives all that way and the map turns out to be …'

'He's determined to go, and I'm determined to go with him.'

Later, I returned home. Orwell was due the next day, so I found a clean sheet of paper and started writing, incorporating the corrections. Then I heard the door slam, footsteps in the hallway and Pop at the door. 'You didn't?'

'What?' I could see it in his eyes. 'I let it slip.'

'I've told you, it's just me and you – it's our secret.'

'Sorry.'

'He says, I can help with the driving. He says, *I love that sorta country.*'

'Sorry.'

'Just like yer mother: can't keep yer trap shut. Now everyone in the neighbourhood'll know.'

'We could always let him come.'

'No – bloody – way. That's my reef, my gold, my money. I been waitin' fer years. Forget it.'

He stood fuming, his carotid pounding. I said, 'I'll tell him to keep quiet.'

'What are the chances of that? It's a two-way split: me and you, and yer mum, perhaps. Not him or Ernie, or anyone.'

He stormed out, shaking the floorboards, going out the back to his shed, and map, and dreams of Providence.

Mum had the esky loaded: milk, cold chops and coleslaw – enough for another day. The curry was bubbling on the stove. 'I thought Peter was helping?' she said.

'He did.'

'Well, you mustn't have been listening.'

My fifty-six per cent Modern History exam. I'd explained: waking with a headache, thoughts drifting around the room as I tried to work, a couple of electricians fucking around in the hallway. 'It's just a trial,' I said.

'That's the worst you ever done.'

'No … well, perhaps, but he's a hard marker.'

'Excuses.'

Hill Street Blues from the lounge room. Mum said, 'Dad, turn it down!' As she stirred. 'Fifty-six per cent?' And tasted. 'Dad!'

'What?'

'We're not deaf.'

'I'd learnt the Russian Revolution, but the questions were all about France and Vietnam.' Trying to spread a small amount of knowledge on a big piece of toast.

'What if that was the real thing? You wanna go to university …'

'When did I say that?'

'*You do.*'

'*You* want me to.'

'So? What are you gonna do? Fix cars? Kmart? You gotta good head, or I thought you did.'

She tasted the curry, but wasn't happy.

'I could get a job in a bank. Look at Barbara what's-her-name.'

'*She* studied.'

'Year Ten, teller at a bank, then she's managing it, then an executive.'

'It's not so easy these days.'

'Why not? I could be a copper.'

'Coppers don't write novels about *vaginas*.'

'A detective?'

Dozens of them, busy in our lounge room, with Pop calling, 'Go on, get him. He's behind you.'

'*Let's be careful out there*,' I called.

'Yes, Sarge,' he replied.

'The point is,' Mum said, 'you'd be the first in the family with a degree. We'd always thought that.'

'Who had?'

'Yer father, me, Pop.'

'Should I be worried about what he wanted?'

'*Yes, you should.* It'd be nice if Jen could but …'

And what she wanted to say: three years of Ds for high school maths. All the comments had said she'd been *working hard*. Before she'd seen the ad in the paper for hairdressing apprenticeships and said to Mum, 'How's about this?' and Mum had said, 'You should give 'em a ring.'

She emptied the curry into a Tupperware container and rinsed the pot. 'Even if it's just arts,' she said. 'What d'you need for that?'

'Seventy-eight.'

'You could get seventy-eight. You used to get straight As.'

'That's when it was easy.'

'If you worked hard you could get into law. Imagine how proud Pop'd be, wouldn't you, Pop?'

'Eh?'

'If Clem got inta law?'

'When's tea?'

I tasted the curry. 'I don't want to be a lawyer.'

'They make good money.'

'They're all crooks.'

'Or a doctor?'

'That's ninety-seven.'

'All I'm saying's buckle down. It's not too late.'

I didn't think it was, but I didn't care. It seemed stupid to reduce life to a tertiary entrance ranking, but that's how it was. Your brain produced a number, the number got you into university, this got you a good or boring job. There were more of the latter than the former, so you had to work hard and take advantage of every opportunity. Like Peter. He'd conquered law, but only through hard work.

Mum said, 'I'm no good, Pop isn't. Ask Peter, he knows what it takes.'

'It was easier in his day.'

'There you go again. Val made them boys work. I'd go in at night and they'd be studying. Go into your room and yer listening to John Lennon, playing your guitar.'

'Cos I've finished for the night.'

'Obviously not. If yer gettin' fifty-six.'

'He's behind yer!' Pop said.

Mum packed the curry in the esky. We checked to make sure Les hadn't come home, then set off without Pop noticing. As we went, I said, 'I could do journalism.'

'What's that?'

'Seventy-one.'

'Any idiot can be a journalist.'

'Plenty of authors started out like that: Hemingway, Steinbeck.'

'You bring the sauce?'

'Yeah.'

'Don't say anything to upset her. She's been a bit delicate.'

'She could come stay with us.'

'Doesn't want to.'

'Why?'

'*I dunno*. People got their pride.'

This seemed silly. It wasn't like we didn't know, or care. 'Or even if she stayed in our shed. At least she'd have power and—'

'Don't talk about what you don't know.'

Although the back door was missing, Mum knocked, and waited. It was getting dark and we could see candlelight from what had been the master bedroom. It was at the back, on the opposite side, so Les wouldn't be able to see.

'You there?' Mum called.

'Come in.'

Wendy was sitting on the mattress, covered in the rugs we'd supplied, surrounded by plates of half-eaten food (we'd supplied), listening to a battery radio (Pop had donated). Mum said, 'How you feeling?'

'Good.'

Wendy half-smiled at me and said, 'Not to worry, Clem. It'll all be sorted soon.'

Mum opened the esky and showed her what we'd brought. 'This curry's just come off the stove, so careful.'

'I appreciate it, Fay.'

'That's alright. You'd do the same.'

I wondered if she ever had, in the Dad days. Mum and me and Jen, perhaps, sitting around the telly, as Les and Wendy came over with their esky.

Mum gathered the plates and put them in a plastic bag. 'I'll give 'em a clean.'

'What's he up to?' Wendy asked.

'He's been out since four, wasn't it, Clem?'

Me with my telescope, and log book. 'Half four.'

'Probably down the pub. He's been doin' that of late. Was a time he'd never go.'

I didn't know whether to go or stay. Mum had told me to hang about. She didn't fancy the dramas, or waterworks, and there was safety in numbers. So I slipped down against the wall, and half-knelt in the corner.

Wendy said, 'It's a pity, what's happened to this place.'

'Can all be fixed,' Mum said, smiling. It was important to keep smiling.

'I'd come in when Vicky was little and help out. They had it nice. This room was all wooden furniture. But even then, Oswald was a moper, wasn't he?'

'Yes. Gloomy, but nice enough. Dad says he saw it coming, years before.'

The word was never mentioned. Not even the rope, or tree, or coroner's van in the drive; or the funeral (that me and Jen were kept away from), or any mention of it since. When things died you just buried them and got on with life.

'I think he could've been helped,' Wendy said, and she was really saying *she* could be (with curries, perhaps). 'If someone had sought help.'

'Yes,' Mum said, 'what can you say? *Listen, Tina, your husband's not likely to …*'

'Kill himself?' I asked.

Mum couldn't really deny it. '*Clem.*'

'That's what he did.'

There were piles of clothes in the corner. I'd watched, and when Les had gone out I'd told Mum and she'd told Wendy and they'd gone into number 28, gathering clothes, toiletries and the seventeen jumpers. Wendy noticed my interest and said, 'Gotta put 'em somewhere soon or the rats'll get 'em.'

'They're inside?' I asked.

'Too right. I woke last night with one lookin' me in the face.'

'Wendy, you can't stay here,' Mum said. 'Come with us, we'll sort it. Shouldn't be no need for this.'

'Patience.'

Mum knew there was no point. 'I'll take the jumpers and put 'em in the press. Got some mothballs.'

'No, they'll be right for now. I like having them around.' Then she looked at me, her eyes asking if I knew about the child.

I said, 'Mum told me.'

'*Clem!*'

'That's alright,' Wendy said. 'It's not like I'm hiding it.'

'I wasn't gonna tell him, Wendy …'

But Wendy said, 'I'm a mad woman, Clem.'

'No,' I replied. 'It musta been a shit.'

'Yeah, it was a shit.' She sighed again, like all the bits didn't add up. 'You'd have to be nuts to keep knitting them. That's what Les thinks.'

'If it helps,' I said.

Wendy forced herself to look away from whoever I was. 'These things take time,' she said, turning to Mum. 'All that wool, but I'm willing to wait. I know he'll wonder, one day, and come looking, eh, Clem?'

'You can find out about him,' I said.

'I tried that.'

'There's a government department does it. I could help you fill in the paperwork, if you like.'

Mum said, 'He could. He's gonna be a lawyer.'

Wendy examined the jumpers, stacked neatly. 'Even if I knew, but didn't say anything.'

Mum was about to say (believe me, I could tell), Might be best if you didn't.

I wondered what was worse: a kid not having a dad, or a mum not having a kid, but then realised it was the same thing.

'Gotta have an interest,' Mum said.

'I have,' Pop replied.

'What?'

He had to think. 'Place doesn't run itself.'

'Yeah, I run it.' She squeezed lemon on the chips.

'Man my age oughta expect a bita rest, considering.'

'But you've gotta have an interest now you've stopped fixin' cars.'

We'd already had this conversation, days before, and it had finished with Pop saying, Well, I'd like to get out a bit more.

Like?

You know, places we used to go. Port Stevens.

We'll go on the weekend.

Port Stevens, on the coast, an hour from Gleneagles. We'd bought fish and chips from Soto's and were sitting in the middle of the road on the grassy verge.

Curtis said, 'You want that dim sim, Doug?'

'Na.'

He checked with us before eating it. 'Not as good as Don's.'

'He's got special dim sims,' Pop said. 'Wog ones.'

'How can you have wog dim sims?' Mum asked.

'Course you can. Wogs like 'em too.'

'Don's got the best fish,' I said. He had a fridge for fish fillets, prawns and dim sims, butter for the hamburger rolls, the chocolate bars (on hot days), pineapple fritters and patties.

'It's not butterfish, it's flake,' Pop said.

'What?' Mum asked.

'Don the Greek. He sells it as butterfish, but it's flake. Someone should tell the government.'

'The government?' Mum asked.

'*The government*. Weights and Measures.'

'They haven't had that since the Depression.'

Curtis said, 'I wouldn't eat there.'

'Why?' Mum asked.

'You can see his arse crack. When he's cookin' he scratches it, picks up a loada chips, dumps them in the basket and puts them in the oil.'

'That'll kill anything,' Pop said. 'Anyway, he's a good man.'

'But he's not *clean*,' Mum said.

'There's a lotta clean arseholes in the world. But Don, he's decent.'

'Why'd you say that?'

'He had a rough trot.'

Mum didn't want to buy into it. He was the fish shop man, and Greek, so what did it matter? But she knew Pop talked to Don for hours.

'Germans took his wife and son.'

'He told you that?' Mum said.

'Then she come back, minus the kiddy, and never told him where he was.'

'Where was he?' Curtis asked.

'*She never told him*.'

Quiet. Just cars, seagulls, gathered in a toothpaste-coloured flock, waiting for a stray chip.

Mum said, 'I've seen his wife a few times, but she doesn't talk either.'

It wasn't hot, but there were plenty of kids in T-shirts and bathers headed down to the beach. Pop said, 'Shoulda brought mine.'

'What?' Mum asked, hoping there might be progress.

'Bathers. Used to like a swim.'

'You can go in yer undies.'

'Get arrested.'

'Worse than you along the beach.'

Curtis had worn his, with a loose shirt, and thongs. 'I'll go in with you, Doug.'

He didn't reply.

'Go on, then,' Mum said.

Pop glared at her. 'I dare not.'

'That's why we come.'

'*Why?* Why did we come?'

'So you could ...' But she couldn't say it.

I ate Soto's chips. 'Not as good as Don's.'

Curtis: 'If only you'd seen what I'd seen.'

And Pop barked, 'Not doin' so bad for a man who doesn't know what happened to his ...' He sat, with a chip in his hand, staring at the grass. Lost. Like he was watching television.

'I used to like it when you'd bring me down,' Curtis said.

'Good company for Clem,' Mum explained.

'Dad never brought us. Maybe once, with John.' As he tried to remember. He turned to me. 'Jetty jumping?'

'Yeah.' I smiled.

Off the end, which wasn't all that deep, but deep enough. Into the mire, bathers forced up your crack, barnacle cuts where you'd climb the pylons, over, up, for hours, as your ears filled but you shook your head like an old St Bernard to get it out.

Fishing lines, too. Curtis said, 'Remember, Clem? Pullin' the rods in the water?'

'I never did.'

'That was fun.' Reminding us how he used to swim up the beach to get away from the old fellas who'd come after him.

And all this time, Pop, with the same chip in his hand.

'You okay?' Mum asked.

'Yes.' He ate it. 'It used to be nicer.'

'How's that?'

'Well, for one thing, the old fellas would walk along in a shirt and tie, and their wives in frocks. Now it's just boob tubes, and everyone's fat hanging out. People today got no bloody class.'

'You and Mum used to come?' Mum asked.

'Yes. When there was a train runnin' down the middle, right here. Then it was a big day. The whole family. Now it's just big arses and soggy chips.'

It was like he was trying to convince us. I pointed out a girl with a very small bikini. 'Is that what you mean, Pop?'

'Exactly. How could you hold up yer head? Imagine Nan wearing that?'

Mum smiled.

'What?' Pop said.

'She'd topple over.'

We walked down to the sideshows on the esplanade. Passing the lolly shop, where Curtis had pocketed his first fags. He said, 'What d'you reckon?'

'Not now.'

He conceded. But it seemed easy: one old girl behind the counter reading the *Weekly*, a free pocket and, if you were good, you'd buy something cheap to divert suspicion. As we went I said, 'You're just like your dad.'

'Bullshit.'

'What's the difference?'

He had to think. 'He's got it down to an art. Like dickbrain.'

'What's he up to?'

'Who cares?'

'I saw the cops at your place the other day.'

He searched for answers on the hot, gummy footpath. 'They were asking Mum about ... *stuff*.'

I didn't push it. There was never any point.

'Stuff John'd stolen.'

'But they were talking to your dad.'

'So?'

I remembered the two officers searching Gary's car, talking to him for half an hour, writing down what he was saying. It seemed strange – Gary was always out when the cops came round. Then I said, 'He oughta be careful.'

'Why?'

'You know, stuff that fell off the back of his truck.'

'*Like what?*'

Another of Curtis's gifts: the art of the backwards-walking chicken. You had a story, you stuck with it.

'They were there about dickbrain,' he said.

We waited at the lights, then crossed. The music was tinny, the rides empty, except for a few stick legs in centrifugal motion.

'Long as he's got receipts,' I dared.

'You're so full of shit.'

Curtis was the real Winston, excising and replacing the daily facts. The cubby: steel legs, steel frame, iron roof, wood panelling. And, to quote him (though the words were rusty), 'Didn't cost us a cent.'

'The cops were looking for that grog?' Pop said to Curtis.

'I guess,' he replied.

'Looks like he's back in the shit.'

'Good.'

'Harry's got someone else.'

'Why wouldn't he?'

We sat on a bench. There was an empty ghost ride, and a ferris wheel which had featured in an Elvis movie. Mum noticed Pop, watching his shoes, shuffling them in a box pattern to arrange the sand on the concrete. She said, 'Having fun?'

'That breeze keeps it nice.' As we guessed his thoughts: Nan in a frock, men in ties, girls in bathing suits. Or maybe who had the best chips, or what the Germans had done with Don's boy.

I guessed Mum was getting worried. He was leaving us, but quicker than she'd hoped. She'd bought him a 1:72 model of an EH Holden, sat with him, with the instructions, before she'd lost interest and gone off to cook tea and he'd stuck all the wrong bits together, so she'd put them all in the bin.

Daisy, Daisy, give me your answer do …

Even I could remember the song, scratchy, like it was being played with a knitting needle. Me and Jen, with our bowl-cut hair and sticky fingers, saying, Carn, Pop, let's go on that one! The carousel. Fifteen horses with peeling bridles and fading paint jobs. Going around and around. *Daisy, Daisy …*

Pop smiled. 'Now I remember.'

'What?' Mum asked.

'Why I wanted to come.'

Pop leading us, putting us on our horses and standing between us in case we fell. Round and round. *Daisy, Daisy …* Singing along, climbing on a horse and riding side-saddle. And when the ride ended, too soon, he said, Carn, fella, give the kids a bit longer, which he did, because even back then no one was waiting.

Pop stood, shuffled towards the carousel, and we followed. He didn't buy a ticket, or say a word. Just climbed on a horse and sat waiting.

The man saw what was happening and started the ride. Faster and faster. *Daisy, Daisy, give me your answer do …*

He waved, and Mum turned to us and said, 'See, it's happening.'

Pop stared out, beyond the sideshows, to the sea. It was big. A mystery. But only he understood it.

I'd torn the star chart from the paper, waited for dark and headed outside. Then set up the TK25 in the middle of the front lawn and started searching.

Orion. That was easy enough. Topped and tailed by Betelgeuse and Rigel. Then Ernie walked past, on the way home. He pulled Fi-Fi down the drive, and I told him where to look, but he just stumbled and nearly knocked the whole thing over.

Close by, Taurus, galloping across the sky. Leo. Broken back. Diamondhead. Ron Glasson came down his drive with his bin, parked it on the footpath and saw me. 'Any luck?'

'Some.'

He seemed intrigued. Unusual, as nothing in Lanark II ever interested him. He studied the sky and said, 'Too much high cloud.'

It didn't bother me. It was misty, and you could see through it. 'I got Orion.'

'That's easy. What about Gemini? Castor? Pollux?'

I checked the chart. 'Where are they?'

He crossed the road with a little limp and came down our drive. I handed him the chart and he said, 'This is out of date.'

'It was in today's paper.'

'No doubt, but they put any crap in. Not like anyone's gonna notice.'

I waited as he took out a hanky, spat on it, polished the lens and looked. 'It's very weak.'

'I haven't used it a lot for …'

He almost shook his head, but smiled. 'There, that's something.'

I checked. A couple of big ones, pulsing: one yellow, one white.

'Virgo. Spica. Second magnitude.'

'Virgo?'

'Right on the Milky Way. More interesting than watching Les scratch his arse, eh?'

'I guess.' I couldn't remember ever seeing him up close: his broad nose, white whiskers, little eyes and brows so thin they looked like they'd been shaved. 'You seem to know 'em.'

'I should.'

'Why?'

While he spoke he kept searching: 'Physics degree. Master's. Then the start of a PhD in astrophysics. Taurus. Look, while the sky's clear.'

I could see the bull in full flight, and asked, 'What happened to your PhD?'

'Lots of things.'

Hester came out, saw us talking and waved. Ron said, 'Be in soon.'

'No rush. How are yer, Clem?'

'Good, ta, Mrs Glasson.' And she was gone.

'Like what?' I said.

He seemed surprised I cared. 'Dad got sick, and we needed

someone to take over the business. Make more from car seats than astrophysics.'

'You coulda been a professor, made a tonne of money.'

'Coulda, shoulda, but none of that matters. Mum was sick, my sister wasn't interested, so I got to ...' He'd had enough. The past was so long ago none of it mattered. All of the adults in Lanark II thought like this. I guessed you had to. You worked, put food on the table, watched *The Two Ronnies*, slept, and everything was good.

He said, 'All these years you been lookin'?'

'Only cos I's interested. I wanted to see how people worked. Now I know enough, I'm writing a book about it all.'

'And what did you learn, from all these observations?'

'I dunno. People are hard to understand.'

'*Hard*? And what about me and Hester?'

I felt he was using his scientific skills to examine me. 'You like to stick to yerselves.'

'Why?'

'I dunno.'

'Watchin' us wasn't gonna tell you that. Askin' us might've.' He smiled at me.

'So, why do you keep to yerselves?'

'Mind your own business.' He found more stars, and showed me, then the cloud moved over and we waited, and he found more, but by then I'd lost interest in astronomy. There were other questions needed answering. 'There must be a reason.'

'All these years of looking, and you still don't know. You must be using the wrong method.' He moved the telescope. 'There, Jupiter, just above the bull's head.'

I checked. 'Never woulda noticed.'

'You gotta know what you're looking for.'

His face was flat and his lips were thin.

'D'you ever think of finishing your study?'

'Yep, but I haven't. Won't. I got it pretty good now. If you spend yer time thinkin' you can do better—'

'But you could do better. Gleneagles is a dump.'

'You haven't had much to compare it to.' He reached out and messed my hair, like I was still seven, like he'd been waiting all these years to do it. 'Well,' he said, 'I better get going.'

'And yer not goin' to tell me?'

'No.'

I watched him go. If he'd always wanted to talk, and kid me, and mess my hair, he could've a million times. But he hadn't. Quite the opposite. And there was that look of his, like he thought me and Curtis were planning something.

'Clem?'

A talking bush. I studied the shadows on the diosma.

'Is it clear?'

'Yeah.'

John sat forward, and I noticed his face, cut, smeared with oil or mud or whatever it was.

'Don't look ... you *fucking* idiot.'

I pretended to look at the stars. 'What are you doing?'

'Is Doug in?'

'Yeah.'

'I wanna see him.'

'Out here?'

'No.'

'Wanna wait in the shed?'

We ran across the yard, down the drive, into the shed. When we were there he said, 'Tell him I'm here.'

He wore overalls, and a blue jacket. There was a backpack, with clothes falling out. His hair was shaved, with fresh scars underneath.

'Stop fuckin' staring and go get him.'

I really hated John. I always had, always would. I'd always thought it was okay to fuck up, but when people offered help? 'Do you want something to drink, eat?'

'Yeah, whatever you got.'

I went in, found Pop on the lounge and said, 'Somethin' needs doin' in the shed, Pop.'

'What?'

I couldn't think. 'I'll have to show you. But I need you now.'

He glared at me, then relented. As we went I grabbed a bottle of Coke from the fridge. He said, 'Can't it wait?'

We went in and John was sitting on a pile of tyres. Pop said, '*Jesus*.'

John stood, took the Coke, opened it and drank. 'I got out.'

'Got out?' Pop asked.

'Got away.'

'You bloody idiot.'

'They were moving me from the remand centre, and one of them left the van unlocked.' He didn't seem concerned. Just finished the Coke, and forced the bottle into my hands. 'I had to, Doug.'

Pop moved, and claimed the tyre throne. 'Now they're gonna think—'

John approached Pop and knelt. 'It doesn't matter. Alan said I was in it with him, but I was at home. I didn't steal no grog. I didn't steal anything. I was waiting to start my new job.'

'If you didn't, everything'll be fine. We'll go back and tell them—'

'I'm not going back.'

'What else you gonna do?'

'If I could get some money – get a bus, go interstate.'

Pop took a moment to think. 'Harry's given the job to someone else.'

John sat on the crumbling concrete. 'I guessed he would've.'

'But don't worry about that, there're plenty of jobs. Plenty of places want good people. We'll get this sorted then I'll talk to a few other fellas.'

'It doesn't matter, Doug. They've decided.'

Pop leaned forward so his head was close to John's. 'You didn't nick nothin'?'

'No.'

'Then there's no proof.' He stood and pulled a swag out from its hiding place. 'Here, roll this out. Clem and I'll get you some food.'

'*No.*'

We waited.

'You couldn't lend us some money, could you, Doug?'

He stood with his hands on his hips. 'Why?'

'Got a few people I know.'

'What sorta people?'

'They'll help me get sorted. There's no use staying here.'

Pop thought about this. 'I got a few dollars, but I'm not sure what yer gonna use them for.'

'Don't worry, Doug. These fellas are okay.'

Pop went in. I waited, silently. John just stared at the floor. I said, 'I could drive you where you need to go.'

He bit a fingernail, spat the residue. 'I can walk. Just don't say nothin'.'

Pop returned with a handful of money. He made John stand, then counted out three hundred dollars. 'That keep you going?'

'Thanks, Doug. You're a lifesaver.' He picked up his backpack.

Mum was at the back door. 'You two coming in?'

'Just let us know what's going on,' Pop said. 'Phone us, right?'

'Done.'

Three hundred dollars. I'd assumed his Lasseter money was quarantined. There were plenty of things he could've spent it on, but didn't. Mum hated the 120Y. She'd left the 180B brochures around the house, but Pop had just put them in the bin.

John opened the shed door, checked it was clear, and was gone.

I said, 'Reckon you've done your dough, Pop.'

He didn't argue. 'Sometimes these things are decided for you.'

The skipping woman, again. Around the block, back, never slowing. No singing, no smile, no emotion. I could set my clock by her appearance. This tall, African miracle of locomotion. Mum came in and said, 'Anything?'

'I'll let you know.'

My job: to say when Les went out, so she could head over

with the esky and return with the dirty dishes and washing. This routine three times a day, as we kept saying to Wendy, 'So, what should we do?' And she kept repeating: 'He'll be ready soon.'

I didn't mind so much. Kraftwerk kept me happy, the electro-disco rhythm filling my room with Euro-vibe. *Flat tyre on the paving stones …* I stood, jiggled about, let my head roll and my shoulders sway. Jen came in and said, 'What the hell are you doing?'

'Kraftwerk.'

'*So gay.*'

The bike is repaired quickly …

Mum, in the doorway, 'Are you watching?'

'Yes.'

'You're not. You're dancing. What is that rubbish?'

The skipping woman, again, but I barely noticed, rewinding. *The hell of the north: Paris-Roubaix …*

Pop walked down the street in a sort of counter-orbit to the skipping woman. 'Pop,' I called, but he didn't hear me, just passed down the street, around the corner, shuffling like some sort of prototype robot.

I checked the scope for Les, but there was no sign of movement. Then a face, popping up from beneath my window frame.

Hey, Clem.

Hey, Arnold.

What cher doin'?'

Waitin' for Mr Lawrence to go out.

Why?

You know. Why do I gotta tell you?

You don't.

Arnie's face was dirty, food, gravy, something. He showed me his arm and said, Look.

Nice. A deep graze starting at his wrist and finishing at his elbow. I said, How d'you do that?

I was riding along and saw Cicely and that Rattle girl. I thought I'd be smart and rode up to them at a million miles an hour and jammed on the brakes (thinking, you know, a Dukes of Hazzard skid). But it was blue metal and the bike went from under me and I kept going, on my arm, and …

Pretty dumb thing to do.

You can talk.

Pop, again. 'Pop.'

He glanced back, but didn't stop.

'Pop?'

Past the skipping woman, who seemed to be bouncing even higher.

Written any more? Arnold asked.

A bit.

All that sorta stuff, it's personal … you shoulda asked me.

D'you mind?

Na. Just nothin' about the brown bags.

I'll change yer name.

Promise?

I promised, but I lied. The same brown bags they put your groceries in at Woolies. 'Cept it was your pissy pants and you had to carry them home every afternoon and other kids would ride past and say, Pissy pants! and you'd scrunch the bag and try to hide it but they knew cos they'd been in the room, or their sister had, or someone. Then you'd get home and Mum'd give you that look, but take the bag and put the pants in the wash and say, Take those off, too, we'll have to send them back tomorrow.

I gotta put it in, I said to Arnold. I want this to be honest.

Don't.

It was years ago. It's funny now.

It's not.

The skipping woman hadn't returned. Maybe she'd gone home? And stranger still – no Pop.

Anyway, Arnold said. I gotta go.

Where?

Colin's place. His dad's building a cubby. It's gonna have a pole. So you can slide down, like a fireman.

And he was gone. I was left looking at my arms. One white, the other scab-rashy brown. It'd healed nicely, but they didn't look the same. Never would, the doctor reckoned. Pop approached and I called, 'You coming in?'

He said, 'Which way's the shop?' and continued shuffling.

'Mum?'

She was in the doorway.

'Pop's looking for the shop again.'

She was out the front door, down the road, after him.

No Les. I let my head fall about, looked up, and Curtis was crossing the yard. 'What yer doin'?'

He came in, sat beside me and switched off Kraftwerk. Something was wrong. 'Why you always spying on people?' he said.

'I'm watchin' for Les.'

'She still in there?'

'Yeah.'

Mum appeared with Pop, led him down the drive, inside, into the kitchen.

Then, as some sort of good omen, the skipping woman (although she wasn't much more than a girl). Curtis said, 'She's so fuckin' hot.'

'Something wrong with her,' I said.

'Why?'

'Who skips around the block all day?'

Curtis didn't care; he was studying her extra-long legs, broad shoulders, long neck. 'She's pregnant,' he said.

I knew he didn't mean the skipping girl. 'No fuckin' way.'

'You watchin'?' Mum called.

'Yeah.'

He rested his arms on his knees, dropped his head.

'When ... what?'

'I dunno. She just told me.'

'She might be makin' it up.'

'Na, I don't reckon. We've been doin' it a lot.'

'Like?'

'Her mum starts work at six, so I've been goin' over before school, then at lunch, in the toilets, afterwards ... lots.'

I checked for Les. Nothing. 'What you gonna do?'

'Get rid of it. She says, I need a few days to think about it, and I say, What's to think about? And she says, It's my body and my decision, and I say, You reckon?'

'She wants to have it?'

No more skipping woman. The afternoon had settled. The same as always: trees, dog, bird on power line. But to Curtis, everything had changed.

'If you need help, money ...'

'I'm not havin' a kid.'

'Just tell her: an abortion, or you deal with it. It's your kid, too.'

'Fuck, don't say that. There's not actually a kid yet.'

'Well, after a few weeks it's got arms and legs.'

'Shut up!'

So I did. But then said, 'Your mum'd freak out.'

'Thanks.'

'And what about yer dad?'

He decided. 'It's simple, eh? It's gotta go. None of this *few days to think about it*, eh?'

'Exactly.'

'We're goin' to the doctor.' And he thought. 'Gotta find one Mum and Dad don't use.'

'There's a clinic in the city. Bailey told us about it, remember?'

'*Of course.*' His face glowed with possibility. 'I'll go see her now.'

'Don't let her talk you round.'

Mum stood behind us. '*Clem!*'

I checked the street. Les had emerged, and stood watering his petunias. A few feet away, Wendy, and her shopping, hiding behind a camellia.

'I ask you to do one thing.'

'I've been watching all morning. It's not my job.'

'*Ssh!*' She leaned forward, waved, as though Wendy might see. 'Wait a minute,' she whispered.

'She's not gonna hear you,' I said.

'Well, what do you suggest?'

'I got an idea,' Curtis said. He took Mum by the arm, led her out to the lounge, and told her what to do. I stayed in my spot, watching. Then Curtis ran across to Les. A muffle of words. Les switched off the hose and they walked towards Lanark I. Mum darted across the road, basket in hand, gathered Wendy from her plant and whisked her inside.

Curtis saw it was clear and returned Les to his hose, still leaking on the lawn. I heard him say, 'So that's a magpie, eh?'

'I don't keep them. No one does. You see my lorikeets, you tell me.'

And he continued.

Curtis turned to me, smiled and said, 'Will do, Les. They can'ta just flown away, eh?'

'No.'

I hit play. *Comrades and friendship*. And bed-danced.

Pop had got dressed up, polished his shoes (although Mum told him you wouldn't see them) and oiled his hair. Now, he stood, waiting: red. Next to him, a maths teacher from Melbourne (with a handlebar moustache): yellow. And next to him, a homemaker from Hervey Bay: blue. The three of them, waiting, as Burgo and Adriana had a laugh with the floor manager.

I said to Mum, 'D'you reckon he'll be okay?'

'Just what he needs.'

I wasn't so sure. Television amplified the smallest imperfection. Then again, Burgo was *nice*, and wouldn't make fun of him. There was a warm-up man, and he told jokes he probably told every Friday. (*What's the worst time to have a heart attack? When yer playin' charades!*) Friday, because all five episodes were taped on one afternoon. We'd sat through Monday and Tuesday night, Burgo and Adriana changing their clothes between each episode. Everything, changed. Contestants, banter, prizes. Even references to Ted, from Gladstone, who'd been saving for a year to visit.

It was exciting to see what was normally on telly, there, in front of you. The inch-high people made real, the wheel that actually clicked as it turned, the music, the APPLAUSE sign, cameras, the lot. The opal pendant and antique desk, a designer dress and Atari home entertainment package.

The stage manager quietened us and we sat waiting. It seemed strange: a million mums and dads and kids sitting with their tea on their lap. Old folks in nursing homes, fireys waiting for a call, the nation united in its love of OCCUPATION, seven letters. I'd told the Burrells, the Donnellans, and everyone was planning to watch when it was eventually screened. So every time the camera panned the audience I'd wave so everyone at Gleneagles High, Primary, scouts, Don's, the lot, would see me and think, Wow, Clem really made it. *Wheel of Fortune*!

We applauded and Burgo said to Pop, 'I hear you're a Datsun man?'

'Yes … *indeed*.'

'And, Doug, what's your favourite model?'

He stopped to think. Stopping didn't make good television so Adriana said, 'I used to have a Datsun.'

Burgo agreed. 'I think we all did … before we grew up.'

Laughter.

'The 610,' Pop said, 'Nineteen seventy-one.'

'And what are you gonna do with the money if you win?'

'Eh?' He stared at the lights, and swayed. Again, dead air.

'Maybe take the wife on a trip?'

'She's dead.'

Bummer. Bad, bad telly. So Adriana said, 'You can take me if you like, Doug.'

I was sure he didn't look right. I'd said this to Mum, earlier that morning. 'Do you think we should go?'

'He's looking forward to it.'

'He's a bit vague.'

'It's a long wait for tickets.'

We were going, regardless. Pop would come good, spin the wheel and win some money. Or at least that was the plan.

AUSSIE STAR, two words, five and eight letters. Pop spun first. Sixty dollars. 'I'd like a U please.'

Ernt! Not a good start. It passed to the teacher who spun $240, asked for C and scored the first letter. Then the homemaker, who scored three hundred before she was stopped.

On it went, as Chips Rafferty was revealed. It wasn't hard: obvious stuff a three-year-old could guess. I suppose this had the effect of making the average viewer feel at least partly intelligent. But that wasn't saying much, as they'd all been tested (they'd sent Pop a questionnaire in the mail) and selected because they were between 70–90 on Terman's Classification (Borderline deficiency and Dullness).

Round one drew to a close. Burgo threw to an ad then told the stage manager he needed a piss. Ten minutes later we started again. SLANG. Three words. Seven, two and four letters. Burgo asked the teacher, 'Is it true that people are getting smarter?'

'Not from what I see.'

Laughter, and the stage manager encouraged us.

Blue. The teacher drew second blood. $370. P, please. I could see he knew, but was determined to wait. Then, the homemaker, as Pop waited, his head following the wheel. 'Give it a spin, Doug.'

He did, and as he leaned forward he nearly overbalanced. The teacher went to grab him, but didn't need to, and Burgo said, 'I like a man who knows how to spin the wheel.'

But it didn't help. Sixty dollars, leaving him with the lowest score. 'He's not havin' much luck,' I whispered to Mum.

'That's not what we come for.'

Although it would've been nice. The previous evening Pop had said to me, 'If I get anything, half for Lasseter, half for you and Jen.' I'd had visions of a new Toyota, driving to school in luxury, or at least a trip to Surfers, or enough for the brick cladding Mum had always wanted for the house.

Blue: $270. L.

Red: $90. A. 'I'll solve that one, please, Burgo. *Plates of meat?*'

APPLAUSE.

Off again. Burgo didn't seem interested in the contestants. A girl checked his hair, he loosened his jacket, and Adriana sipped juice.

Pop waved to us. Mum called, 'You're doin' well.'

'He looks lost,' I said to her.

'He'll be talking about this for months.'

I didn't think he'd even remember it. We risked going home with a more despondent Pop. What would happen then? A descent into the lounge room chair, the recliner, the bed? Would Burgo smooth his way to senility?

Burgo asked the homemaker about Hervey Bay and she told him Pialba, with its grassy streets and salty-smelling breeze, was just about the best place on earth. Burgo told her his sister had bought a unit on the beach. Pop said, 'They got that in the *Post*.'

Burgo said, 'Indeed they do, Doug.'

'And them bloody meter maids, eh? They're half decent.'

'Down on the Gold Coast,' Burgo suggested, as all eyes settled, uncomfortably, on Pop.

'See,' I said to Mum.

'Ssh!'

FAMOUS BUILDING. Two words, three and five letters.

The Taj Mahal. Below 70. Definite feeble-mindedness.

The homemaker said: R.

It passed to Pop. He spun, and this time scored $1200. Mum squeezed my arm and, for a moment, he seemed to come good. 'P please, John.'

Ernt!

Red, yellow, blue. Until the Hervey Bay homemaker got lucky. $360 T. $470 M. $390 L.

Burgo risked it. Just as Pop was about to spin he said, 'Get this one, Doug, you might be in for a nice new Sunny.'

But, of course: LOSE A TURN.

Mum leaned on my shoulder. 'Shit.'

I watched as Pop waited, alone under the lights, wiping sweat from his face: a man stripped of clothes, and magic, left for people to poke sticks at. He swayed, and when the teacher told Burgo what he'd like to do with his money, Pop said, 'Doesn't always turn out like it should.'

Burgo didn't seem happy. 'Too right, Doug.' But it was the worst sort of matey *too right*.

'Just cos something looks bad,' he continued.

'That's how the wheel spins,' Burgo said.

'But he didn't, you know, Burgo. He didn't take no grog. His mate did, but he didn't. So they should stop looking for him.'

Burgo listened to his earpiece.

'It's not fair. If people'd just give him a go.'

Mum was sitting forward, biting a thumb nail. 'They should stop it.'

'I think I've had enough,' Pop said, and he turned and walked from the set.

Mum ran down to the studio floor, tripped on a cable, but took Pop by the arm and led him backstage. I was left watching.

The funny thing is, they spun again, like nothing had happened. And it was then I realised how the machine really worked.

Driving home, I said to Pop, 'Purely random. That old cow got lucky.'

'I told you I didn't want to go.'

'It was fun,' Mum said. 'Didn't you have fun?'

'Did it look like I was having fun?' He just watched the road. 'It stopped being fun when I got up there.'

'How's that?' Mum asked.

'When I saw how it was all put together, and realised it was fake. A loada shit made for idiots.' He turned to Mum. 'We should stop them screening it.'

'You signed a form.'

'Did I?'

Although she'd faked his signature.

'Anyway, they won't screen it like that, will they?'

None of us knew, or cared, I guessed. I said, 'At least they got *Happy Days* at five-thirty.'

He agreed. 'Yes, that's a good show.'

Mum never seemed happy. Clothes, quick, for the wash. Didn't eat yer lunch again, Clem. At your age, I'd expect you could make your bed. Dad, turn it down! A noise-generating device placed in our lounge room. Stress, like a Van de Graaff on full, whirring away as we slept, recharging, until the morning: If yer not gettin' up don't expect me to drive you to school or write a note.

Mums lived with this image of perfection: ordered, paid for, full marks, bin out, windows cleaned, telly turned down. They didn't understand that the machine spat out C-grade maths tests, stale bread under the bed, dog shit on the drive.

Even now, standing beside her esky, looking out the front window. 'I wish she'd just go home ... or piss off.'

'That's not very nice,' Jen said.

'I'm not feeding her forever.'

She'd been counting Wendy's days, too. Six. Breakfasts, lunches, teas. Six days of sheets and water, dunny wrap, and Les-watch. 'I got too much else to worry about,' she said.

'Where else can she go?' I asked.

'She's got a sister at Hawthorn. She could go there, but no, she'd rather have me feed her.'

'Tell her,' I said, taking K–L from the abridged and condensed bookcase.

'Can't.'

'Yes, you can. She can't stay in there forever.'

Mum studied the street. 'I think she likes the attention.'

'She's confused,' Jen said, laying out cards to tell her what might be done.

Mum sat on the esky. 'She hasn't even paid me.'

'She will,' Jen said.

'She eats like a horse. You'd think, if she was so upset ... She's costing me a fortune.'

Mum was ready to take the esky over, but wasn't sure where Les had gone. She hadn't seen his car for two days. 'Clem, go knock on his door.'

'Why me?'

'And if he answers tell him we were worried.'

'Go on,' Jen said.

'*He's out.*'

'Na,' Mum said. 'No lights, no movement. If he's not there, give me the thumbs up, I'll deliver the mornay to Her Majesty.'

K–L was best. Lithuania, with pictures of hot women working in a car factory, overalls unbuttoned, cleavage, like some sort of Eastern European porn.

'Right.' I walked from the house, across the street, down the Champnesses' drive, up the few steps, and knocked. There was a pot plant but it had shrivelled and turned brown. Beside this, a small table with smokes and matches and a glass with dried beer froth. I knocked harder. 'Mr Champness?'

I saw Mum standing on our porch, waving for me to go round the back. 'He's not here,' I called.

'*Ssh!*'

Mothers were shame generators, gauging the weather of neighbourhood opinion and posting warnings, making sure the blinds were up, bikes put away, windows closed. In case someone *saw something*, and told someone else, and the sky fell in. There is nothing to be done. You just put your life in a brown paper bag and present it for washing at the end of every disappointment-filled day.

And there he was, in his Falcon, driving towards me. He pulled up, got out and said, 'How are yer, Clem?'

'Good. You?'

'Lookin' for something?'

I thought on my feet. 'Mum hadn't seen you for a while and was a bit worried.'

He lit up. 'That's nice of her. But I've been up the Port.'

'Right.' Up the Port. Whatever that meant.

'You wanna help me?' He indicated a large cage on the back seat of the Falcon. It was full of birds, a dozen perhaps: cockatoos, lorikeets, a budgie, a few others I didn't know. They'd been shitting all the way from the Port, but he'd put a rug over the vinyl. 'Time to restock,' he said, opening the door, pulling out the cage.

Wherever the Port was, it seemed good for birds. They squawked, clung to the metal, went for Les's fingers. But he didn't care. He opened his aviary, took the cage in, closed the main door and released his new birds.

As he waited for them to come out he said, 'How the telly show go?'

'Not so good.'

'How's that?'

'Pop got a bit confused.'

They peeked out, tested the air, and flew around. Les didn't flinch. Birds didn't bother him. 'He's gettin' worse, eh?'

'I reckon.'

'We'll have to keep an eye out for him. See him out wandering sometimes.'

The birds had all come out. Les closed the smaller cage, opened the bigger one, and stopped to admire his menagerie. 'That one there,' he said. 'Took us hours.'

A sulphur-crested cockatoo. But the trip to the Port might've been wasted. There were plenty around Gleneagles.

'And the flame robin. Don't see 'em in the scrub anymore. Was a time, there'd be thousands.'

It was a nice-looking bird: red throat, white stripe above the beak. From the outback to Lanark II. It seemed a shame.

'Of course, she's the queen,' he said, indicating a superb parrot. 'Look at the yellow on that head.' He filled a seed tray from a bag of grain, inserted it between the wire and watched them eating. The superb parrot just sat there; like she felt the dislocation most keenly.

'She's not hungry,' I said, indicating.

'She will be,' he half-sang. 'Wait here.'

He went in, and banged around inside. I watched the birds as they explored their new patch; wire, shitty ground, cloudy water. He came out with two cold beers, pulled up a bench and motioned for me to sit. Then he gave me a beer and I said, 'I dunno.'

I looked down the drive. The angle obscured number 31, so in theory … I took a swig, and liked it (I'd got the taste from a few strays in the cubby). Les just said, 'You're old enough?'

'Nearly.'

'Close enough. I's drinkin' at eleven, and it never hurt me.' There was a crimson rosella, but he didn't seem that interested. 'Nice selection. I had plenty more, but I only want one of each, so I let the rest go.'

Then he explained: a family shack in the mallee, and a trapping expedition with his brother. 'He's clever, see. Sets out a net, connects it to these long branches then waits. One strays in, *whoosh*, got it.'

He drank half a bottle in one go. 'So then you got a couple of mallee parrots. Don't want 'em, let 'em go. Wait a bit longer. We were there most of the night, but we got a nice selection, eh?'

'I reckon.' Once you got the taste, it slipped down the throat. I kept checking, but there was no way Mum could see.

'That how you get all your birds?' I asked.

'Yep.' He finished, went in and returned with another two bottles. He cracked his and said, 'My brother loves his birds. He's got an aviary the size of our house. Hundreds of 'em. Sells 'em to the shops.'

'I didn't know you had a brother.'

'He never moved to the city. See, smart. I shoulda stayed there.'

The scratching of small feet.

'That's what we did when we were kids,' he said.

'Trapped birds?'

'Go out for days at a time.' He was remembering. Two boys, bare feet, thorny acacia and frogmouth. 'We had to, Clem.'

'How's that?'

He held up his beer. 'The old man was permanently pissed, so Mum relied on us. No school past ten. That's why I'm always on at you to keep going.'

'I will.' I drank. I could feel the happy numbing, as slow as test cricket.

'He'd clobber her, so we preferred it out camping and trapping.'

He seemed to lose interest in the birds, and studied the ground beneath his feet. 'Anyway, it was a bita money, so it helped.'

I finished the first and cracked the second. I could feel my head loosening on my shoulders, and felt sentimental, but had little to feel sentimental about.

'Family's what matters,' he said.

'It is.'

'But I buggered that up, eh?'

'No.'

'Can't blame her. She's living next door.'

'*She is?*'

'Seen her in the yard a few times. Don't think she knows I know. But when she's ready ...'

'Why don't you go in and talk to her?'

'Na, that wouldn't work.'

It seemed like a different Les talking. Some old, fat-bellied Buddha. With infinite patience, and wisdom. But this wasn't the man Mum or Wendy had described.

'Do you want me to say something?' I asked.

But he was still in the mallee, with his brother, and their scratched legs. 'Waiting's good too. Just lying there, lookin' up at the stars. That's the best part. Gets to the stage you don't care if no birds come. Eventually, Harry, my brother, would fall asleep and I'd cover him with a rug, and the birds'd come and eat all our grain, but I wouldn't pull the pin, cos that'd spoil it ... you know, being out there together.'

As their mum stood on the porch, calling, Harry! Les! Where are yers?

'Long as she's got enough to eat,' Les said. 'Your mum's been cookin' her decent stuff?'

'Yes.'

'I'll fix her up for it, after. Don't expect her to pay.'

'She doesn't care.'

'I know, but it must be takin' time. That's what makes this street special. Which is why we gotta look out for Doug now, eh?'

'I guess.'

'You'll have to be careful. That's what happened to Dad.'

'Dementia?'

'Just wandered off most days, and of course, Mum let him. Then one day he didn't come back, and she called the coppers, and they found him. See, you wait long enough, problems take care of themselves.'

I hoped this was true.

He lifted the dregs of his beer. 'Finished the old man, and probably finish me.'

It was finishing me. Nearly to the bottom of my second bottle.

He said, 'We'd wake up, and the net would be full.'

This seemed like a nice idea.

Wendy came walking up the drive, bag packed, slippers, petticoat showing under her dress. 'You coulda told me,' she said.

'Break's as good as a holiday,' he replied.

And she went in, saying, 'Clem, tell Mum I'll fix her up.'

It was a sunny afternoon. Pop decided to open the shed door. He'd stolen another one of Mum's bedsheets, spread it on the floor and drawn outlines for the items on his Lasseter list: dehydrated curry, roadmaps, the map, coolant, oil, shovels. Then he'd sat with the list, checking them for the tenth time. 'Guy ropes?'

'Here.'

'Grate?'

He kept insisting, saying, preparation's the key to success. I'd suggested success had more to do with finding the gold, but that was a given, apparently.

'Boots?'

He'd taken me to town, got some kid to measure my feet, fit them properly. 'That's what Blamey said.'

'What?'

'If a soldier's got good boots …'

I had no idea who Blamey was, but what did it matter?

'What about my spare teeth?'

I checked the choppers he'd had made, leaving his loose ones with the dentist overnight, staying in his room so Mum wouldn't notice. Dad, you comin' for tea?

Not hungry.

He stopped, lit a smoke and said, 'I reckon we got it all.' He surveyed the gear, and inhaled deeply, like everything was as it should be. 'Course, we prob'ly forgot something, but we can stop on the way.'

I wondered if the idea would fade, or if he'd back out, as the time approached. Then he said, 'I got you a birthday present.'

This seemed strange. To Pop, birthdays were like ponies, or Disneyland holidays.

'It's in the toolbox.'

I extracted a small parcel, done up in newspaper. Then I sat down beside him. 'Ta.'

'I didn't want to give it to you when we did the cake.'

A week before; as we ate little boys and sausage rolls, Jen sitting with her arms crossed, Mum lighting the candles.

'Go on, open it,' Pop said.

I don't think he'd bought a present in his life. That was Nan's job, then Mum's, or there wasn't a present at all. But I knew he gave Mum money and she bought stuff for us and put his name on the label. I opened it: Old Spice, of course. 'Ta, Pop.'

'It was on special.'

'Thanks anyway.'

'Make sure you use it.'

'Did Mum buy it?'

'No, she did bloody not. I bought it.'

I studied the little blue bottle. It was the best present ever. My Pop had bought it for me, his grandson. He'd walked to the shops, thought, purchased, and even wrapped. Imagine that? Pop wrapping something up. I knew, then, I'd never use it. I'd keep it to show my kids so they could understand how people worked.

'I thought Mum bought the presents?'

'You thought wrong. Anyway, since we're travelling together ...'
He checked his list. 'Toiletries?'

'Inside.'

'Don't let your mother see.'

Maybe I was grinning.

'So what?' he said. 'I bought you something. Tyre pressure
gauge?'

'There.' I pointed.

'There's something else in there.'

A one pound note. Old. English. I smelt, felt it, examined the
fading image of the king. 'That's an old one,' I said.

'You'll need to look after it.'

Why give someone a pound? What was a pound even worth? A
dollar? Two? Was he trying to be generous, somehow?

'Thanks for that, I'll buy something with it.'

'You can't.'

'No?'

'No one'll accept it. Anyway, it's not for spending. It's so you
remember.'

'What?'

He took a moment. 'When I was nineteen I went to England.'

'I never knew that.'

'Got a job and saved a bita money. Bought a ticket, six weeks on
a steamer. The *Orion*. Heard of it?'

'No.'

'Anyway, arrived in London, got drunk, worked in a meat-
packing store, saved some more money, travelled around –
Stonehenge, Edinburgh – all over the place.'

'Why'd you never say anything?'

'Met a nice girl, but a week or so later ...'

I studied the pound note. I thought I knew why.

'Time was up. I came home, met yer Nan, got a job and settled
down. And that's how it's been, ever since.' He took the note. 'And

this … this was the last pound I come home with. The only one I didn't spend.'

'So it's pretty old?'

'Pretty.' He returned it. 'You keep it.'

'Why?'

'To remind you.'

'What?'

'Fifty years I been lookin' at it, and every time I've thought, I shoulda stayed longer, or shoulda gone back, travelled to America, France, all over the place. It's a big world, Clem.'

'I've heard.'

'Staying here, that's okay, but you only live once, eh?'

I put it in my wallet. It seemed strange, carrying a regret in your pocket for that long. 'You reckon I should travel?'

'Yep, go see it all. Don't believe what they say about university, or getting a good job. That'll all come in time, but you gotta go. Sit on the lion in Trafalgar Square.'

'You reckon?'

'I think back now, that was the happiest day of my life. Sittin' there, nothin' to do, no money.'

Silent, again. He wasn't forgetful. There was no Alzheimer's.

'Mortgage, that's what kills a man,' he said. '*Mort*, from the Latin for death. That's what it is: a little death, every day, till you forget.'

He'd given me a present. But old blokes like Pop only did something for a reason. Old Spice, because he wanted to give me a pound. And now it was done there'd never be another present. Which was okay.

He'd had enough. 'We need to fill those water drums, make sure they don't leak.'

'Done it.'

'Righto. We'll need plenty of warm clothes, even in September. Middle of the desert. Plenty of them explorers died of exposure.'

We saw the dog first: Fi-Fi, staring at us, a little yelp, then Ernie looking down the drive. 'Hey, Doug.'

'Quick, shut the door,' Pop said. He stood, dropped his smoke and reached up.

'What you up to?' Ernie asked, starting down the drive.

'Nothing.' He turned to me. 'Help, will yer?'

I reached for it and started pulling it down, but Ernie was already there.

'What's all that gear?' he asked.

'Nothin',' Pop said, giving up on the door.

Ernie came in the shed, inspected the equipment and said, 'Like yer gonna invade Russia.'

Pop refused to comment.

'Doug?'

'I told you, we're goin' camping.'

Ernie sat down. 'You promised, Doug.'

Pop lit another smoke, looked down the drive and said, 'We gotta finish up. Fay comes home she'll see this lot.'

'So?'

I could almost hear him grinding his teeth.

'I won't take up much room.'

'You won't take up any.'

'This isn't fair.' He squeezed my arm. 'You got yer licence yet?'

'He doesn't need a licence to drive a Datsun. Any idiot can do that.'

Ernie said, 'You're too old for them thousands of kilometres, Doug.'

'Bullshit.'

'And Clem, it's a lot for someone still at school.'

'We'll manage.'

'Easier with three.'

'Two's enough.'

'You'd regret it.'

Pop turned on him. 'Regret it? What? Not takin' you?'

'We had an agreement.'

'*When?*'

'You've got a selective memory.'

'*Bullshit.*' He closed the door, then returned to Ernie. 'Look at all this. How we gonna get it in with you takin' up half the back seat?'

Fi-Fi pissed against the wall. Pop used his foot to lift her off the ground, but even this didn't bother Ernie. He said, 'What about my trailer?'

'What trailer?'

'Come on, I'll show you.'

Pop stood firm. If he went, he was conceding. 'This is my trip, mine.'

Ern just waited.

'Pommy bastard!' He kicked a water container. 'Right! Show us!'

A few minutes later we were in Ernie's shed. He removed a tarp and revealed his trailer, rusted, flat tyres, uneven from broken springs and suspension. 'That Datsun got a tow bar?'

'Yes.'

'Good-o. Bita spit and polish. Was a time you'd fix somethin' like this in an afternoon.'

Pop shook his head. 'I'm not takin' that dog.'

Ernie shrugged, but then said, 'She sits in my lap.'

July

Somehow, Curtis had convinced the owner of the North East Road BP to give him a job. Mr Haslam had been one of our childhood idols. Mum'd pull up in the Datsun, he'd be waiting (never busy with anything else), pop his head in the window and say, 'Usual, Fay?'

Usual, because everyone filled their car with fifty-fifty. As a kid you'd watch the little cups stirring the pink water, passing it into the tube as Mr H stood smoking, watching the road for something different, although there never was. He wore a shirt with a BP logo; a proud company man (I guessed). Grey hair, slicked back, and a carpenter's pencil in his pocket. As he filled our car he'd take my nose between his fingers and twist it and say, 'Careful, it might drop off.' Then he'd get bored, put out his smoke, ask for Mum to pop the bonnet and check the oil.

Once, in 1977, there was a raffle. A Christmas stocking that touched the station's ceiling. Being Whelans, we never won anything. Mum had given up buying lottery tickets. It was, she said, like God had painted a cross on her forehead. Anyway, Mr Haslam convinced her to have a go (because it was for the crippled children), and we won. I can still remember Gazza (not that we could call him that) helping us tie it to the roof of the Datsun, driving home, unloading, Pop saying something like *fuck me*, taking it in and standing it beside the Christmas tree. And Mum saying, 'See, if you live long enough everything happens.'

July 2: the middle of a warm, dry winter. It was quiet, so Curtis opened a pack of Winnie Blues, offered me one and said, 'He doesn't care.'

We smoked. A few people stopped, so he went out and served them, came in with the money and returned with their change. Ernie and Fi-fi walked past on the way to the Windsor and I called out the door, 'Ernie, Pop's got new springs.'

He smiled and gave a thumbs up, but continued, because cold beer would only stay cold for so long.

The newsstand had the paper and the *Post* and some titty mags. Curtis opened one, showed me Mrs July and explained how they injected pig fat to make them big. 'You gotta admit, it'd be nice.'

'Not her.'

'Taken.' He read: '*Glenda studies hydraulic engineering at a Queensland university* … yeah, right.'

'So what about Tracey?' I asked, placing my smoke in a tray, eating a handful of teeth.

'All sorted.' He continued studying the magazine, then approached the staff toilet.

'I'm not serving no one,' I said.

'*Fuck.*' He went in and locked the door.

'Hurry up.'

No reply. Of course, a car pulled up. 'You got a customer.'

'Can you?'

The car tooted so I headed out, undid the cap and said, 'Fill her up?'

An older woman with what must have been her grandkids. I started, waited, stopped and took her money. I went back in and said, 'Don't worry, I got it.'

Nothing. I returned, gave her the change and another car pulled up. I did this one too, but when it'd gone, I knocked on the door. 'How long's it take?'

He came out, zipped up and returned to his half-done smoke. The magazine didn't seem to interest him anymore. 'What was I saying?'

'Tracey.'

'I think that's resolved.' He opened the fridge, took out a Coke and cracked it. 'So we went to the clinic and there's this doctor, and he gives us a talk about contraception, looks at me like, You dirty little prick. Which was fair enough. Then he says, Once it's done it's done, and he asks her what she thinks.'

Curtis served another car, then continued. 'She says, I reckon I'd make an okay mum.'

'Fuck.'

'Exactly. He asks me and I say, Maybe if we could … take care of it, we'd heed your advice next time.'

He found a Bay City Rollers best-of in the carousel and put it on. *I only want to be with you.* 'S'pose I should do some work.' He found a broom and started sweeping the lino. 'Anyway, then it was on. Tracey saying I should support her decision, it was *her* body, *our* child. But I just said, Na, forget it, and asked the doctor about our options. He gave us this leaflet, and explained the process, and Tracey starts again. I'm not doin' that. I told her she should, and she called me an arsehole.'

He swept the dust, butts and pull tabs out the front door. It was strange to see him working, with his sewn-on logo. He wasn't the logo type. He danced with his broom. '*It happens to be true ... I only want to be with you.*' Then he grabbed my arm, and we waltzed, sort of. I gave in and sang, '*You stopped and smiled at me, Asked me if I'd care to dance ...*'

And then, in a squeaky chorus, like we'd done a hundred times in the cubby, as the batteries slowed the music: '*I just wanna be beside you everywhere ...*' On and on, until the bell rang, and we climbed down the steps his dad had welded.

When he came back he said, 'The doctor looks at her and says, Miss Smith, bringing a child into the world is a very big responsibility. Like that, like he was on my side.'

The smokes were finished, the pornography, Coke, Rollers, so we helped ourselves to a couple of Gaytimes.

'She huffs and puffs but eventually takes the brochure.'

'And she's ... done it?'

'I dunno.'

'Why?'

'When we went out she calls me all these names, storms off.'

'So she might still be preggers?'

'I guess, but in that case it's not my responsibility.'

The phone rang and Curtis answered it. 'Yes, Mr Haslam ... not very busy, no ... just cleaning up, then I thought I might hose down the driveway ... yes, I know ... righto, see you at seven.'

'And what if she doesn't ...?'

He finished his ice cream. 'She had the choice.'

He hosed the driveway. I sat on a pile of tyres. 'I reckon your Mum'd be happy.'

'I don't want to talk about it.'

'She loves kids. But she just got stuck with you and John.'

'There's a secret.'

'What?'

'How Gazz holds his smoke, but doesn't blow the place up.'

'It's probably got eyes by now. Yours. And a nose, stubby—'

He turned the hose on me.

'Or maybe it's a chook? And it can walk backwards?'

He kept wetting me, but I ran, laughing, across the driveway. *'Dad, can we go to the footy?'*

A car pulled up, but he didn't care.

'Think I shat me nappy. Dad, can you change it?'

It was a Torana, a girl on her P-plates. She got out and said, 'Fill her up, please, Curtis.'

Harris. Something Harris. One of Tracey's mates. Curtis unscrewed her cap and began.

She said, 'Trace told me you worked here now.'

'Yeah?'

She waited, deciding. 'Told me to tell you she's gonna fix it.'

No expression, but I could tell he was smiling inside.

'But she said she's gonna make you pay.'

'Yeah?' He finished, replaced her cap and said, 'Ten fifty.'

She gave him the correct change. 'You didn't check my oil.'

'D'you want me to?'

'Na.'

'Well, why'd you ask?'

She was enjoying it. 'You're a creep.'

'She never said no.'

'That's disgusting!' She took a folded piece of paper from her pocket, opened it, and showed him. It was his photocopied bum, blown up to a full page, and the caption: *This is the arse of Curtis Burrell. Big, smelly and full of shit, like him.*

Curtis said, 'That's very grown-up.'

'Cost her twenty dollars.'

'What?'

'To have five hundred copies made.'

His face went white.

'And it took us four hours to stick them up around school. What d'you reckon about that?'

He studied his arse. It seemed familiar, convincing.

'And she reckons there's more to come.' She smiled, got in her car and drove off.

'Five hundred?' I asked.

'She's bullshitting.'

It was a decent arse, with a long cleft, dimples, and a shadow that might've been one of several things.

'Come on!' He went inside the shop, wrote a note (*Back in 10 mins*) and locked the door. We ran down North East Road, past Don's, the salvage yard, Cara-Rest campers. Faster, through the back streets, past the semi-detached houses and cracking fibro. I called for him to slow down but he paid no attention. Five hundred arses. If they hadn't been named, it might've been okay, but Trace had made it clear.

We arrived. She wasn't lying. On the front fence, the staff room door, the main doors, the arbour, stapled to trees. Every square inch of weatherboard building. Arses, hundreds of them, flapping in the breeze, blowing along the ground, caught in lavender bushes. Arses on the change rooms and arses on home economics. Bums all over our art room, where the year had started with such promise.

'Come on.' He started pulling them off, gathering handfuls, stuffing them down his BP shirt. This proved inefficient, so he fetched a wheelie bin and we started filling it.

Later, we walked around the school checking. He was sure we hadn't found all five hundred. Then we heard a voice, looked up, and Tracey and Something Harris were sitting on a fire escape eating what might have been popcorn and drinking Diet Coke. Tracey said, 'I still got the original.' And she held it up.

'You're such a fucking idiot,' Curtis said.

We walked back to the BP with the bin. It took us an hour, but Curtis was determined to destroy the images. When we arrived Gary was waiting in the shop. 'Ten minutes?'

When Curtis explained, Mr H laughed so hard he leaked (or so he said). He was good like that. He might've missed a few sales, but they'd be back. What mattered was that this Curtis kid, this strange, slightly idiotic boy of the suburbs, had learned his lesson.

There was a forty-four-gallon drum behind the workshop. Gary helped us unload the pictures, and he tipped a little petrol on them, threw in a smoke, and we watched them burn. Over twenty minutes, we fed the flames. Gary took care of the customers, and we overheard him telling one what we were burning. They laughed.

It was getting dark and I said, 'I'm going home.'

'I'll come with you.'

The fire died down.

Gary won out, because he got a bin, and it was handy (once he painted over the school name) for the driveway.

That's how it was done back then. There was no point worrying about anything. It was only a bum. Everyone had one.

I got out, closed the door and Pop said, 'Tomorrow, practise yer parking.'

The L-plates were still L. Curtis was in his yard, and called over, 'How did it go?'

'Nine points,' Pop said.

'Bad luck.'

Seeing how you were only allowed eight.

'What did you do wrong?'

'Plenty,' Pop continued. 'Reversing, parking …'

'*Pop*,' I said.

'And we'll keep going until you get it right.'

He went in, and I could hear him telling Mum and Jen before he was even through the door. I didn't want to face another half-hour of analysis. The fact was, Pop was pissed off he'd have to spend more time preparing for Lasseter.

Luckily, there was a voice. *'Clem?'*

I followed it into Val's yard, over the lunar landscape, to David, sitting in the shade. He said, 'Don't worry, I failed three times before I got mine.'

This is what I wanted to hear. Dave was a sage, stranded under his Bodhi tree, contemplating life's possibilities.

'I'm in the Datsun waiting,' I said, 'and he gets in and looks at me like, *You're* gonna be trouble, writes something down, says, Reverse, turn right and enter the left carriageway. Who says that? The left carriageway?'

I noticed a boot on the footpath, half-burning, half-smoking. 'Is that yours?'

'No.'

'I pull out and this guy comes burning along, pounds the horn and old four-eyes writes something down. I say, I did check, but he was speeding. And he just looks at me like, I'll be the judge of that.'

I sat in the grass beside him. It was one of those indecisive winter mornings: sun for a few minutes, overcast, a few spots of rain. 'Who sets a boot on fire?' I asked.

'Go on,' he insisted.

Ernie, from next door: *'Worker competes with worker, and the employer takes advantage of this. Wages are driven down ...'*

We turned and saw, through the bushes, Ernie in his singlet and shorts, sitting on his porch, reciting (what I assumed to be) more of his soapbox speeches. *'The effect of this is a weakening of the workers' rights.'*

Blah, blah. The boot burned, the sun broke through. 'Go on,' David insisted.

'Reverse parking. It was an impossible gap, no one coulda got their car in. I said, Seems a bit small, and he said, Plenty of room. I said, I dunno, and he scribbled again.'

'The covenant of minimum wage is a temporary construct.' I noticed

the four bottles of dark ale. 'Comrade Sharpe is speaking,' I said.

David smiled. 'I've heard them all. What else?'

The flames had died down, but the boot was still smoking. 'Did you see who put it there?' I asked.

'Mum.'

'Why?'

'She threw it, from the backyard. You should put in a complaint about him.'

'I should. I had three shots, but couldn't get it in.'

'*Idealism becomes materialism.*' Ida came out in her leotards and said, 'Get in before everyone sees you.'

He didn't respond. It didn't need dignifying. When the time came, certain people would be put against a wall.

So Ida went in. 'How'd you feel if I sat on the porch in my underwear?'

'There were a few other things,' I said.

'Go on.'

'A school crossing.'

'*Ah.*'

'But … but … it said to slow *if children present.*'

The boot was shitting me off. I went over and picked it up, filled it with dirt to stop it smoldering, and brought it back. Then I sat in my spot, and read the tag: *Sid Donnellan.*

David said, 'Mum and Peter had a disagreement.'

Apparently Peter had decided to burn some of Sid's old gear in the backyard. Val had gone out, seen the clothes and shouted at him, picked up a poker and tried to remove them. Some were destroyed, others half-burned. But she'd got them out, stamped on them, and said, 'What made you think …?'

'It's like living in a museum.'

'*They were your father's.*'

She'd continued dragging underwear from the ashes, reaching in for the boots, but had flicked one high into the air, over the house and into the front yard.

'Why today?' she'd asked.

'This is the problem,' he'd said. 'Like he's still here, and you won't move on.'

David said, 'Peter's always reckoned that.'

'What?'

'Mum won't move on.'

This made sense. Sid was on the walls, his watch on the sideboard. There was even a pile of his magazines beside his recliner.

Ernie was snoring. The boot was cold. The fugue had ended. I noticed something shining in the grass, walked a few steps on my knees and examined it. Pond's Powder. It was an old tin, the paint flaking, the borders rusted.

'That came over, too,' David said.

I emptied some of the powder, smelt it, blew it into a cloud.

'Even that. She'd never part with it.'

'Why?'

He told me the story of how his mum had prepared for her first child. Sid had helped with a nursery, a homemade cot, reflective stars on the ceiling. A change table, cloth nappies, pins, powder. Pond's.

'I reckon they had the name picked out.'

'Who?'

'Clement.'

It dawned on me. The conversations I'd had with Mum. 'Why'd you give me such a crappy old name?'

'It's not crappy, it's nice.'

'Mum got pains too early,' David said. 'Dad rushed her to the hospital. Bombs dropping everywhere, but he just drove, cos it was coming. *He* was coming.'

'Clem?' I asked.

'Yeah. They arrived and out he comes, and they're celebrating, but then he stops breathing.'

'Shit.'

'The doctors tried to help, but they couldn't … and he died.'

Now I got it. Me asking Mum, 'Can I change my name?'

'To what?'

'Trevor? Gary? Darren? Anything but Clem.'

'No, you cannot. It's a nice name.'

I smelt the talc again; felt it on my arse. 'So, we should give it back to her?'

'I guess.' I held the tin, studied the floral design, and wondered about this dead baby, lying on a stainless steel table, as Hitler went about his business.

'So she asked my mum …?'

'No, she didn't ask. But your Mum knew, and offered.'

I handed the tin to Dave, but he returned it and said, 'You hold onto it, eh? I'll tell her. I think she'd like that.'

'What sorta idea's that?' Ida asked.

'Mind yer own business,' Ernie told her.

We removed the tarp, examined the trailer, and Pop said, 'She'll need a bita work.'

'Nothin' major,' Ernie explained.

'You're too old for this, Ern,' Ida said. 'If you want another heart attack.'

He didn't reply, but I guessed he was thinking it was better than sitting around listening to her.

Pop said, 'I'm a lot older than Ernie, and I'm going.'

'Well …'

'And whatever you do, not a word to Fay,' Ernie said.

She just shook her head. 'Man your age, Doug, should be relaxing. Put your feet up, bowls …'

'Couldn't think of anything worse.'

Pop threw the tarp aside and we pushed the trailer. Nothing. Again, and we managed a few inches. And again, and it rolled on its flat tyres out of the shed.

'You two should know better,' Ida said. 'What if something goes wrong? It'll all be down to Clem.'

'He's up to the job,' Pop said.

'How will Fay know what's goin' on? Once you go, she'll be worried sick.'

'She'll be fine.'

'How you gonna keep in touch?'

'Give it a rest,' Ernie said. 'We'll ring you.'

'And when we come home with a boat loada gold?' Pop asked.

'I'm not holding my breath.'

We pushed again, and the trailer emerged into the sodium-lit night. It was warm, overcast, and blowy. That's why Pop had chosen his moment. No one would hear the commotion. The trailer ground on its flat tyres. The springs amplified every bump in the concrete. There was no suspension. The whole thing shook and wobbled like it might fall apart at any moment.

Ida wasn't finished. 'What if I tell Fay?'

'You won't,' Ernie replied.

'If it's the only way to make you lot see sense.'

'She won't,' he told us.

'I will.'

'You do, you watch. Whose name's on the deed?'

'You can have it. Loada shit, anyway.'

She'd always thought this. Always wanted brick, or a nicer street, suburb, life. Ernie was the eternal disappointment. She'd tell anyone who'd listen. *I chose bad. I shoulda waited, seen what else was available.*

'You tell anyone, you see,' Ernie said.

'Yer mad, the lot of yer. You haven't thought it through. I wouldn't mind if yers were goin' fishin' or somethin', but *gold*.' And with that she turned and went in, slamming the door.

'She'll be okay,' Ernie said. 'Now come on.'

We got behind the trailer, pushed it down the drive and onto the street. Then the skipping woman buzzed past, singing. Ernie said, 'At this time of night?'

Pop shooshed him and we continued. Ernie said, 'Saw you on the telly last night, Doug.'

He didn't reply. He'd refused to watch. Mum had made popcorn and cracked fresh Coke and we'd laughed, and Pop had come out of his room and switched it off, but Mum had switched it back on. Then he'd said, 'Think it's funny?'

'No, but it's strange to see you on the telly.'

Back on the road, Ernie said, 'You hada bita bad luck.'

Pop shook his head. 'I don't know why I agreed.'

'Every time it spun me and Ida were rootin' for yer. Woulda been nice if they'd given you some sort of prize. My sister went on Tony Barber.'

'She win?' I asked.

'First night. They offered her a trip to Tassie but she turned it down. Always regretted it. Second night, put on this professor, and that was that.'

'Never been to Tassie,' Pop said.

'No,' Ern agreed. 'They reckon it's nice.'

Maybe, I thought, this was Pop's Tasmania. The trip he'd never taken, or continued. Maybe he was still trying to get back to the bronze lion.

We kept going, and I thought I noticed the curtain move in the Donnellans' lounge room. 'Don't look now,' I said, indicating.

Pop checked and said, 'He can mind his own business.'

We arrived at number 31. Turned the trailer, lined it up with the drive, and pushed. It went forward, then back, forward, back. We stopped and Pop said, 'We'll have to do better, gents. Three thousand kilometres, and we can't get it in the shed.'

We tried again, and this time made it along the drive, past the front door and into the shed. Pop closed it, and said, 'Gonna take a bita work, Ern.'

'Bita paint, get it registered, coupla wheels.' He sat on Pop's chair, took out a smoke (just one, for himself) and lit it.

Pop said, 'I reckon we take turns cooking?'

Ernie didn't reply.

'Ern?'

'Yes, I reckon.'

Pop had already explained his concerns. Ernie was a strange

sort of communist; he had the theories, but not the practice. Pop'd said, 'That's why I didn't want to take him.'

'Cos he's lazy?'

'Exactly. He was sacked, and no one'd give him another job. Just complained, agitated. People'll listen for so long. Not sure that's the sort of man we need along.'

Pop watched him smoking, like a budget Ho Chi Minh. 'And we'll take turns driving, eh, Ern?'

'In for a penny in for a pound.'

'And a ten per cent cut?'

'*Ten?*'

'Considering … I think that's quite generous.'

Ernie reclined and thought about it. 'Risking my health, and heart, for ten per cent?'

Pop shook the trailer and a light fell off. 'I could get the gear in the back.'

Then the side door opened and Peter Donnellan looked in.

'Jesus!' Pop said.

'Saw you go past.'

'Well, we're just talkin'. Aren't we, Ern?'

'I guess so, Doug.'

Peter came in, examined the trailer and said to Ernie, 'Long time since you've had this out?'

'Few years.'

'He asked if I could fix it up,' Pop said. 'That's my next project.'

Peter was having none of it. 'Why bother?'

Ernie didn't seem concerned. It wasn't his reef of gold.

'Like I said,' Pop repeated. 'A project.'

Peter said, 'I don't want nothin', assuming you find something.'

'*Fuck!*' Pop glared at me. Then Peter. 'I'm fixin' the trailer. That's it.'

'I like that dry country. And if you remember, you told me—'

'*I never told you nothin'.*'

But he must've told him something. Maybe, over the decades, he'd told everyone.

'Four seats,' Peter said. 'You takin' the Datsun?'

'Where?'

'The reef?'

'*What fuckin' reef?*'

'Lasseter's?'

'There's no bloody reef, and no bloody trip. There's nothin'. And if there was, I wouldn't go with you lot.' Pop glared at them, then me. 'Got it? It's my map, and my gold.'

'I'll drive, cook, navigate, anything,' Peter said. 'And I don't want an ounce of your gold. I just wanna come along. With my mate, Clem. Exams coming up. We gotta lotta work to do, eh, Clem?'

I dared not speak.

'I'm very useful, Doug.'

Ernie continued smoking. He didn't care. Someone in the back was company, even if it was the cat woman's son. He said to him, 'She's got another one, hasn't she?'

Peter didn't want to start on cats. 'Doug?'

Pop was fuming. 'I don't even wanna go,' he said, turning, storming from the shed and going inside.

Ernie finished his smoke, put it out on the shed frame and said, 'What's she call it, Providence?'

Peter didn't care. 'Keeps it inside.'

'Figure it'll take her another ten years to breed a colony. By then I'll be dead.' He stood.

'So?' Peter said.

'Don't ask me.'

I found Providence in our garden, and headed next door to return him. Jen was sitting in the garden, tanning herself, 'Too shy' coming through the window. She said, 'Whose is that?'

'Val's.'

'I thought they took 'em all?'

'Missed one.'

She slipped on her sunglasses and reclined. She'd *tried* Ida's Figurama, set up in the lounge room in her old leotards, jumped about for half an hour before retiring to the fridge, and low-fat yoghurt. Tried.

I knocked and went in; down the hall of many photos.

'In here,' Val called.

I went in, and Wendy sat at the table, nursing tea, smiling. 'Hey, Clem.'

'Mrs Champness.'

Unusual. There was an interchangeability of parts in Lanark II. Things fit where they fit, depending on what was needed. But Val and Wendy were a couple of positives, giving off too similar a charge.

I handed Providence to Val and said, 'He was in our yard.'

'Let him go,' she said, already fixing my tea.

'I thought you were going to keep him inside?'

'Why bother? Ernie knows.'

I sat down and noticed an official-looking form on the table. Wendy said, 'I got it.'

'What's that?'

'The form they said I'd need to fill out. To find out … *Name, address, contact, year of birth, place of birth, sex of child.* And that's about as far as we got, Clem.'

'You gonna send it in?'

'Oath. Val's been helping me, haven't you?'

Busy with tea.

'Then there's this bit about … circumstances, but I know what I'm gonna say.'

Val gave me my tea. 'That's easy enough. Mother needs her kiddy.'

Wendy said, 'I'm gonna write about the nuns.'

'Seems fair,' I ventured.

'Then, the next bit says: *Reasons for seeking information.*'

'Seems obvious,' Val said. 'You shouldn't be expected to say.'

'No, I can see it,' Wendy said. 'Assuming the kiddy's settled in somewhere else, grown up, maybe even had his own family.'

'I suppose. Could be a bit of a shock, comin' out of the blue.'

As she imagined Clem, perhaps, busy mowing his lawn when the postie arrived.

Wendy said, 'What d'you reckon, Clem?'

I remembered the promise I'd made in the Rosie house. 'I guess you gotta say you *need* to know.'

She slid the form in front of me. 'That's it. You write it.'

Maybe I was a writer, but this was beyond my expertise. I picked up the pen. 'You want me to just …?'

They both waited.

It's been years since I last saw my child. I never felt like I had any choice. I read it back.

'Good start,' Val said.

Since then, there hasn't been a day when I haven't wondered …

'Oh, you can write,' Wendy said. 'Can't he, Val?'

'He's workin' on a novel. Aren't you, Clem?'

I nodded. This was the strangest story of all.

Of course, if he agrees to see me, I promise I won't interfere with his life. As long as I get a chance to explain.

Wendy said, 'I can still see my mum in a frock, with her long white gloves, telling the nuns it couldn't be avoided.'

Val had cupped her tea in her hands.

'And the glass-fronted cabinets full of … instruments.' She was there, I guessed. The sheets all white, with little Calvary crosses, the nuns all pale and pink and forced smiles. And her mum (when the nuns had left the room) saying, They reckon a couple of hours. Or can you get up now?

'That enough?' Wendy asked me, and Val.

'Pretty clear,' I said. 'Seems natural that someone would want to …?'

They were hanging off my every word. But what did I know? Wendy reread it and said, 'That flows real nice, Clem. Just what I wanted.'

'Just hope they let you,' Val said. 'These government departments have a peculiar way of thinking.'

'How's that?' Wendy asked.

'Well, that money we applied for ...'

And she explained. The form, like this one, where you had to say why you needed three thousand dollars.

'I wrote down that David couldn't get in the bathroom. Well, he can't.'

'No,' Wendy agreed.

'That me and his brother had to lift him out of his chair, and I'm old. I wrote that we couldn't do it no more, and we couldn't afford for someone else to come in.'

'Seems fair,' Wendy agreed.

'It's like a circus of a night. Me takin' off his daks, Peter gettin' him under the arms, dragging him into the shower, dumpin' him on that chair. All I asked for was a few thousand. But, of course, it comes back no.'

'Disgrace,' Wendy said.

'They got enough to fly politicians around the globe, but a few thousand for a shower.'

There seemed to be a consensus: hard-working people paid taxes, asked for little, but when they did need help it was always no. Still, Wendy wasn't put off. 'Where there's a will there's a way.'

My mind was ticking over. A will. A way. In a street of handymen, and foreignies.

'Maybe we should tell them about my mother,' Wendy said to me.

'How's that?'

'How it wasn't *my* choice. How she had the car out front, running, and got them Catholic hounds to take me down the steps, out the door, the ramp, in a wheelchair.'

I could see this too, and hear the chair's flat wheels grinding on the asphalt. Arriving at the car, brakes on, Come on, Wendy, help us a bit.

'I suppose it might help,' I said.

The choice had been made for me. My mother and the nuns had decided they knew best. Although I was young, I thought I might make a good mother.

'In the car on the way home,' Wendy said. 'I started kicking and screaming, but then I musta fallen asleep. I reckon they'd given me something.'

My son was forcibly removed. The shock is as great today as it was then. I've never stopped thinking about him, wanting to hold him, to see his face, hear him talk. All of the things any mother expects. To see him walk for the first time, write, sing, start school.

Wendy nodded. 'You got it just right, Clem.'

I felt ashamed, because now I was just writing.

'There's a lot we could say,' Wendy explained. 'Like how when I woke up Mum was sittin' there and she said, All done. Like that. Happy as Larry. All done. Now, Wendy, she said, we gotta move on.'

I was taken home and told to forget about my boy. I was told it was best that way.

'It was a week later. Mum went out and I called a taxi, went back to the nuns, and they told me he'd gone. Put that, Clem.'

So I did.

'How can I be denied a sight of my boy when none of this was my fault? Say that.'

Again.

'Even just seeing a photo. His hair – could you imagine? – how it'd part in the middle.' She stopped, exhausted by the thought. 'Can you say all that, Clem?'

'I think I've got enough,' I said, showing her how we'd filled the half-page allowed. 'I reckon when they see what we've written …'

She waited. 'But if we got one more line, I'd like to put down that my husband's supported me, all these years.'

I put it on the back.

Providence had climbed onto Val's lap and fallen asleep. The tea was cold. I'd barely touched mine.

'Know what I'd like to say,' Wendy managed.

'What?' Val asked.

'The way it was done.' She looked at me, but guessed it was okay. 'How they made sure I'd never have another one.'

As a whole load of things were explained. Les's faulty plumbing laid to rest.

The prison-bar memory of a thousand days. Handball, losing interest, the Stephenson twins putting away milk benches, Pop's chalkless map (for now), walking along the fence line, and an old man smiling at me (stranger danger) and Mr Gottl saying, 'Oi, Clem, what cher doin'?' Sherrin thumping across the afternoon, as sprinklers drizzled, boys fell, teeth chipped, and the bell ... in.

Walking home. A handful of seed pods, high in the air, hitting Jen and her friend, an earlier Tracey. The same driveways, bushes with holes where cats slept, stumped cars and onion weed. As though the world would go on like this forever. The hot-steel smell of burning rosemary, and loin chops, perhaps. Mum, as I fell asleep, as I fell asleep.

A Datsun 180B pulled up. Chariot hubcaps, fresh liquorice tyres, chrome trim and bucket seats. A man got out and headed into the Glassons'. The car was left alone, waiting. For me. Squat, solid and angry-eyed. Ernie and Fi-Fi walked past, and she pissed on it. He waved and said, 'Howya, Clem?'

Then footsteps on the path. John approaching, jumping our fence and running towards me. 'You there, Clem?'

'What?'

'Doug around?'

'Go to the shed.'

He disappeared. I went into Pop's room and found him, half-asleep on his bed. 'He's back,' I said.

'Tell him I'm not here.'

I waited.

'Where is he?'

'The shed.'

I followed him out and as we went Mum said, 'Where you goin'?'

'Work on the trailer,' Pop said.

'What's Ern want a trailer for?'

Pop unlocked the shed door and we went in, John carrying his backpack and a plastic bag. He sat on the floor, glared at me and said to Pop, 'Why's he gotta be here?'

'He's meant to be helping me with the trailer.' Pop noticed the bag. 'What you got there?'

'I founda place to stay. Williamstown. In a shed. George's old girl cooked for me.'

'Who's George?'

'Friend. But I couldn't keep livin' there, Doug.'

'Righto.' Pop sat and rolled a smoke.

''Bout the worst thing of all, listenin' for who's pullin' up in the drive, who's knockin' at the door.'

Pop lit up, stood and examined the welds he'd made on the trailer's wheel wells. 'You shoulda been doin' this.'

'So I's thinkin' I should give myself in?'

'It's an art, welding. Harry woulda taught you.'

'Doug?'

Pop picked up the bag and emptied it out. Twenty or more cartons of cigarettes fell to the ground. 'Gary Haslam?'

'Didn't have much choice, eh?'

'He's given Curtis a job.'

I knew Curtis had a key, but wasn't sure if, or how.

'I can get ten bucks a carton,' John said.

'*Think*,' Pop growled. 'How does one thing fix another?'

'How else was I gonna—'

'*Think*.' He put the cartons back in the bag, and handed it to John. Then he looked at me. 'Is there a camera?'

'No.'

Then John. 'So, we'll fix it.'

Pop helped John up. We went out, down the street, past the substation and the glass shop, reflections of three shabby figures in the low-light dusk. I never liked what I saw. Mirrors had a way of distorting. We stopped before the servo and Pop said, 'Go on, take 'em back.'

The servo was dark, the concourse empty. John refused to move. 'I need the money.'

'I'll give you the money. How did you get in?'

He took the key from his pocket and showed Pop.

'Come on.' Pop took him by the arm, dragged him to the door and waited while he unlocked it. They went in and replaced the smokes, locked the door and returned. John handed me the key and said, 'Give it back to him, will yer?'

As we walked back he explained how he'd made up his mind to go home. Knocked, but there was no one there. Went in, searched Curtis's room and found the key with Haslam's BP tag. 'I's gonna see what Dad thought,' he said.

'Well, come on then,' Pop replied.

'No, not now.'

Back to our shed. Pop picked up a set of new shockers and started bolting them to the chassis. For a while, John watched. He lit his own smoke and said, 'I don't care about nothin' no more.'

'Yes, you do,' Pop said.

'I could string up a rope from the rafter there.'

Pop didn't even look up. 'You could.'

'Save everyone a lot of trouble.'

Pop turned on him. His voice was solid, determined. 'Since *I* gave up, I been watchin' a lot of telly. That one where they stand talking at each other. Tess and Eugene and Carrie.'

John just listened.

'Pathetic. But it's not real. Some idiot wrote it, for stupid housewives.'

John said, 'I coulda stood in front of a train. I's watchin' the other day, for an hour, just thinkin' …'

'Why didn't you?'

'Just didn't.'

'Well, stop goin' on about it. I coulda done it, Clem coulda, we all coulda.'

Pop kept working. John stood, helped him with the springs and waited until he had them fastened.

Pop tightened the bolts and sat down. 'So, what's it gonna be?' he said. 'Wanna rope, or you gonna go ask your parents for help? They're the ones made you, wiped yer arse, drove you to footy when they'd rather be sleepin'. But if you wanna believe they hate you.'

'Didn't say that.'

'Or you wanna go to the cops, and do it properly. I've tried for you.'

John waited.

'I went with him,' I said.

'Wrote a letter,' Pop explained. 'Clem drove me to the station. Gave it over, asked they give it to the right person.'

John sat up. 'What d'you say?'

'Said I seen you, and you didn't take nothin' or do nothin' but you were too scared to come forward, seein' how you thought they'd already made up their minds.'

'And d'you hear back?'

'No. But we'll go see them now.' He stood.

'No.'

I think Pop was too tired to argue. He took his swag from the shelf, rolled it out and said, 'You can sleep there.'

John seemed happy with this. He could see the trailer, examine the work, smell the grease, and dream, perhaps, of how this was his future.

'Wait here,' Pop said. 'I'll get you somethin' to eat.' And he went in.

At first, John ignored me. He settled into the swag, placed his hands behind his head and closed his eyes. 'How's Curtis been?'

'Okay.'

'Still got that list?'

'I reckon.'

'I'm number one. He was always strange. I remember parent–teacher nights, and we'd get dragged along, and they'd say how smart he was.'

'Say that about everyone.' Then without thinking I said, 'He got this bird pregnant.'

'No fuckin' way?' He sat up.

'In the tunnels under the main wing. Then she wouldn't deal with it, so it got nasty.'

'Randy little shit. Who was it?'

I explained. Tracey, the Inferno, the revelation, the five hundred bums.

He said, 'Serves him right. See, he's not so clever.' He stopped, but not because he understood the irony. 'But she ... you know?'

'Yeah.'

'Well, I gotta hand it to him. Even I haven't done that.' He lay down again. 'Why any girl would let *him* fuck her. Jesus.'

I don't know why I said it, but I asked, 'You ever been into the Glassons' place?'

A long pause. Then he turned his head and looked at me awkwardly. 'Why would you ask that?'

'Dunno.'

'The Glassons'? You're like Curtis ...' And settled.

Nothing.

'The Glassons'? Why not the Donnellans', the Sharpes'? Why would I have gone to the Glassons' place?' He sat up again, glared at me. 'What, cos there's something missing?'

Pop returned with a few slices of bread, ham, cheese, and the dregs of a bottle of orange juice. John started eating, all the time looking at me.

Pop said, 'I'll take you in the morning. Go in with you, yeah?'

'Okay.' But he settled before he'd finished. I guessed there was a lot to think about.

People had always been saying bad things about John, but it was the first who'd done the damage, and the rest had followed. He hadn't done a thing, really. It wasn't, isn't, fair that some people get a fibro childhood, some brick, some ivy. Years later, I learned that Barry Davidson (I'd been in his class in Grade Six) hadn't given way to a truck on Eastern Avenue, and the eighty years we'd been promised wasn't to be. And Matthew Jolley's cousin had driven through a wall. And a couple kids in Year Eleven had crashed into a tree on the way home from band practice. And Smithy, whose mum had deadlocked the front door, but forgotten the key, and the firemen had found them on top of each other, trying to open it. I'd like to say to this supposed God, Well, you need to explain. I used to share school milk with them. And I don't feel glad that I survived when they didn't.

'I don't think it's too late for you and Harry,' Pop said. 'He'll need someone else, eventually.'

John didn't reply. The concrete under his head didn't bother him. He didn't complain. He didn't say a word.

And the next morning he'd gone.

Lucky bastards, the Burrells. VCR. And Beta, too, which was the best sort. Gary had come good and bought it. Now they could settle in for the night, pop a bit of corn, suck back the Passiona. They'd had me in for *The Woman in Red*, but what was that? Taken me to Focus Video, where I'd scoured the shelves, unsuccessfully, for half an hour. 'It's just a fad,' I said.

'Bullshit,' Curtis replied. 'Who's gonna go to the movies when you can watch it in your living room?'

'It's better without your dad cutting his toenails.'

We turned into Lanark Avenue. The Cohens (37), next to the Sharpes, although they never talked to anyone. Word was they were *very* Christian and only mixed with other Godbodies. Ern had said he'd seen them invite the Jehovahs or SDAs in one Saturday morning. Something no one *ever* did. Ida reckoned a couple of Mormons, too. The God theory must've been right, because no one was *that* hard up for friends.

Curtis checked their perfect roses and said, 'John taught 'em.'

'Who?'

'The Mormons. They were comin' up the drive and he told me to let them in, keep them talkin'. So they were sittin' there saying Jesus this and Jesus that and I see John (he'd gone around the house) taking their bikes, wheeling them down the drive and (I later found out) putting them in our shed.'

'Nice work.'

'So I piss these fellas off. *No, our bikes!* And John comes out: What's up, fellas?'

We laughed. It's what John had been like when breaking rules was a pastime. When most things could be gotten away with. I remembered, searched my pocket and handed him his key. 'I found it.'

'Thank God. Where?'

'On the footpath.'

'I was putting off telling Gary. He woulda freaked out.'

'You owe me.'

He studied it, thought about it. 'I coulda swore I left it in me bedroom. I do the same, every time: wallet, keys, frangers.'

'Frangers?'

'She'll come back.'

'You're delusional.'

We approached 31. There was a car out front, and a figure, pacing. Status Quo pounding. I assumed he was waiting for Ron. Curtis went home and I went in, looking back at this man, who turned his head to look at me.

No one home. Jen had trade school, and Mum was probably shopping, leading Pop like a lost dog. I went into my room, threw my bag in the corner (the work could wait) and checked the street. The man was studying our house. I closed the blinds so there was a shredded-cabbage view of the world. Then I thought of John. One of his mates? He was unshaved, wearing a T-shirt, long brown hair and a stubby nose, like a curious pig.

I went to the toilet, and when I returned he was gone. A knock. Fuck. Who? What?

Calm, Whelan. Wrong address.

Knock.

I could just ignore it. He'd go away. Unless he didn't go away. And what if he started shimmying (was that even a word?) up the windows, crawling in, prowling around the house?

Knock.

Having spent my life complaining about the dullness of our suburb, I'd finally got some action. I walked down the hall, waited, and peered through the bubble glass. It was him. The hair, nose, broad shoulders. The jaw, even, big, Clutch Cargo. Bulljaw. Yes, he'd arrived, at last. My mythical hero, come to save the day. I opened the door and said, 'Hello?'

'G'day. Is Fay around?'

I didn't want him thinking I was alone, but he must've already tried the empty house. 'She's gone down the shops. She'll be back in a minute.'

'You Clem?'

'Yeah.'

Fuck, the voice. I knew.

He said, 'Guessed you were.'

Now I was really confused. It wasn't meant to happen like this.

'I's hopin' she'd be here, but it doesn't matter.'

'D'you wanna leave a message?'

He waited. 'What are you now, Clem? Sixteen?'

I knew I shouldn't, but had to tell him. 'Seventeen.'

And I could hear him doing the maths.

'Of course, seventeen. Sorry.'

Sorry. Maybe that was the apology. *Sorry.* I recognised the tone, the timbre, and knew it just as surely as Mum's or Pop's or Val's. I was in a bassinet, sitting in my unfurnished room, new carpet, Status Quo playing on a tranny in the corner as this man stirred paint, tipped it into a bowl and worked on my lime-green walls.

'I used to know your mum,' this strange man said.

'Yeah?'

'Haven't heard a word for donkey's … so I thought …' He studied my face.

I opened the screen door. I don't know why, but I did.

He said, 'Fuck, you look just like your mum.'

'You reckon?'

'Yer forehead, the way your hair falls.' He indicated, but stopped short of crossing the threshold (I guessed) he'd built. 'How long you say she'd be?'

'Little while.'

'Right.'

I wasn't sure Mum would want to see him, but I wasn't about to tell him to leave.

'She's a good woman, your mum.'

I couldn't ask him. He'd have to tell me. Those were the rules.

'Long time ago,' he said, 'I painted this room.'

'Were you a friend of Dad's?'

He waited. 'How's yer sister?'

'Good.'

'Still do calisthenics?'

'Na.'

'She a hairdresser, isn't she?'

How do you know? How long have you been watching? How many people have you been asking? 'Yes.'

'Good she's got somethin'.'

'Do you wanna wait for her?'

'No.'

'Leave your number?'

Bulljaw wanted to do it on his own terms. 'What you gonna do when you leave school, Clem?'

'Might be a writer. Although Mum reckons that's a dumb idea. Although Peter, next door—'

'How is he?'

'You know him?'

'Used to.'

'He reckons I should. Reckons I'm pretty decent.'

'Good. That's what you should do then. What you want. Don't listen to anyone, Clem. Just what you want, yeah?'

'I guess.'

'I'll pop back.'

'I'll tell Mum you came.'

He couldn't make up his mind about this. He just turned, got in his car and drove off, leaving me wondering if he'd ever return.

I sat on the porch thinking. *Why now?* But in a way, it didn't matter. Like Pop said, Everything happens if you wait long enough. He was tall, but no taller than me. Had a smell, but not a bad one, or strong, or inviting or off-putting.

Mum pulled up, dragged Pop from the car and said, 'Shouldn't you be studying?'

'Done it.'

'Half an hour? Year Twelve?' She went in, shaking her head. Pop stopped and showed me a pack of beef jerky he'd hidden in his jacket. 'I'll buy somethin' every week.'

I'd never eaten it. No one had ever eaten it, not since the Eureka Stockade. He went in and she came out for more groceries. 'You gonna help, or supervise?'

'Someone came to see you,' I said.

The frozen stuff. She handed it to me. 'Who?'

'Some bloke in a Kingswood.'

She dropped a bag, and sugar and flour and rice fell out. She knelt down and gathered them. 'And?'

'I asked if he wanted to leave a message, but he didn't. He wanted to know about me and Jen.'

She sat down beside me. 'That's strange.'

'I's thinking, he looks familiar.'

'How?'

'The photo.' I looked at her, but not accusingly. 'Same person.'

She stood, but left the groceries on the porch. A moment later she returned, sat and unfolded a piece of old paper. 'Read this.' She handed it to me. There was no name, address, nothing.

Dear Mrs Whelan

I was in two minds about writing this. Sometimes its best not to know. But seeing how Wilf had talked about you and Clem and Jen. He'd told me all about you. And the place hed put up in Gleneagles. He was very proud of it.

Me and him had been working together for three years. Freighters. Hed done so well theyd promoted him. Last month we had a free night in Callao. We split up, but agreed to meet at eleven to get back to the Joyita by midnight. I waited for Wilf until quarter to twelve, but he never arrived, so I went back to the ship. He'd been found floating, in the water. Dead. The police were called, they took the body, and we sailed later that morning. When we checked, after, they said they had no record of him.

Sorry that's all I can tell you, but I thought perhaps I should write. Good luck, Mrs Whelan. I hope it all works out.

Yours: A Friend.

Mum waited as I read. I turned to her and said, 'That's bullshit. I don't believe it.'

'Why would someone send it?' she asked.

'Dunno. But it was him, clear as day, from the photo.'

She shook her head. 'I wish it was, but he wouldn't wait this long.'

I just sat, studying the letter, trying to work it out.

'Here,' she said, handing me a small card.

It was the same man from the photo. And the same, perhaps, from the porch on which we sat. He was younger, side-burned, narrow-faced. It was a Maritime Workers' Union membership: Wilfred Albert Whelan. Born 10 December 1938. 'He'd included this,' Mum said.

I studied the face, the eyes. 'I know it was him,' I said.

'Your dad's dead,' she said. 'Unless …'

I waited.

'It's a sick joke.'

But that didn't explain it. My dad was either driving around in a Kingswood, or buried somewhere around Chacaritas.

Ern had brought beer, and wanted to make a night of it, but Pop was having none of that. Regardless, Comrade Sharpe cracked a stubby for himself and Pop, and Pop sipped it, but said, 'We've gotta keep our eyes on the ball.'

In the form of the stripped-down trailer, new springs, tyres ready to go. Pop handed Ern a brush and he continued painting, smoke in the corner of his mouth so he could move it with lips, inhale, exhale, drink, talk, and repeat the cycle until he was down to the stub and an empty bottle. He said, 'MacDonnell Ranges, not far from Alice Springs.'

'Long way,' Pop said. 'Under the stars, Ern. No motels.'

'No?'

'Unforgiving country. Read yer book of explorers.'

'Mad, that lot. Who'd head out with a coupla camels?'

'Or a Datsun?' I suggested.

I was studying a wiring diagram. That, Pop had explained, would be my job. Apparently, the ability to use a VCR qualified me.

Ern said, 'The map makes it clear, doesn't it, Doug?'

'Yes.'

'I mean, what roads, where to turn … *exactly*.'

'Exactly.'

'So we couldn't get lost?'

'No chance.'

'So, you got it handy?'

'Yep.'

'Can I have a look?'

Pop sipped the warming beer. 'I don't show no one.'

'But if we're gonna go, eh, Clem?'

'If Pop says,' I explained.

'Right. But, Doug, I've committed, I'm willing to put in …'

'Your choice.'

'Right.' He kept painting. 'But the thing is, if we're in the middle of the outback, we gotta be able to trust each other.'

Pop seemed to be enjoying it. 'Listen, Ern, you wanna take yer beers, you can go home.'

'No.'

'I've compared the map to proper ones, army ones, and it checks out. Whoever done it must've known the land.'

'Right.' Ern thought about this. 'So what happens if we go out there, have a look-see, and find nothing?'

'If yer gonna say that, why go?'

I sat on the ground, studied where the wires would go, emerge, screw into their plug. It didn't seem so hard.

'That day on North East Road,' Pop said, 'when I just about got collected by a truck. After, I heard a voice.'

'Whose?'

'*Come on, Doug, what are you doin' waitin'? I've been sittin' here for years. I need a bita help.*'

'Who was that?' Ern asked, finishing his grog.

Pop tapped his nose. 'I'd assumed he'd given up, gone off somewhere, but he'd been there all along, in the desert … waiting. Bita faith, that's what you need, Ern. You don't haveta see a map, it's up here.' And he tapped his head.

'Map'd help. It's a big desert.'

'It's a good map, Ern. Latitude, longitude, the lot. Why would someone draw a map to nowhere?'

I noticed the newspaper Pop had put down to catch the primer. *What's Your Problem?* It was Curtis's arse. I picked it up, studied the grainy photo and read: *Dear Ms Attitude. I was wondering if you could help. My boyfriend, Dane, enjoys photographing his privates …*

'You wanna start?' Pop asked.

'Hold on.'

This photo, for instance. 'Dane' attends Gleneagles High. He's a Year Twelve, but has the brain of a Grade Two. He has trouble controlling his urges, and I'm worried he'll get into trouble.

I held up the photo. 'Hey, Pop, look, it's Curtis's arse.'

He almost spat out a mouthful. 'In the paper?'

I read aloud: '*I was wondering whether you could suggest help? A psychologist? Ever since starting work at our local service station he's got worse.*'

'Who wrote it?' Ern asked.

'His girlfriend.'

'I always reckoned he wasn't quite right. And the brother. The whole family.'

Because, apparently, thirty years of walking to the Windsor had left him with an encyclopedic knowledge of everyone in our street. There was nothing he didn't know. 'See him sittin' on the roof sometimes, and I'd say, What you doin' up there? And he'd say, What you doin' down there?'

Ms Attitude hadn't minced her words. '*Dear Tracey. 'Dane' is the worst sort of adolescent male: infantile, self-absorbed, narcissistic, completely unaware of others.*'

'Why's he takin' photos of his bum?' Pop asked.

'He thought it'd turn her on.'

He examined it. 'Not much of an arse.'

I tore it out, folded it, and determined to show him. The war was continuing.

'So, what d'you reckon?' Pop asked.

'Looks easy enough.'

'Them schematics help,' Ern said, still not convinced.

'Not if you know what yer doin',' Pop replied.

Mum was at the door. 'What you lot up to?'

'*Busy!*' Pop growled.

She wasn't happy with this. 'What you gonna do with it, Ern?'

'Ida wants some gardenin' done.'

She didn't buy this for a minute. 'Only costs a few dollars to get yer mulch delivered.'

'Why? When there's a trailer handy?'

Mum turned on me. 'Haven't you got an essay due?'

'Peter helped me with it. All done.'

'Well, man's gotta have a hobby,' she said, happy (perhaps) that Ern had done what horse racing and Baby Burgess had failed to.

She went in, and Ern said, 'If I'm in this deep, least you could do's show me the map.'

'You wanted to come,' Pop replied. 'Only doin' this to make room for you.'

'You *needed* it.'

'*Bullshit.*'

Silence. I folded my schematic.

Pop was staring at him. 'Carn then.' He grabbed his box of chalk from the bench and stormed out, down the drive, the road. We followed. It was the usual Saturday afternoon, a distant mower, Gary loading steel onto the back of his truck, Val (her colour almost completely grown out) pulling a few weeds, hoping for a miracle. Pop almost ran and we jogged to keep up. Val went in, said to Peter (I guess), Doug and Ern and Clem are goin' somewhere, and Peter replied (I guess), Watch the tomatoes, don't let them catch. A few moments later he was calling after us. 'Wait on!'

Pop wobbled, tripped, but kept on. Over the mound, in through the primary school gates. When we arrived he was already working, drawing roads, tracks, ranges. Ern said, 'What's he doing?'

'You wanted a map.'

He didn't get it. Why not just show him? And how could he remember a map as detailed as Doug claimed it was?

The lot: the telegraph station, the Todd, Waterhouse Range, Owen Springs and even Imanda, Talpanama, Tjikara. He'd memorised it all. The path we'd take, the turnoffs (*323 more yards, sharp left, beside a gidgee tree*), rocky outcrops, the Finke, Idracowra, Mborawatna and finally, Horseshoe Bend.

Peter appeared, exhausted, and said, 'What is it?'

'The map,' Pop said. 'You wanna see? Here it is? Don't believe me, look!'

He kept going: the names of stations, wells, springs, creeks (*dry from September to March*), and even the cross to mark the spot: Lasseter's Reef.

He faced us, but really just Ern and Peter, because they were the ones who needed converting. 'This one here,' he said, indicating Horseshoe Bend. 'That's what learnt me.'

We waited.

'This kid, fourteen years old, lived with his dad, here.' He moved north, over hundreds of kilometres. 'Hermannsburg Mission. The dad was the pastor. And for thirty years he said, Listen fellas, Jesus is here, in the desert, and he wants to help yers. Of course, he was bloody nuts, wasn't he? But that wasn't the point.'

Ern faced what might have been his second revelation.

'The dad gets sick and the kid and a few of the blacks have to harness some horses and drive him all the way to Horseshoe Bend. This dad's fading fast (heart failure) but the boy's determined he'll survive, so they go on and on, through the heat, broken wheels, dead horses. The boy refuses to admit his dad's gonna die.'

Peter was silent, fixed.

'Because the kid knew if his dad died it'd all be over. They'd have to move, start a new life, and all the people who relied on the pastor (cos he'd got the blacks working, makin' money from cattle) would be finished.'

Pop was there, in his concrete desert, urging the horses on, checking his dad with his swollen legs and red face and lack of breath, saying, This time tomorrow, I reckon, as his dad (who knew he'd never make it), replied, That's it, son, keep going.

Pop said to Ernie, 'Can't you hear the voice?'

Ernie had no idea what he was talking about. The dementia, no doubt.

'He's waitin' for us, Ern. He's saying, Keep the faith, son.'

As the cart and horse continued, over roads that were no longer roads, bogging in sand, as the horses strained, and managed to get free.

'The old man?' Ernie asked.

'No,' Pop replied. 'Can't you see? The son.'

Since the government weren't going to help, we, the inhabitants of Lanark Avenue, had decided to do it ourselves. So Peter and Pop had knocked out a dividing wall, removed the shower screen and peeled back the original tiles. We'd all helped barrow the debris out the door, down the drive, into a skip. Now we were left with blank walls, and twelve boxes of tiles, ready to be stuck on, little plastic toothpicks to get the spacing right. Peter had started at the bottom. This didn't seem right. Surely any imperfection would be amplified as you worked up? And it was. What had started slightly out of plumb had become very obvious. He'd stopped, stood back, squinted (apparently this helped) and said, 'Nothin' you could actually notice.'

Although you could.

So we continued. I smeared the adhesive, handed him the tiles and he worked his way up, saying, 'I reckon it's gonna look great.'

I couldn't argue. Providence came in, sniffed around, licked the walls and left. Val, saying, 'Look at this: plenty of room for the wheelchair.'

The rubbish had been removed and the tiles and paint and new shower fittings delivered. Peter had said to Val, We could get the whole place lookin' nice.

How?

Bita paint, new carpet. You don't have to spend a lot of money.

She'd shaken her head, Carpet's got a coupla years in it yet.

The rows were getting wonkier. 'You'll be twenty degrees off at the top,' I told Peter. 'How you gonna finish it then?'

'Cut a few to size.'

'Should we just take these off, start again?'

'I'm not startin' again.' He showed me his claggy hands, glue and grout under his long fingernails. 'Doug doesn't *really* think there's a reef?'

'Course he does.'

He laid another tile. '*You* believe?'

'I thought by the time he finds the spot, nothin' there, he'll say, Fair enough, gave it a go.'

'But if he …?' But then he just shrugged. 'I'm lookin' forward to camping out. It's been years, remember?'

The tent in the backyard, Peter snoring, Davo scratching his arse, Val coming out and saying, You better get up now. Clem's got school.

But we were in the jungle, swinging from tree to tree. Davo: *Gentlemen, our food supplies are gone.*

Val: Come on, you lot.

I'm just stepping out. I may be some time.

And Peter, *Mr Burke, there seems little point in fooling ourselves. That was the last of the water. My eyes are done, I cannot see, I have not brought my specs with me, I have not brought my specs with me.*

Come on, Clem, yer mum's waitin'.

And together: *My eyes are dim I cannot see …*

Davo looked in. 'Nice work.'

'God bless Gary,' Peter said.

'And Ernie,' Dave added.

Sometimes in life talking is the most important thing. Val believed it was all Ern was good for. Hence the soapbox speeches, the career in the union movement. Like Marx, Lenin, and the rest, you didn't have to be smart, just persuasive.

Like Ern, at the Windsor. With Alan. He'd latched onto him right away.

What line yer in, Alan?

Steel fabrication. Cabinets, switchboards, whitegoods.

Steel, eh? And he'd thought about it. That stuff don't come cheap.

No.

Unless, of course, it does.

How d'you mean?

Ern had looked around, made sure it was safe. I got this neighbour, friend, who's come across a whole heap of steel.

Have, eh?

And now he has to get rid of it.

Why's that?

Nothing illegal, it's just in the way.

The next day, he'd approached Gary. They were both men of the world. So there was no point mincing words. The cops been around, eh?

What's it your business?

Must be hard to offload so much stuff?

No reply.

The easier way's to back in a truck, load it up ... one night, when the street's quiet.

Gary had been about to go in when Ern had said, I can get a good price, long as there's ... ten per cent for me.

Gary had waited, unsure. Ern had explained Alan's offer: two grand the lot. Then, a few nights later, the truck had arrived, the steel was brought out, loaded, an envelope offered, money counted, two hundred slipped into Ernie's hand, and all was good. Gary was an innocent man, again, and he'd learned his lesson, so no more foreignies. The company had taken a hit, admittedly, but it was doing well and wasn't about to miss a few rolls of steel, and after all (Gary explained later), considering the hundreds of hours of unpaid overtime he'd put in ...

The next morning when Peter pushed his brother out to the yard he found the envelope under the screen door. He picked it up and read the front. *I reckon this should cover the bathroom.*

All because of Ernie, and his ability to talk underwater. Alan, and a set of new switching units for the Railways, made for nearly a hundred per cent profit.

As I've said before, that's the way it was done back then. People weren't crooked – just practical.

I stood, stretched and made for the kitchen. Val had been rearranging photos. There was a new one. Our backyard, an empty paddock, before (even) Frontline Ford. Hills in the distance, blue sky, suburb-free country. Mum, glaring at the camera like she was saying, Go on then, take the bloody thing. A man in the mid-distance fiddling with what might have been a pipe. And at the back, in front of the new fence, the figure, I guessed.

Val came up beside me. 'I found that one, too.'

I indicated the small man, his face turned away from the camera.

'Wilf,' she said.

The hair was the same. A slight wave. Right height, and broad shoulders.

Val said, 'He'd just done yer fence, and ours. Sid helped him.'

No me, or Jen, but two little boys looking over the fence from number 33.

'He came to our place,' I said.

'Who?' she asked.

'Dad.'

'You sure?'

'Yeah. That's him.' And I pointed again.

'What'd he say?'

'Wanted to see Mum. I said she was out, but he didn't say who he was.'

'Didn't ask how you were going?'

'No.'

'That's strange. Why he'd come back, after so long. You sure it was him?'

'I'm sure. Although Mum said it couldn'ta been.' And I explained the letter.

'Well, it mustn'ta been,' she said.

'I reckon it was. I reckon the letter's wrong.'

She didn't seem so happy talking about it this time. Maybe she knew what would come from his return. 'Like I said, there was a lotta bad business.'

'But he wouldn't say what he wanted.'

'Even if it was him, how's it gonna help if …' She seemed to put it out of her head. 'Wanna cuppa?'

'Please.'

'Davo, Pete, wanna cuppa?'

And they said they did.

She went into the kitchen. 'That coulda been a hundred people.

If it was yer dad, don't you think he woulda said somethin'?'

'I guess.'

'Couldn't just stand and look at yer kid, all grown up, and not say somethin'. Probably just someone she called for a quote. I know you're probably interested but ... lotta fellas look like that.'

As the kettle started hissing I kept studying the photo. The neck, the cheeks, all black and white and blurred, but the same.

'I gotta bita sultana cake, wanna bit?'

'Ta.'

'And you told yer mum?'

'Yes.'

'Pity. Just the thought'd upset her, I guess.'

I sat while she filled the pot, covered it with its beanie, set out the cups. Providence slept on the floor in the little bit of sun that had turned the lino white.

'I should thank Ernie,' she said.

She knew. Gary had told her.

'Perhaps,' I replied.

'You don't reckon?'

'Na ... that's why he left it under the door.'

She thought about this. 'Yairs.' And more. 'Coulda kept it for himself.'

'I reckon he's got plenty. Reckon when he dies they'll find millions under the floorboards. Union money.'

She stared out of the window at number 35. 'He reckoned he was gonna sell his Val Doonican collection, but he still plays them.'

'Wouldn't get much for Val Doonican.'

'I dunno.' She could hear him, as she'd been hearing him for years. 'Only the Heartaches'. Or 'O'Rafferty's Motor Car'. They were her favourites. She'd stand, cooking her cakes, singing along to Ern's records. Like they were one, dancing in his front room, while Ida looked on angrily.

I saw another envelope sitting among the brochures and bills and knitting patterns. And on the front: *Clem*. It was open, and a few strands of fine, blond hair poked out like she'd been looking at them, holding them, smelling them, even. She turned to me and saw I was interested. She sat, picked up the pot and started pouring. 'Just a keepsake,' she said.

I didn't know what to say.

'If I's smart I'd throw it, and forget. That'd make sense, wouldn't it?'

'No,' I said. The couple of photos of the stranger; his smell as he stood at the door; his voice. Small, real, knowable. 'You can't forget.'

She just looked ahead. She'd tried to explain about Wilf; that was something. But some things defied explanation. The jumpers. The lamb's wool, soft on the cheek, and arse. The powder. I told her about it and said, 'I reckon I oughta give it back.'

'No,' she said. 'It's yours. I shoulda given it to you a long time ago.'

And we just sat, silently, drinking tea. In time Peter wheeled his brother into the kitchen, which was the heart of the house. He said, 'Nother coupla days.'

Davo smiled. We were still feigning sleep, and Val was still saying, 'We gotta get Clem to school.'

Mrs Masharin was our own commissar, Soviet discipline made word in the Gleneagles Steppes. Short skirt and unforgiving pantyhose, knee-high boots (always polished) and an industrious shirt; hair up (bun narrowly avoided) and a slight accent that could've been anything European, but we were so white-bread we didn't know. She looked at me and said, 'Nice big voice.' Each word separate, in her usual permafrost accent.

The new radio studio (Mr de Weerd's idea) had started broadcasting across the school grounds every Monday, Wednesday and Friday at recess and lunch. Light classics, mainly, courtesy of Ms Field's expansive Comoesque record collection, but the powers that be had conceded, allowing a pop segment (Spandau Ballet, Boy George), an electronic music corner (there were other Kraftwerk fans) and Mrs Masharin's literature salon.

'I don't know,' I said.

'It will be fine,' she replied. Not even *it'll*, just *it will*. That's what I was up against.

Dwayne Schuit had been made producer. He sat at a control desk outside the studio. Dwayne of the Komputer Klub ('Fun Programming in Basic'), debating and chess club. Dwayne, who'd missed out on a private education, but wore a tie and jacket to school anyway. Quoting Python ten years before anyone else; topping Year Eleven Latin (narrowly beating Curtis) and Classics, making it clear he *wanted* to study arts. He said, 'Nearly ready, Mrs Masharin.'

I clutched the pages of my new novel. She'd read the first few chapters, declared them genius and said, 'I insist, a reading for the Wednesday salon.'

'No, I don't reckon.'

'This week, you see, everyone will hear and love.'

Maybe she thought I was some sort of Black & Gold Gogol, but I knew this couldn't help my reputation, what there was of it. Curtis sat beside Dwayne, looking in, grinning. I mouthed a *fuck off* and he bit his lip. A strangely out-of-place Rachmaninoff vesper played to a yard of 1100 Darrens and Kerrys as I thought, Please, let it be over quick.

Mr de Weerd was a marvel. Back in Holland, apparently, every school had its own radio station. When he'd arrived at the beginning of the year (on an exchange) he'd told Curtis's class, 'I don't understand where the culture lies.' They'd got a big laugh out of this. Curtis had said, 'It doesn't lie anywhere,' and (I guess) de Weerd had wondered what the hell he'd got himself in for. Then (so I've been told) he'd caught Wendy going her hardest behind the hall with a Year Nine. Sports day: a muscle-fest in the century-plus sun. The change room fire (two burned down). A teachers' strike. George Bullock's Torana through the school fence. By which time he would've known exactly where it lay.

Not to be put off, he'd decided the transmission of culture would solve everything. He'd spoken to the principal, who'd loaned him a room for six months, and the school council, who'd given him a few thousand dollars. Next, a whole-school egg carton drive to insulate the walls. Carpet, desks, chairs, microphones and reel-to-reel wired into the school's PA. Then, in March, he'd brought us culture. Mr Thorpe making a little speech on the first day of transmission. 'Welcome, students, to Radio Gleneagles. Thanks to the hard work of Mr de Weerd we have a suitable medium to provide entertainment during breaks.' Then he'd said how it was only a trial, and how they'd need the room back when the typing class moved. A cultural disclaimer, like this music and poetry stuff was all well and good, but don't get too used to it. Remember who you are, children of the proletariat. Deep down (I guess) he didn't think we'd appreciate it. Someone would cut some wires, or steal some equipment, or piss on the carpet. He'd said, 'To get us started, Mrs Masharin will read from Prowst.'

But, with the help of Dwayne, and the suffering of our own audiophonic-Gogh, Radio Bogan was still on the air. Mrs Masharin was there every week, reading student work to the masses. Some of the ball-kickers had complained to Thorpey (*Why d'we gotta listen to that shit all day?*) but he'd kept on keeping on.

The vespers faded and Dwayne indicated to Comrade Masharin. She said, 'And now we have an excerpt from new novel of Clem Vhelarn …'

I could hear the distant jeers.

'Clem, what is your novel to be called?'

'*This Excellent Machine.*'

'And to what does that refer?'

'It's a bit hard to explain but, you know, like life's a machine, and we go in one end and come out the other, changed.'

'So without further ado, *This Excellent Machine*, by talented Year Twelve student, Clem *Wee*land.'

Dwayne gave me the thumbs-up. He shared the delusion that this place could be improved. The food scattered over the ground after lunch, the crows picking at old salami; the girls tattooing their legs with stolen markers so the grunters would look at them. Mr

Hunt, on yard duty, studying the form for the Harold Park trots as he scratched his arse and shouted, Youse kids piss off outa there. Dwayne was wandering Datsunland in search of a new Volvo, but there'd never been a Volvo, and anyway, he couldn't afford one.

I thought it best to get it over with. '*Barry Ruge looked at his grandson, Arnold, and said, I remember you. Arnold was surprised. Barry said, You used to deliver the milk, didn't yer? Arnold said, No, Pop, I never delivered milk.*'

Curtis had settled back. He was talking to Dwayne. Dwayne who would've and should've been Head Boy at St Andrew's Grammar School. Curtis had put him on his list (number 41), with the comment: *Pretentious twat who hasn't accepted his lot in life. Cicero will save him apparently.*

I finished in a sprint, and Masharin started a book review.

Curtis and I wandered the yard. There were a few comments. *Loved yer stuff, Clemmy. Gotta getta copy when it comes out.* But even the bile didn't last. Netball practice was underway, and a dozen short skirts were some consolation. Curtis said, '*Ah, a bear in its natural habitat.*'

'*A Studebaker.*'

1979. The Blacks Road drive-in. Mum had taken me, Jen and Curtis to see *The Muppet Movie*. It was a hot night, so we'd sat on the bonnet, and I'd said, 'Not bad, Kermit,' and Curtis had said, 'It's not *Star Wars*, Fozzie,' and Jen had told us to shut up and Mum (sitting in the car reading) had said, 'Any arguing and we'll go straight home.' Then we'd sang, '*Opportunity knocks once let's reach out and grab it, together we'll nab it ...*'

Twelve years old, under the stars, thinking it would go on forever. As it had, in a way, the short skirts flying up, revealing California's promised palm trees.

'How'd it go, Fozzie?' Curtis asked.

'*Movin' right along ...*'

And it was like it had been, and not so long ago.

Crackle. Mrs Masharin's voice trailed across the car park. 'And now for our final book review of the day.' Then there was a more familiar voice. Tracey. Mrs M asked her what she'd been reading.

'*Glory Days*,' she said. 'It's about a young girl, and she stupidly falls for a boy called Curtis.'

Curtis's mouth formed a little o, and his eyes narrowed.

'Anyway, it's quite involved, but eventually she falls pregnant.'

'Please, begin.'

'*In today's world a girl needs to be careful. As this book shows, many boys care only for one thing. Curtis Durell is such a boy.*'

For once, he was lost for words.

'*Glory Days*?' I said.

'She's not gonna give up.'

So it seemed. I'd given him the newspaper clipping. He'd screwed it up, threatening to march around to her place and have it out, get a lawyer, call the police, but decided he was only giving her oxygen.

He was off across the compound, the library verandah, Home Economics and the bike quad.

'*In a way, it's not Curtis's fault. He was never taught right from wrong. But the girl, Kerry, suffers from his selfishness. Her mother threatens to throw her out.*'

He arrived, opened the door and said, 'Turn it off.'

Mrs Masharin came out and said, 'What is it?'

'That's not a book, she's made it up.' He approached Dwayne and started flicking switches.

'Out!' Masharin demanded. 'Clem, take him out.'

Curtis just looked at Tracey.

'*We are left with the feeling that some boys will never become men. Never grow up, learn responsibility.*'

'It's about me!' he said to Masharin.

'Out!'

He just stared at Tracey. She finished, came out, and walked past. 'Thanks, Mrs Masharin.' And exited the control room.

August

A shopping date. Jen was at work, and Mum out to lunch with some of her friends. Ernie and Peter arrived, and we climbed into the 120Y. Pop drove us, parked over two spots (crooked) and we went in. Peter saw the photo machine and said, 'We should have a record.'

Pop said, 'Don't be stupid.'

But Peter insisted. We dragged Pop into the box and arranged ourselves – me on my knees, my head popping up between the three stooges. Flash, and four copies. Peter promised to chop them up, share them, and Pop said, 'Don't worry about mine.'

Aisle four. Ernie put two bags of flour in the trolley. 'Who's cookin'?'

'We can take it in turns,' Pop said. 'I've been doin' some research.'

He told them about the file he'd created: a collection of easy-to-cook recipes, courtesy of Margaret Fulton. 'Lotta pork.'

'Pork?' Peter asked.

'Keeps best in the esky. Spare ribs, sweet and sour. You two like pork?'

'Fatty,' Ernie said.

'Bad luck. Chicken doesn't keep.'

'Bita beef?'

'Pork's best.'

Ern left it there. The details could wait. He put a few bottles of Coke in the trolley and Pop said, 'We can't take those.'

'Why?'

'Weight.' He put them back.

Ernie didn't like this, and returned a single bottle to the trolley. Pop took it out. They stared at each other. Ern said, 'It's not just what *you* want.'

'It's what's practical. You agreed.' He showed him a list he'd made: water and sugar, flour, curry powder (everything tasted better with curry), gravy (as with curry), croutons, carrots, potatoes, turnips. Most of which could be used for stew.

Ern said, 'It's not the Calvert expedition. We can still eat decent.'

'I'm happy with stew,' Peter said. 'Long as we don't go hungry.'

Ernie hated this about Peter. Compromise. That's why lawyers didn't start revolutions: they didn't believe in anything, except money, and even that had eluded Pathetic Pete. So the issue of Coke was avoided. We continued, Pop searching his list, saying, 'Still alright to put this lot in your shed, Ern?'

'Yeah,' he mumbled.

'Fay'd sniff it out in five minutes flat.'

'*It's alright.*' Short, sharp, Cokeless.

I loved the Gleneagles Woolies, especially on weekdays (like today) when I should've been at school. Pop had picked me up after recess. He'd said I didn't need to come, but I'd said I did.

School days had their own pace. The government was taking care of the kids; grown-ups could get on with important things. A couple of old blokes standing in front of the newsagent checking their keno tickets; Clarrie and Ruth sharing a sandwich in the snack bar, the slow, no-rush cuts of the knife, the plate slid across the melamine, a single bite, chewing, as Clarrie wiped his chin with a napkin and said to Ruth, That ham's nice, and she replied, Special, continental, and he nodded as if to say, Yes, they know how to do ham.

Peter chose a few cans of tuna. Pop consulted his list and said, 'I hadn't thought of that,' but allowed it anyway.

'I hate tuna,' Ern said.

'If yer gonna complain the whole time,' Pop replied.

'Do you like tuna, Clem?'

Pop. 'It's not a council meeting. Tuna's filling, and light, so we can take it.' He turned and continued, refusing to argue facts. Cocoa. Milk powder. Peter said he'd prefer tea, so we bought bags, and Ern wanted coffee, and Pop said, 'It's not on the list.'

'Bugger yer list. I don't like cocoa, I like coffee.'

'Well, you can bloody well drink cocoa. It's not gonna kill you.'

'Coffee relaxes you.'

'Well, why don't we take one of them machines?'

'Now you're being difficult.'

'*Am I?*'

We continued. In the next aisle, Ern selected beans and sausages. Pop said, 'It's dearer like that.'

'Twelve cents? For snags? I don't think they're gonna weigh us down any more, eh?' He held the can in front of Pop's face.

'That's it, forget it.' Pop turned, abandoned his shopping and walked towards the checkout.

Ern called, 'What, you havin' a tanty?'

Pop didn't reply. We studied the trolley, the groceries forming a small mountain of canned everything. 'Leave it,' I said.

We followed a few steps behind. Peter said, 'Carn, Doug, we haven't even left.'

'We're not gonna.'

'We gotta get along.'

He turned. 'No, we don't. It was *my* trip. I don't gotta get along with no one. I'll go by myself.' He continued, past the butcher, into the car park.

Peter said, 'What about I shout us all a coffee?'

'Piss off! Don't know what I was thinking. Five minutes with him!' And he pointed at Ernie.

Leaving the car park, he crossed Blacks Road and headed down the back streets towards Lanark III.

We stood beside the Datsun. Ernie said, 'He's got a two-second fuse.'

I suggested we let him go, cool off, and tackle it later, but Ernie was determined. 'Come on, we'll pick him up.' He held his hand out for the keys. I said, 'You okay with a Datsun?'

'For god sake, Clem, you're as bad as him.'

I surrendered the keys. We got in, and he reversed, straight into some old girl's trolley, narrowly missing her. He got out and said, 'Jesus, I'm sorry, missus, I didn't see you.'

'You didn't look.'

We examined the scratched paint, and Ern said, 'That'll buff out.'

A few minutes later we found Pop walking past the primary school. The kids were out kicking balls, shouting, and Mr Gottl was half-asleep on a bench. Ernie slowed, told Peter to wind down a window and said, 'Carn, Doug get in.'

He ignored him.

'Come on. I promise, I'll keep my trap shut.'

Nothing.

'You and me can work things out. We have before.'

Peter said, 'He paid for the tiles, Doug.'

Pop said, 'So what? It didn't cost *him* anything.'

'I needn'ta.'

'*So what?*' He kept on.

A small boy followed him along the fence line. 'Youse havin' a barney?'

Pop told him to go away.

Peter wasn't finished. 'You could go by yourself, Doug, but that'd be a big trip. Clem's only young.'

I kept my mouth shut. The kid said, 'My dad's got a Datsun.'

Pop ignored him. Peter said, 'Well, that's okay, if you wanna go by yourself. We can stay here. But it might be nice, the four of us.'

Pop stopped, like something had occurred to him.

Peter continued. 'I didn't wanna come for me, but I thought, us blokes from Lanark Avenue. I reckoned that's what it was about.'

The car idled. I guessed Pop agreed with him, but couldn't agree. The kid said, 'Youse got any money?'

'No!' Pop said. 'Piss off!' And the kid ran away.

Ernie said, 'You got a short fuse like me, Doug. We gotta know our limitations.'

'I know mine.' He kept walking.

We started after him, but I said, 'Go home, Ern, he won't be far behind.'

So we drove home, parked in our drive, and I said, 'I suppose I better get back to school.'

'What's the rush?' Ernie asked. 'Come on.'

He led us into his backyard, and a fire pit he'd dug in the middle of his buffalo. He'd set up a camp oven, and lit a fire, and it had burned down to embers. 'What cher reckon?' he asked.

'All ready to go?' I said.

'Wait here.'

He went inside. Peter and I sat on stools he'd set out. He'd made it like it might be in the desert. A sort of 1:72 scale adventure.

We waited, and Peter said, 'Years they drank together, down the Windsor.'

It seemed hard to imagine.

'Doug'd wander down to Ernie's, they'd watch telly together.'

Ernie came out with a handful of dough. He opened the camp oven, plopped it in and nestled it in the remains of the fire. Then he covered it with the glowing embers. 'I thought we'd have a dry run.'

Ida wasn't far behind. She had water and tea in the billy, and put it in the fire beside the damper.

'Once he smells it,' Ernie said. He sat down.

In the Ford dealership, the wheel-nut machine whirred, and someone dropped a spanner, and the radio murmured with talkback.

Peter said, 'Just tellin' Clem about you and Doug.'

'He knows, don't yer, Clem?'

I nodded.

'Doug just needs half an hour.'

Ida said, 'Call us when it's ready,' and went in.

I told them how Pop had changed, and how, of a night, he'd sit reading the encyclopedias out loud, as if this might help him remember. 'I reckon if you fellas came down and sat with him and had a talk it might help.'

They thought about this. Ernie said, 'Encyclopedias?'

'Yeah.'

'Well, I guess I could.'

'It's a shame, when he just sits there all afternoon.'

'It's always better, isn't it,' Ern said, 'if there's someone with you? Even if they don't say nothin'.'

'Makes Mum sad, I reckon.'

Ida brought out five mugs, and Ernie filled them. He took the damper from the fire, tore it into pieces, and left some. And we ate, without talking. Eventually Pop appeared, sat down, picked up his mug and rescued the damper from the oven. 'That's a new scratch,' he said to me.

I turned to Ernie, and smiled, and he said, 'It wasn't me.'

And we laughed, and Pop said, 'Jesus, y' didn't let him drive, did yer?'

We put the Datsun on the lawn and hosed it. Pop started with a bucket of sudsy water. Every square inch of its fading red metal and caramel-coloured duco. I told him I'd been reading about Lasseter's Reef. 'These three fellas made a pact when they were ten. Every year they've gone to look.'

'Well, they don't know what I do.'

'They've used special maps, remote sensing, satellite images, the lot.'

'You could get ten thousand men, but unless you know.' He finished his scrubbing and I hosed it down.

'Quartz, with lumps of gold as big as plums?' I said.

'That's what he reckoned.'

'And he just stumbled across it?'

'That's what he reckoned.'

He refilled the bucket with water and wax, then handed me a chamois. 'You practised your parks?'

'Coupla times.'

'I'm relying on you.'

'Don't need a licence to drive.'

'Helps.'

He sat on the front verandah, deciding, perhaps, if the old girl looked any better.

'They reckon it's near the WA–NT border,' I said.

He almost laughed. 'No wonder they haven't found nothin'. Too far west.' He stood. 'You alright to finish off?' And went in before I could answer.

I hosed the car, emptied the bucket and parked in the drive.

When I got out I smelled smoke. Ron, perhaps, at his incinerator, burning his wool scraps. No – it was coming from number 28.

I thought I'd risk it. I crossed the road, walked down the drive and saw Wendy, alone, beside the incinerator, feeding a jumper to the flames. And beside her, the others. I approached her, but she didn't acknowledge me. I could see she'd been crying. 'I thought you were gonna hold onto them,' I said.

No reply. She picked up another, let it drop into the flames, and watched it.

'All those years,' I said.

She didn't even turn and look at me. She was intent upon destruction; the wool flickering and flaring and glowing before becoming smoke, making a column that rose above the house, street, suburb.

'Wendy?'

She wouldn't reply. I took it to mean I should leave. I turned, headed for the drive, but Les was standing at the back door. He motioned for me to come in.

He dropped into his recliner, and I sat beside him. He said, 'Look.' He handed me a letter. Three folds, on white paper. Black and blue ink.

Dear Mrs Champness

Thank you for your letter. The request was considered, and approved. The young man, now eighteen, was contacted. Although unable to provide specific details, I can say that he presently lives interstate.

Mrs Champness, I am sorry to say the young man declined your invitation. He explained that he has settled, and is happy, and believes any contact would upset his adoptive parents, whom he holds close. He did say, though, this was not a reflection on how he feels about you and Mr Champness. He understands the circumstances, and wishes you well. He says he is curious about those days, and might, in time, change his mind.

I understand this is difficult news. It might be some consolation to know his adoptive parents have been honest with him, and explained his earliest days. I have left an 'open invitation' for him to contact us, and you, so, for now, all we can do is be patient.

I returned it to Les. 'That's bad luck.'

'I guessed it'd happen. Wanna drink?'

'No, thanks.'

'I put myself in the same position. If yer happy, it's a loada baggage to have to open.'

The smoke was coming in the door.

'I helped her with the application,' I said.

'I know.'

The television was on, but the sound was turned down.

'I hope that's okay?'

'Of course.'

I stood, and walked away. Les said, 'You couldn't turn it up, could you?'

So I did.

I emerged into the sun. Down at the back fence, Wendy was nearly finished. She picked up the second-smallest, and dropped it in.

'We tried,' I said.

Now, she looked at me. 'That's the main thing. And he said he wasn't angry with us. That's a good sign, eh?'

'I reckon.'

'And, later, maybe a year or two …'

She picked up the last jumper. So small. Dog-sized. 'This was the first. You can see where the silverfish got to it.' And she showed me.

It was beautifully knit, cable pattern, unlike the shit you bought in Target. 'Maybe you should keep one,' I said.

'No.'

'Six months, he might change his mind.'

'I don't reckon.' She went to put it in, but I held it, tried to take it.

'I reckon if it were me, and I was living somewhere, I'd wanna know.'

'You reckon?'

'Cos you'd think, Maybe she had to ... and maybe she felt bad, all this time.'

She let go, and I took it.

'What d'you reckon, six months?' she asked.

'Maybe. Maybe a bit longer.'

Wool burns quickly. So the flames had died, and the smoke had slowed. She reclaimed the jumper, walked over to the tap, and rinsed it under a slow stream. Turned off the water, held the jumper up and said, 'Hard to imagine anyone being that small.' She pegged it on the line.

The smoke seemed to have quietened the bees. That's how it was in nature, especially with bees. They all assumed their home was burning, so they flew back, to see. But now, they started up again. And Les came out to look.

Wilton wasn't the flashest suburb. The bus ride had been a descent into Curtis's Latin hell. A couple of kids sucking each other's face, saying, 'What's your fuckin' problem?' when I looked around. The bus driver wasn't about to buy into it. I got off and walked past a row of empty shops, the doors boarded up, VapoRub signs from the fifties when (I guessed) it was still safe to bring your family shopping. The streets were dirty, the footpaths, too – some sort of vomit–claret–urine mixture.

Thomas Street. I studied my mud map, walked past yards full of washer bodies and crates of empties, stumped cars and stuffed water features. You could see down hallways, into dark kitchens blaring finals footy and fuck-the-reffos talkback. Like any moment Virgil would step out from behind a fuse box and say, Come on, I'll show you the way.

I wanted to turn, retrace my steps, get on a bus and head for the city, but couldn't. Something was pushing me, saying, You've come this far.

Gould Street. Easy, I told myself. He'll know. And anyway, what's my choice? I'd looked up the Maritime Workers' Union, called, and said, 'My name's Clem Whelan. My dad used to be a member, I think.'

'Go on.'

'I have his membership card, but it's pretty old.' I explained how he'd been a builder (probably), then stopped, worked on freighters (or some other type of ship), stopped in Callao and then …?

The woman said, 'We can't give information over the phone.'

'This was a long time ago.' I told her how I hadn't seen him since I was a kid, but how I'd found his membership card, and how there didn't seem any other option. And she said, 'You checked Births, Deaths and Marriages?'

'No.'

'If he's dead they'd have some record.'

I wasn't sure I wanted to know. 'I could, but I was thinking, if you had some sort of record?'

'Right … what was your name?'

I told her. And Dad's. How it would've been the late sixties, early seventies, judging from the age of the letter. She asked, What letter? I told her. From a shipmate he'd been with on the night. She said, 'If that'd happened there'd be some sort of record. Newspapers, even?'

'I guess. But I thought, for a start, if I could find out?'

She'd taken a deep breath, thought about it and said, 'Hold on.' Putting down the phone and walking away. I'd waited two, three minutes before she returned. 'Got it.'

'Great.'

'You're the son?'

'Yes. What's it say?'

'Wilfred Albert Whelan. Joined September 1971.'

'That's it?'

'Signed up, paid his dues, that's the last we heard.'

'So there's no way of finding out?'

'There's a referee: Bob Jones. Wilton.'

'Wilton?'

'It's a suburb, down the Port.'

And that was it. I looked him up: Jones, B 34 Gould St, Wilton. I spent the next few days wondering what to do. Call? It was a hard decision, but I made it, and waited until Mum took Pop to the shops, then sat, dialled, and listened to the voice: *The number you are calling has been disconnected.* So, then, whether to bite the bullet. What could he tell me?

Thirty-four. Per square inch, the neatest house I'd ever seen. I opened a little gate and walked down the path. Old concrete, but clean, swept, sinking into the perfectly clipped lawn with its six or so gnomes. The screen door vented roast beef into the afternoon. I knocked. 'Hello? Mr Jones?'

The races, of course, from the back room. 'Mr Jones?'

A chair scraping on floorboards. 'Hold up.'

The silhouette of a stooped man, emerging from the darkness, claiming a halo and approaching from the kitchen. 'Hold yer horses.'

He opened the door and said, 'None today, thanks.'

'I'm not selling anything. I'm Clem Whelan.'

His face screwed into a little ball. All shaved, of course. 'Whelan?'

'I think my dad used to work with you.'

He smiled. 'Wilf?'

This was enough to get me into the kitchen, and a beer, the radio turned down. He sat and said, 'I seen you before.'

'When?'

'Just a bub. Few months old. We were working somewhere, and yer mum brings you in … and yer dad's showin' you off.'

'Mighta been my sister, she's two years older.'

'No, it was a boy, I remember. Clem, you say?'

'Yeah.'

'Nice to meet you.' And we shook.

Half a glass later (with the form put away) he said, 'I gave yer dad that job. Sixty-eight, nine, when I was foreman with Blackie's.' He squeezed my arm. 'Look at you, all grown up. I remember that day. Your mum brought you along and yer dad's sayin', Number one son … not bad, eh? Like that. Not bad? Proud as punch. Course, a man is with his first son.'

'I can't remember.'

'Why would you? Bet you've done him proud.'

'Haven't done much yet, till I get out of school, anyway.'

'You will. Lay bricks, like him. What a worker.'

I waited, and drank. The beer seemed natural, and I could already feel my head.

'Got nasty when he left.'

'How's that?'

'Let's not talk about it. Everything worked out okay.'

'He was sacked?'

'Not me. Mr Black, the owner.'

'Why?'

He paused, wiped beer from his mouth. 'He laid around a bit, left work to others. Then when Mr Black challenged him he'd give him a mouthful. I stayed out of it, cos he could lay bricks real good. But you know … some blokes are their own worst enemy.'

It sounded like Mum had said, but Mr Jones seemed apologetic. 'Don't worry about that. Blokes came and went. That was the business. Yer dad'd had enough anyway. Reckoned he'd make a good sailor.'

'And that's why you went referee?'

'Yeah. Old Blackie sacked lots of fellas, didn't mean they weren't decent. He was short-fused, and if you come up against him, like your dad did, that'd be the end of it. But you ask him, he'll tell you about Blackie.'

I wondered what he meant. 'But he's dead.'

Bob looked confused. 'Blackie?'

'Dad.'

'Dead?' He almost laughed. 'Not less he's a ghost.'

Then I told him about the letter.

'Someone's pulling your leg.'

'How?'

'How old's the letter?'

'Seventies some time.'

'Last time I saw your dad was three, four years ago. He dropped by, sat there, drinkin' a beer, like you. Even looks like you.'

'Here?'

'I seen him plenty of times over the years. Stops by, asks how I'm going.'

I didn't get it. The letter. Mum's words.

'And he never mentions me ... Mum, Jen?'

'I knew he'd moved on but ... Told me about you. Like books, don't yer?'

'Yes.'

'And yer sister, she's a hairdresser?'

I didn't know what to say.

'He's been tellin' me about you kids for years. You grazed yer arm, didn't yer, riding yer bike?'

'Yeah.'

'And you were in scouts at one point? Won some trophy?'

It didn't seem real.

'He never held it against me, you know, him gettin' sacked. Said I'd done what I could.'

This seemed to go against everything I'd ever heard about him.

'Wanna another beer?' Bob asked.

'Why not?'

I no longer felt the need to escape from Wilton. Whatever it was, it was an honest place, and a place of honesty. Maybe I'd remain forever, discovering more of the truth the suburbs had denied me. Over the next hour I heard about Dad's bricklaying records, how quickly he could cut and nail up asbestos, and how, in a way, he'd built our fibro dream. How he was good at sport, and how women liked him. How he could get along with almost anyone, unless he was backed into a corner. 'What's he do now?'

'Works for a plumber. Fella he gets along with.'

'And he's ...'

He leaned forward. 'She's a nice girl, coupla years younger. Yvonne, I think, or Yvette.'

Damn. 'You got his number?'

Bob just looked at me. 'You sure you want it?'

6/viii/84 Technically, I had failed another driving test. I say technically, because I didn't really fail. There was a stop sign, and I stopped but (apparently) rolled, so that I hadn't really stopped. But, according to any reasonable human being, I'd stopped. So after turning the corner, the examiner (a nose picker who whistled when he breathed) said ...

'Okay, Mr Whelan, you can head back to the office.'

Not a good sign. We'd only been out five minutes. 'Is something wrong?'

'You failed to stop.'

'But. I. Stopped.'

'You need to come to a *full* stop.'

'I did.'

'Turn around, please.'

I was destined to remain licenceless. It seemed unfair. Girls always got theirs first go, but there was some unwritten rule about suburban males. The minute we got our licence we were off drag racing, drunk driving, wrapping our parents' cars around poles. So they kept failing us. All of which proved it was a woman's world. Pop, particularly, subscribed to this view. Germaine Greer. It was all her fault. If only she'd kept her trap shut everything would've been alright. And Helen Reddy. *I am woman.* So bloody what? I am man (nearly).

Pop was pissed. 'Three fuckin' times. You're a perfectly good driver. Revenue, that's what it's about.'

We were driving down North East Road after the test. Pop couldn't see the problem. 'Hundred and fifteen dollars each time. That's ... three forty-five. *That's* what it's about.'

I just drove.

'You stopped, you reckon?'

'Yep.'

'Course you did. I taught you to stop. Full stop?'

'Yep.'

'I'll write to the paper.'

'What's that gonna do?'

'Gotta be a limit, doesn't there? You can only fail so many times.'

'Thanks, Pop.'

'A statute of limitations. What is it? Ten, twelve?'

'I'm not doin' it ten times.'

'You might have to.'

'I don't need a licence.'

He thought about this. It was just a bit of paper. 'Well, bugger it.'

'Y' reckon?'

'What's the fine for driving without a licence?'

'Dunno.'

'Gotta be less than doing that test a hundred times.'

A hundred? Maybe he thought I really *was* hopeless. 'Annoying, cos I had it all down pat. The reverse parking, three-point …'

Pop was caught up in his own thoughts. His fist clenched, his head shaking. 'Not gonna let this stop us?'

'Eh?'

'The trip. You'll do.'

I pulled into Lanark II, slowed, wondering what Mum would say. I noticed a car parked in the Rosies' drive. Pop got out, slammed the door and went in. I heard Mum saying, 'How'd he go?' and Pop replying, 'Failed again,' and Mum saying, 'What this time?'

But I wasn't interested. A car in the Rosies' drive. No one parked there.

I waited. An older woman came out, took something from the boot of her car, and went in.

Tina …

Inside, Mum was saying, 'They oughta give him his money back. No one stops at stop signs.'

'But yer meant to.'

How many years? Surely someone had bought it?

Then, a second figure. Fifteen. Sixteen. Seventeen. Short brown hair and an oval face (at least from this distance). I reckoned ... but it had been so long.

Vicky.

No, it couldn't be. The girl took bedding from the boot, brushed hair from her face and went in.

Mum called, 'Clem, come and tell us about it.'

That was the last thing I felt like doing. I walked down the drive and slowly crossed the road, just in case I was wrong. I thought, Fuck, if it's them, we've got a full house again. I stopped to think. *Vicky*. Standing together in this same spot on the morning the ambulance came to take him away. Me saying something like, That's pretty rotten.

They reckon he was sick, and it just got him, quick.

Sorry 'bout that.

Not your fault.

Where do they take him, d'you reckon?

No point goin' to the hospital, is there?

Guess not.

Those were the sorts of conversations I remembered. Probably all imagined, later, in some sort of fantasy, as I lay in bed, dreaming of touching her smooth skin, kissing her, holding her hand, telling her how much I loved her.

I walked up the drive and stood beside the car. The boot was full of blankets and pillows, and clothes, stacked half-neat in the wheel well. In the back there were a couple of suitcases, and books, stuffed in the gaps. Some of Oswald's, perhaps?

The girl came out, looked at me, then smiled. 'No way.'

I said, 'You're kidding.'

'Clem?'

'Vicky?'

She half-ran down to me, but stopped, realising we hadn't seen each other in the best part of a lifetime. She put a hand out, and I shook it. She was so bloody beautiful. The same round face, big cheeks and perfect teeth. I managed, 'It's been years.'

'You're so tall.'

'And you … you were one of those midgety-looking kids.'

'Thanks.'

And she did touch my hand, squeezed it, then released. 'You were so scrawny, and now you're … beefed up?'

'Shit … what are you …?

'Yeah,' she said, smiling. 'We've come home, Clem.'

Then Tina came out and said, 'Clem bloody Whelan!' She hugged me, and examined me like I was some sort of prize bull she was thinking of buying. 'You were so weedy.'

'Was I?'

'Ossie used to …' She didn't really know what to say. Maybe she just wanted to say his name, so he'd be there, with us.

They'd cleaned out the rooms, and there were boxes and mattresses. Mum had already been over, apparently, and helped them mop. They'd made a few trips. A couple of pictures, ready to hang. Tina explained how they hadn't thought it would be in such bad condition, and I told her about the vandals, the local kids, rats, birds, Mr Champness's rabbits (probably). 'It was a real pity, cos I remembered how you and Mr … how you and Ossie had it. But we assumed you'd sold it.'

'Nope, never sold it,' she said.

I looked at Vicky, and she was looking at me. She was so beautiful. It didn't seem right, things like this never happened to me. Years of staring out of a telescope, waiting for something to happen, and I'd accepted it'd be like this forever. But now. 'You doin' matric?'

'Yeah. You?'

'Stopped end of last year. Mum wants me to do it.'

'Not want, you will.'

'Maybe.'

Tina started making up her mattress with sheets. Vicky went around the other side to help. They were a team. Maybe this is what it had been like, since the lemon tree. 'Me and Pop used to chase people out, or call the cops,' I said. 'I said we oughta board it up, but he said it wasn't our business.'

'Thanks anyway,' Tina said.

Not only beautiful, but athletic. Tallish, with long legs joining a bendy torso topped with melonish boobs. Little Vicky standing in the backyard, me, coming out from a talk with Oswald, watching her flatten her chest and say, I reckon they're coming.

What?

Tits.

Don't they come later?

Depends. What you got?

Kidnapped.

I read that one. Stupid. Haven't you got yer own books?

No.

You should tell yer Mum to get some. See, here, boobs.

I can't see nothin'.

You're not looking.

She'd had a controlling streak. Estella and Pip, to a lesser extent, although she was never really nasty. Just like she had the potential to be a bitch. Pop had warned me about this. Fancy her, eh?

No.

You do. Give her a chance. Wait till she gets her claws in.

Don't like her.

Fair enough. You smell like her, though.

Do not.

She lend you her perfume?

There was an esky in the corner and Tina fetched a Coke and poured three glasses. We sat on the mattress, and floor, as the afternoon breeze fought with the sepia curtains.

'Mrs Champness stayed in here,' I said.

'She did?'

'When she had a blue with Les. He knew she was here, but didn't say nothin'. Then she went home.'

'They well?'

'Everyone's well, except Pop.'

'Fay was telling me. That's a shame, eh? He was always independent.'

'Still is, but he leaves his keys in the letter box. After a while you work out where things are gonna be, so it's okay.'

Tina wanted to know about the Donnellans, Sharpes, Burrells, even Ron and Hester Glasson, but I kept it brief because I really wanted to know about them. It got to a pause in the conversation, and I guess she knew it was her turn. 'Donath,' she said.

'Where's that?'

'Coupla hours' drive north, coupla thousand people. Places like that get smaller after a while. I guess that's why we're back.'

Why so long? But I didn't have to ask.

'I can see what you're thinking, Clem.'

'What?'

'I could always tell what you were thinking. And Ossie. He could read you.' She'd found her mark. 'He thought you were a top kid.'

'He was great, wasn't he?' I checked with Vicky, to make sure. 'Got me readin', and I'm still doing it. Writing a novel.'

'*No?*'

'Done over a hundred pages.'

'See, he woulda known that was coming. He could tell.'

Then there was a little silence. In memoriam, perhaps.

Tina said, 'Took us a while to get back. Thought we'd give it a bita time … and that got longer and longer, and now you're all grown up.'

We've missed so many years, I wanted to say.

'So we're gonna fix it up, paint it, aren't we, Vick?'

'Yep.'

'You can help with the garden, if you like.'

An invitation! Me, in overalls, and Vick, in short shorts, taming the wilderness, planting cabbages and tomatoes, sweating, together, in the summer sun. 'Course,' I said. 'It's a lotta work.'

'We're in no rush.'

Then Mum was at the door, esky in hand. She ignored me, sat on the bed, got sandwiches out and handed them around. 'What d'you reckon, Clem? You and Vicky used to get on real nice, didn't they, Tina?'

'Yes.'

We ate. Cheese and pickle. Ham and chutney.

'I couldn't believe it,' she said. 'I said to Dad, I know that car, and he said, Bugger me, it's the Rosies.'

Tina said, 'Just sayin' how big he's got.'

'That's cos he never stops eatin'.'

'You oughta be proud, Fay.'

'He has his moments, though not today.'

She told them about my history of failed driving tests. Mum was good at amplifying failure.

'Wasn't my fault,' I said, as I explained the rolling stop.

Vicky was laughing, at me. Praise Jehovah! She said, 'I got mine first go.'

'Exactly! See, Mum, girls always get it first go. They hate boys.'

They all laughed, but I really didn't care. 'I did stop.'

Vicky tried to be nice. 'I remember you, Clem.'

I waited.

'You were always a bit clumsy. But that was sorta nice. Curtis, he was an idiot. Is he still an idiot?'

'Oath,' Mum said, and she gave her a potted history of his idiocy. 'And his brother, John, remember him?'

'He was horrible.'

'You wouldn't believe the trouble he's been in with the law.' As she ate half a samby in a single bite. There was more about John, the coppers, Gary's foreignies, Peter's bathroom renovations (courtesy of Ernie, who, she explained, had softened a bit).

I was glad Mum had come. This way, the Rosies listened and I got to study Vicky's face. It was like we were five again, throwing a ball from one side of the road to another, her saying, Dad's gone to bed early.

He tired?

He always goes to bed early.

Why?

Just does. Then, perhaps, she picked soursobs, and sucked them and I, perhaps, said, Dog's pissed on them.

So?

You can get tuberculosis from dog piss.

Bullshit.

Pop said.

What's he know?

He can strip a 240Z in less than hour.

So what?

I seen him.

So what?

So what? She was back, and like that, the years disappeared. What did it matter that we missed the Bay City Rollers, Sherbet, *Grease* and *Xanadu*? Because there was the potential for more, from where we'd left off, sucking weeds.

Jen stood, plastic apron and gloves, waiting for Curtis to sit. She'd made sure he'd washed his shaggy hair, and she'd cut it, so the perm would take. 'You sure?'

'I wouldn't have asked.'

He sat on an old chair in the middle of our kitchen.

I said, 'I haven't seen anyone with a perm.'

'At Gleneagles High … but in the real world.' He invoked the names of a few telly stars who, apparently, had permed hair.

I said, 'What are people gonna say?'

'What do I care?'

I could see and hear the reactions: Curtis walking through the front gate, peals of laughter, before the insults. *Are you an absofuckinlutelygaypoofda?*

He'd bought the rods, solution, neutraliser, told us how he felt he was growing stale. It'd come out of nowhere. Gleneagles males didn't have permed hair. Not unless they'd changed sides, or developed some sort of mental condition.

Jen smeared Vaseline on his neck and face. 'How wavy?'

'Wavy.'

She told me to sit, wrapped a towel around his shoulders, and combed his wet hair. 'This to impress your girlfriend?'

'Don't have one.'

'Tracey?'

'She's not my girlfriend.' His eyes settled on the floor. '*In digito clavus*. Nail in my toe.'

Another aspect of his growth. A Latin phrase book he'd stolen from the school library. Now, he'd set himself the goal of learning every phrase. He'd already started incorporating them in his essays, not that anyone was impressed.

'*Plurimus hic aeger moritur vigilando.*'

'What's that?' Jen asked, with her you're-a-bit-of-a-tosser look.

'Most sick people die from insomnia.'

'What's that mean?'

'Yeah,' I said, 'what *does* it mean?'

'Whatever you want it to.'

Jen split his hair into four sections and fixed them with metal clips.

'Like a cuppa?' I asked.

'Piss off.'

She rolled the strands onto the rods, smiled at me and said, 'You're next.'

'Bullshit.'

'Clem!' Pop called, from the lounge room.

'Vicky'd love you permed,' Curtis said.

Pop came in, went to the fridge and poured himself a Coke. 'I thought you were joking,' he said to Curtis.

'No. I am very definitely *in medias res*.'

Pop had never understood him. At least John could fit a tyre, but Curtis just talked bullshit. Seventeen years of garbage, and what did he have to show for it? 'They'll be calling you a nancy,' he said.

Jen and I laughed. Curtis replied, '*Frontem tabernae sopionibus scribam* ... I will draw *sopios* on the front of the tavern.'

'See,' I said, 'that has no relevance to anything.'

'*Helena amatur a Rufo.*'

Pop just shook his head and left. 'Hope yer mother knows what yer doin'.'

Jen finished rolling and said, 'Right, let's go.'

Curtis sat up, determined.

'Once I put this stuff in, that's it. You're happy for me to continue?'

'Happy, and excited.'

She popped the tab on the solution, drizzled it over his hair, then started rubbing it in.

Curtis grimaced. 'Burns a bit, eh?'

'That'll go, just doin' its job.' She said to me, 'Vicky's not so friendly to me.'

'You weren't friends.'

'She wasn't interested.'

The two of them, standing in her room, Jen putting on *Dancing Queen*, showing her the moves, but Vicky just standing there. 'She was always a bit stuck up.'

'Bullshit.'

'Language!' Pop.

'She was, wasn't she, Curtis?'

'I remember yers, Clemmy, on the shed roof,' Curtis said. 'And me saying, Can I come up? And you saying, I'll see yer later. I's sorta glad when she went.'

'That's horrible,' I said. 'Her dad killed himself.'

'We don't *know* that,' Pop called.

'She'd come in and sit as you made your models,' Jen said.

'Didn't.'

'I heard yers. *You gonna stick the wing on, Clem?*'

The perm twins laughed.

'*D'you reckon I should? D'you wanna have a go?*'

'What a loada shit.'

'Clem!'

Jen finished. 'Now, time to wait.'

Curtis checked in the mirror Jen had provided. 'You're doin' a good job, Jen.'

She smiled, might've blushed, but we hadn't seen the result yet. She took off her plastic gloves and threw them in the bin. 'Half an hour.' Setting the timer on the oven.

Curtis and I sat with Pop, busy with Tony Barber. He'd given up on Baby Burgess and Adriana and the rest of the crooks on the *Wheel. Sale of the Century*, he explained, was classier. Intelligent questions. You had to have a few brains. 'I reckon that Delvene Delaney's not as good as Victoria Nicholls,' he said.

'Why's that?' Curtis asked, settling in with a magazine.

'She was homely. This one's vulgar.'

Capital of Japan. I said, 'The questions are pretty easy.'

'They get harder.'

A noble gas that glows in the night.

'See,' Pop said, 'most people wouldn't know what a noble gas was.' Staring at Curtis again. 'Never heard of a bloke havin' a perm.'

'It's all the go. Women love it.'

'Couldn't see John gettin' a perm.'

'Well, we're different.'

'Too right. Your mum heard anything?'

'Not a word. Nice and peaceful. Hopefully that's it.'

'What?'

'*It*. Hopefully he won't come back.'

Pop shook his head. 'Nice thing to say about your brother.'

'Just being honest.'

'Some of us make bad decisions. Bet you'd hope, if you did, people'd stand by you.' He returned to the television.

'It's not that simple,' Curtis replied.

'He was brought up just the same as you. No different. Like Clem and Jen.'

'But I didn't steal from people.'

'*So?*'

'And I didn't ...' He backed off. 'This stuff's burning.' And called. 'Is it meant to burn?'

'A bit.'

He returned to his magazine. 'I guess you're right, Doug. *Ars longa, vita brevis.*'

'Yes, it bloody well is. You should try and remember.'

We settled and waited as the solution did its work. I went to the dunny, and listened from the half-open door. The square root of 144. Flushed, came out, and remembered. Mum wouldn't be home for hours, so I went into her room, sat on her bed and opened her bottom drawer.

I remembered it from years before; the repository of everything old, yellow, mouldering. On the top, a few cookbooks to cover the past. Digging down through the years, birth certificates, the paid-off mortgage (they wouldn't tell me, but I knew it was Pop, surrendering his final pay-out to make sure we'd never lose the house), family photos (the scissor marks of history), the letter. The story of my father's fall from grace, and Callao. I studied the small, clipped letters, the dotted i's and crossed t's. I found a loose sheet (*Clem was born on 10 June 1967 at Calvary ...*) and compared the two. It wasn't the same author.

So who'd written it? Who'd tried to convince my mother (or was it just me and Jen?) that my father had gone missing? What could be gained from that? I knew who'd come to my door; who'd shared ale with Bob Jones.

The timer. I replaced every layer, closed the drawer and fled the room. Curtis was already sitting in the kitchen, and Jen was lowering his head over the sink. Pop had come in to watch. 'We gotta wash up in there.'

Jen filled a bowl with water and rinsed the solution, again and again, as Curtis said, 'Imagine what Mum'll say.'

'She'll kill you,' I said.

'Na, she's used to it.'

Then, the neutralising solution. Jen said, 'This helps to fix all the broken protein in the hair.'

Curtis didn't care. He just wanted to be funky.

Pop was grinning. 'I got the clippers if it goes wrong.'

Finally, it was at an end. Jen towel-dried his hair, sat him up and started to remove the rods. One by one the curls tumbled out, and Pop said, 'Jesus fuckin' Christ.'

'Language,' I said.

'Come on,' Curtis said, as Jen released the last of the rods, stood back, and smiled. 'Not bad.'

He grabbed the mirror, studied himself and said, 'Fantastic.' Half-hugged his stylist and continued his self-admiration. 'You gotta admit, it's pretty hot.'

I held a box while she made a selection: glasses, plates and cutlery. We kept looking around the Gleneagles Vinnies. 'But why now?' I asked.

Vicky led me around the shop. Maybe she'd always done this; but I felt happy to follow. 'I'd had enough. I said to Mum, Either we go home or I find somewhere in town, or interstate. I knew she'd come.'

Because, she explained, Tina wasn't about to let her go. They'd started, and would finish, together.

Vinnies smelled like Val's house: naphthalene-dipped collections of old crap that'd survived the years. For sentimental reasons, I guessed. Easier to keep than throw. Maybe that applied to people, too. Racks of old jackets from the sixties: leather, velvet and denim.

'You'd had enough?'

'Nice place to grow up, but every day you'd go to the same shops and some old girl'd say, Hi, Vicky, how's your mum? She got her knee fixed yet?'

'Like Lanark Avenue?'

'Much worse.'

I waited as she put a few tablecloths in the box. 'It'd be easier to get them new.'

'Pre-loved's the go. Like me.' And smiled.

'By whom?'

'He knows his grammar. We're all pre-loved, Clemmy.'

'God, don't call me that.'

'*Clemmy.*'

I remembered this streak: like being tied down before something pleasurable.

'Like your dad,' she said.

'How?'

'He doted, didn't he?'

'Like Ossie?'

'Exactly.'

Coincidentally, we came to the old books: car manuals, romances with broken spines and an old *Planet of the Apes*. 'That was such a bummer how ...' It took a while to choose the right words. Ossie had always said that, too: choose the right words. '... how your mum sold all his books.'

'I told her not to.'

'*Swiss Family Robinson* one day, Tolstoy the next. Not that I got beyond the first chapter.' I studied the titles. 'I always looked forward to getting a new book.' Robert Graves. I'd heard of him, checked the price, and read the back. 'Compared to the cultural wasteland of number 31.'

'But yours was the best place in the street. Everyone'd just pop in. Mum, me, Wendy. Saturday morning scones. It seemed a *happy* place.'

'Happy?'

'No stress. Doug clanging away in the shed, your Mum and Val in the kitchen.'

I studied her arm and wrist. Not too bony, or fat. Just the right length. Long, piano-playing fingers and short nails, the sign of a smart woman. Leading up to strong shoulders and a pre-loved ebony neck, with one little freckle, and I remembered this too. Ears, not too small, or big, and whispy hair that curled in and around the lobes. 'You loved coming over for scones?'

'And books?'

'Not just that. For your mum ... and you.'

'Do tell.'

'You were more intelligent company. Curtis was for climbing trees.'

'You liked to talk?'

'Are you trying to get me to say something?' I remembered this. You had to stop the conversation, and send it off in another direction.

She said, 'I had other friends.'

'Me too. Just the scones?'

'Yep. Then you'd drag me into your room, to show me your models.'

'That's not how I remember it.'

'Well, you remember wrong. You stickin' bits of plastic together. *Look at this. A Stuka. The Germans used to dive-bomb everyone.*'

'Like that? I spoke like a spaz?'

'I'd ask to have a go and you'd say, Na, I gotta do it properly, cos the glue sets quick.' She laughed.

I suppressed a smile, but it did sound like something I'd say.

She stopped in front of the dresses. One, a light, summer frock. 'I reckon this'd fit.'

'Try it on.'

I stood with my box as she went into the change room, re-emerged, modelling it. I noticed the tag and told her and she said, 'Why not?'

She returned, took it off, and I could see through a gap in the curtain. Skin. Peach-coloured, flawless, glowing. The valley down her back, not too deep, too shallow, the bra strap with its metal clip. *Jesus.* Shoulder blades designed by the gods. Like I'd filled out a requisition, and been given exactly what I'd asked for. The dress slipped to the floor, she turned ten or fifteen degrees, and I could see part of the covered breast. Nothing wasted, or denied.

A few moments later, she emerged, put the dress in the box, and continued. We passed the men's jackets, suits from wartime weddings, glossy vests that reflected every bit of sun coming through the window. 'What a loada shit,' she said.

'I feel like your butler.'

'You want me to take them?'

'No.'

'Well ...'

I'd been put in my spot. I didn't mind. Vicky Rosie could punish me all day, every day. The high forehead, full of brain, the high cheeks, full of breeding, the perfect teeth, and lips, that I'd kissed. Or was I dreaming? I could remember a time when she'd said, Come on, just so we can see what it's like.

I hadn't taken a lot of persuading. The slow coming-together of faces, the warm breath, the touching lips. No, I must have been dreaming.

She said, 'Curtis came over.'

'Why?'

'To say hello.'

What right did he have? He'd fancied her too. This was something I'd have to deal with immediately. Unless she was saying it for effect? 'And?'

'Came in for a drink.'

'And?'

'That's it. A drink. That's okay, isn't it?'

She put a salt and pepper shaker in the box.

'Why should I care?'

She smiled. 'Why should you?'

'You used to like him.'

She didn't like the game she'd started. 'He was an idiot. He's still an idiot.'

Relief. Second kiss, first encounter, marriage, second encounter, babies, new house, as the whole thing repeated, everyone in someone else's house eating their scones.

'Why's that?' I asked.

'He has a perm.'

'Jen did it.'

'What boy gets a perm? Is he a poof?'

'No. He thought it'd look good.'

'See, still an idiot. He looks ridiculous.'

'I tried to tell him.'

'Does stuff just to annoy people. He told me he has a list of things and people he hates.'

I waited. It was all music to my ears. I was everything Curtis wasn't (hopefully).

'But he said I'd never be on it. How creepy's that?'

'It's his way of telling you he likes you.'

'*Jesus.* Keep him away from me.'

'I don't see him much any more.'

'And his creepy brother.'

I brought her up to date. She said, 'We're getting new locks on the doors tomorrow.'

We paid, and started walking home along North East Road. 'So, what now?' I asked.

She shrugged. 'Who knows? Do you know?'

'Arts, journalism, something with writing.'

She didn't reply. I struggled with the box. Maybe I'd always be struggling with the box, but that was okay.

'*Swiss Family Robinson*?' she said.

'I guess.'

'After all these years. That's nice.'

'Well, I didn't have a dad.'

'You had Doug.'

She wasn't going to help. I said, 'I'd look forward to Saturday morning. Your dad must've thought I was a pain in the arse, standing there for an hour: *What's this one about, Mr Rosie?* But he'd tell me, then he'd read me a page, put it in my hand and say, Next Saturday, come back and tell me what you think.'

We continued: the smell of fried chicken, curry from the Paki place, sirens up and down the road, a couple of wogs arguing out front of the newsagent.

Vicky said, 'Maybe I shoulda read a few. End up smart, like you.'

Good sign. Only a few days in and she was already impressed. 'He just sat, read, and you never knew what he was thinking.'

We crossed the stadium car park, passed the Sharpes', the Donnellans', and I said, 'Come in, for a drink.'

'Mum's waiting.'

'A few minutes.' They all counted.

We went in and Ernie was sitting in our lounge room, beside Pop. It was another first kiss. Had Ernie even been into our house before? 'G'day, Ern.'

'Clem, Vicky. How's yer mum goin'?'

Like that. Like he'd sit there every day, and ask after everyone's mum.

'Good, Mr Sharpe.'

'Me and Doug are gonna do some jobs for her, aren't we, Doug?'

'Eh?'

'For Tina?'

'Yes.'

Ern had come through. Maybe it was Lasseter's Promise. But what did it matter? Bernard King was trading pavlova for talent. A kid in a country outfit, yodelling. Bernard said, *Can I take my earplugs out yet?*

Pop almost laughed. 'Who'd teach their kid to yodel?'

We went into the kitchen and shared Coke. I whispered, 'Company for Pop.'

She leaned back against a bench and gave me a sort of smirk-smile. 'I prefer Diet Coke.'

'Tastes like shit.'

She didn't reply. More smirk than smile. She hadn't done her top button up, and it was easy to use a bit of imagination.

Pop muttered, 'Day three's gonna be a bit of driving.'

'How far?' Ernie asked.

'Five hundred, I reckon.'

'We can do it. Clem's young.'

'Where you going?' Vicky asked me.

I wasn't thinking. I told her. 'Just don't tell anyone. Mum can't know.'

She zipped her lips.

'Tough country, but,' Pop said, as Bernard laid on the camp.

'Let a bita air outa yer tyres.'

'That's what they reckon.'

Vicky said, 'He doesn't actually think …'

'Why else would he wanna go?'

'Why don't you tell him he's wasting his time?'

'Is he?'

'You've got exams coming up.'

She said it like I couldn't afford to fail. Like I'd need to pass, go to uni, get a job, if I was gonna buy a house for … us? 'It's so far,' she said.

'So?'

'What if he gets sick? What if something happens?'

I explained this, too. My gradual coming-to-see that a man had to do what a man had to do. Like me, surveying my melamine future, and knowing I'd do anything, no matter how irrational. 'At least he'll die happy,' I said.

'You should tell your mum.'

'No. And you can't. I'm trusting you.'

She smirked again. Like, how do you know what I'll do?

'If she stopped him he'd just sit there, give up. At least if he goes, and finds out …'

Less smirk, more smile. She knew I was right. That's what I liked about Vicky (one thing, anyway). The joke lasted as long as it should, no more.

Pop said, 'Curtin Springs … they got water, so that's the best place to camp.'

'How much we taking?'

'What?'

'Water?'

'Plenty. We can refill at Coober. Don't worry about all that, it's sorted.'

We took our Cokes and went to my bedroom. Not something you could get away with if Mum was home. As we passed them, Pop shooshed Ernie.

'Don't worry, we didn't hear a thing,' I said.

Vicky sat on my bed and looked across at her home, Tina busy clearing weeds from around the water meter.

'I've sat watching your place for years,' I said.

She just studied her mother's efforts.

'Like I said, there were prowlers, but we moved them on.'

Again, nothing.

I was unsure what to do, so I sat close to her. 'I've been watching the street, all these years.'

'That's a bit creepy.'

'Not much else to do.'

She noticed my telescope. 'With that?'

'No. For the stars.'

But she wasn't convinced. 'So I should make sure my window's shut of a night?'

'It was just out of curiosity. I'm a very curious person. You remember that?'

She just grinned, like she'd known me forever. 'You're just a little boy still, aren't you?'

'How?'

'Like you used to be. A little mouse, watching.'

'Well, I think you'll find I'm capable of much more now.'

She almost laughed. 'Really?'

I wanted to explain, or demonstrate, but dared not.

'Like what?'

'Like plenty of things. My novel, for instance.'

'Do tell, Clemmy.'

A moment later I had it out, and turned to a passage I thought she might enjoy.

'Arnold's view of the world was really quite simple. Everyone was in need of help. Rescuing. And only he was able.' I explained. How it was Arnold, not me, who'd rescue the world. *'This could happen in a physical way (for example, rescuing people from high-rise fires) or in a simpler, more domestic way.'*

She turned towards me. One leg (don't look, don't look, Whelan!) across my unmade bed, the other sticking out like a snag, ready to trap me.

'*Arnold woke to screaming. Then, smoke. He jumped from bed, saw his neighbour, Joan, on the roof of her house, the flames licking at her feet.*'

'You imagined this?' Vicky asked.

'That's what writers do, Vick.'

'Go on.'

'*Arnold donned his tights, adjusted his tackle, and flew from the window of his small room. Across the road. He hovered above the gal, took Joan in his arms and rocketed upwards, and at that instance, the house exploded, disintegrating in a ruin that would lay unrepaired for more than a decade, until Joan returned, determined to fix her future.*'

I waited. 'Well?'

'I'm Joan?'

'Perhaps.'

'You're a good writer.'

I had a thought. A stroke of genius. My hand was on the bed, and if I moved it, and a finger or two accidentally touched hers, then it was like I was actually … trying.

I had to do it before I reasoned it away. I touched her hand, and every nerve in my body tingled. Stasis; the shared warmth of skin. Although she didn't reciprocate, she didn't do anything to stop me.

Ernie held a small pistol, taking the magazine in and out, showing us how it worked. 'You can't be too careful.'

'We're not taking a pistol,' Pop said.

'You wanna catch rabbits?'

Pop showed him a small trap he'd already packed in the trailer.

'You won't catch nothin' with that.'

'I used to get plenty.'

Ernie loaded, cocked, and pointed the pistol at the roof.

'Put the bloody thing away,' Pop said.

'Don't worry, it's on safety.'

Pop took a few steps, grabbed the weapon and slammed it down on the tool bench. 'Let's get it clear: *I'm* running things.'

Ernie and Peter waited, unsure.

'Right, let's get this done.'

This being the trailer, sitting in the cheesy light from our sixty-watt globe. Welded, primed, painted, and the wiring working, praise Clem! It'd taken me a while, following the diagrams, and then we'd hooked it up to the Datsun, but the brake triggered the blinker, the blinker the running lights, so I'd tried again, and eventually it worked. Pop had been pleased, hair had been ruffled. New tyres and a rego disk we'd arranged from the office of my many failings (the licence could wait).

So under Pop's direction, it began. Firstly, the tent, packed in the bottom. I sat on it. Then, the groundcovers and swags, cooking pots and digging tools. As they were slipped into the gaps, Pop said, 'I can hear the clunk.'

We waited for him.

'As we dig down ... through the sand. Quartz. Can you hear it, Clem?'

'I reckon.'

'Pete?'

'Gold-bearing, eh, Doug?'

'Oath. Ernie?'

He took a moment. 'I can hear it, Doug. I can hear it.'

Like we were all being asked to take a pledge, to believe in Lasseter's gold. We'd had it all explained: the hills that looked like sun bonnets, the sacred waterhole, the razor-sharp mallee protecting its gold. The dozens of doomed expeditions. Amateurish efforts, destined to fail. Lasseter's son, even, driving west every year in search of his father's slippery dream.

'This is what we'll do,' Pop said, packing an esky. 'Take a picture and mark the spot. Then, cover it up and head back to town to make the claim.'

'How'd you do that?' Ernie asked.

'Department of Mines and Energy.' He took a sheet of paper

from his pocket and showed us. 'Application for Mining Claim'. We examined it. He'd already filled in certain fields: name, address, type(s) of minerals under consideration.

'It's just got your name on it,' Ernie said.

'Correct. I make the claim, then we come to an agreement.'

Ernie was unsure. 'Agreement?'

'Pete draws up a contract, saying who gets what.'

'I do?'

'We agreed on this.'

Ernie. 'But why can't we have our names on the claim?'

'It's *my* claim. *I'll* discover it. That was the agreement. Me and Clem were going, but you two wanted to come.'

This didn't go down well. Maybe they'd reconsidered. After all, it was a long way to go for a few scraps, especially if the lode was as big as Pop was saying.

'You could pop our names on the claim, and make the percentage clear,' Ernie said.

'Easier this way.'

Peter said, 'Maybe we should agree on it now?'

Pop. 'Fine.' He sat, placed the claim on the bench, found a carpenter's pencil and wrote: '*I, Douglas Currie …*' Then turned to Peter. 'Come on, you're the lawyer.'

'You can't do it that way. It wouldn't hold up in court.'

'It's never gonna get to court. We've agreed, haven't we?' He handed Peter the pencil and he sat down and wrote.

'*I, Douglas Currie, holding the claim on this gold, do hereby state that all earnings and royalties will accrue ninety per cent to me, five to Peter* (add yer middle name) *Donnellan and five to Ernest –* what's yer middle name?'

'John, as if it matters.'

'*Ernest John Sharpe, all of Lanark Avenue, Gleneagles.*'

Ernie said, 'Five? Coupla weeks ago it was ten.'

'It was never ten.'

'This yer memory going?'

'*It was never ten.*'

'It was.'

'If you want, there's the door.'

Again, a stand-off. Ernie mumbled, 'Five?'

'Five.'

Peter didn't say a thing. Maybe he was thinking that five per cent of nothing's still nothing. He finished writing, signed the bottom then presented it to Pop, who signed, and Ernie, who looked miserable, made a few more comments, then signed.

I reclaimed my spot on the trailer and they continued packing lanterns, saucepans and camp oven, Pop finding spots, squeezing them in, me jumping up and down.

Pop said to Peter, 'You haven't told anyone?'

'No.'

But he didn't look sure. 'Not even Davo?'

'You gonna trust *any* of us, Doug?'

'I do, only I don't want Val knowin'. She's in Fay's ear five times a day.'

I knew Pete would've told Dave, and he would've said, Can I come? And Pete would've explained: only four seats in a Datsun. They would've whispered and laughed and Val would've heard and said, What you two talking about? Maybe they'd told her, and she'd agreed to keep mum, seeing it as Pop's final, grand delusion.

'We're a team,' Pete said. 'It's not just you, with us along for the ride.'

'*Exactly*,' Ernie agreed. 'We got a stake too. We believe, don't we, Clem?'

I nodded.

'Righto,' Pop said. 'I'm tryin' to make it happen. Can't just talk about it. Planning, that's how you find gold. Less you wanna end up like Burke and Wills.'

'They didn't have a Datsun,' I said.

'Camels,' Pop replied. 'And their radiators don't overheat.'

We were nearly there. The last of the food, bottles of water, a box with powdered milk, custard and cordial. Then Ernie picked up the dry goods. 'Shit.' He put them down on the wheel arch.

Flour everywhere, and biscuit crumbs from the few packs we'd wrapped in foil.

'Rats?' Pete asked.

Pop looked at him like, Yes, from your shed.

'No,' I said, watching the little red eyes.

Everyone followed my stare. A rabbit: grey, fat, buck-toothed. After years of hearing about them, here was the proof. Les's mythical bunnies. 'One of Les's,' I said.

Ernie moved towards the bench, picked up his pistol, slipped off the safety and lined it up.

Pop pushed his hand down. 'Don't be stupid.'

'I can get him.'

'Everyone in the street'll know.'

Ernie wasn't happy. The rabbit just watched us.

'What we gonna do?' Peter asked.

Pop took a step towards it, but it didn't move. 'Come here y' little shit.' He lunged, but the bunny darted behind the shelves.

When we were done, Pop produced a bottle of brandy and paper cups and insisted we all drink. More of the pledge, or some sort of blood-mixing. He spread a map on the bench and used the pistol as a pointer. 'Day one, here … here. Ern, you rang the hotel at Port Augusta?'

'Done. Single room. Put the swags on the floor.'

Mum was at the back door. 'Dad, Clem, you comin' in?'

Pop stuck his head out. 'Gis a minute, will you?'

'What you doin'?'

'Fixin' that idiot's trailer.'

We waited, listening, as she went back in. Then Pop folded the map and said, 'That's gonna have to do for now. We'll talk again tomorrow.' He raised his cup and said, 'To success.'

And we repeated it, half-believing, half-dreading. But sometimes you just had to sit on your egg, regardless of its chances of hatching.

Fig trees were bastards. Even if you managed to remove them, they were back a few months later. But Pop was determined. He'd dug around the base, loosened the trunk, and now, him and Ernie were rocking it.

'Must be an easier way,' Ernie said.

'Keep going. Clem?'

I joined in, the three of us, back and forth, but it refused to yield.

Tina came out and said, 'Drinks?'

'In a minute,' Pop grumbled.

'Don't damage yourselves.'

He didn't reply. He'd never liked gardening, but it was something that had to be done. Why people planted trees, he didn't know. Grass was the go. Run the mower over every couple of weeks, everyone's happy. 'Who planted this?' he asked.

'Ossie. He liked fig jam. Reckoned we could make our own.'

As Pop thought (I guessed), Well, why the hell isn't he here removing it?

'Gis a call when yer ready,' Tina said, going inside.

Back and forth, but it wouldn't yield. Ernie took the pruning saw and started on the trunk.

'That'll take hours,' Pop said.

But he kept going.

Pop sat back, his legs in the hole. 'Why can't she get some-one in?'

'Can't afford it,' I suggested.

He surveyed the yard – overgrown trees surrounded by dead or feral shrubs; four-foot lawn full of thistle and wireweed. 'She can't expect us to do it all.'

'You offered.'

'No, your mother offered me. While she sits in there havin' a cuppa with her.'

Ernie's saw slipped, grazing his hand. He examined it, and licked the blood.

'Go easy,' Pop said. 'That gets infected, you won't be coming.'

'It's not gonna. Anyway, who says who's goin' or not?'

'I do.'

Vicky had helped for an hour: short shorts and work shirt, borrowed boots and hiking socks. Quite the modern woman, although I did keep my eyes to myself. Then she'd had to go in, shower, and get a bus for a job interview. Secretarial, although she couldn't type or take shorthand. But she'd just said, 'Don't worry, I'll convince them.'

'Despite not knowing what to do?'

'The right person, Clemmy. You can teach a monkey to type.'

'*Really?*'

She'd punched my arm, hard enough for a bruise. Which, I guessed, I'd wash lovingly every night until it faded.

Back and forth. Pop said, 'I'm too old for this.'

Ernie'd had enough. 'A hundred and fifty for the day and he'd clear this lot out. I'm too old.'

'*You're* too old?' Pop said.

Silence, as the wilderness was contemplated, and we listened to the ladies, inside number 26, laughing and talking about whatever women talk about.

'Bita spirit,' Pop said. 'That's what we're gonna need: bita spirit. Let's get it started.' As he pushed, pulled, spat on his hands, wiped sweat from his forehead, bulged from his singlet. 'Come on, you two, I'm the old bastard.'

Then, finally, the cracking of wood, splintering of fibre, as the fig groaned and laid itself out, defeated. Ernie cut the sinew and Pop pushed it with his foot. 'One down. What's next?'

'The lemon tree,' Ernie said.

Pop wasn't sure. 'We better ask.'

'She wants them all gone. Her words.'

It was a big tree, with healthy limbs, although, since it hadn't been watered in years, its fruit was small, scrotal. I said, 'Bita water and fertiliser, it might come good.'

'*All gone,*' Ernie repeated.

'Strange she left it,' Pop said.

'Why?' Ernie asked.

He didn't reply.

'That's the tree he used,' I said.

'You don't know that,' Pop growled.

'See, that big branch.'

'Don't say what you don't know.'

Ernie was a gossip. 'How do you know?'

'*We know*,' Pop said.

We all saw Ossie moving in the breeze, his feet brushing against the trunk.

'Pity,' Ernie said.

'Pity,' Pop agreed. 'He was a decent sorta fella, wasn't he, Clem?'

'Yeah.'

'Gave you them books, eh?'

All this made me wonder whether we should chop it down. 'Maybe we should ask Tina.'

Pop wasn't so sentimental. He stood and said, 'Yer gotta move on,' took the pruning saw from Ernie and approached it. Picked the narrowest part of the trunk and began.

It felt strange. The object of my and Curtis's fascination for so long. The number of times we'd examined it for rope marks, imagined the day, the moment, the result, the ambulance, the crying and screaming and shouting, the neighbours (some we'd never met) gathering with their arms crossed, asking what had happened. Pop sawed without pausing, determined.

Ernie said, 'He was never quite right, was he?'

'Just different,' I said. 'Thoughtful.'

'Doesn't pay to think about things too much.' Ern had his own orthodoxy, written and spoken on a daily basis. Sensible, fair, equitable. These small, suburban revolutions didn't matter. If Ossie had just got on with things … No one *had* to kill themselves.

Pop's arm pushed saw into flesh, and it cut, and the wet, green tissue fell to the ground. The trunk moved, and he cut it some more, moved some more, and he pushed it with his foot, and it fell.

'Done,' he said, returning.

Good, I thought. Me and Vicky and Tina and everything that

might happen now: all in the future. Books were for memories; stories, too, over a cuppa, but not lemon trees.

Tina came out with a tray and handed us a glass of barley water. 'I do appreciate this, fellas.'

'Glad to help,' Pop said.

As we drank, she noticed which trees had fallen. 'Lotta work, eh?'

'Not so much,' Pop said.

'I was gonna get someone in, but Fay reckoned it wasn't worth it.'

'Na, why pay someone?'

'Yes.' Her eyes lingering on the lemon. 'Good job, I'd say.' Before she went in.

'What next?' Ernie asked.

'I've had enough,' Pop replied. 'Don't wanna pull a muscle, this close.'

Suddenly, a raised voice, from inside. Mum, of course. 'When did he say that?'

'Careful,' Pop said.

Then she was at the back door, hands on hips – never a good sign. 'You got something to tell me, Dad?'

'What you talking about?'

Tina stood behind her, terrified.

'You and yer bloody *reef*!'

Shit, I thought. Vicky. I remembered what Pop had told me dozens of times: They always tell their mothers.

Pop said, 'When you start makin' sense …'

'Packed ready to go?'

'What are you talkin' about?' He turned to Ernie, who played along, and me, although it was more, I'm gonna kill you, you little shit.

Mum stormed across the road towards our shed. We followed. The trinity of naughty boys, and Tina, saying, 'I thought she knew.'

'No, she didn't bloody well know,' Pop said.

Through the gate, to the side door of the shed. Locked, of course.

Mum stood waiting, and Pop had no choice but to let her in. He switched on the lights and attempted an explanation. 'All planned.'

'When?'

'Soon. Ernie and Pete are coming.'

She turned to Ernie. 'He's an old man.'

For once, he had nothing to say.

'Clem – you knew?'

'Yeah.'

'I don't believe … your grandfather … you shoulda told me.'

'He's coming too,' Pop said.

'*He is bloody not.* I don't believe it. All of yers. Behind my back.' She lifted the tarp and said, 'You were gonna look for this gold?'

'Not *this* gold. Lasseter's Reef. I know where it is. You know I know. Nan knew. So, what's the problem?'

'The map? You think—'

'Everyone's been stoppin' me, for fifty years. Now I'm goin'. See, Clem gets it, don't you? If you just keep talkin' about things, where's it get you?'

Mum wasn't about to be swayed. 'How were you gonna get there?'

'The Datsun.'

She laughed. 'The Datsun? Barely gets us to Woolies.'

'Nothin' wrong with it.'

'I can't believe you did all this behind my back.' She glared at me again for good measure.

'Why not?' I said.

'He's an old man with dementia.'

Like he wasn't even in the shed. But he was having none of it. 'So bloody what? I might forget a few things, but I still know what's happening.' He went to the cupboard, opened the toolbox, took out his map and shook it in her face. 'Every detail, down to the closest foot. All we gotta do's follow it. How hard's that?'

She grabbed the map from his hand, tore it in half, again, and again. 'Some piss-pot drew it up as a joke. *A joke!*'

This was his Torah, his Bible, his life. So I was expecting some sort of reaction. But nothing. He just stood there, watching her make confetti. No anger, frustration, disappointment.

Then she said, 'I forbid it.'

But he didn't react to this either, which annoyed her even more.

'Did you hear me?'

Nothing.

She turned on me again. 'And you, you've got exams coming up. What were you thinking of doing?'

'Pete's gonna tutor me.'

Pop sat, lit a smoke, and watched. This pissed Mum off no end. She stood in front of him. 'You lied.'

'How?'

She indicated the trailer.

'Didn't lie about nothin'. You didn't ask the right questions.'

'I forbid it!' She turned and walked out, saying, 'Carn, Tina, let's get this kitchen finished.'

We stood watching Pop. He said, 'You gotta learn, Clemmy. You can't trust any of them.'

'Sorry, Pop.'

'They're welded to their mothers. No man can change that.' He stood, went to the cupboard, fiddled under the tools and pulled out the real map. 'You learn to work them out.' He folded it, and placed it in his pocket.

Ernie said, 'You've been told, Doug.'

'Na, just gotta bring it forward a few days … maybe tomorrow morning?'

'*Tomorrow?*'

'You still in?'

'Too right.'

'Five o'clock departure. Sleep in yer clothes. Go tell, Pete, eh? And whatever you do, not a word!'

Ern took a moment, thought about it, and smiled. 'Not a word.' And was gone.

Pop was left with his smoke, and me, and I said, 'I screwed that up, eh?'

He shook his head. 'Na, that's just what we needed to get us going. No lookin' back now, eh, Clemmy?'

That night, as I was getting ready for bed, Vicky came to my window and whispered. 'Sorry.'

'Don't worry, it's sorted.' I wondered if I should tell her, but remembered Pop's words. *Welded to their mothers …*

She said, 'It just slipped out.'

'Doesn't matter.'

'What's he gonna do?'

'Wait and see. He won't give up. But don't tell your mum'

'No, definitely not.'

'D'you get the job?'

'Of course.'

'You're a shy little thing.'

I thought about removing the fly screen, letting her in, and all the other things that were due. But I had to be strong – the clock was set for four thirty. So I said, 'Might have another go at your garden tomorrow.'

Pop at my door. 'You awake?'

As I tumbled into consciousness. 'Yeah.' And checked my clock: 4.21.

'Come on.'

I pulled the clock's cord from the wall, got out of bed (jeans, shirt and jacket ready to go), slipped on my shoes, found my backpack and emerged from my room. Pop whispered, 'The kitchen.'

Where he'd filled two bowls with cereal and milk; where we ate, silently, by the glow of the microwave clock. He'd dressed, combed his hair, written a note (*Don't fuss, just a few days. We'll call with the good news*) and made tea. We finished, went outside, and Ernie was waiting, jacketed, heavy boots, freshly shaved. 'You're early,' Pop whispered.

'Couldn't sleep.'

He was agitated, but I guessed this was excitement. He wore a woven cap, like he was ready for a bank job, or a week on the wharves. 'Here.' A Tupperware container full of fried eggs and bacon. 'Ida's just done it.'

Pop knew there was no time. 'Come on.'

The shed door groaned, but he slowly lifted it and switched on the light. We got behind the trailer and pushed it to the road, by which time Peter was emerging from number 33. Pop opened the boot and we threw our bags in. No talking; it wasn't needed. Everything had been discussed, arranged, made ready.

I studied the street. A light was on in number 35 and I fancied I could see Ida watching from a window. Ern noticed and said, 'She's going back to bed.' It was a cool morning, and the birds were already at it. Providence sat at the end of Val's drive and Peter said, 'Get inside.'

Pop used hand signals to lead. We pushed the trailer, attached it to the Datsun and I fixed the shackles and plug. Then Pop said, 'Ready?'

Sometimes dreams are bouncy castles, half-filled with air. But this felt good, like the Mad Mouse, ready to fly into the universe. And we four were holding on for dear life, because it was expensive and you only got one go and if you never rode the coaster then how could you know what it was *really* like?

We climbed in. Pop, of course, wanted to drive. He started the 120Y, and it purred, and he stroked the dashboard and said, 'God love yer, Bessie.'

We headed north, into darkness. For a while, no one spoke, then Peter said, 'I hope she finds it.'

'What?' Ernie (sitting beside Pop) asked.

'My note. Thought I better explain.'

'Why?' Pop asked.

'It's gonna be a shock for Mum. Can you imagine? Her running inta Fay ... *d'you know what's happening?*'

We smiled, but it was too early to laugh. Ern opened a loaf of bread and started making sandwiches with Ida's bacon and egg. We each got one, and Peter dropped his egg in his lap, and Pop said, 'Careful, we gotta keep it clean.'

'She'll have a coronary,' Peter said.

'She'll be alright,' Pop consoled. 'They'll all get together, have a cuppa, complain about us, and Fay'll say, I reckon I oughta call the police, but Ida and Val'll say, Na, they'll be fine. Somethin' like that.'

'I hope,' Peter said, licking egg from his fingers.

Bessie loved city roads. Just glided, up and down, loop the loop, as we clutched our handles and Ern said to Pop, 'You got the map?'

'What am I, stupid?'

'Just asking.'

Pop patted his pocket, to make sure.

Then silence again. Petrol stations, suburbs with sleep in their eyes, the road so open Pop started weaving from lane to lane. *'Daisy, Daisy, give me your answer do ...'*

'You won't be so happy when the cops pull you over,' Ernie said.

Pop glared at him. Ern, the destroyer of dreams. 'What cops? No one for a million miles.'

Suburbs became factories, white-fanged hounds drooling as we passed. A yard with a hundred tractors, another with a thousand caravans, another with a million drilling rigs. All lined up, waiting for another dreary day that we'd avoid. 'We're doin' it,' Pop said. 'We're actually doin' it.'

'What, you thought we wouldn't?' Ernie asked.

'Taken so bloody long. When was it we first talked about it?'

'Years ago.'

Pop turned to me. 'You weren't even thought about. How's that? A lifetime ago. Just goes to show, if you wait long enough, everything happens.'

He was glowing, alive, dried egg around his mouth, the shovel already in his hands.

Factories became paddocks, then scattered homes, hobby farms with a couple of horses and goats and sheep. Pop studied every detail: every yard, every stumped car, every olive tree and dead willow. 'The real Australia, eh?'

Peter said, 'Bit early yet, Doug.'

'Na. The suburbs are death. Lock a man in a house, shove him next to a million other people – nothing intended, I did alright neighbour-wise – then you watch him wither on the vine.'

'Reckon you shoulda lived in the country?' Peter asked.

'Reckon. Bita land, few animals, keep a man busy. What d'you do in town? Baby Burgess? That's not a life.'

We passed through a small town. It was already alive, joggers, a rubbish truck trawling the streets. Pop said, 'Never ends, does it?'

Ernie searched his pockets, found the picture we'd taken in town, and placed it on the dash. The four of us, grinning, clutching shoulders. 'Do we gotta look at that the whole way?' Pop asked.

'It's just us boys now, eh?'

Pop couldn't argue. Perhaps, he guessed, it was important.

Soon, the world was gone. Treeless hills stuck out their tongues, thirsting for rain that stuck to the coast. Town-sized paddocks full of sheep and Angus, and vines clinging to hills like old war wounds. Pop put down his window and smelled it. 'That's it ... we've arrived.'

'We've just left,' Ernie said. 'Anyway, I gotta pee.'

Pop looked over. 'Already?'

'Me bladder.'

'This gonna happen the whole way?'

'No, but I gotta pee.'

Pop shook his head, but pulled up. Ernie said, 'Somewhere with a tree.'

Pop got out, stretched his legs and said, 'This'll do.'

'Everyone can see.'

'Who's looking at you?'

Ernie walked a few metres, turned away from us, and waited. A car sped past, and he said, 'Fuck, I need a tree.'

'Just do it. It's not the front bar of the Windsor.'

Ernie zipped himself and walked back. 'Can't piss in the open.'

We drove. The tress turned to stumps, the grass dried off and granite and limestone emerged from the hills. Sheep gave way to wheat, or stubble, or harvesters and field bins. Pop scanned the landscape. 'It's dry this year.'

But we'd already tired of his travelogue.

'Not meant for agriculture. They pump fertiliser into it, but it's not sustainable.'

'What's not?' Ernie said.

'Grain. This far north. Idiot's game.'

'They've been doing it for years.'

'Still …'

Ernie retreated, realising there was no point.

I'd tried some D. H. Lawrence, but it wasn't working. So I found Jen's cards in my pocket and said, 'Who wants their fortune told?

'Me,' Peter replied.

'Not that loada shit,' Pop said.

But I was shuffling. 'Lap of the gods, Pop.'

'Rubbish. Man makes his own luck.'

'Righto, Pete.' I laid the first card on my knee. The Fool.

'What's that?' Pete asked.

'Spirit in search of experience.' (I'd heard it so many times I'd remembered.)

'There you go,' Pete said to Pop. 'D'you hear that?'

'Not listening. Jen's not gonna be happy.'

'She's lost interest,' I said.

On, further. A sagging geography, letting in the sea, so that everything to our west was swamp, brittle land filled with salt, skeletal trees and the smell of rotting vegetation. But it shimmered in the crystal sun, and Pop said, 'That's just about the prettiest thing I seen.'

Low-tide beaches covered in sea grass, and a couple of kids with buckets and spades. Pop said, 'That's where we shoulda taken you, Clem.' Regretfully, like there was a whole life he should've lived, and shared, and shown, but hadn't, because he'd listened to other people.

'Not much of a beach,' I said.

And near this beach, a little town with a jetty that kept going out for miles, trying to reclaim the sea, because the ocean (I guessed) kept receding. Maybe this is what Pop was seeing. A jetty that'd had bits tacked on over the years. But in the end, the sea would be too far way, and you'd have to stop building, and then you weren't a seaside town, but a swampy town, and who wanted to live there?

We arrived at Port Wakefield. The highway had bypassed the town centre and now there was a row of servos and bakeries and public toilets, all smelling swampy. We stopped at the BP and Pop filled up, parked the car and led us towards promised pies. Bursting with molten meat. Splitting open, burning our hands as we sat under a lean-to with a few hundred seagulls. As they got closer, Ernie kicked at them, and they scattered, but returned.

'They're fearless,' I said, throwing a bit of burnt crust.

'Don't feed them,' Pop said. 'Never get rid of them.'

We ate in silence. The conversation, too, surged and receded. Someone would start something and Pop'd say it's bullshit and Ernie would disagree and Peter would try to find a middle path, and I'd just sit and listen, and giggle inwardly.

'She woulda read it by now,' Peter said.

'Wonder what they're doing?' I added.

'*They're all gonna die,*' Pop said.

The park was dead grass and blue metal, and the lean-to produced a pocket of shade the size of a large grave. We kept moving to avoid the sun. Someone had scribbled *vaginer* on the table, and someone else had drizzled sauce over the slats. The wind blew up around us. I said, 'Why would anyone live here?'

'People need petrol,' Pop said.

'But who'd need a job this bad?'

Peter stretched back, breathed the exhaust from the highway and said, 'I could think of worse places.'

In a way, this was the number 33 of Highway 1. Livable, just, full of its own feral cats, and lives. Treeless, loveless, hopeless.

'If you're born somewhere,' Pop said, 'and it's all you know.'

The seagulls were losing interest. They guessed we were a lost cause. Mincemeat had spilled onto the ground, but Pop wasn't letting them near.

'Butcher bird,' Ernie said.

There, in the middle of the gulls, waiting for a scrap.

'Na, that's a swift,' Peter said.

'Bullshit, a butcher bird,' Ernie said. 'You can tell from the beak, and the big eyes.'

'They don't have butcher birds in Port Wakefield.'

'They got 'em everywhere.'

'They're on the east coast.'

'Rubbish. They're all over the place.'

'Who cares?' Pop said, flicking meat from his hand, wiping it from his mouth. 'This is the worst fuckin' pie I've ever eaten.'

Everyone laughed, but Ernie was determined it was a butcher bird. He swooshed the gulls and threw it a crust, but a gull swooped and took it, and he chased it a few steps and said, 'Piss off, yer little cunt.'

We all watched.

'Pardon,' he said. 'Slipped out.' He tried again, almost delivering the crust to the bird. Happy with this, he returned, sat and finished his pie.

We continued, stopping at Snowtown for drinks and more prostate relief, and Port Pirie, because Pop insisted we walk down Ellen Street and find the shoe shop his great-grandfather used to run. Saying to me, 'Have I ever told you about him, Clem?'

'No.'

And surely he would've. The family history had been thoroughly surveyed.

'Maybe it was this place?' he said, studying what was now a laundromat, Ernie asking if we should get going, Peter unconcerned.

'Shoes, you reckon?' I said to Pop.

'Yeah.' He looked up and down the street. 'I reckon it was Pirie. A shoe shop. I remember coming as a kid and …' But then, like he wasn't so sure: 'Or was it Crystal Brook? Maybe not shoes. Maybe he sold clothes, or fabrics? That was him. Mum said ...' Staring into the laundromat.

'Should we keep moving?' Ern asked.

Driving north. When the radio dropped out Pop switched on his tranny (which, he explained, reached further). Stock prices and country music, as we headed up the scoliotic spine of the country. The land flattened and the horizon crumbled, little salt grains dissolving in the haze, as the offing floated towards us, retreated, found new features, came to meet us again.

Peter was determined to help with modern history. The Russian Revolution, although nothing could be further from my thoughts. 'Three reasons why the Bolsheviks won?'

'Lenin?'

He waited. In some places people had put up fences, but they'd rusted through, fallen, tangled with phalaris and rotten posts. 'Why'd they bother?' I asked.

'What?' Pop.

'Farming. You can see it wouldn't work. What's to drink?'

Troughs, overturned and broken, waiting for stock that had wandered off years ago. Loading ramps along deserted roads. Signs of optimism.

'Keep going,' Peter said.

'The peasants were starving. They'd had enough. Lenin says, Blah blah, they say, Righto, let's have a go at that. Then (reason number three) along comes the war, and the Tsar can find plenty of money for that, but as for feeding them ...' I didn't care. School, exams, a future sitting in a small room writing numbers in a large book seemed distant and depressing.

'Of course, Marx's ideas had already spread through Russia,' Ernie said.

Here we go, I thought.

'The Bolsheviks had educated people.'

'That's something you could say,' Peter added.

Bessie just kept going. The temperature gauge behaved, she fired on all four, and as we approached Port Augusta the radio returned. More stock prices and country music, but at least we were nearing civilisation. Electricity towers dominated the landscape, weighing it down, pushing coal power towards town. We, of course, were overtaken by pretty much everything.

'Problem with Russia,' Ernie said, 'is it makes people think it's in the past. But it's not. Everything Marx said is just as relevant today.'

'How?' Peter asked.

But he'd lost interest. Silence, again, as we turned onto a narrowing road, past half-houses, chicken shops and more Rotary signs (*Port Augusta: Top o' the gulf to you!*). Into the town centre, a small patch of watered civilisation in the desert. Stone buildings beside glass-fronted shops beside vacant lots. An old canon beside a granite Anzac. There was a hotel with a four-lane bottle shop, and several men watching a forklift load pallets of beer onto a flat-top. On, past cathedral-sized sheds with skylights, broken-down trains awaiting reassembly, greasy faces strolling yards in search of sandwiches. And on, to the Desert Stars Motel. Surrounded by more barbed wire, and an electric fence.

We parked, paid and unloaded. A single room, but it was big enough for our swags. As the men unpacked I explored: a jungle gym and an empty pool full of deflated toys breeding with wire, leaves, a dead dog, perhaps. There was an attempt at a barbecue area, but the vintage cooker hadn't seen meat for years. Apart from that, it was quite nice. If you looked out the bathroom window you could see the main rail line (you could hear it every few minutes). There was a dining room, but we decided it was probably best to go into town for tea.

It was almost dark when we went into the Lady Grey Hotel. The men (since I was still the boy) had showered, shaved and combed with poppy oil. Like a pack of wolves in search of schnitzel. Which we got. Miraculously, over- and under-cooked, burnt on the outside and raw in the middle.

The dining room was almost full. Surprising, but at least we hadn't picked the worst pub in town. There was a band. 'The

Impersonators' ranged from Nat King Cole to Elvis, and back again. Between songs the singer, Norm, tried to lighten the evening. 'Someone get us a beer, eh? I'm as dry as a nun's nasty.'

'Blue Moon' got the punters going. An old fella in a flannelette shirt and jeans, and his girlfriend in a frock, with a sort of tiara arrangement. The room was mostly men, which seemed difficult, but country people solved every problem. Soon there were blokes dancing together. Not too close, but close enough. 'After the ball'. They moved gracefully in three-quarter time. Ernie, who'd had a few schooners by now, said, 'I reckon that looks okay.'

'Not me,' Pop said.

Peter gathered his beard in his hand and smiled.

'Carn, Ern,' I said.

We stood, I put a hand on his shoulder, and he on mine, and we danced. No idea what we were doing, of course, but that didn't matter. Up and down, round and round, giggling to ourselves, then laughing out loud. I noticed Pop. He was itching, but with Peter?

'Hold on,' I said to Ernie. I approached Pop, asked him, but he refused, so I dragged him up, and we began. He just stood there, but then loosened, moved his feet a few steps either way, swayed with the music. 'Havin' fun?' I managed.

'Heard worse.'

Another hour, another few schooners, before Pop said, 'I reckon that'll do for the grog.'

'Y' only live once,' Ern replied, taking out a twenty. 'Sleep it off,' and he was gone. To the bar, five, ten, twenty minutes, as Pop leaned forward and said, 'I dida bita research at the library.'

We waited.

'I didn't want to say anything before now, but I stumbled across this in an old book.' He took out a hand-scrawled note. 'Two messages. One was an open message, but that was fake, to fool people.'

And he read: *'This is the position of the reef in question ...'*

It seemed strange. More information. When he was finished I said, 'And that's the same position as your map?'

He took a moment. 'No.'

Peter looked at me, then Pop. 'So, where we goin'?'

'Ssh!' Pop said. 'That's the open message. But there was another one, under it, and I don't reckon no one's ever seen it.' He turned the sheet over and read: '*The estimated position of this reef is Lat._S., Long._E. Group of three hills, looking like group of Dickens's women in 'Dombey and Son', one looks like a maternity case, bearing_, dist. 17 miles. Single hill looking like* QUAKER, *bearing_by_, dist. 20 miles.* See, that's the one he was hiding.'

'But it's different.'

He took a moment. 'Could be.'

Peter sat forward. 'But we've come all this way because—'

'*Could be.*'

It was the first time I'd heard doubt in his voice. 'But these directions are close to what your map says?'

'Sorta.'

'Sorta?'

'Day or two's drive. All I'm sayin's, if it's not where I thought, maybe it's here.' He waved the paper under our noses.

This wasn't good, at all. Our odyssey had been predicated on one destination, one latitude and longitude, one cross on the map: the reef. Now, it seemed, he wasn't so sure.

'Whatever you do, don't tell Ernie.'

Who was still at the bar, drinking, saying loudly, 'You lot were sold down the river.' Six or seven men were listening, others quietening, interested.

'He's more convinced than me,' Pop said.

'But you always reckoned you knew,' I said.

'*I do!*' He studied the words. 'But you'd be stupid to come all this way without a plan B.'

Ernie was getting louder. 'Marx made it clear: profit comes from unpaid labour. Your mob let them bastards get away with it for far too long.' As he emptied another schooner. 'Now it's cheaper to close the sheds, send the work away, somewhere cheaper.'

Cries of Rubbish, You don't know what you're talkin' about, Who the hell are you, anyway?

'So we just keep going?' I asked Pop.

'Exactly. I thought I might mention it, just in case.'

'In case?'

'You know, I'm wrong.'

Ernie said, 'You lot deserve what you get.'

Now there were thirty or so, jeering, a few at the front pushing and shoving, the publican telling them to settle down.

'The value or price of the labouring power takes the semblance ...'

Then it was on: Ern disappearing into a scrum, feet, arms and fists flying around the front bar, the publican clearing the crowd, saying, 'Go on, out of it, the lot of yers.'

We reclaimed Ern and left. He hadn't been too badly injured. A small cut on his cheek and a few bruises that ripened on our walk back to the motel.

Pop said, 'What were you thinking?'

'Buncha idiots. Not the slightest clue.'

None of us knew what he meant. No one cared. But, to Ernie, it was his best speech yet. What he'd been missing, as Ida told him to stop cutting his toenails on the carpet.

At eleven, we were all settled. Pop and Ernie were snoring. Peter lay on his bed, thinking, and said, '*Now* he's starting to doubt.'

There were long gaps. As the trains rolled past; as a couple argued and threw bottles next door.

'He's scared of what we might find,' I said. 'Cos we're getting closer. Like, for the first time, he'll actually know.'

Silence.

'Perhaps he already does,' Peter said.

September

Port Augusta hadn't woken when we pulled out of town. 'Fella tellin' me about the ghost truck,' Pop said, sitting in the passenger seat as I drove.

'What's that?' Peter asked.

'Said be careful if yer out at night. No driver. Up and down the highway, twenty-four hours a day.'

It only took a few minutes for town to become desert. More red sand, low shrubs dipping their feet in waterless creeks, a couple of small trees. More troughs, with their own pumping stations, and stock roaming the fenceless landscape. Like no man, or animal, or truck, needed geography. Pop took the new directions from his pocket and studied them. I didn't say a word. It seemed like a little bit of gold in a very big country.

'What d'you reckon?' I said to him.

'Don't reckon nothin'.' But he was lost, caught up, confused. With a couple of numbers that didn't add up to what they ought to.

'Good to have a plan B,' I said.

'Keep your eyes on the road.'

Which revealed a hill with its top sliced off.

Peter said, 'How d'you reckon that happened?'

'Erosion,' Ernie replied.

'Like that?'

'The wind, over centuries.'

'I reckon someone did it.'

'Who'd do it? Who'd want the top of a hill?'

Niggles, minor arguments, silence. Even this morning, as we woke to a chorus of suffocated farts, Pop saying, 'Come on you lot, we gotta get going.'

'What's the time?' Ernie had asked.

'Six.'

'Why so early?'

'I told you, six hundred kilometres before lunch.'

'Nother half-hour?'

'No, up.'

'Seig fuckin' heil.'

Pop had thrown a pillow at him. 'If you want we can put you on a bus home. It's not too late.'

Showers, rolled swags, me and Pop packing the trailer, and Pop saying, 'Some bastard's stolen the camp oven.' We'd searched, but it had gone. Pop: 'Miserable fuckin' dump of a town. One night and they've gone through our stuff.' But there'd been more. Some of the food, including the dry goods. So, we'd had to stop at Coles on the way out of town, all of the time Pop saying, 'Dump like this. You'd think they'd just dynamite it, and plough it inta the ground.'

Pop was still studying directions, occasionally surveying the flatness, and returning to latitude and longitude.

'Nice to have the Rosies back,' Peter said.

Ern didn't respond. He was working on a crossword, licking his pencil, writing and scribbling out.

'Long time,' I said.

'Guess they thought it was time to face the music.'

Pop looked up, like we'd said it about him. Then returned.

'Musta had bad memories,' Peter said.

'Vicky told me Tina didn't want to come home, but she made her. She couldn't stand the place they lived in.'

'Good-lookin' kid,' Ernie said. 'If I was fifty years younger … You should try yer luck, Clem.'

'Too busy with study.'

'Bullshit. I seen yers, goin' round the shop together.'

'Doesn't mean I'm *tryin' my luck*.'

'Doesn't mean yer not. You could do a lot worse.'

'We're just friends.'

They laughed. Ernie said, 'Friends, eh?'

'Friends.'

'That's how me and Ida started, friends. Her parents had a shop and I'd go in twice a day, spend all me money on smokes. Then when I worked out I couldn't afford to keep doin' it I said, Well, Ida, you probably noticed I smoke too much. The fact is, I never touched fags before I met you, and I can't afford to keep it up. So how's about we go see a movie together?'

'That's how it started?' Peter asked.

'Yep. We went to see this Clark Gable film, which was horrible, last one I ever saw, and halfway through she's snoring.'

Peter, doubting. 'Snoring?'

'And I'm thinkin', Should I just get up and go?'

'You didn't?' I asked.

'Oath, I'd paid. Went inta her shop the next day and she wouldn't talk to me. Another five years before I went in again, and she's still there, and I said, You forgiven me yet? And she said, Just about, and it was all on again.'

What's that got to do with Vicky? I thought. Every story led back to Ernie.

Peter said, 'I reckon you could do worse than Vicky.'

'She's okay, but I got a few more things to do before I worry about that stuff.'

'It's never too early.'

As he said this, and as I saw the nape of her peach-coloured neck, I had to agree: it was never too early.

'Just don't appear to keen,' Ernie said.

'How's that?' I asked.

'If they think you're interested … that was my mistake. Draw 'em out, Clem. Make 'em work for it. What d'you reckon, Pete?'

'I wouldn't know.'

Ernie nudged him. 'Go on, you can tell us.'

'That was a long time ago.'

'What was?'

'Second-year law. But she found someone who'd earn more than me. Lucky she did, or she'd be livin' with Davo and Mum.'

'What was her name?'

'Mandy.'

I guess none of us thought it decent to ask. Anyway, I knew – we all knew – that Peter had made promises to his family.

Pop screwed the sheet of paper into a tight ball.

'Not so sure?' I asked.

Then he flattened it on his knee, refolded it and put it in his pocket. 'No point worrying about women.'

'Why?'

'They come along soon enough. Your nan came in with her dad to get their car done, and she's watchin' me change a tyre, and she says, That's okay, and I said, You like cars, and she said, What's to like? And that was it.'

'What?'

'I got her address from the office, went around that night, said to her dad, Car runnin' okay? And he said, Not bad. And I said, Righto, I reckon me and Trish should go for a ride. And he said, You drive a Vauxhall? I said, Easy. And that was it.'

'A Vauxhall?' I asked.

'Easy. Like everything in those days. Goin' round, gettin' married ... like buyin' a box of Persil.' He felt for the new directions; smoothed them again, in his pocket. 'Problem these days, everything's too complicated. Keep it simple, Clemmy.'

We thundered north, following the pipeline. Pop opened his map and described Hesso and Monument Hill, Bookaloo, Birthday and the crossed pick and shovel that was Ernie's hammer and sickle. To our west, Lake Dutton; east, the sulphur and porpoise-shaped rot of Lake Torrens (Pop claimed he could smell it). Then, Spud's Roadhouse for early lunch: walls papered with number plates from around the world, pubobilia, snake skins and dunny seats signed by Burke and his missus. We sat down with our hot dogs and Chiko rolls.

'We're makin' good time,' Pop said.

Ernie rolled up his crossword book and put it in his pocket. 'No turnin' back now, eh?'

'I got a sore arse,' Peter said, and Pop told him it would get sorer.

You could pin your business card to the wall, add your photo to a gallery, hang your bra, even, in an underwear jungle hanging from the roof. There was a set of stoplights, operational, and a bowling alley beside the men's chunderama. Pop's finger traced the red line from Pimba to Coober. 'Lotta bloody nothing.'

Back in the shed, the gaps had seemed smaller, but now each had to be worked for. Neville Bluff and Glendambo, thousands of strokes of a mapmaker's pen that didn't show the endless boredom or pointless conversations needed to fill the hours, and miles.

'All that today?' Peter asked.

'Today.' He stretched his hand, finger to pinkie, one-and-a-half times, to show us. 'Still up to it, Ern?'

'Don't worry about me, Doug. How you feelin'?'

'Never better.' He glowed, but then dimmed. Dropped his shoulders and said, 'I'll go fill up.'

Peter drove, Pop beside him, me and Ern in the back. Pete was efficiency, upright, ten-to-two. Pop saw it all: 'That one must be Rocky Hill.' Indicating.

I chose Lawrence; Ernie, level four Superword; Pop, the promise of progress towards gold. There were a few outcrops, granite perhaps, but the thought of a seven-mile reef? 'This is the way Lasseter must've come,' I said to Pop.

He looked back. 'I reckon.'

'Musta felt like this, eh?'

'How?'

'Like it was getting closer?'

This didn't seem to excite him.

'Phar Lap outstation … abandoned. Mount Brady.' But then he took out the new directions, laid the crumpled sheet on his map, and descended, again, into doubt.

We arrived in Coober Pedy early afternoon. Firstly, through a moonscape of tailings and shafts. We stopped, examined a few, and Pop said, 'Best place to dump a body.'

A million shafts, according to the information bay on the way in. Then, low, growling fish shops and explosives stores. Another school, with even fewer promises of Byron on his pony.

'Lotta black fellas,' Pop said, as he studied them.

'Don't know if I'd like to live here,' Peter said.

Karl and Paddy, Slobodan, Giovanni and Giuseppe, loading their utes, driving towards imagined fortunes. Ruptures in the earth where underground homes and shops dared to test the temperature, although it wasn't so bad today. Making a fruitcup-coloured town of up-and-downs, sinking gyms and submerged love nests, brave government offices sitting stiff-shouldered in the sun.

We parked outside a row of shops and Pop bought a chicken. We sat al fresco breaking it apart. I got a drumstick, and Coke, and Peter settled for wings, and a little breast. Pop wasn't hungry. He noticed a phone and said, 'I s'pose I better face the music. Wish me luck.'

Ten minutes later we'd finished, and Pop was still talking, and a couple of local kids (shoeless and shirtless) had asked for money. Ernie had said, 'Piss off,' but Peter had given them some change, because you couldn't afford to make enemies in a small town.

Peter said, 'I wonder what she's saying?'

'She's demanding we return, saying how worried everyone is, how selfish it was to just leave.'

We eyed Pop, who was poker-faced.

'D'you reckon there's any gold?' Ernie asked.

'Course,' I said, dutifully.

'You reckon?'

'… perhaps.'

Another minute, Pop returned, sat down, but then cleaned up the chicken, put it in the bin, stood beside us and said, 'Come on, let's see this room.'

'What'd she say?' Peter asked.

'Grizzled, of course. Come on, we got a lot to do.'

'What else did she say?' I asked.

'Doesn't matter. Grizzled. It's all she does. But she'll get over it.'

He brushed his pants, felt the new directions in his pocket then said, 'Would you lot just bloody come!'

'What is it?' Ern asked.

'It's nothin'. If we don't keep going …'

Ernie was driving, his seat back, one hand on the wheel. Pop said, 'Pay attention.'

'Fifty years of driving, not so much as a dent.'

Pop retreated into the landscape.

An early start, again. We'd emerged from our cave room with our bags, loaded the car, returned for the all-inclusive breakfast, but the woman (still in her nightie) had said, 'Dining room's not open till seven.'

'We gotta make tracks,' Pop had said.

'Seven.'

'But we only wanna bita toast, a cuppa.'

She'd shrugged, and he'd said, 'Fuck me,' and she'd said, 'Language,' and he'd said, 'Not much for the tourists, eh?'

So we'd loaded our gear, found a servo and bought day-old pies and sausage rolls. All the time, Pop saying, 'Coupla sticks of dynamite.'

'Can't believe we've come this far,' I said.

'Yeah,' Pop mumbled. A sort of *so what?* yeah.

'Be diggin' soon, eh?'

'Yeah.' As he studied the desert, the last of the slag heaps and signs showing tourists what'd happen if they fell down a shaft.

'How far to the border?' Peter asked.

'Three-fifty,' Pop replied. But not a confident three-fifty.

'That what yer map says?'

'Yes, it's what my map says. Listen, just read yer book or somethin'.'

Ernie tried the radio, and a man told us there might be rain, but probably not. 'Long wait,' Ern said to Pop.

'What?' Annoyed.

'That day at the pub. The map.'

No reply.

'We shoulda done it earlier, eh, Doug?'

'Yeah.'

'We coulda been livin' the high life, eh? Clem coulda had the best schools. Best house, suburb. Wilf. Things woulda been easier.'

'Stop rattlin' on,' Pop said. 'Just keep yer eyes on the road.'

'Trip to Europe every year. How'd you like that, Clem?'

'Okay, I guess.'

'Paris'd beat the coast. Still …'

I wanted to tell him there was nothing wrong with the coast. With Dad, lifting me, throwing me in the waves, laughing as I struggled. I said to Pop, 'Do you remember Bob Jones?'

He thought about it. 'Jones?'

'Dad used to work for him.'

'Yeah, I remember. How do you know …?'

I didn't reply, for a while. 'I went and saw him.'

'Why?'

I explained: my curiosity, the man at the door, the MWU, Bob in his little kitchen. 'First time I heard much about him.'

'Well, maybe there's a reason for that. You weren't there. You don't know.'

'Know more now.'

'Don't be smart.'

Peter was busy with a crossword; Ernie with the road, slowing every few kilometres for cattle grates, or the beasts themselves, sniffing the verge.

'He reckoned he was a good worker.'

'He was.'

'Told me how when I was born he brought me to this building site, showed me to everyone. I never knew that.'

Pop turned to me and said, 'Everything's done for a reason. You didn't see what he was capable of. Think about how your mother feels.'

This is how it had always ended: the censored photos, and memories.

'It's all in the past.'

'It was Dad, at the door.'

'Bullshit. Yer mother explained.'

'That can't be right.'

'*How do you know?*'

Pause. Rubber on road, and a click in the back wheel.

'Who was it then?'

'Coulda been a million people.'

I, too, don't like things staying hidden, I thought. You search; I search. You need to know, and so do I. 'Maybe the letter was fake?'

'*Enough!*'

At eleven am we made camp. A stick fire, the billy boiling beside the highway, and Peter opening the biscuits. 'Why'd we get gingernut?' As we worked, Pop paced up and down the highway. Ernie poured the tea and said, 'Carn, Doug.'

But he wasn't listening. Up and back, smoothing his hands on his pants, mumbling to himself.

'Lasseter died looking,' I said. 'He tried to convince everyone but …' It didn't need saying.

Pop took the new directions from his pocket and studied them.

'How we going?' Peter called.

But he just kept pacing. A truck hurtled past, only a metre from where he walked, and the dust blew up around him.

Ern said, 'He must be onto something. Maybe not like Lasseter said, but *something*. A chunk, big as your fist.'

'You reckon?' I asked.

Pop returned to the car, took his map from the glove box and came over to us. 'I just worked it out.'

He tore the map into pieces and threw them into the fire. Peter sat forward, tried to brush them out, but then looked at Pop, and stopped.

Pop shredded his new directions, and tossed them to the wind. 'I worked it out.'

'What?' Ernie asked.

But he just stood looking at the desert, turning a circle, his mouth wide open. 'It's not meant to be found,' he said.

'The gold?' Ernie asked.

'That too.' He turned, walked to the car and got in the driver's seat. 'Come on, you lot. We can get lunch back in Coober Pedy.'

We drove back to town in silence. To Port Augusta. Home.

Each of the timbers burned beautifully. The roof, with its exposed wooden frame; the pine floorboards, crackling in the mid-morning sun. As the fire brigade unwound hoses, the Year Eights ran screaming, and White and the other teachers tried to hold the cheering students back.

Curtis couldn't give a shit. 'I was civil, after what she's done. I coulda told her what I thought of her.'

We sat on a shaded mound on the edge of the oval, beside the water fountain. A great view of the fire.

'You gotta move on, don't you?' Curtis asked.

'I guess.'

'So I said, I hope it all works out, Trace, and she said, I reckon, next time, look out for your *woman*.'

'*Stand by your man …*' I sang.

'Though I reckon she's going out with that Duncan guy in Year Eleven. You know, the state footballer.'

The art room popped and crackled; one of the walls had already collapsed. The paint had blistered, and you could see a Bulljaw outline, and the remains of our mural. 'I suppose it doesn't matter that they painted over it,' I said.

Another unit arrived and parked. More hoses, more men running around in search of hydrants, flame and smoke and small spray-pack explosions. 'Pity, we had some good times in there.'

'She seemed sorry.'

'Who?'

'Trace. Probably wanted to get back together.'

'Perhaps she *is* sorry?'

The roof fell in, lifting a sea of embers.

'Best teacher I ever had,' I said.

'Nick?'

'Said it like it was.'

Miss White came over. 'Clem, Curtis, you Year Twelves could help, keep the little ones back.' She gave us a look, turned and ran away.

'Fuck off, you old slag,' Curtis said.

Another wall collapsed, crushing tables and chairs. 'My sculptures,' I said.

'My paintings,' Curtis added. 'My charcoals of Trace … from the early days.'

'You sittin' with a stiffy.'

'Jealous.'

'Of Tracey?'

'Vicky?'

'She's classy. Intelligent. Motivated.'

'Do tell.'

'On Saturday she asked me to go on this bushwalk. Eight kilometres, gradients like this.' I might've exaggerated. '*Come on, Clem, keep up.* See, she's driven.'

'Had any luck?'

'It's not like that.'

'Bullshit.' He studied the flames. 'It was probably John. He hated this place.'

Two firefighters finished disconnecting gas bottles and rolled them away.

Curtis was caught in the orange glow. 'Long way to go for nothing.'

'Wasn't nothing.'

'No gold?'

'Wasn't about that.'

'What?'

The water stopped, and the captain said, 'Fuck it, let it burn out,' and the firefighters stood watching the last of the flames.

'We got home and Mum storms out and says, You coulda killed yerselves.'

'I heard,' Curtis said. 'The whole street heard.'

'She went quiet for a couple of days, then last night it all comes out. I's sittin' with Pop and I said, Maybe we shoulda kept going? Even if we looked, and it wasn't there? Then he told me, his phone call in Coober Pedy, Mum telling him there were plenty of maps. The fella at the pub had sold dozens of copies – and she'd seen them. *Eggers, round the block, had one, and the Irish fella, across from the stadium, him and his brother had one. Nan told me, but she wanted you to think* ... I asked him how he felt and he said, Not bad, Clemo. I wondered why he seemed so resigned, and he said, Least we got to see a bit of country.'

Down, down, she burned, our acrylic Valhalla.

'So, Baby Burgess'll have to do,' I said.

Curtis smiled. 'You can use it for one of your stories. Then you can show it to Masharin, and she can tell you how brilliant you are and make you get up in front of assembly again.'

Earlier that morning: me, standing in the wings, as Miss White said, 'Of course, it's not all about sport. Here at Gleneagles High you got artz: painting, music, and literature.'

I'd looked at Mrs Masharin and said, 'Maybe you could read it?'

'No, all sorted. Clem, you, please.'

I'd held my story, shaking; a thousand sets of eyes ready to follow me on. 'People don't usually read stories at assembly.'

'You, first time, please.'

Eventually I was ushered on. *'Arnold's view of the world was complex.'*

Strangely, they were silent. Maybe what I'd written was okay. I noticed Curtis was missing from the spot where we normally sat. As I progressed, I became confident. *'Arnold knew he couldn't tell her, but he could see it in her eyes.'*

Applause, and I lingered, and White came over and held my shoulder and said, 'We might see you in print soon.'

I stood, consumed by the eyes, and then sniffed the air. Something was burning. A door opened and one of the groundsmen ran in: 'The art room!'

Classic schoolboy error. One thousand kids stood, screamed, and ran, and the little ones were almost crushed. Hundreds of Kennys and Narelles running for a squiz, as sirens wailed in the distance, and Curtis came up behind me. 'What's going on?'

'The art room. Let's go.'

We made our way across the school and settled on our shady mound. As the first unit arrived I said, 'What did you think?'

'Of what?'

'My performance?'

Now, the fire had burned down. Unfortunately, it hadn't spread, so the party was over. The school drifted away, to the oval, canteen, ignoring the bell and reclaiming lost recess. A few kids were already arriving for art, looking at the firemen and asking what to do. 'That's so fucking pathetic,' Curtis said.

Round the block with Davo, pushing his chair over tree roots and lifted driveways. Peter, walking a few steps behind, carrying my notes, asked, 'March 1949?'

I had to think. 'The Elysée Accords?'

There was another car stripper in his driveway, wiping grease on his singlet. He said, 'How are yer, gents?' and Peter replied, 'Good, you?'

'It's a pity,' Davo managed.

'What's that?' his brother asked.

'Doug. What's he gonna do now?'

'Went to the pub with Ern the other night,' I said. 'First time in years.'

'He should get back to fixin' cars.'

'We tell him, but he's lined up at midday for the movie.'

A regular, but depressing sight. With his Coke and chips, saying, 'This one looks okay. She murders her husband.'

'April 1954?'

'Nixon says America should send troops?'

'Nice work. We're ready to try a practice essay.'

'I guess.'

'Maybe you shoulda made him continue?' Dave said, as I pushed hard to get him out of a crack.

'We tried,' I said. 'Didn't we, Pete?'

'He was determined.'

As we described the trip towards Coober Pedy. Pete saying, 'What's happened, Doug?'

Nothing.

'I reckon we oughta keep going.'

'I don't, and it's my trip.'

Then I'd had a go. 'Come on, Pop, what's there to go home to?'

'I don't wanna talk about it.'

'So we get home, switch on the telly, that's it?' Ernie had asked.

'Do what you want.'

'But you said—'

'*Do what you want!* I'm not responsible for you, Ernie.'

Who'd said, 'That's not the point. We been planning this for months. We believed what you said, Doug, and now, in the middle of nowhere, you change your mind and don't even think it worth telling us why.'

Dave was listening carefully. 'I never could work Doug out.'

'What?' Peter asked.

'Gets something in his head …'

Back on the highway, Pop had said, 'The map was unreliable.'

'How do you know?' Ernie had asked.

'Was it Mum?' I'd asked.

'No!'

Although I knew it was. Mum would've found a way to get him home.

'Has she called the police?'

'*No.*'

Although I reckoned she might've. Said, He's convinced half the street there's a reef of gold in the middle of the desert. I'm worried they're gonna end up in an accident. My son's only seventeen.

Back on Lanark III, Dave said, 'Pity. I seen him moping in the garden yesterday. Asked if he was goin' back. He said it was time to move on.'

'He's pissin' Mum off,' I said. 'She reckons, if it continues, he might have to …'

'What?' Peter asked.

'You know, a nursing home.'

People in Gleneagles didn't use nursing homes. Firstly, no one could afford one, but mostly, you looked after your own, as long as you could. I said, 'He got upset when she said it, then she said sorry, but if someone says somethin', then it's in their head, eh?'

Silence, as they agreed. There was a bit of a hill, and I let Davo roll.

'Later, me and Jen told her we reckoned it was a pretty rough thing to say, and she said sorry. But she'd said it.'

Peter looked at me strangely and asked, 'How's the novel going?'

'Good.'

'I was thinking, why wait?'

'What do you mean?'

But he turned, and headed home. 'Follow me.'

He parked Davo in his spot and said, 'Come on, before he grizzles about this too.' A minute later we were in the shed, admiring the Jag. Peter walked around it, wiped the bonnet and said, 'This'll be great.'

'I can have it now?'

'Why not? Encouragement, to get the book finished.'

He got behind it, tried to push, and said, 'Come on.'

I helped. It moved a bit, but wouldn't budge.

'More muscle!'

Again and again, but the flat tyres weren't helping.

Peter went out, called, 'Mum!'

A few moments later Val joined us, and we all got behind it. Heave-ho, two, three times, then it moved.

'Keep going,' Peter said.

We rolled it down the drive, narrowly avoiding Providence, past Dave and onto the road. Then into 31. I ran ahead, opened the shed, and the Jag rolled in. Val and Peter stood admiring it. Val said, 'What you gonna do with it, Clem?'

'Like new,' I said.

'Give Doug an interest, anyway.'

'What will?' he said, appearing at the side door, Mum and Jen following.

I approached it. 'Look, Pop, our next project.'

At first, he didn't say a thing. Just walked around it, looked inside, then turned to Peter, 'What, you reckon …?'

'I've given it to Clem,' he said.

Mum seemed happy enough.

'You've given it to him?' Pop said. 'To keep?'

'That's the deal. My driving days are over.'

Pop examined the dash. 'No gauges, leather's gone, wiring's shot.' He stood back. 'In fact, nothing's any good.'

'I guess not.'

'And you want Clem, me, to …?'

'Either that or I sell it for scrap. But it seems a shame.'

'It'd cost thousands.'

'I'll pay,' I said.

'With what?'

'I can help,' Mum suggested.

'Thousands! We could buy two new cars with what it'd cost us to do this up. All that lifting and bending and gettin' down on the ground. Come on, Pete, I'll give you a hand takin' it back.'

'No,' I said. 'It's mine!'

Everyone looked at me. I said to Pop, 'If you couldn't be bothered helping me …'

'It's not that—'

'Then I'll do it myself. It's staying right here.'

Pop waited. 'Righto, whatever you like.' Before storming off.

Silence. Just the gal, expanding in the sun.

'That coulda gone better,' Peter said.

'I can remember this,' Vicky said.

'*No.*'

'I can. You and me used to come around.'

'We did?'

We stood waiting for Don. He was taking a phone order, shouting down the line: *How many? Salt?* He finished, greeted us and I said, 'Don, do you remember Vicky? She used to live round the corner.'

He shook his head. 'What'll it be?'

Minimum chips. Always. He should've known. Hated us, I guessed, because you couldn't get rich making minimum chips.

As he worked, Vicky said, 'He still doesn't say much.'

I wanted to tell her about the wife and kid, the war, but now wasn't the time.

'Mum kept busy,' she said.

'How?'

'His name was Frank, and he was a prick.'

She explained: the man who'd been coming in and out of their house since they moved north. Frank, with his PE teacher's moustache, body hair and Ralph Lauren glow. 'Every night: *Frank's coming over for tea.*'

'Bit of a wanker?'

'Lots.'

Don stared at the cooking chips. He could've turned, asked what she'd been doing all these years, but didn't. That was just him.

Vicky said, 'When I was about eleven he'd say, Well, Vicks, what say we get you in the netball team? And I'd reply, What say we don't?'

'A PE teacher stepfather?' I said. 'That'd be about the worst thing of all.'

'Well, Vicks, how about we go fishing next *Saturdee*?'

Don shook the chips and waited while the oil drained. His cleft was showing.

'Then when I was in Year Nine Mum said, Me and Frank are

thinking of getting engaged. I said, Over my dead body. And they sat me down for the talk.'

'The talk?'

'Mum said, Vicks (he'd got her started), me and Frank have grown quite close.'

'Disgusting.'

'And it's been a long time since yer father … hush, hush, cos we never talked about it. Then Frank said, I reckon your mother deserves a bit of happiness, eh, luv?'

'Luv?'

'*Vicks* and *luv* and *darlin*'. I told them they could do what they want and Mum said, We wouldn't do it unless you were happy.'

Don wrapped the chips, and said to Vicky, 'I remember you, this big.' He showed her. 'You and Clem, kissy-kissy.' And for the first time ever, he smiled.

'No kissy-kissy,' I said.

'Long time,' Don said, remembering, at last, the pair of us with bottles and mixed lollies.

We left, past Ford, ripping a hole in the bag and eating chips.

'So, no Frank?' I said.

'He pissed off, and Mum blamed me. Then the lecture about love coming in different sized packages.'

'But not with a bushy mo.'

'Or hairy back, big, muscly legs and single eyebrow.'

'Disgusting.'

'I said, Frank, why don't you shave the bit in between, but he said, Na, Vicks, this is how God made me. I didn't mention that: he was religious, and everything happened for a reason, and that's why Mum had run into him at the butcher's, because God wanted them to be together.'

'A *religious* PE-teaching stepdad. Shit.'

'Don't worry, he wasn't around long. Look!' She indicated a motorised scooter parked in front of a Housing Trust unit.

I knew the look, and smiled. '*Vicks.*'

'Come on.'

'No.'

But she was off. 'Once around the block. They'll never know.'

'She's disabled.'

'She'll never know.'

I ran after her. She sat on the scooter, turned the key, and motioned for me to dinky.

'No.'

'Get on, you pussy.'

Why, I wondered, did I attract friends like this? Even Curtis wouldn't hijack a scooter, although John would've stolen it. 'You'll get yourself in a lotta trouble.'

'You comin' or not?'

The eyes, the dimples. You couldn't say no. I got on and she drove down Lanark III, over the mound, at maximum speed. I held on to what was left of the chips. The suspension wasn't so hot, and every bump was amplified up my arse and backbone.

'That's enough, let's take it back.'

But she wasn't listening. Past the primary school, narrowly avoiding a man walking his dog (and the dog). Over a raised drive, and we nearly went flying, but held on, and passed onto the road, in the middle, left, as we were overtaken.

'Okay, you've had yer fun.'

'Where's yer spirit, Clemmy?'

Back onto the footpath, across the basketball stadium car park, down Lanark II, past our homes (thankfully everyone was inside), around the corner, past the Colonel, Don, Ford, back across the car park. As it started slowing, and she worked the throttle. 'It's running out of electricity.' She thought better of it, and returned. By the time we parked it was barely going. We ran off, and I said, 'What happens when she comes out?'

'She can plug it in.'

'What if it's an emergency?'

'What are the chances? You need to chill out, Clemmy.'

She ate the cold chips.

'What else did you get up to in your little country town?' I asked.

'My little country town?'

'Did you have your own tractor?'

'Fuck off. They had *real* men.'

'Like?'

'Daryl, a Year Eleven. Driving a tractor since he was seven. No scribbling novels in your bedroom. *Real* men.'

'So, you and Daryl ...?'

'Yep. Every night, for a coupla hours, in the hay shed.'

God, she'd said it. We'd crossed some sort of barrier. 'You and ... *Daryl?*'

'Yes, but he was smart, and funny.'

'Perfect Daryl?'

'Perfect.'

'Imaginary Daryl?'

'He was real, believe me.'

We turned into number 26, up the drive, the front steps, and into the lounge. Mum, busy painting, said, 'Righto, break time.'

Pop got down from his ladder, stood back and said, 'Couldn't tell.' The panels he'd replaced, the gaps he'd filled, sanded, and undercoated.

Tina came in and said, 'Like new.'

Vicky opened the chips, laid them on the floor, and Tina said, 'You've eaten them all.'

'A few.'

Pop started picking at them. Mum said, 'I'm not hungry.' But she always said that when there wasn't enough.

'Ask you to do one thing,' Tina said to Vicky. 'Get some chips for lunch, and you eat them all.' She sat down, tried a few. 'And they're cold.'

'It's Don, not me.' She turned to me. *Don't say anything, Clemmy.*

As we ate and drank weak cordial, Mum said to Vicky, 'After they lay the carpet it'll be like new.'

We admired the fresh walls, and smelled the paint.

'New job?' Pop asked Vicky.

'Start next week.'

'Excited?'

'It's money. It'll be good to have some coming in, eh, Mum?'

Tina just smiled, searching for something resembling a chip.

'Where did you learn to type?' I asked her.

'I didn't.'

'*Really?* That might be a problem. Just as well you've got shorthand.'

She sort of smiled.

'No? Dear me, *Vicks*. I hope they don't mind.'

'They know. Maybe they thought I'd pick it up quick.'

'You will,' Mum said.

I said to Tina, 'Vicks was just telling me about Daryl.'

Tina turned to her daughter. 'Daryl?'

'You know, you met him. We went to the movies that time?'

'Did you?'

'What movie was that?' I asked.

'How the hell should I remember?'

The conversation turned to blinds: venetian versus vertical, but all the time, Vicky just looked at me, pissed off.

'Peter's been helping Clem,' Mum said.

Tina said, 'It's a miracle Val is still alive. She used to get through a pack a day. I couldn't believe she still lived there with her sons.'

'Peter looks after his brother,' Mum said.

'He never practised law?'

'For a time, but apparently he wasn't very good. I mean, you gotta have a nasty streak to do that job, don't you?'

'Yes.'

'You *do*,' I said, still looking at Daryl's girlfriend.

'Never thought either of them would make good lawyers,' Tina said.

Then, I saw it. How her lips parted, and something resembling a smile emerged.

'Vicks was telling me about Daryl,' I said.

Mum just ignored me and said, 'I think Val's worried.'

'How's that?' Tina replied, scraping the crumbs from the greaseproof paper.

'You know, when she's gone, what'll happen to Davo.'

'As long as Peter outlives him.'

'Apparently Daryl was *smart*, and *funny*,' I said.

'Who?' Mum asked, shitty.

'Daryl.'

She couldn't see what this had to do with the Donnellans, and the Donnellans were being discussed, so I should just keep my mouth shut.

'Daryl,' I repeated. 'And, *and*, he was driving a tractor at eight years of age. When I was still playing with my toys, *he* was driving a tractor, ploughing stuff.'

'What's that got to do with anything?' Mum asked.

'I was just tellin' yers. This Daryl (whom you've never met, Mrs Rosie) used to go out with Vicky.'

Tina looked at her daughter.

'Not go out,' Vicky said.

'But you told me—'

'*Not go out, Clemmy.*'

And that's how it ended – me, and her, unlikely magnets, repelling and attracting at the same time.

I wasn't about to buy into it, so I sat in bed and listened. Mum led him into her room, and I heard her say, 'It was painted about five years ago,' and he said, 'Four bedrooms, that's where the value is. Big families, you know?'

I didn't get it. Why was she showing him through our house? Earlier, she'd said, 'I got someone coming to give me a price on the place.'

Pop had said, 'An agent?'

'Just a price.'

'But you don't get a price unless you're thinking of selling.'

She'd taken a moment, like that might or might not be true, and Pop had said, 'I'm not havin' no one through.'

'Just for a look-see. I'm curious to know … if we had to.'

'Why?'

'If we *had* to.'

They were in Jen's room. Mum said, 'Ignore the colours, and the mess, of course.'

'Don't worry, I got my own teenagers.'

Piss off, I wanted to say. Don't you *dare* come in here.

'And this is my son's room,' Mum said, showing him in.

He stood smiling, playing with his mo. 'How are you, son?'

I just glared at Mum, but she didn't care. 'Like the other room, nice view out the front. We hada coupla big trees but cut 'em down. Nicer that way, don't you think?'

'Of course. Brings light into the room.'

I guessed he'd agree with anything if it might help his chances. He checked the ceiling, walls, tried my window, the carpet with his shoes. 'You got it nice in here.'

'Of course, it's a hovel,' Mum said. 'I asked him to clean it …'

'I did.'

'That's okay,' the agent said. 'I got a bloke too. He's growing potatoes in his room, I reckon.'

And then he was gone, up the hall, into the lounge room, and I heard Pop say, 'We're not sellin' it,' and the agent reply, 'No, I understand the situation. Just givin' yer daughter a price.'

Les's car cruised into the drive of number 28. He and Wendy got out, and talked to each other. Him in a suit, like he'd just been to a funeral, her in a long frock, like she'd just been to the sales at Myer. He used his hands, but descriptively. Then leaned forward, held her arm, kissed her cheek. Like that. And she let him. Like he was saying, You wouldn't be dead for quids, would you?

They went in, closed the door, and I was left wondering. Why we'd carried the esky across the road, given her the mattress, tea, milk and cold chops. If something was wrong, didn't it stay wrong? John never got better; Dave didn't improve. It was like the whole street was in a permanent state of decay. Soil shifted, houses crumbled, weeds grew, cats and rats bred; the arguments at dusk; the mowers at eight on a Sunday morning.

'I'll just give you a look in the shed,' Mum said.

'No, that's private,' Pop growled.

'Just a look,' and I heard her and the agent disappearing out the back door, Pop following, saying, 'If you don't mind.'

Too good to miss, I followed them out, and waited at the shed door. The agent said, 'Beautiful Jag. My Pop had one.'

I could see Pop's face.

'As you can see,' Mum said, 'plenty of room. My father's been fixing up cars for years. Like a business.'

'Yes, I can see that. You're well-stocked, Doug.'

I could see him, fuming.

'Good concrete floor,' Mum said. 'My husband laid this.'

Suddenly it was my husband. Suddenly he'd come back to life.

They stepped out, and Mum seemed surprised to see me. 'What's wrong?'

'Nothing.'

She showed him the yard. 'Plenty of room for the kids to run around.'

He made a note.

'You and Jen, eh, Clem, you've had plenty of good times out here?'

She said it like they were about to come to an end.

'But you got this factory?' the agent said, as some machine started whirring.

'Yes, but you don't notice it after a while.'

He examined the lifting concrete paths, and Pop said, 'It was never mixed right. Not enough gravel.'

Mum was a volcano, building.

'You could rip it up, start again.'

'And what about the neighbours?' he asked.

Pop told him. Gary the klepto and his criminal son on one side, Catwoman, and oh, of course, Ron, across the road, works from home, so every Saturday morning you got cars coming out yer arse.

Mum said nothing; she looked pissed. I stopped, because I didn't want to be anywhere near the eruption.

'Course, these places,' Pop said, 'weren't built to last. The soil cracks, so you can't build in brick unless you can afford the footings. No one round here could, so we stumped, and had fibro. But they'll all be coming down soon. See it starting.'

We went in, and Mum showed him the kitchen, with its lack of modern features, but explained, 'The lino's only a couple of years old.'

They settled in the lounge, and I returned to my room. He was doing the numbers. Mum was waiting anxiously. Pop was watching the news.

Les and Wendy had come out, sat on the porch, drinking coffee. I checked with the TK25 as she stood, noticed something on his jacket, picked it off, went in, and returned with her knitting.

The agent said, 'I'd put it on the market for eighty-five, Mrs Whelan.'

'Is that all?'

'Market's down. Hard movin' anything these days.'

'Might as well give it away,' Pop said.

'Right,' Mum said. 'We'll have to think about it.'

'What?' Pop asked. 'You said—'

'Alright!'

Silence, as they retreated.

'Course, if you painted it, got in some modern furniture, you might get ninety.'

'That's a bit disappointing.'

'Lotta stock on the market, Mrs Whelan.'

Mum showed the agent out to his car, and I came out to the lounge, watching them through the blinds. 'Why d'you reckon she did that, Pop?'

'We're being punished, Clem.'

'You reckon?'

'Me and you, for crossing her.'

I sat down. Sport on the telly; questionable hamstrings. I noticed Mum waving to Les and Wendy, and Les calling back, 'Sellin' up?'

'No, just gettin' a price.'

And the agent getting in his *Danny Moore: We Sell for More* BMW and driving off.

The moment Mum came in the front door, Pop was ready. 'I'm not going anywhere.'

'I's just curious.'

'No, you weren't. You haven't been curious all these years.'

She sat, folded arms, watching the telly.

'I don't wanna go nowhere,' I said.

She ignored me and turned to Pop. 'In the future, you might need more than we can give.'

'Me? Cosa me?'

'If you—'

'Nothin' wrong with me. I'm not going to some nursing home.'

'Never said—'

'You did.'

'*If.*'

'No,' and he turned to her. 'Cos I got in that car and—'

'You wanna know? I got responsibility for everything. The kids, you, this place. So *someone's* gotta think logically.'

'Just cos you couldn't see the point of going.'

'I couldn't give a shit about your little *trip*. If this thing progresses, Dad, I'll be left to …'

He seemed to calm. 'Even if … that's years away.'

She touched his arm, and settled. 'That's all I was thinking, Dad. It comes quick, doesn't it?' She looked at me. 'You … little while ago I was changing your nappy.'

Life has a way of making you live it. Not the one you wanted, since you were a kid, but the one that needs doing. The potatoes that need peeling. I looked out, and Les and Wendy had gone in, leaving their coffee cups on the little glass table. Wendy's knitting, too.

'Bit of a dweep,' Vicky said.

'How's that?'

'*Um cumnia probus.* I mean, who's he trying to impress?'

'Told me he likes the sound of the words.'

'Or his own voice. He said to me, Miss White's number three on my list. I said, What list? And he said, *my enemies.*'

I pulled the first seat from the Jag, placed it on the ground and examined it. The leather had been shredded by cat paws, bleached by piss.

'Making a list doesn't seem very well-adjusted. He looked at me like, You've just moved up a few slots.'

'He feels threatened,' I said.

'Why?'

'Cos of … you know, us.' At last, I was worth fighting over. 'He just overthinks things.'

'And John's at the top of the list.'

'Well, he's earned his spot.'

'I used to like him.'

'Used to. He turned into an arse.'

'I like a bita that. Bad boys.'

'Me?'

'No, you're a mummy's boy.'

'Fuck off.' I tried to release the latch on the other side, but it had seized. 'Gis a hand, will yer?'

Vicky came over, squeezed beside me, and we shook the seat until it came loose. This close, I could smell something nice. I wanted to turn, kiss her, lay her across the shitty leather. Instead, I removed the seat and placed it beside the other one. 'Maybe I could get them re-covered.'

'With whose money?'

'I got money, *thanks.*'

Next, I opened the bonnet and examined the engine. She said, 'How long since he drove it?'

'I can't remember seeing it on the road.'

Pop walked in and said, 'You can forget about that.'

I wasn't about to argue. He'd come around, I guessed. 'These plugs have seized. What do you reckon I should do?'

He shrugged, determined to keep his distance.

'Don't wanna break 'em off.'

'Tell him to get it towed. It's not our problem.' He reached into the toolbox, found a spanner and said, 'I got other jobs.'

'Reckon you could get 'em out?' I asked.

He walked over, checked the engine, and thought better of it. 'Once you start you gotta finish it.'

We waited.

'And you got other jobs, Clem. Like studying.'

'Can't do it all day.'

'It'd have to be sanded, gaps filled, sprayed … that'd cost you a Corolla, there.'

'I could do it.'

'Windows need new glass, windscreen's cracked. You'd have to be stupid.'

'Maybe I am.'

Vicky said, 'I told him, Doug, but he won't listen.'

'Exactly. *He* just wants it gone, so he can make his wine.'

There might have been something to that. Since he'd cleared his shed, Peter had started fermenting. A couple of tables with plastic vats, and breathers. A box of bottles, ready. Labels, and bags of tartaric acid and oak chips. 'You ever done it before?' I'd asked him.

'Na, but it looks easy.'

As we watched the gas bubble to the top.

'What you gonna do with it?'

'Drink it.'

'All of it?'

'You can have a bottle.'

Shiraz. Although he reckoned he wanted to do whites, too, but had to wait until he got enough money to buy more gear.

'Anyway, gotta fix the sink for your mother,' Pop said.

'So what do you reckon?' I asked.

'I reckon yer stupid. Even someone with the skills, it'd take years.' Then he walked out.

I removed the old battery. It'd leaked acid for a few years, I guessed, before drying up. Now it was a shell.

'And what about Curtis's backwards-walking chicken?' she asked.

'You remember?'

'I remember the television crew, and watching it. He was like that back then too.'

And he was there, in the doorway, saying, 'Like what?'

'Vicky was just talking about your chicken,' I said.

He studied her suspiciously, like he knew why she'd brought it up. 'A disbeliever?'

'You can tell us, Curtis.'

'It's all true.'

'Really?' With her arms crossed.

'*Sis dubius.*'

'We're not impressed. Use English.'

'The chicken walked backwards. Mum saw it. She's the one told me to call them.'

'And what happened to it?'

'We ate it.'

'Cos it wouldn't walk backwards?'

'It had its chance.'

There was something between them. Something not-so-nice, or friendly. It'd started with a tennis match, me in shorts and old sneakers, Vicky in a skimpy dress, hair up, the full package. She was winning, of course. Aces, impressive returns to the back corner, as I stumbled and fell, ran out of energy, and will, saying, 'Carn, let's get some something to eat.'

'You're such a slob.'

'Thanks.'

At which point Curtis had appeared again, like he'd been stalking us. 'Tennis?'

'Wanna go?' I'd handed him my racquet but Vicky had said, 'No, we're playing.'

'I need a break.'

So Curtis had tried, missed every shot on purpose, and she'd got shitty and refused to continue until I took over. Then he'd sat in the shade and said to Vicky, 'Did you play in Tumbletown?'

She'd ignored him.

'You've got all the moves.'

She'd stopped, come over and said, 'You haven't changed, have you?'

He'd shrugged.

'Just sit there with your opinions, bullshitting about … with your list. But no one's listening.'

'Clem listens.'

'He has to. He hasn't got a choice.'

Back in the shed, they were still at it. Curtis lit a smoke and sat opposite her. 'I still remember that play we all did.'

She just said, 'Do we have to breathe your smoke?'

He blew it up.

'That's not gonna help.'

But he gave her the same look. 'Do you remember? I was a tree. You were a post box.'

'I wasn't a post box.'

'Stop it, you two,' I said. 'Curtis, help us, will you?'

We ripped the pissy old carpet out of the boot.

'But what I do remember,' Vicky said, 'is you having to wear that sign around your neck because you'd damaged a teacher's car.'

'Accidentally.'

'And it said: *I have misused someone else's property.*'

'That was John.'

'No, it was you.'

Stand-off. I remembered it. Gottl had come up with a scheme whereby students were given a dollar for washing teachers' cars at lunch. Curtis had removed bearings from a wheel, and it had wobbled, and been discovered. Anne and Gary were notified (and guessed they'd produced a second John), and he'd been made to wear the sign.

'You remember, don't you, Clem?' Vicky said.

'Not really.'

And she just looked at me. 'I gotta go help Mum.' And left, without a word.

October

A knock. I ran to the door, and he was there, again. 'Wilf?'

'How are you, Clem?'

'Mum's out again.'

'She's always out. Trying to avoid me?'

I could feel my heart racing, and imagined Mum pulling up, and the fireworks. 'D'you wanna get an ice cream?' I said.

'I reckon.'

I locked the door and we walked all the way down Lanark, and he said, 'Someone's moved inta the Rosies' place?'

'They're back.'

'No?'

'How did you know?'

'Don't worry, I've kept track.'

He was slender, a long neck leading up to a lean face with sunken cheeks, and what I guessed were my eyes peeping into the day. We went into Don's, and Don said, 'Hi, Wilf,' and I wondered.

As we made our selection, I summarised my search, my Wilton odyssey, Bob, and the confetti of information that had rained down since our last meeting.

'You were determined,' Dad said.

'I wanted to know, but Mum reckoned ...'

'Let me guess: he was a bad seed, drank, ran around with the wrong people ... close?' A half-smile. 'Stole, got in trouble with the police?'

'That's pretty much it.'

'That's one version.'

We got our choc-tops, and Don said, 'He's been asking about you for years.'

We crossed onto the grass in front of the basketball stadium and sat at a smoking table, covered in burns. 'You like writing?' my father asked.

I wondered who'd told him. Don? Me watching him, making notes, him saying, 'What cher doin'?' Me saying, 'They reckon you should write about what you know.'

I licked chocolate from my fingers. 'I didn't believe everything.'

'Good. When me and yer mum first come here, all this was countryside.' He indicated, with a sticky hand. 'Everyone thought it was the future. Then we got building, and I helped Sid and Ernie, and they helped me, and it wasn't long before we had a street.'

He said it like, I built it for you and Jen.

'And that's how it was at the start. Don built his shop a little while later, and he was the only place on this stretch of North East Road.' As we watched the traffic pass.

'He never talked to me that much.'

'There was a reason.'

I got it. Don refusing to tell tales.

'I just met a few dickheads,' Dad said. 'But that happens.'

'I know a few.'

'John?'

'He ran off.'

'I know all about it. He's still around.'

'And Curtis.'

'You don't always choose your friends, eh?'

I could hear Don: Hi, Wilf. Seen your boy, and this Curtis, the other day. Don't want to talk, but he was smoking a cigarette.

'So how you been, Clem?'

What could you say? There were too many years to summarise. 'Gettin' along.'

'You always did that. You were placid. Jen'd cry and scream, but you'd just sit there watching everyone, like you were making your mind up.'

'What's Don told you?'

'Enough. Every coupla weeks. In there for an hour sometimes. You came in once, and I just read a magazine.'

'*No*. What'd I say?'

'Nothing. Minimum chips. Didn't even see me watchin' you.'

The ice creams had collapsed, but we kept going.

'Why'd you wait so long?'

He explained, the letters (which she'd burned), saying, No, I haven't found anyone else, and maybe I could take them out someplace, and if it worked, move back with yers. 'Did that for a coupla years,' he said. 'But it never made no difference.'

'She knows how to hold a grudge,' I said.

'You're telling me.'

'She was pissed off when I went with Pop, on this trip.'

He almost laughed. 'I told him, years ago, It's a fake, but he wouldn't listen. So, when yers left …'

'You knew?'

'Don said Pop'd bought a couple of pouches of tobacco, told him he wouldn't be back for weeks.'

Providence wandered across the car park.

'Long time,' I said.

'Sorry, Clem.'

'I often wondered why you didn't just stay.'

'Bit hard when there's a court order.'

Providence came over, wanting food.

'Pop's been doin' a good job,' I said.

'I know.'

'When I was in scouts, he came camping a few times, until he twisted his ankle, and that was that.'

'The Cohen Cup?'

I realised he'd always been there, watching. Providence jumped on the table, sniffed it, licked some dry food, and jumped down.

'Then there was this letter … some place called Callao …'

He grinned.

'*You* …?'

'I wrote it so she could get on with things, without worrying about me. She was friendly with some bloke. Harry … Don told me.'

'You made up the story?'

'Good one, eh? I knew she'd got it, cos Don said she'd told him I was dead.'

Neither of us spoke for a while. There didn't seem any need. There were plenty of crows in the scribbly gums along the road.

'So long,' I said again.

'I know. But I's thinking, we could catch up a bit now?'

'Without Mum knowing?'

'I could try again, but I don't reckon ...'

The Datsun, in the car park, skidding to a stop. Mum got out, and waited to make sure.

'Christ,' Dad said.

She ran towards us, slowed, stopped. 'What the hell are you doing here?'

'Popped by to say hello.'

She glared at me. No words, but I knew. 'Home.' And she pointed.

'We were just talking.'

'*Home*!'

Dad said, 'Go on, maybe we can catch up later?'

I walked away, hearing Mum saying, 'Keep yer distance.'

'I have ... but he's my son.'

My son. At last, I was someone's son. It felt good, like everything was and always would be alright, cos my dad was back. I turned, watched them arguing, and felt like calling, See you, Dad, but knew I couldn't.

When I walked in, Jen was there, and I said, 'I just talked to Dad.'

'What?'

I explained.

'He came to the door?'

'Yep.'

'And you ...?'

'He's arguing with Mum, down the stadium.'

She was torn between wanting to go and wanting to stay, to tell me I was a selfish prick. 'What's he look like?'

'Me ... you.'

'Should I ... would he still be there?'

'Go look.'

But in the end, the girl was with Mum, and Mum was with the girl. You couldn't separate them with a wrench.

Then Mum came in and said, 'Clem, outside,' and I went out and stood in the drive.

'If he comes to the door, you tell him to go away.'

'We were just talking.'

I could see Jen in the doorway, trying to decide.

'You just do it,' she said.

'He seems okay.'

She shook her head, opened the Datsun and took out a bag of groceries. 'Every day I done this, cos he hasn't been here.'

She had a good point. She went in, and I followed. 'I'm not saying any of that was right, but—'

'*Seventeen years*.' She dropped the groceries on the bench.

'I know but—'

'Clem,' Jen said.

'Get the other bag,' she said to me.

'Maybe it's best to know.'

'*Now*!'

'Like the letter … he wrote it so you could … with Harry. That was a good thing to do, eh?'

Jen looked confused.

Mum turned, went out to the car, and got the groceries. 'I don't ask a lot.'

'He wrote it, Mum. He did it so you could start again.'

She threw the groceries to the ground, stormed down the drive, the street. Jen went after her. 'You're such a selfish prick.'

'Here's to our Jag,' Peter said, filling two coffee mugs with his first vintage.

My first wine, although it didn't seem right. It was bitter, sitting in my mouth like a dead dog.

Peter swilled, swallowed and said, 'Not bad. What d'you reckon?'

'Nice.'

'What, you don't like it?'

'No, it's nice.'

As we sat against the shed, in full sun, Peter in his overalls, me in my old T-shirt and shorts, both of us covered in putty dust.

'Might need a bit longer,' he conceded, examining the first of his bottles.

'How many'd you make?'

'Two dozen. I gave Doug a few.'

I tried again. There was no way I was gonna make it. 'For a first go,' I said.

'You refine,' he replied. 'Like restoring a Jag, eh?'

'I guess.'

Another few days we'd be there: a bumping hammer to take out the dents, holes fixed, rust sanded down, built up. Me and Pete (in the absence of Pop) using fine paper to smooth it, ready for the canary yellow I'd chosen. Pete had said, 'I think you'll regret it.' I'd said, 'No, it has to be yellow.'

I had another sip. 'Maybe I'll finish it later.'

'You don't like it, do you?'

'Well ...'

He emptied his cup onto the lawn. 'It's bloody awful, isn't it?'

I knew he had his next lot brewing. Sauvignon, which, he explained, you couldn't get wrong. 'I'm gonna watch the pH this time,' he said.

'That helps?'

'They reckon.'

Then he picked up my exam notes, and we started again. 'Definition of GDP?'

'The whole value of a country's economy, including exports.'

'GNP?'

And on it went, for another ten minutes. He was determined to get me through, and with good marks. 'What about your essay?'

'Keynes.'

'Go on then.'

Again: the man, the theories, criticisms. As I talked, he took a tissue-wrapped object from his pocket and handed it to me. 'Open it.'

I did as I was told, and found a Jag hood ornament. 'No way.'

'But, *but*,' he said, 'promise me? It'll be the very last thing you do.'

'How much did it cost?'

'Don't worry about that. You gotta have one.'

It was heavy, perfect, polished. 'I can give you something for it.'

'No, you can't. She's gonna cost a lot. I'll help out where I can.'

A few minutes later we were back at it. More Lenin, and how I'd structure an essay on Bruce Dawe. 'It'd be better if Pop helped,' I said.

'We'll be okay.'

'When it gets to the engine. He'd be the one.'

'Well, he's decided.'

'I keep asking him.'

'That's all you can do.'

'I thought, after the trip, things might change.'

We sat silently, thinking.

'It's the keeping going,' Peter said. 'When you can't see the point.'

Then, Val, in the distance. 'Pete, you comin' in?'

Like he was seven, still, out on his bike, and she'd cooked his tea.

'Comin'.' He stood, took his bottle, and said, 'Bout another week and it'll be ready. I promise, drinkable, at least.'

And was gone.

Perhaps I was complicating life. I'd already learned, it was all about asking the right questions. Meeting Ron on his way to the shops the previous day, saying, 'Mum only goes to Tom the Cheap now.'

'Why's that?'

'Reckons those girls are rude down at Woolies.'

Then he'd said, 'You thought about that problem I posed you?'

I'd taken a moment. 'The subject almost completed his education; almost received a scholarship; almost secured a teaching position. But life had other plans.'

'Keep it scientific.'

'And with the death of both parents, what *had* seemed important, no longer seemed important.'

He'd said, 'And who told you that?'

I'd just smiled. He knew, of course. Don had the answers to everything.

'So?'

'I guess that's enough to make anyone rethink things?'

'At some point you lose your ambition and settle on something. But car seats, that's something I enjoy. Something my dad taught me, so I guess, in a way, I owe it to him.'

So maybe Pop was asking the God of Datsuns what really mattered? And maybe He was saying, Spend time with your family, Doug. Plenty of other people know how to fit a timing chain.

As the big, white (lost) rabbit of the universe sniffed about for food. Les, in the distance, calling, Carn, Susie, I gotta lettuce leaf for you.

I remembered Pop saying, Somewhere near the hutch. Stripped-back Pop, covered with a fine layer of dust, wandering the backyard looking for something he'd lost. Me saying, What is it? What are you looking for, Pop?

The rabbit.

There must have been hundreds, millions of them by now. Ernie's inbred bunnies, spread across Gleneagles. But why was it you never saw them?

Near the hutch …

As I wondered, stood, walked behind the shed, and sorted through the wood pile. Old fence posts, eaves, the lot, and a little door, with a back and sides and bottom, with shit on it.

I tried to remember. Had we had rabbits?

There was wire, too, off the front, and you could see where teeth had tried to chew it.

I couldn't remember a hutch. I walked behind the sheds, searched, around the sides, the concrete ring where the pool had been, the fence line, where me and Jen had put up the ladder to get to Don's. And there, in the back corner, the sawed-off bottom of four posts. The size matching the timber. I scratched it with my foot, and wondered.

Near the hutch …

Dead grass, cracking soil, and sand. In all these years, I'd never noticed, but there was a thin layer of sand, like it might've been a pit.

I ran to the shed, found a shovel, returned, and began. A foot down, two, then a metallic clang. I dug until the truck took shape: a Tonka tipper, rusted, but still operating. I dragged it from the earth, sat it on the ground, pushed it around, even put some sand in the tray. Trying to remember, sitting here, in my pit, running my hands through the soil, building cities, as the rabbit watched me, as Pop came out, sat with me and said, We should start a quarry.

And me, wondering what a quarry was.

I couldn't remember, but it must have happened. A million things I didn't know about, because they were too long ago. I reckoned I could stay in my sandpit forever: filling, moving, tipping, listening to Pop saying, These things can carry fifty tonnes. Maybe we could drive one? What d'you reckon, Clemmy? You and me?

I could see him, squeezing my hand, flicking sand from my face, and getting me ready for the world. No words. Just the noise of the factory, the flapping of wet clothes on the line, not-so-distant traffic, Sherbet playing somewhere.

I picked up the tipper and went in and showed it to Pop, who couldn't remember it, of course. I placed it on my desk, studied how it opened and closed, the door, even, and how the steering wheel turned, and realised, Ron was wrong. There was no way to find out; no way to explain.

'I can remember,' Vicky said.

'Bullshit.'

'He'd just mowed the lawn, and bent over to pick a weed or

something, and you pushed him and he fell, and then you jumped on his back: *Giddyup!*'

'How can you remember that?'

'And then I got on, and he carried us both.'

It might've happened, I thought, or maybe it just suited the moment. I breathed again, deeply, and saw the green world, and us kids, running around inside its borders.

'And then he collapsed, and Dad said, Leave Doug alone, and Doug said, Na, it's okay, Ossie.'

I sat up. It would've been nice, if it had happened like this.

I noticed Pop come out of the Sutherland wing, stand with the woman who had shown us around, and work his chin in his hand, like he always did before making an important decision. *'It looks very nice, Ms Smith,'* I said.

'Call me Fiona, Mr Currie … Doug.'

I studied the woman's face, her work tunic, with its woven St Margaret's logo.

'If I need to share a room, I wouldn't want a Paki.'

'You're so wrong,' Vicky said.

'They have this terrible habit of passing wind.'

It'd been Pop's idea. He'd pulled me aside and said, 'What you doin' Saturday?'

'Studying.'

'Got an hour spare?'

'I s'pose. What's up?'

'I wanna get your opinion on something.'

'What?'

But he'd just tapped his nose. Then, on our way, he'd said, 'A nursing home.'

This I didn't get. He was a hater of nursing homes. Of order, made beds, people in tunics with woven logos. 'But …'

'Just to have a look. Can't a man be curious?'

Vicky had said, 'You don't wanna go in one of those places, Doug.'

'Didn't say I was gonna.'

It had ended there. We'd arrived, met Fiona or whatever her name was, had a tour of the Bradman wing, before Pop went on without us.

Vicky watched the woman and said, '*We have bingo at five every night, Doug. Oh, I like a bita bingo. And the ladies have Feres in to set their hair. Feres, eh? Bit of a poof, isn't he? Yes, of course, but the ladies like that. Joyrene comes once a month with a selection of frocks, but we can arrange for some gentlemen's wear.*'

'She's not saying that,' I said. 'She's saying, You come live with us, Doug, gis yer pension, meat and three veg every day. How's that sound?'

'What's he thinking?'

'I dunno.' I really didn't. Death was better than Doonican (sorry, Ern). Three o'clock charades (she'd already told us about them). Four o'clock bowls. 'She's saying, None of us are getting any younger, Doug.'

We watched them talk. Or, her talk and him listen.

'I can remember,' Vicky said. 'His back giving way, and us rolling on the lawn.'

'He used to like the races.'

'And us running through the sprinkler, with the clover and the bees and the stings and the Condy's crystals.'

We could hear the old girl; like a lawnmower.

'Pity it's gotta come to this, eh, Clem?'

'It doesn't.'

'But it does. One day you're talking …'

Pop was still a healthy man, and whatever was going on upstairs, it was still early days. 'I don't even reckon they're right,' I said.

'What?'

'Alzheimer's. He's got a good memory, mostly. Except when he goes out with his jarmies on.'

'*Well, you can take yer boiled cabbage and yer pissy carpet and shove it up yer arse,*' Vicky said.

'*Excuse me, Mr Currie.*'

'*Can we have prostitutes?*'

'*What about me?*'

'*No, decent ones. You haggard old sea dog.*'

'*I go like an outboard motor.*'

We laughed, rolled again, and Pop called over, 'What's wrong with you two?'

'Nothing,' I sang, sweetly.

My opinion, apparently. That's all I'd been brought for. But maybe, he guessed, there was a good chance I'd tell Mum something he'd sworn me not to.

'He needs to learn to listen,' Vicky said.

'I reckon he's made his mind up. *Mr Currie, we have a Greek fella who sings, but your grandson says you enjoy a bita that.*'

'*Greek?*'

'*Singing.*'

She grinned at me. 'You're obsessed with it?'

'What?'

'Sex?'

'What'd I say?'

And continued grinning. I wondered, if we hadn't been sitting on St Margaret's lawns …

'Carn,' Pop said, motioning.

We followed them inside. Fiona stopped in front of a door and said, 'This is our wanderers' ward.'

A nurse exited after entering a code. Fiona said, 'You just put in one, two, three, four, but they can't work that out.'

They, I thought. People like Pop. Inside, a few old girls in dressing-gowns wandered, stopped, talked to themselves, blew on their hands.

'Bit depressing,' Vicky said.

Fiona smiled. 'It's how you look at it.'

'Depressing.'

Pop was watching some old man rocking to and fro. 'Better here than Woolies, or the main road.'

Better the main road, I thought.

We continued. The Palmer wing. Double rooms, but bed-bound.

Two old fellas watching car racing. One said, 'Holdens this year,' and the other replied, 'Fords.'

Fiona's pager went off, and she found a phone. I took the opportunity to say to Pop, 'This place is horrible. What d'you reckon, Vick?'

'You're not seriously thinking about it, are you, Doug?'

'My age …'

But Fiona was back.

The first man said, 'Holdens this year,' and his mate replied, 'Fords,' and I said, 'They seem to have made their minds up,' but Fiona just looked at me like, I reckon you're a bit of a smart-arse.

As the girls walked ahead, I said to Pop, 'Me and Jen and Mum'll look after you.'

'I know you will.'

'Is it cosa what Mum said?'

'Na.'

We both knew; when we'd returned from the desert. Mum, on the porch, 'Bloody ridiculous, a man your age. If you can't be trusted we'll have to find somewhere to look after you.'

'I know why,' I said to Pop. 'Cos Mum reckons she'll sell the house.'

'Bullshit.'

'It is. You're calling her bluff.'

Vicky overheard. 'He's right, Doug. You don't wanna go before you have to.'

'You know what Mum's like,' I said. 'Half the stuff she says she doesn't mean.'

'She means it; all of it.'

A small room, smelling of spearmint leaves. A faded poster, with instructions for fitting deadbolts. Light blue walls, for pacifying, I guessed, but judging from the holes in the wall, it hadn't worked.

I could still see the coppers, taking him away. Me and Pop standing in the drive, Pop approaching them and saying, 'Why'd you wanna put him in handcuffs?'

All this before we'd found out what had happened.

There was a small window, and you could see across the road to Gleneagles High. Ted Hunter, smoke in hand, stood watching the Year Eights as they ran around, forming a pattern that'd last into adulthood. Now, I could see the point of the pool hall. Nothing they told you was true; or *necessarily* true. Fitness didn't make you happy, or smart, or get you a good job, or keep you out of this place, apparently.

Pop had said, 'He's not eighteen,' then one of the coppers had replied, 'How about you leave it to us?'

A small table, chipped melamine, with a plastic seat each side. So he couldn't hurt anyone, I guessed.

Pop had said, 'No need to twist his arm.'

But he wasn't talking about John.

Round and round, before he made them start jumping jacks. Like, if the blood flowed, everything would be okay. Exercise and matrices and anaerobic respiration would make us better people.

A fan, clunking, although it wasn't particularly hot.

Pop had said, 'If you'd just stop, let him be, he'd calm down.'

Curtis had looked at him like, Don't worry, Doug. It doesn't matter.

Before they'd put him in the van, bolted the door and driven off, as other cars arrived.

I couldn't believe I was sitting in a spearmint-smelling room, waiting for my best friend. Life has a way of warping, changing, and throwing up piles of caramel-coloured shit, but nothing like this.

Teddy Hunter gave them softballs, and they started throwing them at each other. I could just hear him. Carn, you mob, get yer arses inta gear.

But the oval seemed a long way away; across a road of years, and a thousand front lawns. Whatever had happened there had happened before we could remember.

The door opened and a constable peered in and said, 'You're Clem Whelan?'

'Yeah.'

'Righto. Ten minutes. And careful, you're being watched.' He pointed to a camera in the corner.

Curtis came in and stood, waiting. 'Now this, *this* is like something out of *Easy Rider*.'

But not funny said it. More, observational said it.

'*Prisoner*.'

'*Carn here, you fat slag.*'

But then he deflated, realising there was no point. He sat, waved to the camera, and said, 'You're number three.'

I waited.

'Mum, Dad ...'

'What'd they say?'

No reply. He was wearing his own clothes; his own jeans, and shirt. I wanted to ask about the overalls, and slippers, but knew I couldn't.

'Yes, quite strange,' he said. 'Me, locked away.'

'What's it like?'

'There's a view of the school, so if I can't go I can at least watch.' He wiped his nose on the back of his hand. '*Pessimum.*' And looked at me. 'Doesn't work.'

'Guess not.'

'I was gonna have a top ten hates of the day. Number one: John. He was always the top. Number two: White. Number three—'

'Your own room?'

'For now. Though I've been told ...'

'What?'

'If I'm tried as an adult ...'

We both knew. Strange, that one minute you could be reading a book (I'd seen him, half an hour earlier, on his porch), and the next, sharing a room with a rapist.

'I wouldn't worry about that,' I said. 'It'll all come out. You had to ... yeah?'

'Didn't *have* to.'

Now they had a game going: pitcher, batter, bases. Me and Curtis in the outfield, where we couldn't do any harm.

'Hunter,' I said.

'He was okay.'

'You never had him.'

'Yes, I did. Year Eight.'

But it all returned to the room, and the spearmint smell. He was watching the game. 'They should tell you what happens after all that.'

Or during. Since John had first jumped down from his tree, beat his chest, stolen a few packs of chips while Don was out the back.

'... it's nothin' like that, eh?'

'Guess not.'

'*Guess not.* You always say that, *Clemmy. Guess not.* Little Tom Sawyer, eh?'

'Fuck off.'

'With yer little dimples. *Guess not.*'

I smiled; for his sake.

'And how's yer girlfriend?'

'She's not.'

'Way she looks at you, like she wants to lay back and let little Clemmy—'

'You didn't have a choice,' I said.

'I did.'

'You're not gonna tell them that?'

He studied my face. 'I can see what she sees in you.'

'What?'

'You're sorta good-lookin', in a non-poof sorta way. Compared to the Burrells, who are all ... blocky. See, that's what the chicks like.'

I didn't know if I could bring him back, or should. 'What, he'd just got home?'

'Walked past me and said, What you readin'? And, as instructed, I ignored him.'

It didn't matter. I already knew. How John had returned in syrupy, smoky clothes, two weeks' growth, needle marks, the lot. How he'd gone in, and within minutes was shouting at his parents.

'What's the food like?' I asked, as if it mattered.

'They like chicken. Roasted, fried … I asked who made it and this prick says, Why do you care? But it seems strange. There's only six or seven of us, so you wouldn't think they'd have a full-time cook.'

He looked down. No thought, it seemed, could cancel out *the* thought. John, on a trolley, wheeled from the house, as Gary comforted Anne, Les and Wendy watched from their lounge and me and Mum and Pop stood waiting for answers. Pop telling a detective, 'He was a bad egg. Anything Curtis mighta done, he woulda had to.'

Then the detective had taken a statement, and our names, and said, 'We'll come back and talk to yers when we got a bit more time.' And went in.

'They can't get you if you *had to* do it,' I said.

'Didn't have to.'

'Yes, you did.'

Moot point. According to Anne, John had said, If you hadn't a rung 'em none of this woulda got going. And she'd replied, What choice did I have? Then Gary had stepped in and John had laid him flat, then his Mum, then Curtis, coming in the door. All of them.

'Got a telly,' he said.

'That's one thing.'

'Yeah … *Fortune*, all to myself.'

'They'll give you bail.'

'No, they won't. Dad reckons next week, if we can get someone decent. But if the judge reckons I might …'

'What?'

'It was a pretty decent whack, Clemmy.'

I'd heard. How Anne had stood, approached John, held his arm, and how he'd hit her again, right in the face, but held her there so he could keep going, a second, third, fourth time. Until Curtis got up, grabbed the smokers' stand (aluminium, but with a concrete base to keep it stable) and struck him across the back of the head.

How John had fallen, unconscious, and how Anne, even then, had knelt beside him and said, 'Why'd you do that?'

'That's the problem with Mum,' Curtis said. 'She never understood him. She couldn't see how biga cocksucker he was.'

'Mums can't,' I said.

'Well, they oughta.'

He was watching the game, and seemed to have settled into the truth.

'What did you do?' I asked.

'Nothin'. Just sat and thought, I hope yer dead, you cunt. See, I needn'ta done it, but I did.'

'He would've killed her.'

'Maybe. Did they say how he was?'

'There's swelling on the brain, so they've put him in a coma.'

'Right. Coma's better than nothin'. If I gotta go to McNally's, might as well be worthwhile.'

'Na,' I said, 'there's no chance of that. They came back later and me and Pop told them all about him.'

He was still looking out the window.

Pop was saying, Curtis wouldn'ta done it unless he had to. He's a good boy, smart, thinks about things, gets good marks. Whereas that other one ...

They'd said they knew about him, how he had a file a mile long. I'd said, Curtis has been my mate for years, never raised his voice, never got angry. And I'd told them how shocked I was. They'd seemed happy, and drank some of the wine Peter had given Pop, and said, Shouldn't be much of a fuss. He was threatening his mum's life.

'I gave him a good whack,' Curtis said. 'I really felt it: muscle, but bone too. Like when you break a length of timber. Just my luck, he'll get better and they'll lock me away.'

'That's not what the cops were saying.'

'Doesn't matter what they said. Matters if someone's dead, and who did it.'

'Your parents'll say—'

'I don't give a shit what they say ... long as he's dead.'

I wanted to ask who'd called the ambulance, because I guessed it wasn't him. What they'd done, said, as they waited, because I guessed he didn't attempt first-aid. How long it felt, sitting beside the body, the blood on the floor. What they said to the ambos when they arrived, and the first coppers. How long it'd been before Gary had come around. All of this interested me, but it could wait until we were sitting on his porch, and he was telling me his top ten.

The constable entered and said, 'I gave yers longer.'

'Ta,' I replied. I said, 'Try get back tomorrow.'

'Na, leave it.' But he was still watching the softball game.

'Pop wants to come, and Mum.'

He half-smiled. 'Tell them not to, eh? Not now, anyway.'

'Right ... keep cool. Coupla days, eh?'

But again, he was lost in the small figures, running.

The handwritten sign on the door said 'Finished'. The freezer had gone, and the fridge, the table with its pile of *Post*s and ashtrays that had never been emptied. I could see the outlines on the floor; the indentations, the decades of dust. The till, too, had gone, but the menu remained: potato and pineapple fritters, fishcakes and flake. It would be there for years to come, a reminder of all the shit I'd ordered, the chips we'd shared around the television, the Cokes John had flogged, the mixed lollies me and Jen had climbed the back fence for. Years, until someone turned it into an adult book shop, with Don's ghost floating between the fluoros.

'He shut up,' the man from the next shop (a home-brew place where Peter bought his oak chips and yeast) said.

'When?'

'Sunday. Fella arrived with a truck and they loaded everything. That was it. Without so much as a goodbye. Maybe he's in trouble with the law?'

'I don't reckon.'

As he went in he said, 'Pity. Looked forward to a Chiko Roll every day.'

The grey-looking fish. The hot dogs. As Don said, Your dad was in here.

Yeah?

I been telling him …

What?

No reply. As he shook the chips, and the burnt bits sunk to the bottom.

All this time? I asked.

He brought you in … few days after you were born. He wanted me to see; he'd promised. You and your fat arms … like Anthony.

More hot chips, his nose wiped on the back of his hand. Ever since then, he said, we've been talking about our boys.

I wondered if Dad was the only one to have asked.

I made off down North East Road. Past the car yard, with its Bulljaw dreamings, and chases around and under the cars, laneway skid shows, as the transformers hummed. It had been a good morning. A three-hour history exam. Me, settling in, sharpening my pencil, turning over the exam paper and reading the first essay question: *Which major historical events led up to the Russian Revolution?*

Bingo! Thanks, Peter. I used my ten minutes to regurgitate the facts he'd made me memorise: Lenin, Trotsky, Bolshevik versus Menshevik … Then, 'Your time starts now.' And I was off, my hand flying across the page, the thoughts cueing, patterns forming and linking across the school's cheapest A4. So that, three hours later, when White said, 'Time's up, pens down,' I sat back, breathed deeply and thought *nice bloody work*.

'Clem!'

I turned, and there was Vicky, in her blue dress and corporate jumper, running towards me. 'So?'

'Beautiful.'

She wanted the whole story, but I couldn't be bothered. 'I don't want to be over-confident but, you know …'

'Good, Clemmy.'

'Clem.'

'*Clemmy.*' She pinched my cheek.

'And what about your job?'

'It's so fucking boring.' She was off: the view of a brick wall from her window, three paper cups per worker per day in the drink fountain, how her boss, Mrs Lange, set an alarm so she couldn't leave early. 'A few weeks,' she said. 'That's it.'

'But you've just started.'

We reached the Polish hall and stopped and sat on the steps, and had a smoke.

'Here's the plan,' she said. 'You go to university, get a good job and make lots of money.'

Ernie and Fi-Fi walked past. I hid the smoke. Ern said, 'How's school?' I said, 'Good.' School. Like I was still in Prep, and drawing dragons. That's all he knew: Clemmy, in short pants, heading off with his satchel. 'Just had my history exam.' And I told him about revolutionary Russia.

'Just as well we had that talk,' he said, as Fi-Fi dry-pissed.

'Just as well,' I replied. 'Even used a few quotes from the manifesto.'

He walked on, waving, realising my smoke was burning down and we had better things to talk about.

'Say hello to yer mum, Vicky.'

'Will do.'

I smoked, she smoked. 'But I thought *you* were the ambitious one,' I said.

'*Ambitious*? But Evans loves me, if you know what I mean.' She raised an eyebrow.

'So the job's safe?'

'No, few weeks, then I'll tell them to shove it.' She lowered her head to the smoke, took a puff, smiled.

The door moved in the breeze. 'Look.' I went in, and she followed. Dom Polski watched from the wall, and there was a flag, and a coat-of-arms. A rack of clothes, folksy. She put on a coat. '*Attention, comrade!*'

I saluted. I remembered the hall, from an earlier Sunday school experience, me and Jen in a circle of plastic chairs as someone told us about fish and loaves. But now it was middle Europe. There was a record player, and Vicky switched it on. 'Dance!' she demanded.

So I approached, and we joined arms and waltzed to orchestra and accordion. Little circles, big ones, close, arm's length, running around, chasing each other, throwing off coats and trying on jackets, until we were together, again.

'So, that's the plan: you keep me in luxury.'

I felt her lips on mine, and her tongue, and then, the floor dropped, and we were sitting in a pile of fur and velvet.

'What if someone walks in?' I asked.

It was like I'd rehearsed it a thousand times. Where the hand went, how quickly it moved, where it lingered. She, too, seemed to have the same knowledge.

'Not a good idea,' I said.

'*Not a good idea.*' She giggled.

'Remember what happened to Curtis?'

She knew how every button and latch functioned, how my belt had to be pulled tight before it was loosened, how then everything fell away.

'I can't afford to …' But all I could think of was Bob Grummet's chemist, me, walking in, pretending to look at the bandages. And the girl, 'Can I help you?'

'No, ta.'

As I thought, What are you thinking? Stepped towards the door, but stopped, thought, It's easy. Pick up the box, place it on the counter, hand over the money. *Come on.* She must sell a hundred packs a day … to dirty little boys … *Come on.* As I moved to a spot between the condoms and the tampons, and the girl walked past, again, and smiled, and must have known. As I thought of why I was here: Vicky smiling, running a finger along my collarbone, saying, 'Thing about boy scouts, they're always prepared, eh?'

'I reckon.'

As I picked up the box, walked to the counter, but saw Hester Glasson.

'Hi, Clem.'

'Hi, Mrs Glasson.'

'How's yer mum?'

'Good, ta.' As I turned, so the box was hidden, and trawled the aisles until she was gone.

But, of course, I hadn't taken them to school, so I didn't have them now. Luckily (perhaps), she said, 'It's okay, there's no chance.'

Encouraging, but I thought of Tracey, and how *she'd* apparently known.

Still, there was no point fighting it. The revolution had been fought, and won, or lost, depending on your view.

We walked home in dusky light. Vicky had spearmint leaves and said, 'There were always fewer of these.'

'Where?'

'Don's mixed lollies. Always more jubes, and cheap shit, and less spearmint leaves and milk bottles.'

'And teeth?'

'Exactly. Teeth.'

As we commiserated the last of the lino, a gold chain on a hairy chest.

'They used to have them at school,' she said.

'Teeth?'

'Spearmint leaves.'

'They never did.'

'I remember the smell of them when you went in, at recess, in winter. It's strange, but I only ever remember it being winter.'

'With their five cent mugs of soup,' I said.

'That's right.'

As we celebrated the moment: every girl and boy with his or her mug, lined up in the rain waiting for cheap soup.

'And the smell of pasties, and you, with yer half pie and chocolate doughnut.'

'Courtesy Mum's penny jar.'

'And, best of all, the baker, in the morning.'

We were there, standing in our jarmies in the middle of the road as the baker opened the back door of his van and golden light flooded Lanark Avenue; fresh bread, rolls, finger buns – the lot. Us, breathing it, the day, too; ready to be buttered, cut, and wrapped in greaseproof paper.

Although it was only a short walk home, we made it last. Every rose, and mock orange, the smell of Pop's feet when he cut his nails, dog shit when you stepped in it, vomit, which never really washed out of sheets, piss, too, on the pants in the bag.

We passed Peter in his shed, testing wine. He didn't see us. It didn't matter.

'What's tomorrow?' Vicky asked.

'Economics.'

'Better let you go learn.'

I waited. There was no kiss, just a squeezed hand.

As I approached the door I heard a gravelly voice. '… on a coat hook … and he was only a few inches above the ground.' I stopped and listened, but there were no more words.

I went in and Mum and Pop were sitting at the table. No one had put on a light, and I couldn't make out who was sitting with them. Then everyone turned. Anne had been crying, and Gary's face was set hard. He looked back at the table, at a smoke, burning in the ash tray.

'You better have a seat,' Mum said.

And I knew. Straight away.

Later, after Anne and Gary had left, and Mum and Pop had gone across the road to tell Les and Wendy, and the whole street, I guessed, I went to my room, put my novel and my notes and my book of observations, and everything I'd ever written, in a box. Then I went out and lit the incinerator, and started feeding the flames. None of it meant anything.

I turned, and Vicky was there. She stood beside me, watching the blue tops. I took the last document, the novel, and went to drop it in, but she took it, held it against her chest, said, 'You might regret it later.'

I did the Economics exam, and again, seemed to know what I was talking about. Praise the Lord of Shiraz, and his gentle, whispered ways. For three long, hot hours I'd heard him in my ear, telling me what to write, the best way to weld a sentence, and make a paragraph. The next day was English, and Mrs Masharin was there, saying, That is not an original thought, Clem. That is not a relevant quote. But: Now, that's a point.

Then, one day in early November, when it was all over, school done at last (shorts and knobbly knees, Venn diagrams and pissy toilets), I lay on my bed and thought of the past few months; 1984, with its dodgy predictions, all and none of which had come true. The Fool and the Magician dancing around my room as Curtis (at the window) said, You got lucky yet?

Mind yer business.

Just remember, I beat you by six months.

I'll remember.

As long as you live, you'll always be second, *Clemmy*.

That seemed fair. He was the mould, and I was the copy. Always had been, always would be. And no one, really, would ever know. My grandkids, perhaps, saying, Pop, he's a bit strange, eh?

Me replying, There's a reason.

Why?

Fella I used to know.

And they'd lose interest and run off and I'd be left looking out of my window, saying, You got any smokes, Curtis?

Plenty. Under the floorboards. Come on.

Anyway, the house was silent. I imagined the moment. The sound of the postie, me in the drive, at the letterbox, opening my results, Mum looking over my shoulder. *Come on, then.* As all the promises, threats and persuasions came home, at last, to roost. Every hope and half-wish of every teacher and relative and neighbour, Jen, Pop, Mum, Val, Peter, especially, because he was hoping the most (or maybe Mum, seeing something better, but the same). Curtis saying, Ninety-three ... you prick. No way you're that smart. Mum, Pop and Val, and all of them, dancing across the Santa Ana (freshly mowed, always freshly mowed). And me, nonplussed, cos when you grow up fibro everything's a bonus. And anyway, my life was already planned. Who I'd love, where I'd live, how I'd think and feel about everything and everyone I ever met. See, that's the thing about Gleneagles: you finished where you started. The machine kept working, regardless of any reason why it shouldn't. It just kept going, day, night, and the bits in between.

A hot day. A walking day. So I set off past David ('Any word yet?' 'They reckon December three. I'll let you know.'). Ernie, asleep on his porch. To the corner of Lanark II, the spot where street became car park. Falcons everywhere, but there was no point complaining. That's just how it was, and always would be. That's what made this place perfect: the fact that it was so dull, lacking culture, intellect, nature, beauty, enlightenment, history – pretty much anything anyone might want. Yep, we had it all, if you know what I mean. Across the road, past the stadium, with its sub-floor vents where me and Curtis dumped our uneaten lunches. I said, What cher doin' tonight?

Wanna come over, make some Twistie necklaces?

Packets shrunk in the oven, laced together and worn around the neck.

Na, they look shit.

Just walking, because there wasn't a lot to say, cos not much had happened since yesterday, or the day before, or the four thousand three hundred and thirteen others we'd known (Curtis had calculated).

Down the road that led to the primary school. Past Mrs Porter's place (her husband dead at thirty-seven). My old school. Another million smells, and things to remember, but I want to write another book about that. I stopped beside the fence, watching the usual ball-kicking. Mr Gottl was there, and he noticed me. 'Clem?'

I was a bit embarrassed, hanging around like I had nothing better to do. But it was too late. He came over and said, 'How are you?'

'Good, you?'

'Jesus, come in.'

I did as I was told. You always did with your old teachers, no matter how much water had passed under the bridge. As his class played football he said, 'You musta just finished ...?'

'Year Twelve.'

'No? And me here, still doing the same thing.'

'Same tops,' I said.

'Well, they wash them. But five years, that's not so much when you're my age.'

Then he asked me for the highlights, and I said there weren't many, and I asked if he ever noticed maps drawn in chalk in the lunch shed, and he said yes, and I explained. And he asked after Curtis, and I said he was okay, still a pain, but okay.

Then he said, 'It's good to see you. You know, kids come and go, and you never see them again, but you always remember.'

'All the stuff me and Curtis did?'

'Too right. You, with your hand in the cookie jar.'

'Shit ... you remember?'

'I do.'

'I's hoping ...'

'I knew you'd come good, and you have, eh?'

He told a couple of boys to stop arguing, but didn't seem too concerned about the game, falling apart.

'I was shitting myself,' I said. 'All the way across the yard, and when you stopped and said ...'

He smiled, and held my shoulder for a moment. 'Do this long enough, you can tell. But I always wondered why you did it.'

I said, 'Maybe I wanted to know what it felt like.'

'There's nothin' better. Middle of a sunny day. Green grass. Sherrin's pumped up, and we're alive, eh, Clem?'

'Yeah.'

He looked at his kids, and took a deep breath.

'Wouldn't be dead for quids, I reckon.'

'No.' As I saw Curtis, fighting for the ball.

'Carn,' Mr Gottl said, pulling me towards the oval. Me, the shit-kicker, the weed, the hater-of-sport. But the little kids welcomed me, and I let them tackle me, and pretended to fall and knock my head on the sprinkler, and Mr Gottl joined in, and it was like it had been, and always would be, amen.

I headed home, smelling the viburnum, and feeling happy. That was the most important thing of all: viburnum. The smell I'd smelt trying to get the footy, or throwing pine cones at Jen on the way home, or riding with Curtis to Woolies, the edge of the city, our world, the universe, perhaps. Like a tumble dryer, full of colours: Curtis, burning down the art room; David, noticing a tremor in his hand; Pop, losing his teeth when he spoke at his daughter's wedding; Ossie, handing me another book; Curtis, reciting Canto II. Everything. Socks and jocks and the lemon tree in the Rosies' yard, sprouting; Wendy opening her door to a stranger, embracing him, showing him what she'd been knitting; her and Les packing up and leaving to start a new life (all of those birds) in Harry's shack; Providence, the father of a miraculous litter of twelve; Val, living forever, or at least long enough to know her boys would be okay; me, sitting on a bronze lion, holding Pop's pound note, lighting it, watching it burn, and telling Vicky it was something I'd promised to do for him, years before; Me and Pop, sitting on a reef of gold, Pop saying, See … and you thought I was nutty.

I headed home, past everything I'd ever known. I guessed the future would be just as uncertain as the present, and past, but that didn't matter. All these people, these strange, rough-edged people, would always be with me. I'd think of them every day, and talk to them, and they'd give me advice and tell me to stop worrying about nothing, and Pop would say, Just do your best, Clemmy, and if they're not happy with that, fuck 'em.

I realised that's all I needed to know: fuck 'em.

I approached the door but heard a spanner drop. And whistling.

So I walked down the drive, passed through the gate and into the shed.

Pop was in his overalls, bent over the Jag, removing a manifold.

He didn't even look up. He knew I was there.

'You're gonna have to get out the imperial spanners,' he said.

I waited.

He looked up. 'Come on then.'

I found them in the cupboard, in the box he'd kept his map in. I took them to him, and said, 'What size?'

'Half inch.'

And we began.